KILL TO GROW

Will Freeman

Chapter 1

'I'll see you guys tomorrow in Economics,' I shouted to my rugby buddies Declan and Jamie as we went our separate ways outside the Jigger Inn. I was heading towards town along the side of the Old golf course, the two of them inland to halls. Despite it being spring, a cool breeze swept in off the sea across our ancient university town, St Andrews.

'Aye, see you, and don't forget there's rugby training tomorrow at 4.30 sharp,' shouted back Declan, our captain.

We were the last ones to leave the pub. Our 7 p.m. meet-up for a 'swift pint and a chat' to strategise about the team's next few matches had turned into six or seven pints finished off with three sambuca shots. It had been impromptu and great fun, but now I was feeling annoyed with myself. I'd probably miss my early morning run and I had classes to attend, studying on top of that, and I knew I'd struggle like hell to get through the day. Still, maybe if I downed a couple of pints of water and took an Alka-Seltzer, I might wake up feeling OK … but I very much doubted it.

I hurried as best I could through the car park, climbed over the little wall onto the path situated just behind the seventeenth green, then headed towards the famous eighteenth hole. God, my head was spinning.

What an idiot to have got so rat-arsed. My father, who was back in Hong Kong, always said to me, 'Have a few drinks now and then, but don't overdo it. People do stupid things when they're drunk.'

All I could think about was getting myself home. So instead of following the path around the course perimeter, I cut onto the eighteenth fairway itself—not strictly allowed, but it was midnight and pitch black, and I'd save myself ten minutes. *Stuff the old codgers who make up the rules!*

I spotted the little Swilken Bridge and staggered onto it, but a barnload of puke was on its way, and I clutched the old stone wall and forced my head over the side just in time. God, it was ghastly, splattering in the waters below. After a few more volleys, I found myself on my back, rolling around on the cobbles. But in no time I was up on my feet and half jogging, half staggering up the fairway towards the distant lights. I needed my bed so, so badly.

The breeze seemed to be stiffening, and as I dug my hands into my pockets, other than the sound of seagulls at the beach and the occasional sound of cars in the distance, everything was quiet.

'Hey, you!'

I jumped. Who was that? A woman? I stopped and looked around, swaying. But I couldn't see her.

'Over here!'

I lurched to my left and there she was, ten metres away but scarcely visible in the darkness.

'What's up … everything OK?' I could feel myself slurring.

She was moving closer. 'What's your name?'

Should I engage in conversation? This was kind of weird.

'I'm Peter. And you?'

Now she was much closer. 'Peter who?' Did I pick up a bit of a Midlands accent or no? Maybe she wasn't a native speaker. Was she on drugs or disturbed? Best just to get going.

'Listen, I'm sorry, but I'm drunk as a skunk and need to get going. Have a really nice walk.' Stumbling, I turned and set off for home.

'*Stop.*' Her voice was harder now, and louder. 'I've got a gun.'

'What the—?' I stopped, spun around and peered at her. *Oh my god, is that* really *a gun pointing at me? It can't be!'*

'What's your last name, Peter?'

'Black,' I fired back. 'Do you need some money? If you do, have it—have it all!' I started reaching into my inside jacket pocket for my wallet.

'Get on your knees.'

Did she really just say that? That I should get on my goddamn knees? My anger kicked in.

'No fucking way. Just take the damn money and be on your way.'

All of a sudden, there was a flash. Something whizzed past my left ear. The gun was for real! Now I was on the ground, cowering, staring up at her. My legs felt like jelly.

'Get up on your knees. *Now.*'

I immediately complied.

Then my heart almost stopped beating. She was holding an enormous knife in one hand, the gun in the other.

She's totally nuts. I've got to do something or I'm dead!

'What's with the knife? Let's talk. Let me help you.' I tried to sound as sympathetic and kind as I could.

But she wasn't listening. She made a sudden move. I was up in a flash. *Slam*—I mowed into her, flattening her with a rugby tackle and sending her sprawling. Now it was time to run.

But no, she was up on her knees fast, lunging at me, blade first. I dived clear. But like a crazed machine, she just kept coming. I couldn't get away from her.

As she came at me again, I managed to grab her knife arm, but her forward momentum was too strong, and I fell backwards. Fuck, now she was on top of me, the blade inches from my face. This was it. The end.

Survive! Do fucking anything.

I went berserk, attacking her face. Punching, mauling, gouging. Anything, everything. Life and death.

Finally, with my right fist clenching her throat, I managed to fling her off me and now I was on top of *her*, clinging to her back, ramming her face into the ground.

She crumpled and instinctively, judo style, I spread my entire weight over her so she couldn't budge a fucking inch.

'Who the fuck are you?' I hissed in her ear, my head pinned against hers. 'You're fucking nuts.'

But wait—what was she doing?

She was heaving. Gasping. Gurgling. Then she let out a terrifying groan, and a second later she went limp. *Jesus Christ, what the hell have I done to her?*

It was tactical, surely? I'd jump off her and for sure the crazy bitch would go for me again.

But no. She wasn't breathing.

Holy fuck, have I gone and killed her?

Now I was off her, sitting a few feet away, staring, my hands shaking uncontrollably. I managed to pull out my phone and, after fumbling around, I got the light on and shone it on her.

Holy Jesus!

I jumped to my feet.

The knife was wedged deep in her throat, right under her chin. Her face was covered in blood, and the patch of grass by her head was scarlet and sodden.

I retched. Again and again and again.

Head in my hands, I tried desperately to suck air into my system. *Please let this be a horrible drunken dream. Dear god, don't let it be real.*

But it wasn't a dream. There in front of me was a dead woman, and I was her killer.

Oh my god! My life was over. Uni would be finished. I'd go to jail. Black & Co.'s name would be dragged through the mud. I'd be branded a killer. What would Mum, Dad and my sister, Sam, say? And my flatmates? No one would believe she'd attacked me. I was utterly screwed.

I took a closer look. Maybe I could still revive her?

But no. Her eyes were sticking out like stalks and her face had a look of terror on it. Blood was bubbling and oozing out of her mouth. She was dark, maybe Asian. Holy shit, I was covered in blood too. My left hand, the arm of my grey sweatshirt and probably my dark jacket too.

I ran.

But I'd only taken a few steps when I kicked something solid. When I flashed the light down, I saw the gun, complete with its long silencer. Hell! What if I'd touched it during the fight? What if my prints were on it? My sweat. My DNA.

Not knowing what to do, I grabbed it and legged it. First I headed towards the eighteenth green, then I changed my mind and turned back the way I'd come.

How could this possibly have happened to me? How could this happen to anyone?

Chapter 2

Someone was gently shaking me. 'Peter, wake up. Wake up, Peter.'

I tried to open my eyes. God, my head was thumping, and my throat was like sandpaper. Sweat was pouring off me. A waft of perfume hit me. It was my flatmate Trudy's—she was sitting at the foot of my bed.

'Hey, what's the time?' I rasped, propping myself up on my elbow and trying to focus.

'Oh my god, Peter, look at you,' she said. 'You've puked on your bed, there's an empty bottle of whisky on the floor *and* there are filthy, muddy footprints all over the house. What the hell were you up to? *And* when I walked by your room earlier, you were yelling and swearing in your sleep—something about a, quote, "psychotic fucking bitch."'

I sat thinking for a moment, desperately trying to kickstart my brain. Sure enough, there was mud all over the carpet and there, beside my pillow, was a heap of congealed puke. Housemate Shaun's precious bottle of Oban was lying empty on the floor.

I stared blankly at Trudy, but still I couldn't get my brain in gear.

'Oh god, *look*,' she said, pointing. 'There's blood all over your neck. Dear god, are you OK? Are you hurt?'

Then it all hit me. The golf course, the woman, the fight for my life, and then the manic hours afterwards when I'd charged around like a headless chicken—dumping the gun, washing blood out of my clothes in the sea. I'd even gone way out of town, across the fields, then circled around to enter St Andrew's as far from the golf course as possible. When I finally got home, I'd scrubbed myself in the shower, but clearly not well enough.

'Oh, I'm just fine, Trudy,' I said, trying to be casual. 'Far too many beers with the rugby lads and I got a nosebleed on the way home. Give me a few minutes and I'll come down to tidy the place up.'

'It's just so *unlike* you to get so wasted.'

'Yep, bloody stupid of me.' As I said it, my father's 'people do stupid things when they're drunk' words of wisdom flashed through my mind. I could only imagine how he'd react when he found out about the catastrophic mess I'd got myself into.

'You'll feel much better after a shower. I'll go put the kettle on and I'll see you downstairs,' she said soothingly, and as she left, I gave her a little smile. I had absolutely nothing to be smiling about.

Five minutes later, after looking at the dishevelled wreck of myself in the bathroom mirror, I hauled myself into the shower and re-scrubbed myself from head to toe, desperately trying to work out what on earth to do next. But rather than coming to any conclusions, I simply worked myself into a traumatised frenzy until finally I sat in the shower basin and cried my eyes out. I never *ever* cried, but I was in the deepest shit of my entire life.

Deep down, I knew there was only one thing to do. I'd go straight to the police, tell them the truth, and then hope and pray that they'd believe me. I wasn't a murderer; I'd been in the wrong place at the wrong time, and after accidentally killing the woman, I'd totally freaked, like any mortal would. It was a tragic case of self-defence against a person who quite clearly had severe mental health issues.

My parents would rally round, especially my father. He was a successful and incredibly well-connected Hong Kong-based businessman. He'd hate to see the name of the family firm, Black & Co., dragged through the mud, but when the chips were down, he was always there for me. And his connections went all the way to the very top of British government.

Surely, oh, surely everything would be OK. But what if it wasn't? There were endless cases around the world of completely innocent people being wrongly implicated in horrible stuff and sent to prison for years. Hell, there were numerous TV series dedicated to the topic.

But I *had* to believe that justice, common sense and decency would prevail.

I began pulling on my running gear. I'd have a quick jog around town to get some of the booze out of my system, then I'd go straight to the crime scene and hand myself in.

I imagined the cordoned-off golf course, blue-and-white tape, incident vans, white-suited forensics experts down on their hands and knees looking for every scrap of evidence. They'd probably already found my DNA. Maybe they were already on their way to get me.

Deep in my own world, I went downstairs and walked through the kitchen, barely noticing that Trudy, Shaun and Diti were having their breakfast. 'Hey, wait up,' said Diti. 'Where are you going?'

I hardly looked up. 'For a run.'

'Mate, did you hear about what happened last night?' said Shaun. *That* stopped me in my tracks.

'What do you mean?'

'Hockey team got jumped on Market Street by locals. Ugly, real ugly. Our goalie is in the hospital getting his jaw wired up. Another's got busted fingers. Apparently it was close to all-out warfare.'

'Right,' I said, trying to hide my relief. 'Very nasty.'

'Something's not right. I've never seen him acting like this,' I heard Trudy say as I left. God, how right she was. Maybe that was the last time I'd ever see them again.

Tears streaming down my face, I turned left outside our house and just before hitting North Street, I broke into a slow jog and headed right towards the castle. From there, I'd swing round and run down South Street to the arches before cutting over towards the golf course.

As I ran, my mind began to clear, and I remembered more. Dumping the gun at the breakwater. Wading into the Eden Estuary to wash my clothes. Walking through endless fields and trying to dodge CCTV cameras as I made my way back into town. When I got home, I'd stuffed my shirt and jacket up the chimney in my room, somehow believing that no one would find them up there.

As I neared the golf course, I stopped running and walked, my pulse pounding, sweat running off me. At the corner of Golf Place, I held onto a lamppost and took long deep breaths. Another twenty metres or so and the view would open out onto the golf course.

I stopped again, not yet able to confront what lay ahead of me. *Just do it!* I shouted at myself, scaring an old lady pulling one of those shopping baskets. *Believe in yourself.*

I took the final few steps.

'What the hell ...?'

There were no police cordons or white tents. No police cars. No white-suited people crawling up the fairway. Just a group of golfers casually coming up the eighteenth. In fact, close to where I reckoned I'd had my life-and-death battle, there was a guy lining up an approach shot.

How was it possible? Had the body already been taken away and they'd reopened the course? Surely not. Wait. Maybe she hadn't been dead and maybe, just maybe, she'd got up and staggered off somewhere else. Or, hell, maybe I'd imagined the whole thing. No, that just *wasn't* possible.

'Hi, mate,' I said to a passing caddy. 'I heard the course was shut earlier?'

'I dinnie think sae,' he said, stopping. 'I started just efter six and it's been open all morning.'

'You're joking,' I said, shaking my head. 'It *must* have been closed and the police must have been out on the eighteenth searching ...'

He looked at me like I was bonkers and walked off to join his buddies down by the clubhouse.

Then I was off, sprinting for the police station on North Street not five hundred meters away. I had to come clean. If I didn't, I was going to go completely mad.

'Nice morning for a jog,' said the amiable-sounding front desk officer as I tumbled into the reception in a flustered daze. 'Me and the Mrs had a run last night as well—we're trying to shift some weight.' He laughed, pointing at his rather large frame. 'Now tell me, what can I do for you, son?'

It was time to face the music. I took a long deep breath.

'I'm here to talk about last night, sir. I can explain everything, and while it's all going to sound horrendous, I can assure you that I'm completely innocent.'

'So you wish to report an incident, do you, lad?' he said, squinting at the *Dundee Tribune* sitting on his desk. 'Just let me grab the log.' He swung his chair round and grabbed a huge black book. 'Fire away, then,' he said, but at that moment, the main door opened and a senior-looking officer and two younger ones walked in and headed off down the corridor. They were laughing and joking—not what one would expect on the day a small university town had suffered a grisly killing.

'Is it about the fight in Market Street?' he asked, taking his glasses off and staring at me. 'It was a very nasty episode, and we're looking for witnesses to come forward.'

My voice wobbled. 'No, it's about the thing down at the golf course. I was there and sort of became ... *involved*.'

'The golf course?' he said, sneaking another glimpse at his newspaper before casually turning it over to the sports section.

'Yes, sir. The woman who ...'

I stopped. None of this was registering with him. He was more interested in his fucking newspaper.

'Go on, then.' He strummed his pencil on his notebook. 'What's this all about?'

'You know what, sir, it's nothing. I shouldn't be wasting your time.' I made for the door.

'OK, then, son,' he said, standing up and smiling, 'but feel free to come back if you change your mind. As far as I'm aware, we haven't had any problems down at the golf courses or the beach—not for a couple of weeks or more. Take care now, and enjoy your jog.'

Outside the police station, I stood on the pavement, my head spinning. What was I going to do? What on earth was going on?

Chapter 3

I made it to Economics at 2 p.m., but it was a write-off, as I sat there stewing, trying to figure out what on earth had happened to the woman's body. Business Management wasn't much better.

Maybe I'd got it wrong. Perhaps she'd survived and was now on life support in Dundee's Ninewells Infirmary. It wasn't completely unknown for people to cling to life, but how on earth would she have made it to the place? She'd had to have had help. And if she had died there on the eighteeth, someone must have taken her body away. But who? And where? It was doing my head in.

However, one thing was for sure. The whole hideous event *had* happened. Straight after the police station, I'd gone and double-checked the chimney in my room and sure enough, the bloodstained clothes were there, as well as her unmistakable odour.

My anxiety levels were thankfully beginning to moderate as I began to reconcile what had happened. I was no killer. In fact, I considered myself to be quite a gentle soul, and I think my friends did too. I'd gone for a couple of pints with my buddies and in a few terrible minutes, my life had been wrecked by a nutcase. People would believe my story. Would they not?

Coming out of class into the quad, I spotted Trudy sitting on the lawn. Most days I'd have gone and sat on the grass with her and her admirers, but today I wasn't in the mood. I felt her worried stare on my back as I walked, head down, to the bike racks. Five minutes later, though, I was tanking down the hill to the out-of-town sports complex, the brisk East Neuk wind in my face. God, if only one's worries could magically float away on the breeze. I was dog tired, but rugby training would keep my mind off things, and after that, I had my evening shift in the pub.

'Right, lads,' bellowed Declan in a broad, glorious Belfast accent as we congregated in the changing rooms. 'No rugger today. It'll be fifteen K along the sands with Coach McDougall meeting you at the halfway mark for squats, press-ups and tyres. The last one to the Dunvegan will be buying the pints!'

A fifteen K run! Christ, maybe I should've stayed in the flat! But no, a long-distance run was very much my thing, and within a few minutes of setting off, a group of five of us had broken away. It wasn't long before we reached the top of North Street. God, it felt good.

North Street meant passing the police station, and as we went tanking past, it looked just as sleepy as when I'd left it. And once we got all the way down to the golf course ,the crime scene circus which should have been camped out on the eighteenth was still nowhere to be seen. It really did defy belief that the woman who'd come so close to murdering—yes, murdering!—me had somehow managed to perform a Houdini.

Even the dogs on the beach stopped playing for a moment as the five of us, shoulder to shoulder and splendid in our rugby kit, raced out onto West Sands, and after the initial shock of the North Sea breeze, we soon found our pace. It was going to be a hell of a hike to the far end of the beach, and our banter soon gave way to silence, each of us consumed by our own thoughts.

Oblivious to the pain of the run, I got thinking about Hong Kong, my home for the first eighteen years of my life. God, how I wished I'd never left the place. My father's life's work had been the creation of Black & Co. He'd become a billionaire in the process, and we lived in a beautiful old house perched on Victoria Peak. He and my mother were the most happily married couple I think I'd ever met, and Sam, my big sister, worked for a couple of NGOs. I loved her to death. Christ. What were they going to think of me?

'Almost there. Two K to go,' shouted one of the lads, and sure enough, snapping back into the real world, I found that we'd already turned onto the Eden Estuary stretch of beach. Now we were sprinting from the high water mark towards Coach's jeep on the shore. The race was on.

As we splashed through the shallow pools, I noticed something lying way off to our right, back out at the water's edge. What was it? I kept peering and slowed down a bit. A washed-up seal? Just some debris? *Hell, let's take a look.* 'Catch you all up in a moment,' I shouted, veering off.

As I got closer, just at the point of abandoning my detour, something caught my eye. Had whatever it was just moved? I slowed, straining my eyes, trying to figure it out. It moved again. Got it! It was a big black dog sitting beside a big brown thing. And now it was barking at me. A bark for help?

I suddenly realised what it was. Hell, it was a person! *Good god, surely it couldn't be …?*

Now the person was moving as well, laid out there on the sand. Male—green jacket, brown trousers, boots, flat cap—and he was in the process of propping himself up on his elbow. I pulled to a halt. 'Hello, excuse me, sir, are you all right?' I said, kneeling beside him. Had he had a stroke or a seizure or something like that? I mean, who lies out on the water's edge in the freezing cold?

He stared at me for a moment—quite a long moment. 'Sir, are you OK? Should I go for help?'

Still, he stared at me, studying me before he finally spoke. 'You'll find that when you hit the grand old age of 85, you occasionally have to sit your arse down to get your breath back.' He was well-spoken. 'It's such a damn lovely day too, isn't it?'

'I do apologise.' I nodded towards the lads in the distance. 'We're running, and I saw something out here and came to check.' His dog got up, tiptoed over and put his head under my hand, and I patted him and ruffled his ears. 'He's a nice dog. Looks like a great companion.'

'So you thought I was a corpse, did you?' He laughed, fixing his surprisingly youthful eyes on mine. 'More than a few deck hands have been washed up here over the years. I'm here most days with Bullet and we've seen all manner of stuff.'

'Not at all, sir. I thought maybe a dead seal or debris off a boat.' His mention of a corpse had sent a shiver down my spine. For sure it had crossed my mind that it might have been *her*.

'Mmm.' He sighed. 'Indeed, my old friend is a grand companion, although his master is somewhat decrepit!' He nodded towards my teammates, who were now about 750 metres from the coach's 4 × 4. 'You don't look like the kind of chap who likes to lose a race.'

'Absolutely,' I replied. 'I better be heading off. Now, are you sure you don't need a hand?'

He most certainly didn't. Remarkably quickly, he pulled himself up to his feet, and when he stood in front of me, he seemed to tower above me—and I was six feet tall! 'I'm grand, thanks. But a pleasure to have met you.' He held out his hand. 'The name's Bob McPherson.'

I shook it. 'Peter ... Peter Black.' I began jogging off, Bullet running the first few metres with me before pulling up. Then I picked up my pace and ran flat out, arriving moments behind the rest.

What a strange encounter! And come to think of it, hadn't I seen the old guy somewhere before?

'One hundred and fifty push-ups and fifty squats,' yelled Coach. 'Get on it, lads.'

As I started my push-ups, finally it came to me. Months back, he'd dropped into the pub, and someone had joked that he was an ex-army type who recruited for British Intelligence. I hadn't bought it, but now I wasn't so sure—there was something really quite mysterious about him.

On to my squats. In the distance, I watched as he got into his car. The dog jumped into the back and then, just before he climbed into the driver's seat, I saw Bob glance in my direction for a brief second. Then he closed the door and drove slowly off.

Something didn't feel quite right.

But then again, *nothing* felt right. It was less than twenty-four hours since I'd been attacked by a crazy woman whom I'd gone and killed.

Chapter 4

Dog tired, I virtually crawled into the flat and found Diti writing furiously at the kitchen table. 'Feeling a bit more like it?' she asked without lifting her head. 'You'll be late for your shift if you don't hurry!'

She was from Mumbai, and few knew that her father was one of India's richest men. He was self-made, incredibly well connected, and presided over a conglomerate covering everything from ports and mobile phones to mining, financial services and retail. We four flatmates had been in halls together and we'd clicked, and, like many others, we'd taken the plunge and moved out from year two onwards. The fact that all of us had very successful (and embarrassingly wealthy) parents was perhaps the thing that had brought us together, but it was also something we all tried to downplay.

'Feeling a bit better, thanks,' I replied, 'and sorry about earlier ...'

'No worries. Absolutely sure you're OK?' she asked, still not lifting her head from her scribbles. 'Trudy's convinced you are hiding something.'

'Absolutely sure,' I said, taking a yoghurt from the fridge. I wished I could tell her about my horrid, wretched black cloud of uncertainty. She was the one we all went to with our problems.

'After training, a yoghurt won't take you very far.' She'd finished writing and was looking at me.

'You sound like my mum, Dits. But don't worry, I'll grab something more substantial at the pub.'

'I've spent the last three hours on this Psychology essay,' she moaned, 'and no end in sight.'

'Let me do your dishes for you.' I scooped them up from in front of her.

'You're a dear'—her eyes twinkled—'and just why I chose you as a flatmate!'

'Right.' I smiled, remembering how she'd begged to become the final member of our quartet.

My room was at the top of the first flight of stairs, and as I climbed wearily up, Shaun was on his way down, humming happily. 'Pete, old boy! Have you got the wind back in your sails?'

'Yep, better than I was,' I replied cagily. 'What have you been up to? You're looking chirpy.'

'Yes, life's pretty good, actually.' Then he lowered his voice and whispered, 'You know that German girl I've had my eye on?'

'Katerina?'

'That's the one. Well, I asked her out for a drink, and she said yes. I'm totally psyched.'

I gave him a solid clap on the back. 'Well done. You old rogue. Couldn't have happened to a nicer chap. Let me know how it goes. Got to rush …'

In my room, I quickly switched on the iron, then ducked into the bathroom for a quick shower. As I closed my eyes under the deluge, I found myself thinking about Bob McPherson and Bullet. Was he really *The Recruiter*? And just what kind of stuff would people do in British Intelligence and who fitted the mould? Most of the folks that I knew would be going into advertising, accounting, law or banking. Working for Her Majesty's Secret Service definitely sounded a lot sexier!

With ten minutes to go until the start of my shift, I dashed out into my bedroom—fortunately with a towel around me—to find Diti finishing ironing my shirt. 'You're running late. It's the least I could do,' she said a little awkwardly, putting it on its hanger and heading for the door.

'God, you're a total gem, Diti!'

I pulled on my black trousers and the shirt, grabbed my crested pub tie and bounded down the stairs into the kitchen just as Trudy opened the front door. 'Peter, darling,' she said in her typical exaggerated manner. 'Don't you look dashing! But good lord, I still don't understand why you work in that dingy dive when you don't need to.'

'It's real life, Trudy.' I grinned as I gave her a quick peck on each cheek. 'You should try it sometime; a bit of hard work is good for the soul, you know.'

'Oh, don't give me that rubbish,' she scoffed. 'Anyway, my soul is pretty perfect the way it is.' On that point, I couldn't disagree. Trudy was perfect in all respects—stunning, smart, sporty, and, luckily for her, her family owned the Land Rover franchise across half of Scotland. More importantly, underneath all her outlandishness, she was a *thoroughly* nice person. As were Diti and Shaun.

'Come on, I'm feeling really sorry for you,' she said. 'I'll drop you off, shall I?' I gratefully accepted. 'But only if you speak to me in Chinese on the way. Right?'

We often spoke Chinese to one another, she a beginner, me fluent due to growing up in Hong Kong and having a dad who insisted on me learning 'tomorrow's global language' from the day I could walk. I'd also been incredibly lucky to have Mr and Mrs Peng, our housekeepers, who had tried hard to make sure that my Chinese was as perfect as it possibly could be. Saturday mornings in particular had always been very Chinese, with Mr Peng taking me to judo classes in Wan Chai. He'd played a big part in helping me to secure my black belt—not that I practised it anymore.

'You still look like total shit, Peter,' she said in reasonable Chinese as we set off. 'You're worrying about something, and I want to know what. Come on, get it off your chest. I've been figuring you might have woman problems—we can be such horrible bitches, can't we?'

'Wow, Trudy, you articulated that incredibly well. Grammatically spot on. Have you been practising?' She was right, though. I did have woman problems—dead woman problems.

'Stop evading the question, would you!'

But after a few more attempts to open me up, annoyed, she gave up, and when she dropped me off, she gave me short shrift. 'Bugger off, Peter.' Then, with a screech of wheels and a middle finger gesture at me, she sped off. That was Trudy to a T. God, she made me laugh!

For a Wednesday, the bar was quite busy, and after a briefing and handover from Tommy Schneider—the American guy who did afternoon shifts—I did my usual scout around to get the lie of the land.

Sitting at the bar itself was old Jock, a permanent fixture. Along from him were two fourth-year guys enjoying a pint and a chat, and down at the far end there was a well-dressed, stocky Indian chap wearing a turban. Maybe he had a son or a daughter at the university? As I looked at him, I remembered a Sikh visiting my father many years ago at our home in Hong Kong and the two of them demolishing a bottle of Macallan to celebrate the signing of a business deal. Sikhs must really love their whisky, and this one, as per Tommy's briefing, was drinking Johnny Walker Blue Label.

Noticing his empty glass, I went down to his end of the bar. 'Another one, sir?' He nodded, instinctively tapping his second and third fingers on the top of his glass. Pouring, I noticed that on his left index finger he wore a massive ring with a black stone. I wasn't a fan of man rings, and certainly not big ones, but this one looked quite at home on his massive hand.

Each shot was eight quid, so I gave him a decent measure, and with a loud slurp, he took a large sip. 'What do you think of it, sir?' In reply, all I got was a shrug, then—as he'd been doing before—he fixed his stare on the whisky display behind the bar. Maybe his English wasn't very good.

'Laddie,' said old Jock to me from the other end. 'Another chaser, please. But not that fancy Blue Label stuff. Just gie me Grouse.' He raised his glass to the Sikh, who completely ignored him.

'Back in the war, in my regiment, there were a few of you turbaned lads,' he went on. 'Damn it, you boys was good fighters. Hard as nails.' At this, the Sikh turned his head a bit, as if he wanted to say something, but then he seemed to decide better of it and went back to staring at the booze display.

The main door suddenly burst open with an almighty bang. *Oh god, that's all we need.*

Two local lads, fuelled up, came storming in and started rushing around the place, clearly looking for someone. When they didn't find him or her, they came marching up to the bar.

'Are any of those wank hockey players here tonight?' shouted the taller one. Then, seeing the two fourth years, he went straight up to them. 'Are you fuckers from the hockey team?'

'You're the Johnston boy, aren't you?' cut in old Jock with a snarl. 'Now, why don't you go home to your mammie and stop causing trouble? And you, Jimmy, you should be aff hame as well.'

'Fuck off, auld Jock,' shouted Johnston. 'What's it to you?'

'Aye, fuck off, Jock,' chimed in Jimmy. 'What the fuck is it to you?'

Johnston then turned his attention to me. 'Gimme a bottle of vodka or I'll beat the shit out of you.'

I didn't say a word. The very last thing I needed right now was this.

'*A fucking bottle, ye cunt!*' he yelled.

I shook my head.

Wrong answer. Sending drinks flying, he was over the top of the bar in a flash and raining furious punches on me.

All I could do was put my elbows up and take the blows as best I could. Then, in the mayhem, I lost my footing and *crash*, I fell back onto my arse. Before I knew it, he'd snatched a bottle of Finlandia and the two of them were sprinting for the exit.

It had all happened so incredibly quickly that I just sat there on the wet floor in disbelief, trying to process what had just happened.

Then the anger hit me, and it surged off the Richter scale. *I'm not taking this bullshit.*

Now it was my turn to go over the top of the bar, and in no time, I was out the door. 'No, Peter, leave it to the police!' someone shouted.

But I was already out on the pavement, and nothing—no, nothing—was going to stop me.

Chapter 5

There weren't many who could outrun me, and fifty metres up the street I closed in on sidekick Jimmy and tripped him, sending him crashing face first into the side of a parked van.

Ahead, his taller, uglier buddy stopped and started stomping menacingly back towards me.

Smash. On a lamppost, he broke the head off the vodka bottle. Now he was coming at me. Brandishing the weapon. Screaming every obscenity under the sun.

I darted out between the cars into the middle of South Street to give myself space to manoeuvre, and he immediately did the same.

Now he was thirty metres out and closing. Stomp, stomp, stomp.

'Come on, you lanky piece of piss. Let's see how good you are, then,' I shouted.

He wasn't stomping anymore. He was charging at me like a deranged bull.

Just before he got to me, I saw the blade in his other hand. It wasn't enormous like psycho woman's, but I knew that any mistake could be deadly. Thank god for my many hours of judo training.

I ducked as the broken bottle flew at me, and as he slashed wildly with the knife, I grabbed his forearm with perfect timing and launched him over my shoulder. A nanosecond later he was face down on the tarmac, my foot rammed into the base of his neck, his knife arm pointing to the sky, twisted to near breaking point. He screamed like a woman.

Just then, with half the bar out on the pavement staring, a police Transit van came screeching round the corner. Before it had even pulled to a halt, three policemen stormed out. Irrationally, it flashed through my mind that they were here for me about the previous night, but within seconds Johnston and Jimmy were being cuffed and dragged, cursing and screaming, into the van.

Before the door slammed shut, Johnston yelled, 'You're dead. When I get oot, I'm coming fer ye.'

'Just ignore him,' said the senior officer. 'By the time he's sobered up, he'll have forgotten about you and all of this.' I recognised him. He was the senior of the three I'd seen walking into the police station when I'd been trying to confess to the front desk guy. 'Where have we met before?' he asked as we walked back to the bar. 'I never forget a face.'

I tried to contain my nerves. 'Actually, I was in the station this morning, but it wasn't anything particularly important.'

'Right,' he said, looking me up and down with a slightly quizzical look on his face.

'Quite a show, young Black,' said a loud, familiar voice as we walked into the bar, and there, standing at the counter, was Bob McPherson with Bullet. What the hell was he doing there?

'Thanks, Mr McPherson,' I said, hiding my surprise at seeing him. 'A show I probably shouldn't have been a part of.'

'Rubbish, lad. He didn't stand a chance, and you taught him a valuable lesson. Mark my words, the only way to deal with bullies like that is to bring them down a peg or two.'

'I don't know,' I said, turning to the remaining customers. 'Apologies, everyone, for all the excitement. The next round is on the house.' It was the very least I could do, and a cheer went up.

As I passed Jock a Famous Grouse, he beckoned me closer. 'Don't underestimate that wee shite Johnston. He and his delinquent father are bad news, but I tell you what. Let me visit the auld grandmother tomorrow to see if she can help talk some sense into the pair of them.'

'Thanks, Jock. Much appreciated.' He was a gnarled old alcoholic who I'm sure had a past he'd rather forget, but underneath it all, I figured he was a good man.

The Sikh appeared not to have moved an inch despite the commotion. 'Here's one on the house,' I said, trying to act as normally as possible. As I poured, I noticed Bob McPherson studying him. The Sikh must have felt his stare and turned, and for a second or two they both looked at one another.

Bob broke the silence. 'It's a beautiful time of year to be visiting the old town.'

'Very nice indeed,' responded the Sikh in surprisingly good English. Then he turned away and stared once again at the bar display.

Hang on. What was that strange low-pitched sound I could hear? Where was it coming from?

I peered over the bar. It was Bullet. Growling. Hackles up. Radar ears. Eyes fixed on the Sikh.

'Quiet, Bullet' snapped Bob McPherson. 'What's got into you?'

But the dog kept growling and, if anything, it was getting louder.

'Enough!' shouted Bob, pointing at the entrance. 'Go sit at the door.'

Like a shot, the dog scampered off and sat obediently by the coat stand. But the growl continued.

'I do apologise, my friend,' said the old man, looking puzzled. 'The old hound was retired early from active duty after a nasty accident. Hasn't been quite the same since.'

The Sikh simply ignored him and kept looking ahead, thinking about whatever he was thinking about.

Bang. The door burst open again.

I swung round, fists clenched. Were there more of them?

This time, thankfully, it wasn't a pack of locals baying for blood; it was my three flatmates led by Trudy. 'Peter. *God*, you're OK. We were worried sick. We heard that someone had tried to stab you!'

'You look OK, thank goodness,' said Shaun. 'Let me at the bastards!'

'Oh, I don't think you need to worry.' McPherson guffawed. 'Your able-bodied friend handled the hoodlums marvellously. It was an exhibition in some rather fine judo, and they're now locked up over on North Street courtesy of the boys in blue.'

'Well done, old son,' said Shaun, shaking me by the hand. 'What a bloody star!'

'Do you need to see a doctor?' said Diti, staring me up and down, looking very concerned.

I put my arm around her shoulder. 'I'm 100 per cent fine. There's nothing to worry about.'

There was something really comforting about my flatmates being by my side.

After statements had been taken and I'd locked up the bar, the four of us didn't get back to the flat until almost midnight, and despite their efforts, I politely turned down the offer to share a bottle of wine. Instead, I headed for my room and lay quietly on my bed.

What on earth was going on? In the last twenty-four hours, I seemed to be living in a totally different world. The attack on the course. The missing body. A chance encounter with The Recruiter.

The hoodlums' fight. Bob reappearing. Hell, even the Sikh was weird. Not to mention Bullet's behaviour.

Could any of these things be connected or was it all random? I tried putting my logical hat on, but if some or all of these things were linked, I most certainly couldn't work it out. With my gut telling me it was all coincidence, I felt myself beginning to nod off until I heard a little knock on my door.

'Peter, it's Shaun. Are you still awake? Can I come in?'

'Sure, mate.'

'Bad news, I'm afraid,' he said poking his head around the door. *Oh god, what is it now?* 'Footage of your scrap with those two townies is out on the net and spreading like wildfire! You're famous.'

'Oh god. Tell me it's not true,' I groaned. I could only imagine the field day that the press would have with this. Sam and I had always been warned to maintain an ultra-low profile to keep out of the gossip columns and avoid inflicting damage on the name of the family or on Black & Co.

Still. It could have been a zillion times worse. Although I couldn't work out how on earth I'd miraculously managed not to have been found out. A full day had passed … and so far, nothing.

Chapter 6

The first thing I did when I woke up in the morning was call my father to warn him about what was going around on the internet. I didn't, of course, have the guts to tell him about the other thing.

'I'll get comms and legal on it immediately,' he said, 'and thanks for letting me know.' He then went onto the internet and watched the clip as I listened. 'You dealt quite nicely with the imbecile!' he remarked after a few moments.

'I suppose so, but I know what you're going to say next, so I'll save you the effort. I shouldn't have got myself into the fight in the first place.' Kindly, he didn't lecture me, but he did have a bit of a rant.

'You know, Peter, Scotland used to be a great place, full of youngsters going out into the world and making their mark. Now it seems to be a nation full of drug pushers, wasters, freeloaders and complainers. Anyway,' he went on, 'I'm glad to see that we got a return on all those judo lessons.'

'Oh, Scotland's not so bad,' I said, laughing at his overly downbeat assessment. 'It was just a one-off, and even those two thugs will find their way in life eventually.'

'I'm not sure I share your optimism, Peter, but, saying all that, I hired an excellent Scot into the business a couple of years ago and he's coming through *very* nicely. Gavin's his name. You should meet him on your next trip. Frankly, he's the only person I've met who could take over the reins if ever I keeled over. Not that I'm planning to snuff it, especially with the deal I've got in play.'

'Deal? I didn't know we had something cooking.' Being a shareholder, I was privy to quite a lot about what was going on in Black & Co.

'I've probably already said too much.' He laughed. 'But I tell you what. I'll be in London over the weekend trying to conclude things. It'll be hectically busy, but why don't I send the jet up to Leuchars to collect you and we'll grab some dinner and I'll tell you more?'

His offer could not have come at a better time. 'Deal, Dad. Count me in. London it is!'

'Fabulous. Listen, I'm dashing into a meeting now, but Peng will make all the arrangements and will be in touch. Can't wait to see you on Saturday. Bye for now!'

'Dad, *wait*. Are you still there?'

'Yes, I am, but I only have a minute, son. Can it be quick?'

'Yes, yes. Listen, Dad ...' I swallowed hard and, almost squeezing my damn phone to death, I started. 'I've gone and got myself into ...' But then I stopped. I couldn't. It just wasn't going to come out. 'You know, it isn't too important. I'll fill you in on Saturday over dinner. Don't worry.'

'OK, then,' he said briskly. 'Saturday it is. Bye!'

I walked through to the bathroom. I had so, so badly wanted to confide in him, but how could I detonate a nuclear bomb right in the middle of what sounded like an incredibly important deal? It just wouldn't be fair. Plus I didn't know to break the news—it was just too difficult.

But as I was taking my clothes off to take a shower, my phone rang. It was Dad again.

'Dad?'

'Is everything OK?' I heard lots of voices in the background and pictured him in the boardroom, an important meeting about to start. 'I don't know why, but I feel a bit worried about you.'

'I'm 110 per cent fine,' I replied cheerily. 'Absolutely nothing to worry about! Now get back to your meeting.'

'OK, until Saturday, then.' And he hung up.

I stared at my stupid self in the mirror. 'You total idiot, Peter,' was all I could say to myself.

After showering, I found Trudy and Diti in the kitchen. 'Here he is. Our very own boy wonder,' said Trudy, sporting a big grin.

'Shut up, please, Trudy.' I smiled, 'Today is a new day. Let's not talk about last night, OK?'

'You know, you two,' said Diti angrily. 'It never ceases to amaze me just how uncivilised your apparently civilised country is. My country has a utopian view of the UK—a supposed land of prosperity, manners and civility—but frankly, I'd feel safer walking Mumbai's back streets than I would the hallowed streets of your boroughs and towns. Where I'm from, people don't have time to be out picking fights. Everyone's just trying to eke out a living. What is it about this strange island?'

I couldn't disagree with her. 'It's the same in China and HK. Everyone's busting a gut trying to better themselves, plus there's no dole or social security to bail them out. Still, changing the subject, and on a more cheery note, I'm off for breakfast at McGregor's. Any takers? Oh, and I'm going to London to see my dad on Saturday if anyone wants to cadge a lift on his plane.'

'Can't,' said Diti. 'Too much studying to get through.'

'Ooh, I can't either, but I would have loved a weekend of retail therapy,' said Trudy. But I did get her to come to breakfast, and after a brisk two-minute walk, we arrived at the little café on

Market Street. Pretty much anything of any significance in St Andrews was within two minutes of the flat. Two minutes to Tesco, two minutes to the Union, two minutes to the quad, two minutes to the Scores, the bus station, the off license, the Indian and about ten different pubs. At a stretch, I could almost be on the first tee of the Old Course in two minutes.

As we waited for our food, Trudy reminded me about the massive Save the Planet eco march that would be taking place on Saturday in London. 'Watch out, it's going to be mayhem, especially around Hyde Park. Supposedly a big contingent's going from here too—they're all going to hitch it, believe it or not.' She gave her naughty little Trudy chuckle. 'You'll be taking Daddy's corporate jet while they're sticking their thumbs out in the pissing rain on the M1.'

I didn't like the contrast one bit—in fact, it was quite embarrassing—but the way Trudy delivered it made me burst out laughing. Then my laughter set her off, and in no time we were both in stitches.

Christ, it felt *so* good to let go after the misery of the last thirty-six hours. That was the great thing about Trudy. One never failed to have fun in her company, and deep down, beneath her silly jokes, occasional outrageous comments and theatrical eccentricity, there was a heart of pure gold.

She suddenly became more serious. 'Global warming is just such a huge topic, isn't it? I'm not a person who worries about much, but this thing worries the crap out of me. My god, I even lie awake at night thinking about it. It's scary and, as a world, we seem to be doing zilch to deal with it.'

'I totally agree with you, Trudy. And the big-time politicians who *could* do something about it *don't*, either because they're in denial or conflicted. Worst of all, we've all become used to wanting *more and more and more* of everything when we all need to be consuming and using less.'

'*Good on our St Andrews marchers,*' she whisper-shouted, raising her fist in the air.

Having put the world to rights, we finished up, and out in the street we went our separate ways, Trudy to Psychology, me to the Union to meet my Business Management team to work on our entrepreneurship project.

About a block from the Union, I heard the toot of a horn and the rugby captain, Declan, drew up in his famous old banger. 'A bit of scrap last night, I hear?' he said with an Irish twinkle in his eye.

'News travels fast.'

'The whole place is talking about you. That's the net for you.'

'Fucking nightmare,' I grumped. 'I wish the internet had never been invented.'

'Don't worry, old son. It'll blow over, and I'm sure you'll take it on the chin like the top bloke you are. See you around,' he said before waving and driving off.

Like the rest of us, I greatly admired Declan. He'd never mentioned it, but we all knew that his father, a top policeman, had been killed by an IRA car bomb many years ago. Worse, Declan and his mother had been at the front window seeing him off when it detonated, and the fact that he'd made it to uni, never mind captaining the team, was remarkable.

As I approached the Union car park, I saw that it was a hive of activity. Trudy was right about there being a St Andrews contingent heading south, and I watched as what must have been at least a hundred people got ready to set off, complete with placards, rucksacks and, of course, tons of booze. It was going to be a hell of a road trip, that's for sure, and already groups of them were breaking into song. I almost wished I could join them—what fun they were going to have.

But my feelings of happiness and solidarity were short-lived. A small contingent knew me, and when they spotted me, they let out a massive cheer. Before I knew it, all one hundred were chanting my name over and over again. Shaun was right. My fight had made me famous.

I sprinted into the Union and hid for fifteen minutes before going to find my teammates.

Chapter 7

'Hello, old friend. What a surprise to see you sitting here.'

After lying low, I'd found my teammates and we'd worked hard on our project for a couple of hours. Then, still feeling extremely agitated, I'd headed homeward up Market Street. Outside the supermarket, by chance, I'd spotted Bullet tethered to a post and my mood had instantly lifted.

'Where's your master, old boy?'

I peered through the shop frontage. Ah, there he was, picking up his bag from the checkout counter.

'What a pleasant surprise,' said Bob as the sliding doors opened. 'And hasn't Bullet taken quite a shine to you! He doesn't greet everyone like that, I can tell you.'

'Especially the chap in the pub last night.' I laughed.

'Well, funny you should say that,' he said, pulling his bag down on the pavement. 'I was so surprised, and quite frankly confused, at Bullet's behaviour that I called his old handler first thing this morning. It turns out that the dog has been trained to growl like that when he whiffs firearms! Isn't that quite remarkable, Peter?'

'Maybe the Sikh had been out on one of the shoots,' I suggested, thinking on my feet. 'There are quite a few, run by the big estates, and tourists like him flock to them.'

'Indeed, and I thought that too, but when I quizzed him further, he said that Bullet was trained to growl like that when he catches the scent of *handguns*, not *shotguns*. The latter have a woody odour, you see. It's all rather strange, isn't it? But I'm sure there's a logical explanation.'

'Strange indeed, sir.'

'Anyway,' he said, changing the subject, 'what are you up to for the rest of the day? Anything interesting?' God, he was nosey, but you couldn't help but quite like him.

'Just a quiet day, especially after the silliness of last night.'

'Oh, just take it in your stride, lad, which no doubt you will. And don't worry about all that social media nonsense. It'll all blow over.'

Christ, even this ancient soldier was tuned in to the latest gossip on social media.

'I don't worry.' I smiled but with an air of defensiveness.

'Please don't think I'm prying, but I picked up that you're the son of James Black of Black & Co. My goodness, what a marvellous company, and what a grand job your father has done over the years, building the firm into what it is today. You should be enormously proud of what he's done—a Scot taking on the Asians on their home turf!'

'You don't miss a trick, do you?' I laughed. 'Yes, I'm very proud indeed of him. In fact, I'm off to London tomorrow to see him, as it happens.'

'Interesting,' he said, giving me the same piercing stare that he'd given me down at the beach, and he started untethering Bullet and picked up his shopping bag.

'I'm walking that way,' I said, pointing up Market Street. 'And you?'

'That way, son,' he replied, pointing the other way, and then he paused for a moment, looking a little uncomfortable. 'Peter, as you're going to be in London, I don't suppose you could ... erm ... if it's not too much of an imposition ... consider doing an old man a small favour?'

'Sure,' I replied. 'Happy to help if I can ... I think?'

'Well,' he started, 'I have a granddaughter, Christine, in London, and she's not much older than you, in fact. She's simply marvellous, but I *do* worry about her, and I was wondering if you might drop in on her and perhaps buy her a coffee and sort of ...' He paused, searching for words. 'And sort of check that she's OK. To be frank, Peter, I haven't heard a sausage from her for weeks.'

I didn't quite know what to say. It was quite a big ask, and I hardly knew him from Adam. 'I'm only going for two days and London's a pretty big place ...' I replied politely.

'Don't worry,' he said quickly. 'She lives in the West End, and I can't imagine that you and your father will be staying far from there. A quick twenty-minute coffee should do it.'

The pushy old bugger wasn't giving me much choice, and I couldn't really say no, could I? 'Sure, Mr McPherson.' I smiled. 'Of course I'll do what I can if I find some spare time.'

'Oh, marvellous,' he said, looking relieved. 'You see, her parents were ...' Then he stopped. 'Perhaps another day.' He rummaged in his pockets and pulled out a dog-eared card. 'These are her details. I'm sure you that you'll like her—a little headstrong at times but razor sharp and a computer whiz. She's doing a post-grad at Imperial—data analytics and high-tech stuff.'

When I got home, I decided not to procrastinate and immediately sent her a text. 'Hi, I'm Peter Black texting from St Andrews, where I'm a student. Incredibly sorry to bother you, but I'm going to be in London this weekend and your grandfather (whom I recently met by chance) suggested we meet up for a coffee. He's keen that I check you're OK. Let me know where we can meet— I'll be staying at the Mandarin Oriental Hotel in the West End.'

Up until dinner time, I tried my best to take my mind off things, bashing out the final part of an Economics essay due on Monday. In the evening, after a fabulous Diti curry, the four of us hung out with a few glasses of wine, watching that movie where Liam

Neeson goes on a mission to rescue his missing daughter. Now there's a guy who can kick ass!

Before turning in for the night, I saw that Christine had replied. 'Hello, Peter. Good grief, Gramps can be a pain!! OK, let's meet up tomorrow at the Arabic Café at the rear of Harrods. What time?'

After a flurry of messages, we fixed on 11 a.m.—I'd go straight from the airport—and I nodded off thinking about her grandfather. I seemed to be bumping into him all over the place and now, almost bizarrely, I was going to be meeting his granddaughter.

Chapter 8

By 7 a.m. I was in my Uber heading to Leuchars airbase. By 8 a.m. we were airborne, and as soon as we had reached our cruising altitude, I was tucking into breakfast with a stack of newspapers by my side. Dad's plane always had a well-stocked larder, and the sausages, bacon and eggs were amazing. All the dailies had the Save the Planet march front and centre, and I hadn't really appreciated just how huge it was going to be. It would start in Hyde Park, near my hotel, make its way through Green Park, past the palace and on to Parliament and Downing Street. There were estimates of between 500,000 and a million people, making it the capital's largest ever march!

'World's biggest hot air balloon,' proclaimed the *Daily Mail*, describing the gigantic 'distressed planet' themed hot air balloon which would symbolically rise into the air at the start of the march and then gently float over the city. What a powerful marketing stunt, and all crowd-funded.

'Fears of violence,' headlined *The Times* in its sombre front-page article, suggesting that elements of the eco movement might go radical in the same way that members of the anti-animal-cruelty movement once had. The paper's view was that it was only a matter of time, with politicians, petroleum and mining companies, and airlines potential targets. I wasn't really surprised.

I'd read bits and pieces over the last few months about a Cambridge Uni duo called Green and Jo who had emerged as the main driving force behind the movement, and the papers had pages and pages dedicated to them. *The Telegraph* described Green as a genius frontman who was becoming globally recognised for his views on climate change, and the paper opined that, given time, he could become *the* icon for the global climate change movement. He was a brilliant student who spoke English,

French, Spanish and Chinese and, notably, was adept at going head-to-head with highly experienced politicians. He could expose weaknesses and pick arguments to pieces, and even the US president was now avoiding debates with him after a recent knockout performance by Green.

The Guardian, on the other hand, viewed his girlfriend Jo as the true driving force behind the movement. I scarcely knew anything about her, and a photo showed a plain, bespectacled, dungaree-clad student. However, she was rumoured to be very intelligent and, beneath the hippie exterior, supposedly quite beautiful. She had allegedly been courted by top modelling agencies as a teenager.

I nodded off mid-flight, waking with a jolt as we landed at City Airport. I hadn't had pleasant dreams, though, and I awoke drenched in sweat. The crazy woman had been chasing me all over the golf course with her knife, shrieking like a deranged witch, blood spurting out of her mouth. It wasn't my first dream about her and I was sure it wasn't going to be the last.

The trip from City Airport to the West End was uneventful. London was looking superb, the sun shining after the early morning rain, and the whole city seemed fresh and clean. Cranes dotted the skyline, a good indicator that a boom was under way, and while there weren't too many people about, those who were looked happy and relaxed, in weekend mode. As I sat in the car, I wondered whether I should consider working in London after uni but concluded that I probably loved Hong Kong too much. There were other incredibly exciting Asian cities too, and Black & Co. had offices in pretty much all of them. I felt blessed to have so many different options.

Chapter 9

Traffic was light and having made good time, I changed my plans ever so slightly. The driver took me straight to the hotel, where I dropped my bags in my room before heading down to the lobby for the short walk to Harrods.

As I exited the huge revolving doors into the drop-off forecourt, I was suddenly met by the sound of arguing. *'Fucking tosspot!* Don't tell me where I should or shouldn't park. Useless *wanker,'* snarled a late twenties/early thirties guy from his soft-top sports car.

'Take your fancy car and piss off,' retorted the furious doorman, who was no spring chicken.

Shit! Now the driver had leapt out of his car and was storming towards the doorman, and it looked for sure as though he was going to thump him. I darted forward and just managed to put myself between the two of them in time. 'Stop. Cool it!' I shouted, pushing them apart.

The driver sort of grappled with me, then stopped and stared. He was about my height with a shock of black hair, an entitled sneer on his face. What was he going to do? Was he going to thump me instead of the doorman? My adrenaline was doing its stuff, but I was holding back.

To my relief and immense surprise, he quickly backed right down, then walked briskly to his car. Seconds later, he roared off without so much as giving us another look.

'So sorry about that, sir,' said the doorman, still staring down the car as it left. 'These rich kids think they can park anywhere, and when you tell 'em that they can't, they turn real nasty.'

'Don't worry, Jack,' I said, reading his name badge. 'He's gone now.'

'Do you know him, sir? He took one look at you and scarpered.'

'Never seen him in my life, and thank god he came to his senses. It's a little too early in the day for a scrap,' I joked, trying to lighten the mood. Saying that, when our stares had met, the guy's reaction had been a little strange, and he'd backed down almost immediately. Had he known me? Or maybe he'd mistaken me for someone else. I'd probably never know.

The old chap, though, looked pale and was trembling. 'Apologies for my language, sir; it wasn't very professional of me,' he said shakily.

'What language?' I smiled. 'I didn't hear a word. But more importantly, are you OK?'

'I'm fine, thank you,' he replied, putting his chin up stoically. 'I'll be right as rain in no time after my tea break.'

As I headed to Harrods, it occurred to me that I'd been a whisker away from getting myself into *another* fight, and this time right outside one of London's top hotels. Like with the other stuff, I'd been in the wrong place at the wrong time, but it just seemed to be one thing after another. It would be good to see my father later and feel a bit of normalcy.

Chapter 10

Walking into the Arabic Café tucked behind Harrods was like walking into another world. It was one of huge plush armchairs and sofas, men wearing elegant white dish-dash, and little groups of veiled women deep in conversation. A musky scent wafted through the place along with an aroma of coffee and spices. I took a seat giving me a good view of everything that was going on, and within a few seconds an impeccably turned-out waiter appeared.

'Good morning. I'm Ahmed. May I take your order?'

'Hi, Ahmed. I'm waiting for someone, but in the meantime, please could I have an espresso?'

He gave a tiny bow, then looked at me thoughtfully. 'Sir, if you've never tried it before, could I suggest our delicious Arabic coffee? It's very smooth on the palate.'

'Espresso will be fine, thank you.' I hoped I hadn't sounded too brusque.

'Right away.' Ahmed gave another little bow.

A few minutes later he appeared with my espresso, and as he put it in front of me, he said, 'Sir, I've taken the liberty of also bringing you some Arabic coffee, courtesy of the house. As a good Arab, I feel it is my duty to introduce you to something from my culture, and it also comes with three of the finest dates that you can find—all the way from Liwa.'

'I'll take an Arabic coffee too,' said a voice, and I turned to see a young woman coming up to the table in a wheelchair. 'Ahmed, take that espresso away. Nobody drinks that filthy stuff in here.'

'Ms McPherson, what a great pleasure to see you, as always,' said Ahmed, smiling broadly and giving yet another little bow as he subtly removed my espresso.

'I'm Christine,' she said, thrusting a hand in my direction. 'And you must be Peter Black. Well, now that you've seen me, you can tell the old boy that I'm just fine, can't you?'

Wow. From her grandfather's comments and the tone of her texts, I had expected feisty, but nothing quite like this, and I totally hadn't expected her to use a wheelchair. I was utterly lost for words.

'Well, say something,' she snapped. 'Have you never seen a woman in a wheelchair before?'

'I, um … I, um …' Then I composed myself. 'I guess you're not quite what I was expecting.'

'You expected what? A pretty thing in a miniskirt with a nice pair of boobs? You men are all the same!'

'No, absolutely not,' I said, half laughing, half taken aback. 'Of course I knew you'd be in a wheelchair. I just didn't expect it to have 'Save the Fucking Planet' written on the side of it.'

She glanced down at her chair and seemed to relax a little. 'I painted it last night. Perhaps not the world's greatest artistry, but it captures what I wanted to say, I guess! Maybe the F word was a little too strong, though, especially if there are children around.'

'Oh, I don't know. One can feel the emotion in the statement. Personally, I quite like it.'

'OK, introductions over, Peter. Gramps is the greatest man I know, so if he thinks you are a good chap, then you most probably are. What brings you to London? Are you marching?'

'No, I wasn't planning to. It's just a quick trip down from Scotland to spend some time with my dad. He's in from Hong Kong for the weekend.'

'I've read up on him on my thing,' she said, digging down by her side and producing a small, very sophisticated-looking tablet.

'He's quite the Hong Kong tycoon, isn't he? I also found some interesting footage of you.' At that point, she beckoned Ahmed over, who was loitering close by. 'Ahmed, you better not be giving Peter too much caffeine! Take a look at this.' She started showing him my and Johnston's fight clip.

I could feel my face going red with embarrassment. 'Oh, please. What are you *on*? I've known you for all of ten seconds and you're already showing my new friend Ahmed here videos of the one and only fight that I've ever been in. And by the way, it was self-defence.'

'Don't worry.' The waiter grinned. 'Ms McPherson is always joking and playing with us. She's our favourite regular and she's so very kind to us.'

'Relax. I apologise.' Did I see the hint of a smile? 'My shrink is always telling me to tone it down.' But then a look of guilt tinged with sadness suddenly spread over her face. 'Maybe it's time I started heeding her advice instead of pissing off everyone I come into contact with.'

'No worries from my side, Christine, and you certainly haven't annoyed me. So please don't worry.'

'You'll of course be wondering how I ended up in the chair?' she said abruptly. Now she was looking straight into my eyes with the same piercing look I'd got from Bob down on the beach.

'No, no ... I hadn't, like ... given it any thought.' God, this was awkward, but yes, of course it had crossed my mind. The second I'd seen her.

'Oh, don't worry,' she replied. 'It's simple. I was sitting in a café in the Green Zone in Kabul with my parents—my father the was ambassador to Afghanistan at the time. One of the waiters turned out to be a suicide bomber. He detonated the thing. *Bang*. That was that. I ended halfway up the street tangled in a tree, with a broken back.'

Jesus Christ. Is she being serious?

Yes, she was. It was written all over her face, and I sat quietly for a moment or two, just looking at her. Bizarrely, an image flashed through my mind of a young Declan watching his dad's car explode.

'My god, Christine, I had no idea. I'm *so* sorry,' I said quietly. 'Your grandfather didn't say a word.' But now his 'story for another day' was beginning to make sense.

'It was ages ago and I've come to terms with it,' she said stoically. Her bravery impressed me, but I wasn't sure I was convinced.

'And do you mind me asking …'

'My parents?' she cut in.

'Yes, although I feel awful for asking. It's not really my place …'

'It's fine, plus my shrink would love all this "opening up" nonsense.'

She took a sip of Arabic coffee, closing her eyes for a moment or two, savouring the flavour. Then, as I tried mine—taken aback by just how good it was—she answered my question.

'Mother and Father died instantly. My father had been in post for five years—he loved the place and its people. He'd given it everything. I sometimes wish I'd died too, but it seems God had other plans.'

A horrible chill shot down my spine and all I could do was stare at her in disbelief. Oh my god, what unbelievable hell had this poor young woman gone through?

'Enough of all this misery!' she suddenly announced. 'What's done is done! Now, changing the subject. If you happen to have some spare time this afternoon, why don't you come to the march with me? As a disabled, I, plus one other, get to the very front of the march, and having a bit of able-bodied help to get me to the starting point would be great. The grass is so long in Hyde Park, the paths are all rooted and falling to pieces, and the whole place is littered with dog shit.'

'I'd be happy to,' I said, laughing at her choice of words. 'I can't promise I'll stay too long, but I'll certainly help you to get there.' Reading about Save the Planet in the papers had piqued my interest, but more, how could I *possibly* say no to her? I suddenly had the utmost admiration for her.

'Can I let you into a secret?' Now she had lowered her voice and was looking cautiously around.

I leaned in closer. 'Sure.' What was this all about?

Animated, her eyes darting around the room, making sure there was no one in earshot, she pulled me even closer.

What on earth was she about to tell me?

Chapter 11

'Peter, I've got a *really,really*, bad feeling about the march.'

'What do you mean? I don't understand?' I whispered back, looking around cautiously.

She gripped my arm. 'I've spent months snooping on them and I just know that something *bad* is going to happen. I can feel it. I've been to the police about it, but they just ignore me. Gramps too is tired of me wittering on about it. But I tell you. *I can feel it.*'

'Do you think things might get out of hand—like looting and pillaging and that kind of stuff? I'm sure there'll be a big police presence to keep things under control, so maybe there's no need to worry.' What she was saying sounded a bit bonkers.

'Worse,' she said more loudly. '*Much, much* worse.'

'I'm not really getting the gist of this,' I said, sitting back in my seat. She sounded pretty flaky.

She beckoned me forward again. 'About a year ago,' she whispered, 'genuinely interested in sustainability and the way we're wrecking Earth, I started hanging out with Jo and Green's group. The movement was interesting; progressive, smart people, front-page news, going places. But all of a sudden, after a few weeks, they shut me out just as I was beginning to get into the inner circle.'

'Why would they do that?'

'I think they realised that *McPherson* had a mind of her own and couldn't be brainwashed.' I quite liked the way she called herself McPherson. 'The closer I got to the whole thing, the more I began to feel that Jo and Green—but Jo especially—were beginning to manipulate people. But before I could put my finger on it, I became an outcast.'

'Manipulate? What do you mean?'

'The dialogue was becoming militant—things like "we'll make a statement" and "let's really wake them up". At the same time, there were more and more hushed conversations and shifty looks. Things were changing, and something was beginning to build.

'Jo too was beginning to wrap them all around her little finger, including her boyfriend Green. I'd also go as far as to say that Green wasn't the only one she was sleeping with. She used "that" to control people. And not only the males!

'After being shunned, for a short while I was still able to snoop on them electronically, but then, from one day to the next, it became impossible. That meant one thing—they'd stopped using phones, computers and anything else electronic for internal communication. A massive red flag!'

'Your "snooping" ... was it legal?'

'Of course not,' she said dismissively, 'but I'm good at it, and if I have reasonable grounds for doing it, I don't see any problem with it! After all, this could be in the national interest, couldn't it?'

I raised an eyebrow. Jesus! Grandfather (quite probably) recruiting for British Intelligence. Granddaughter a tech genius, out looking for bad guys. What a family!

'So what's your theory, Christine? What might they do to wake us all up? Won't the size of the march itself and that kick-ass balloon of theirs be a wake-up call? With that level of support, the politicians are going to wake up and take notice for sure.'

'No, Peter,' she replied, shaking her head. 'My theory is that that isn't going to be enough for them, and especially for Jo. I think they'll do something really major, and possibly horrible, today. They feel that the world has gone to sleep on climate change, and they could be about to give us all an almighty jolt. *What*, I don't know. But if they do something, Jo will be the one behind it all.'

'Oh, come on. These are Oxbridge-educated kids from good middle-class families, and surely—'

'You don't believe me either, do you?' she snapped, pushing her chair away from me, her face suddenly going red with fury.

Wow, what a reaction! She really believes all this nonsense.

'It's not that I don't believe you. It certainly sounds as though they've become disillusioned and angry, and maybe there will be some messy stuff this afternoon. But I can't imagine it'll be something that water cannons and mounted police can't sort out. Don't you think?'

'Well, I hope that's all it is.' She sighed, backing down a bit, the redness subsiding. 'But don't forget that behind most terrorist groups lie smart, highly educated people. Anyway, you have an appointment to keep, don't you? I shouldn't take any more of your time.' She signalled for the bill.

'Yes, I must dash—to see Dad. But we'll still meet later, will we? I really am more than happy to help you get up to the march, and I've really enjoyed meeting you and our chat this morning.'

'I suppose so,' she said with an air of resignation. 'I guess some help and a bit of company would be nice.'

'Christine, don't worry, OK? Everything is going to be just fine. You'll see. No need to worry.'

The piercing stare was back again, and she leaned right forward in her chair.

'I hope for all our sakes you're right. Those two are not to be underestimated.'

Chapter 12

As I entered the hotel lobby, I saw Peng waiting for me. He was a small, neat man dressed, as always, in black slacks and a white shirt.

'Master Peter,' he said in his usual soft, calm voice. 'It's good to see you after so long. You look well, although do I sense that you are carrying some worry on your shoulders?'

'I'm fine, Mr Peng, and it's *so* good to see you too!' We shook hands, formal as ever.

There wasn't a person on the planet with better powers of observation or ability to read people than this man. My father knew it too and, over the years, had sought his opinion on countless matters. His observations were rarely wrong. He'd probably studied me as I walked into the hotel and spotted that my shoulders were tight with stress and worry. Now he'd be trying to work out why.

My father appeared, walking across the lobby followed by an entourage of businesspeople in suits. He was the tallest by far, and his healthy tan stood out. 'Right, ladies and gentlemen, go and grab some lunch and we'll reconvene in the Lotus room at 2 p.m. sharp. But *please* run those projections again. Factor in the full upside potential of our combined Brazilian units. Ah, look there, there's Peter! Peng, please look after everyone, would you?'

He gave me a huge hug and looked me up and down. 'You don't look too bad, son. Perhaps a bit pale, but that'll be the grubby weather up there on the Fife coast. It's *so* good to see you after such a long time. Now come on, let's go upstairs to their Japanese place.'

'You're hyper, Dad,' I said with a laugh, hurrying into the lift behind him and giving Peng a little sorry-we-didn't-get-much-chance-to-talk wave as he bustled off with the team.

'It's all go,' he whispered as the doors closed. 'This thing is huge and we're getting very close to clinching it. Perhaps best we don't discuss it over lunch in a public place, though—you just never know who's listening in.'

'Sure, no problem.' Now I was intrigued to know what the deal was all about, not just because I was a shareholder but because of my growing interest in all things business.

The rear of the Mandarin had views out over Hyde Park, and as the lift door opened, we stared in astonishment at the ocean of people milling around the huge expanse. 'Goodness gracious,' gasped my father. 'They did say it'd be big, but this is quite unbelievable. What a job those two students have done; that chap Green can have a job with us any time he wants it. He'd be perfect in comms!'

As we ordered, my father felt obliged to take me through everything that Black & Co. was doing to make itself more sustainable. I hadn't realised just how much. Then it was on to family. My mum and Sam were both doing well, the overhaul of the old Morgan car was complete, Mrs Peng was doing fine, the yacht racing season had just started, and so on. What was clear was that he was as busy as ever, if not busier. The main thing on his mind, though, was the big deal.

It was then my turn to update *him*. First—of course—it was exam grades, followed by an update on my flatmates, and then it was on to the bar job. He'd been so proud when I'd told him a year ago that I'd taken it on. Sport, the most important part, I left until last, and he listened eagerly as I talked him through the ins and outs of my recent rugby and golf matches. He had been an amazing athlete in his day and peppered me with questions.

'So, what's on your mind?' he asked when I'd finished. 'I mean the thing you wanted to talk about the other night.'

'Oh, it was nothing at all.'

'Sure?'

'Sure,' I replied, although I felt I should say *something*. 'I really can't remember, but it might have been something to do with an old guy that I met by chance. His name is Bob McPherson, and rumour has it he recruits for British Intelligence. Do you think that kind of thing really goes on in unis?'

He paused for a moment or two, pondering, drumming his chopsticks on his wasabi dish.

'I'd strongly advise against a career as a spook,' he said quite sternly. 'Sounds glamorous, especially for you youngsters, but it's a mug's game. One minute you're in and the next minute you're out and, from time to time, I'd imagine you do some rather nasty things to earn your keep.' It almost sounded as though he was speaking from experience.

'Don't worry, Dad,' I replied. 'Trust me, I've zero intention of joining up and haven't been asked. Plus, as I said, it was nothing more than a chance encounter.'

'Son'—he pointed a friendly stick at me—'the Firm doesn't do "chance encounters", so don't be naive. Now for god's sake don't do anything stupid—your future lies in our firm, not the government's.'

'OK, Dad, OK.' I laughed and we left it at that. I thought better of telling him that I'd be meeting granddaughter McPherson in less than an hour.

Peng then appeared and after profuse apologies, he and my father headed back to the advisors, who seemed to be working themselves into a bit of a state. We'd be meeting up again in the evening for a beer or two, though.

With twenty minutes to kill, I went to my room to unpack. When I switched the TV on, to my surprise I found that the news channels had wall-to-wall coverage of the build-up to the march.

Flicking through them as I pulled my stuff out of my bags, I suddenly froze and sat on the edge of the bed, fixated on the screen. The BBC was just starting a live interview with Green and Jo.

Chapter 13

'Green and Jo,' opened the correspondent. 'Thanks for visiting our mobile studio here in Hyde Park, and many congratulations on succeeding in pulling together this incredible event. You must be extremely pleased that this day has finally come and over the moon with the response?'

'Ecstatic is the word I'd use, Gerald'—Green grinned—'and huge thanks to the BBC for inviting Jo and me to speak and for giving us global coverage. And yes, it has been one hell of a journey. But the day has finally arrived, and we now have this opportunity to let the world know how important this cause is. Climate change is something that every human needs to be utterly preoccupied with.'

He had blond, almost white, hair and olive skin and was dressed in ripped designer jeans and a crisp white T-shirt. Jo, on the other hand, was unbelievably scruffy, almost grimy looking. She wore ancient cargo trousers, a filthy grey sweatshirt, a woolly beanie hat and little round spectacles. Could she really have been a model in her former life?

Green spoke eloquently, with charm and passion, but—and maybe it was because of what McPherson had told me—I did think that he looked just a little uncomfortable. Throughout, he would often glance across at Jo as if seeking her approval for what he was saying.

'Green, tell us, is there likely to be any trouble or violence out there today? There has been quite some speculation.' I stood up. What a great question! What would he say?

Green paused, slowly rubbed his cheek with his hand and then glanced at Jo. Was the master lost for words? Or was he perhaps hiding something?

'Maybe I can answer that one,' said Jo in a very quiet, soothing voice. The camera zoomed in on her.

She seemed in no hurry. Why would she be? Millions of people were looking at her. Me? I was now on my knees, inches from the TV screen, desperate to hear what she would say. And, like probably many others, I was peering at her, searching for her alleged beauty.

She took off her beanie. 'Give me a moment, please,' she said softly. Then she took off her little round glasses.

'Please take your time, Jo,' replied Gerald as she undid her ponytail and gave her head a little shake, letting her long dark hair fall on her shoulders.

What a transformation. Good god, she *was* beautiful—and it was a unique, simple beauty. 'I think what Green would like to say is that it is quite possible that …' She paused again

'Quite possible that *what*, Jo?' promoted the captivated interviewer, almost begging her to continue.

'Quite possible that there is anger in people's hearts. Anger that the world might simply revert to normal as soon as our beautiful march is finished.'

'So just to be clear, Jo,' said the interviewer, looking a little puzzled. 'Are you in effect signalling that there *could* be violence out there today? By your own group … by your supporters?'

'No, Gerald, all I'm saying is that there are many millions of angry people out there in our precious world. They see our so-called "leaders" doing so very little to guide us all out of the catastrophe that is now upon us. Those leaders should be ashamed of themselves, don't you think, Gerald?' Then suddenly she stood up, nodding to Green to do likewise. She was petite—almost fragile.

'Thank you, Gerald, and the BBC,' said Green. 'We must go on to our other appointments with the other stations.' He seemed to have regained his confidence after his wobble.

What was I to make of what I had just seen?

There was no doubt at all about who was calling the shots—McPherson was dead right on that. What was also clear was that Jo truly was beautiful, and one could easily imagine her having bucketloads of besotted admirers quite willing to jump through hoops for her.

And was there going to be violence today at the hands of Green and Jo's people? She had deftly avoided the question, blamed politicians and talked about the groundswell of anger. But for my money, she had—in a roundabout way—hinted that something might happen. The police were used to managing rowdy demonstrations, though, and I didn't worry too much about it.

Chapter 14

Walking to Knightsbridge to meet McPherson was a nightmare, but getting from there to Hyde Park was even worse, as tens of thousands of people were making their way to the starting point of the march.

McPherson hadn't seen Jo and Green's interview, and when I told her, she pulled it up on her tablet in a flash. 'There, Peter! Do you believe me now? She's got him by the nuts. Now I'm more convinced than ever that they're scheming something.'

'You know, I really don't know what to think'—I sighed—'but why don't we get up to the start of the march and we can see what's what?'

As if the crowds weren't enough, the heavens suddenly opened, and while McPherson had a special see-through contraption to drape over herself, I hadn't brought anything and ended up resorting to wearing a bright orange waterproof she had spare. Three sizes too small, zipped up to my nose and the hood down to my eyes, I looked like a complete tool!

As we made our way along the edge of the park, McPherson was in quite some mood, verbally lashing out at people right and left as we tried to make headway. 'Clear the way ... we haven't got all day, have we? Make way for the cripple ... don't you know how to control your kids?'

She was right about one thing, though. The path was tree-rooted and crumbling, and it took us almost half an hour of hard going until we finally saw signs for the disabled area near Hyde Park Corner. There, a lady police officer gave us a helping hand.

'That was simply ghastly,' said McPherson as we reached the enclosure. 'But thank you, dear Peter. I quite simply couldn't have got here without you.' I smiled to myself, thinking about the carnage she had left in her wake.

Never had I seen so much human life in one place. As far as the eye could see, deep into Hyde Park, there were hundreds of thousands of people, singing, dancing, drinking and beating drums. The rain hadn't dampened their enthusiasm one bit. The noise was utterly obscene.

Close to where we were was a vast cordoned-off area, and laid out on the grass in the process of being inflated was the *ginormous* hot air balloon. Maybe five to ten minutes away from getting off the ground, it was made of a very thin tin foil-like material, and one could clearly see its blue oceans, green land masses and grey mountain ranges. Attached to it was a massive passenger basket perched on a launch platform with about twenty steps leading up to it.

A red boiler-suited security team patrolled the entire cordoned-off zone, and there were two of them in the basket itself helping two smart-uniformed pilots to manage the inflation. One thing was for sure, once fully inflated and in the air, the balloon was going to be an incredible sight.

Close to the launch site was a vast stage looking out over the crowds from where Green and Jo would presumably make an address.

'Look, there they are!' shouted McPherson, pointing, trying to make herself heard above the noise.

She was right. Off to our right, three electric buggies were making their way from a tented area which must have housed the media village. Green and Jo were sitting in the middle one, and there were 'boiler suits' in the first and third, with more running alongside, presidential bodyguard fashion.

'They get death threats from right-wing groups,' shouted McPherson.

'A bit over the top, if you ask me!' I shouted back

A chant began to break out as word got out that the two 'superstars' had arrived. 'Green, Green, Green ...' and like a chain reaction, more and more people joined in. Within half a minute, every single person in Hyde Park was joining in. I could scarcely hear myself think.

I yelled in McPherson's ear, 'I've never seen anything like this. It's unbelievable! *Overpowering.*'

'Bloody scary, I'd say,' she yelled back. 'And did you see Jo? She looked like a zombie on a mission, and I tell you, Peter, something's going to happen. I don't know what. But it will.'

'Everything'll be fine. Trust me.' This got me a fierce, withering look in return. I felt so sorry for her—she was the only one in the park that day not enjoying herself.

Seconds later, their buggy drew to a halt by the stage and Green bounded up the rear steps, followed by Jo, and the crowd went utterly berserk as they burst into view. World-famous pop stars would have struggled to receive such a rapturous reception.

'Silence please for Green. Green is going to speak,' shouted Jo, but it took her numerous further attempts until, finally, the crowd began to quieten down. 'Let's have total silence for Green. Total peace and silence for our beloved Mother Earth.'

Green embraced her, then took the microphone and stood for a few moments as a deathly hush spread across his audience.

'Students, children, ladies, gentlemen, workers, good ordinary people, citizens and comrades.' He then gave a long pause ...

'In a few minutes, this march will begin. The biggest march the world has ever seen. From this day forth, the world will change forever, and *we*, the normal, humble people on Mother Earth, will have made a statement. This day will go down in history, and I ask that each and every one of you, from this day forth, *commit* to making this cause your life's mission.

'Politicians, big business, the G20, the wealthy. They will *never* do what is necessary to save our planet, and instead we must all take up the struggle ourselves. We must do *whatever it takes* to avert the catastrophe that humanity now faces.'

He pointed out across the audience before bowing his head and putting his right hand across his heart. '*You, we, us* are the *only* ones who can save the planet,' he said quietly and emotionally. 'Now please afford two minutes' silence to show our respect for our Earth.'

At that point, dramatically, he went down on his knees, bowing his head and holding his hands in prayer. Jo and the entire team of boiler suits did the same, and like a vast army of dominos, so did the entire park.

'Brainwashing at its best.' McPherson laughed ironically, shaking her head.

Midway through the two minutes, I noticed an electric buggy quietly pull up at the foot of the steps leading up to the basket, and two 'boiler suits' got out carrying two large red backpacks. 'I wonder what's going on there,' I said, nudging McPherson, who was still fixated on Green and Jo, and we both watched as the men climbed the steps.

Back on stage, with the 120 seconds almost up, Green got up off his knees just as, in dramatic unison, the balloon began to pick itself up off the grass. Then, as if by magic, the sun made an appearance from behind the clouds. The Green and Jo PR team would undoubtedly be beside themselves with joy.

'Everyone,' screamed Jo, raising her fist to the heavens, 'let our march begin!' and with a deafening roar, the crowd slowly started to move forward and the chanting began.

'Save the planet, save the planet, save the planet, save the planet ...'

With the balloon now visibly straining at its tethers, Green and Jo dashed off the stage, across the grass to the podium and up the steps to the balloon. 'What the hell do you think they are up to, McPherson?' Something really didn't feel right.

She didn't reply. She was just staring, desperately trying to work out what was going on. As we looked on, we suddenly saw a scuffle break out on the platform as Green and the boiler suits jostled with the pilots, fists flying. Down below, at ground level, the tethers were being released and take-off was imminent. What was going on, I didn't know, but I could feel my adrenaline doing its stuff, ready for fight or flight.

What on earth is McPherson doing? Frozen in shock, I suddenly saw her shooting out across the cordoned area in her chair. *'Police, police ... stop them!'* she was shouting.

I didn't know what to do. Follow? Stay put? But before I could do anything, I watched in horror as two boiler suits ran at her, ploughed into her and knocked her flying out of her chair. Then, as one kicked her savagely in the guts, the other pounded her face with his fists. *They're going to kill her!*

I sprinted like a man possessed and *crunch*, flattened one with a flying kick to the head, then threw a frenzied volley of punches at the other. Now there were four more running at me. What on earth was I going to do? Where were the police? I was seconds away from annihilation. Blood gushing from her face, McPherson suddenly yelled at me, 'Just leave me! Stop Jo and Green! Stop them from doing something terrible!'

Chapter 15

I desperately wanted to help her, but she was right—something awful was going down. With more boiler suits closing in, still sprinting, I veered away from her and went all out to try to get to the balloon and Jo and Green.

Dodging and wrong-footing the musclebound thugs one after the other, I got closer and closer until only a huge fat guy guarding the podium steps stood between me and my goal. There was no time to think. No stopping. No discussion. *Bang.* I floored him with a throat punch, and as he went down, I hurdled over him and tore up the steps. I'd never been more focused in my entire life.

God, *no*! Was I too late? Just as I got to the top of the steps, I watched as the balloon—with its two pilots, Green and Jo, and two boiler suits inside—began to lift off. Surely there was no way I was going to make it. It was moving fast. Really fast. But I wasn't going to give up. I just *couldn't*. With a final burst of acceleration, I sped across the platform and dived out into the abyss.

Miraculously I got my right hand onto the mesh exterior at the base of the huge basket, and for a few seconds I just hung there, gasping in shock, as we soared into the sky. Then, pulling myself together, I got my left hand securely in place, hauled my legs up and began scrambling up to the basket lip until I was able to peer inside.

Jesus. What was going on? One pilot was motionless, out cold on the floor, while the other was being held down by the two thugs. But more worryingly, Jo and Green now had the packs on their backs.

'What's in the packs?' I yelled at Jo and Green as I jumped in. 'What in god's name are you planning?'

'Deal with him,' snapped Jo, looking at the two thugs and pointing at me.

'In a minute,' yelled the taller of the two boiler suits. He looked really agitated and was peering over the side. 'We need elevation. *Now!* We're too heavy.'

'Get rid of the pilots,' barked an emotionless Jo to the stockier boiler suit, and without a moment's hesitation, the bald little thug grabbed the lifeless pilot, jerked him above his head and simply tossed him overboard. Seconds later, pilot two, frozen rigid with fear, was bundled barbarically over the side, having given not an ounce of resistance or even a shout. Green just stood there staring, barely comprehending what he'd just witnessed.

'Him too, ma'am?' grunted the stocky little bastard, nodding towards me.

There wasn't a hint of hesitation. 'Yes, him too,' she said before calmly looking over the side.

A second later, like a deranged robot, with his head down he slammed into me, and solid rib and abdomen punches started battering into me. Clearly his plan was to weaken me before hurling me over the side, and very soon his onslaught began to take its toll on me.

The only thing I could do was grab his ears. I went for them, happy to tear them off if I could, and with a massive bellow he stepped back, grabbing his shiny head in pain. Then, just as he was thinking about coming back to give me more, I slammed the base of his nose with the flat of my palm. It was a solid hit and he lurched backwards like a drunkard.

With a manic growl, blood spraying from his nose, he charged at me again, and we both went down in a heap. The floor, though, was my domain, and in no time I'd got him in a headlock. With my arms and legs wrapped around him, he wasn't going anywhere. Advantage Black.

As I squeezed his airway, I kept my eyes on Green and Jo and the other boiler suit. If I was going to have any chance of dealing with them, I'd have to fully disable this one. But he was strong as an ox with a neck like a damn tree trunk, and I was using every ounce of my strength to hold him down.

Now Jo was peering over the side again. 'Keep guiding us to Parliament. No mistakes.'

Then I got it. I understood what they were going to do. Green had a device in his hand with wires coming out of it leading all the way up to the top of his backpack. Hers too. *Holy shit.* Jo and Green were suicide bombers, and Parliament, the very seat of the UK government, was their target.

Before I could do anything, though, Jo was coming for me as I lay there holding the boxer.

'Bitch,' I screamed. 'Fucking bitch.' She stamped on my head again and again and again, and when I tried to bury myself under my prisoner, she changed tactics and started stamping on one of my hands with her heel. Christ, my fingers were going to break!

But as she paused for just a second, I snatched at her ankle with one hand and got it. I yanked it hard. She came crashing down beside me, and in flash, I grabbed her throat. Wrenched her towards me. Pulled her in tight. Now we were eye to eye, our faces millimetres apart as she fought for air. On my other side, my chokehold on the boxer held rock solid.

'If I have to kill her, I will, Green,' I shouted at him. 'In the name of God, stop this madness!'

'No turning back. It's our destiny,' squealed Jo, somehow finding breath, and I clenched her slender throat even harder.

'We can stop it, Green. No one else needs to be hurt,' I gasped, my strength beginning to wane.

But now it was the other boiler suit's turn to have a go, and he tore across the basket and booted the shit out of me for a few seconds. But in a flash, thank god, he was back at Green's side, staring over the edge. 'Now, Green!' he screamed. 'Parliament in twenty seconds. Prepare to jump.'

Tears flooding down his face, Green began climbing onto the rim. He was going to do it.

Chapter 16

I released my hold on my two prisoners, kicked myself free of them and dived at Green as he straddled the side of the balloon. At the same moment, his boiler suit buddy launched himself at me.

Our heads collided with a sharp crack, but I'd just managed to get a hand on Green's backpack, and he topped back into the basket on top of me as I crashed to the floor.

My head screaming with pain, I was up first, staggering, my vision badly blurred. Green was yelling, struggling to get up on his knees. Boiler suit was out cold. Were we safe? Had we passed Parliament?

As Green tried to get up, I booted him in the nuts, sending him sprawling in the direction of Jo, and as I frantically peered over the side, I got the shock of my life as we passed feet from the clock face of Big Ben. We'd missed Parliament, thank god, but we were losing altitude fast, heading out over the Thames directly towards a wall of buildings on the south side.

Wait. What's Green doing now? He was crawling towards Jo, the detonator in both hands. 'You've killed her. You've killed her,' he screamed.

I had. She was lying lifeless where I'd left her. I hadn't even realised I'd done it, but I must have squeezed her fragile neck so tightly that I'd throttled her to death. I hadn't meant to. She was a monster who had ordered my death, but I felt utterly wretched about what I'd done to her.

'Stop, Green. It's over,' I pleaded with him. 'We've passed Parliament. We're going to crash into buildings. We must jump before it's too late. Save yourself, man. This wasn't your doing.'

'No turning back, my love,' he cried out, embracing his lifeless companion.

Her head now on his lap, he turned and stared at me with a look of pure and utter hatred, and I watched as he closed his eyes and pressed his thumb on the detonator.

Chapter 17

I came to. Was I in a boat? I could hear an engine, and we seemed to be moving at great speed. I couldn't see a thing, though, nor could I move or feel my arms and legs. I tried shouting, but my mouth was gagged. *Maybe I'm dead?* Could I possibly have survived a fall from such a height?

No, I wasn't dead. I remembered the explosion buffeting me into the air literally seconds after I'd hurled myself over the side of the basket. But what about my arms and legs? Did I still have them? I couldn't feel them. Had they been blown off in the blast? I was panicking. All I could think about was my limbs. 'Help, help, help,' I screamed from deep in my thorax. Could anyone hear me? I writhed and twisted until finally I started slamming my head up and down on whatever I was lying on. If anyone was there, they'd surely help me.

'Son. *Calm it!*' Firm hands pinned me down. 'You're safe. Don't panic.'

Whatever was over my head was being taken off. The gag too. My eyes were barely working, but in the blur, I could see a man wearing a black balaclava. As he began to untie my arms and legs, I stared at them, a feeling of euphoria ripping through my system. I was OK. I couldn't believe it. I'd survived fully intact. Bound so tightly I'd lost the feeling in my limbs, but now it was slowly returning.

'Where are we going?' I asked him, but he just ignored me.

The boat was one of those ultra-fast black RIBs that I'd occasionally marvelled at as they pelted up the Thames on drills. Now it was beginning to veer towards the riverbank, heading for a tiny gap between two old river-facing buildings. As it approached, the helm, also balaclava-clad, slowed right down and we slid into a dark tunnel.

The tunnel seemed to go on forever, and after a good five minutes, we glided into an underground docking area complete with pontoons berthing ten or more RIB craft. We must have been deep in the city, probably somewhere between Bank and Monument tube stations.

I was led into a small room where a doctor checked me, and I was given dry clothes before being taken up in an elevator and put in a meeting room with an armed guard stationed at the door. Throughout, despite asking repeatedly where I was, no one would tell me, and all I got was the same script. 'You're safe in a government facility.'

Did these idiots understand what I'd just been through? I wasn't a goddamn criminal!

The room was bare other than a wooden table and six plastic chairs, and I'd barely sat my arse down when in walked a tall man in uniform, probably in his late fifties, followed by a smaller nondescript man. I immediately stood up. 'Be seated,' he said curtly. 'My name is Commander Burke. That's George,' he said pointing at his colleague. 'And you are Peter Black, correct?'

'I am,' I replied. 'Where am I?'

'You were lucky to get out of the balloon.'

'Green was about to detonate. I'm not sure I had a choice.'

'Indeed,' he replied, glancing over at expressionless George.

I suddenly remembered McPherson. 'The woman in the wheelchair. The one who was attacked at the start of the march. Is she OK? Her name is Christine McPherson.'

'She's in critical shape,' he replied bluntly. 'She'll be extremely lucky if she pulls through.'

My body literally trembled with emotion. 'What! When I left her, she was badly beaten but coherent. What more did they fucking do to her?'

'After you ran to the balloon, five or more of them laid into her and left her for dead. They're claiming she was a right-wing radical out to kill Green and Jo. We're interrogating them as we speak.' He nodded over his shoulder as though they were somewhere in the same building.

'Right-wing radical! She was a poor woman in a wheelchair who knew that they were up to something. Without her, I swear to god Parliament would be sitting in ruins right now.'

'It looks like her partner in crime played his part too,' said Burke quietly. 'Well done, lad.'

'Indeed. An outstanding display of courage,' chipped in George. 'Your country owes you an enormous debt of gratitude!'

Emotion suddenly welled up inside me and I stared up at the ceiling, desperately trying to hold back tears. I hadn't really thought about it, but yes, they were right. If I hadn't got into the balloon, the country's seat of power might well have been decimated and people—possibly dozens of them—could have died. It had been harrowing, but somehow I'd survived, and I thanked God that I'd followed Christine's pleas to try to stop them.

'I killed Jo up there, you know?' I suddenly blurted out to them. 'I was holding her down by the throat, and I think I just held on too tight and too long. Maybe she deserved to die, but I feel terrible about it. She was just … just a woman.'

'It's a perfectly understandable reaction, Peter,' said the Commander. 'Killing someone, never mind a woman, takes its toll. We'll be sure to fix you up with someone who will help you deal with it.'

I stared at them. Good lord. If only they knew that she wasn't my first.

'Terrible things happen in battle,' concurred George. 'However, in your own time, why don't you take us through everything right from the very start?'

'Can it wait? I really have to see Christine—I feel *so* responsible.'

'I'll be going to the Cromwell myself later,' said Burke. 'You can join me if you like. I know her grandfather.'

'You know Bob! So do I! Which part of the police are you with, Commander Burke?'

'I run British Intelligence,' he replied dryly. 'You're in our HQ.'

They probably saw me gulp. The guy sitting in front of me headed up the Firm!

Trying hard not to feel too overawed, I took them through everything that had happened. By the end, exhausted, I asked to be excused, and they pointed me down the corridor to the bathroom. 'I'll order teas in the meantime,' said George. 'Milk and two sugars?'

When I got there, I doused my face with water, but even that didn't stop me from nodding off for a few seconds while sitting on the loo. As I dragged my weary legs back up the corridor, some way ahead of me I saw two armed officers approaching, flanking someone in red wearing ankle chains. 'Stand aside,' shouted one of the officers, and I immediately stood back to let them pass.

I froze. *Wait a minute.* As I stared at the approaching prisoner, I suddenly realised that it was one of the boiler suits, still in his red uniform. Then, as he got closer, to my astonishment, I recognised him! It was the one who'd been punching McPherson in the face. The one I'd kicked in the head.

My mind flashed back to the brutal beating he'd been giving her. Then to what Commander Burke had just told me. Fury enveloped me.

He recognised me just as my first punch slammed into his face, and despite the guards, I got a barrage in before I was dragged off him, cuffed and hauled up the corridor. 'Hope you liked taking a beating, you pussy son of a bitch!' I yelled after him. 'If I ever see you again, I'll kill you. Do you hear me? I'll rip the life out of you.'

Roars of hatred and abuse came back at me.

Sirens suddenly blared. Men in balaclavas swarmed the corridor. Medics sprinted. I'd caused the most almighty shitstorm, but it felt phenomenally good to have got a tiny bit of revenge on behalf of McPherson.

But then, as I was frogmarched back into the interview room, I got the shock of my life.

Chapter 18

To say I was speechless was an understatement.

'Dad! What the—? What on earth are you doing here? How did you—'

'James, before we start,' said Burke very calmly, 'please could you tell your errant son that thumping people here in my building just isn't acceptable no matter how odious they are.'

'Sincere apologies, Commander Burke,' said my father, nodding in deference. Then he turned to me. 'I thought I'd come over to HQ to collect you myself. My dear friend Burke gave me a call and suggested I come and give you a bit of moral support. Oh yes, and please can you behave yourself in this place? It's not great to go bashing people in HQ.'

'Friend?'

'We studied at Oxford and rowed together on the team.' He smiled.

'Right. Got it.' I nodded, still in total and absolute shock. My father was friends with the boss of the Firm. And we were sitting together in HQ. Mind-blowing!

'Peter, I watched the Hyde Park footage myself and had absolutely no idea that that the chap in bright orange with a death wish was my very own son.' He suddenly stood, came over to me and gave me a massive hug. 'Have you any idea what you accomplished today? This is really rather significant.'

'I'm sure you would have done the same, Dad.' I laughed awkwardly.

'I very, very, *very* much doubt it. I know very few people who would have done what you just did.'

'Like father, like son.' The Commander sighed. 'Humble to the end.'

Chapter 19

In the Commander's chauffeur-driven Range Rover, I sat quietly up front, browsing on my phone while the two of them sat in the back chatting.

'What's the press saying?' asked my father, seeing that I was scanning the news channels.

'They're looking for the poor bastard who bailed out over the Thames,' I said with half a laugh. 'I hope to hell it never comes back to me. I absolutely *do not* want the press hounding me.'

'Don't worry,' said the Commander. 'George will contain it. He's very good at that.'

I hoped so. In my mid-teens, the HK press had given me a torrid time on account of some mildly silly stuff that I'd done with some of my friends one Saturday afternoon in town, and from that point onwards, I'd avoided them like the plague. They'd twist and distort the truth to their own advantage if they could.

'Mum and Sam? What should I say to them, Dad?'

In the mirror, I saw him look at Burke. 'The usual protocol, James,' Burke counselled.

'The fewer people who know, the better. Let's keep it to you, me, Burke and George.' My father nodded.

'Fine,' I replied.

Usual protocol? Like father, like son? Why was my father so close to the Firm?

We dropped my father at the Mandarin—I'd meet him in the bar later—while the Commander and I went on to see Christine. However, just as we were arriving, he took a call and immediately excused himself. 'Blast. It seems I have an urgent matter to deal with back at HQ. I'll have to go.'

Before driving off, though, he got out of the car and walked over to me with his hand extended. 'Peter, once again, on behalf of the security services and your country, I thank you sincerely. An exemplary performance.' Inside my tired, aching body, I felt myself brimming with pride.

Getting to see McPherson wasn't straightforward, and after being denied entry at reception on account of not being family, I went to the third floor by the back stairs and snuck into her room. But I almost died when I saw her.

She was on a ventilator, hooked up to drips and sensors, her face horrifically swollen. Most normal human beings would already have been dead, but she was clinging on for dear life—for the second time in her short existence. I wished I'd beaten the boiler suited guy to death in HQ or grabbed a guard's gun and put a bullet in his forehead.

Feeling utterly powerless, I stood and stared at her. Would she ever make a recovery or was this it? I imagined them turning the machines off, her grandfather by her side, a long continuous beep from the monitor as she slipped away.

Carefully, I sat down on the edge of her bed and took her hand. 'You were right all along,' I whispered. 'But for you, Green and Jo would have bombed Parliament. I did what you asked me. I got on board. Managed to contain things. But it all started with you. You were amazing, Christine.'

Wait. What was that? Had I felt her hand move just a fraction?

I felt it again. This time ever so slightly stronger. Oh my god, she could hear me.

But now her monitors were going apeshit—beeping, buzzing, ringing—and I heard people running along the corridor. It was time to go. 'Bye, McPherson. I'll be back to see you soon.'

Christ. Now she was holding on to my hand by one of my fingers. She didn't want me to go.

'Christine, I *have* to go. The medics will give me hell, but you're going to be fine. I just know it.' Slowly, she let me go, and as I ran for it, I don't think I'd ever felt so elated. What a fighter! When I got out in the street, I called Bob McPherson so I could give him the wonderful news.

However, when he answered, he immediately tore straight into me. I really should have seen it coming. 'Is that you, Black? I told you to have a coffee with my granddaughter and now I find she's in intensive bloody care. Just what the hell went on today? How did you allow a poor woman to be dreadfully beaten? If she dies, I tell you, when I find you, I'll tear your limbs off one by one. Do you hear me?'

'Mr McPherson, I can explain everything. I've just visited her, and I think she's going to be OK. Honestly, I think she's going to be OK.' I was shaking like a leaf.

'What in the name of Jesus were you doing visiting her?' he exploded. 'And who the hell let you in? No one, I repeat, no one but family is authorised to see her!' he yelled.

'Sir, I came with Commander Burke.'

That made him stop. 'What do you mean, you came with Commander Burke?'

'Yes! Hear me out, sir. It's not what you think. Christine was on to them, and if it weren't for her and her intuition, Parliament would be lying in ruins. Jo and Green were going to bomb it from the air. She—your granddaughter—thwarted it, Bob. She's a *heroine*, and I'm convinced she'll pull through.'

By now he was beginning to calm down. 'I apologise if I may have jumped to conclusions, Peter. I've been at my wits end up here alone in St Andrews, as you can imagine. Burke called me earlier, but he was still trying to piece things together and only gave me a potted version of events. I'll call him immediately. And Peter,' he asked, 'did you get tangled up in the whole mess too?'

'No, I didn't,' I lied, 'but I know enough to know that your granddaughter was key to stopping them. Burke can tell you more, I guess.'

'Oh my, she's one hell of a girl, that one.' His voice was shaking with emotion.

'She is, and according to her you are, quote, the greatest man she knows!'

'Get away! Did she really say that?' He sounded proud as punch, and as I began to walk in the direction of my hotel, we chatted for a couple more minutes. I promised him I'd visit Christine again the following day to check on her.

It was a beautiful warm spring evening in London, and I should have been walking along feeling quite proud of myself, but instead I was racked with guilt and feeling awful. In the space of just a few days, my life had gone nuts, and I was now a double killer. Yes, a double killer! How was it possible that two gazillion-to-one events could have happened? I just couldn't fathom it.

But one thing was utterly, depressingly clear to me. My old life—and whatever trajectory it had been on—was well and truly and cataclysmically finished.

Chapter 20

After a twenty-minute walk, I reached the hotel. Peng appeared from nowhere as I entered the lobby.

'Peter, your father is meeting the lawyers and will be another half an hour or so. He'll meet you in the bar.' He then commented on how tired I looked and suggested I skip it, but while I was dog tired, I badly needed my father's company.

'An interesting day?' he enquired as he walked me to the elevator.

'Quite interesting.' I smiled but gave nothing away. What had he worked out? My father wouldn't have said a word.

'I see you've changed your clothes?' he said, looking at my rather un-Peter-like gear, and I knew fine well that he was on to me. Perhaps he'd watched the TV footage and worked out that the nutcase in the orange mac had been me? I decided to be as honest with him as I could.

'Peng, I'm so sorry, but ...' I thought carefully about what I was going to say. 'Today has been one of those days that I really can't talk about. I do hope you can understand my predicament.'

He nodded thoughtfully, then he did something that he'd never, ever done before. He stood back and bowed his head low, holding it for a good ten seconds or more. 'I am very proud of you, Peter,' he said very quietly.

He knew for sure what I'd done, and once again, I felt the pride brimming inside me. Other than my father, he was the most important male figure in my life. I gave a little bow in return.

When I got up to the sixth-floor bar, it was jam-packed full, but towards the back by the log fire, two huge leather armchairs came free, and I plonked myself down in one of them. For the first time all day, I felt a massive sense of relaxation ripple through my body, and I ordered my favourite ale.

I'd hardly managed to take the first sip when my phone rang. It was Burke. 'Just checking in on you, Peter. Hopefully you're in a nice quiet spot relaxing. You deserve a good rest.'

'Good evening, sir,' I replied a little hesitantly. 'Actually, I'm sitting in the hotel bar about to have a beer and some food with my dad.' I asked him if there was any more news on the day's events.

'Bits and pieces,' he replied, 'but the real reason for calling is to let you know that Christine McPherson, miraculously, has come out of her coma. She's even speaking. It's the best possible news!'

'Oh my god. Yes, it is!'

'However, from what I understand, as a result of the head trauma, she remembers absolutely nothing, so, in time, you may have to help her to fill in the blanks. It will have to be done very carefully, though, and I suggest that you stick to our narrative as much as you can.'

'Sure. I'll visit her tomorrow, Commander.' I saw my father coming into the bar and began excusing myself.

'Peter, before I go …'

'Yes, Commander?'

'Don't forget that you're going to need some support. You might think that you're strong and not in need of it, but don't believe that for a second. The best of us struggle. I've been there myself. Good evening, Peter.'

'Anyone special?' said my father, sitting down opposite me, lounging like a gangly teenager.

'Commander Burke checking I'm OK.'

'Ah, yes. He's a good man. I tell you, though, I almost had a heart attack when he called me today.'

'Like the heart attack I almost had when I saw you sitting in my interrogation room!'

He lowered his voice, looking around to check no one was listening. 'The PM just gave me a call. He was in quite a state about the near bombing of Parliament and passes on his heartfelt thanks to you. He'll be getting you round to Number 10 soon for, and I quote, "a cup of tea and a biscuit".'

'*Me* going to Number 10!' I laughed. 'You've *got* to be joking! What would I say to him?'

'Oh, don't worry about it one bit.' He smiled. 'I've known Andrew for years and he's the nicest chap in the world. It'll just be a friendly chat. In fact, I can never quite work out how on earth he managed to climb all the way up the greasy pole—decent folks normally get cast aside very early on the ascent.'

My father was also one of those rare extremely decent people whom everyone seemed to like, and over the years, on account of his extraordinary success in business, he'd got to know a string of PMs, senior politicians and global business leaders. He had also gone out of his way to promote British business and had become one of the UK's most important 'Global Business Ambassadors'.

'How's the deal coming along?' I yawned as his gin and tonic arrived.

'Despite today's little interruption,' he said with a wink, 'it's been going rather well. The other party is in town from the States, and I met him with his advisors today. It was very interesting, and I'm more convinced than ever about the fabulous synergies our two firms enjoy. He's an excellent chap and we're very much aligned, although, as always, there will be other bidders circling. It's a bit of a nail-biter, and the stakes simply couldn't be higher.'

'Dad, most of your deals have involved you hitting it off with the seller. They like you and trust you. You make them feel very comfortable, and they know that you run a very happy, motivated ship which empowers and respects its employees. Of course he'll sell to Black & Co.!'

'Kind words; however, money often does the talking, and there are plenty of deep pockets out there.' He paused, taking a contemplative sip of his drink. 'Why don't you meet the seller too? I'm due to meet him and his family for breakfast in the morning and I'd love you to join me.'

'Count me in. Anything to help.'

He thumped his fist on the table. 'Deal! 8.30 a.m. at Claridge's it is.'

'I'm going up to the bar to grab one more beer before I conk out,' I said, standing up. 'I've been trying to catch the waiter's eye for some time without success. I'll be back in half a moment.'

As I made my way up to the bar, my phone buzzed with an incoming message, and as I squeezed through to the counter, I saw it was from Trudy. I also had half an eye on a TV screen which was showing 'London eco-terror' coverage. *Jesus, did all this mayhem really happen to me today?*

'Hey, you,' read the message. 'What a mad world. I just can't believe that Green and Jo tried to do what they tried to do—it's unbelievable. Hope you weren't anywhere close when it happened and that all's going well with your dad. Love Trudy.'

'A pint of Timothy Taylor's, please,' I said to the bartender, and I bashed out a reply to Trudy.

'All fine down here, Truds. Just having a pint with my dad. Thankfully I wasn't anywhere near.'

The TV was showing pictures of Green and Jo growing up, and before my eyes, I saw the woman I'd killed morph from pigtailed toothy schoolgirl to beautiful young model to hippy eco-warrior. I looked around me. Little did these people know that her killer was standing amongst them. But I was a killer who profoundly wished he hadn't killed. I felt sick to my stomach about what I'd done to her.

My beer arrived, and as I took a long slug, from the corner of my eye I noticed a young Sikh guy sitting diagonally across the bar from me. We made eye contact for the briefest of moments and then, as the bartender fluttered nearby, I saw him tap the top of his glass in exactly the way that the Sikh in St Andrews had done. Interesting. Did they all do that? It must be a Sikh mannerism.

Immediately to my right, perched on bar stools, two large mid-thirties Americans were talking loudly, commenting on the TV footage. 'Bud, I reckon the security forces should be sued. In plain view those eco-nuts put bomb packs on their backs and flew across London in a frickin' balloon? Can you imagine it? In America, that kind of shit just wouldn't happen. Huh?'

'Yeah, bro, they're just a bunch of fucking amateurs. All they did was send a cripple in a wheelchair to save the day.'

'Right, bud ... and an ugly cripple at that.'

I felt my blood surge to boiling point.

'You could always fuck off home to America if you don't like it here, you fat, useless fuckers.' How *dare* they talk like that about McPherson after everything she'd done. Hell, there had even been a bunch of American senators in the parliament building as the balloon had been going overhead.

'Bro' looked at me and eased himself off his stool. God almighty, he was huge! Then, staring down at me with a look of rage on his huge face, he began pouring his pint of beer over my head, then *swipe*, he swatted me with his other hand and I crashed to the floor.

The whole place went quiet.

'That'll teach you, you little shit,' sneered Bud, pointing his finger down at me. 'Where we come from, we don't take that kind of insolence. Especially from a little English turd.'

'Don't!' I heard my father shout from somewhere over to my right, but it was too late.

With my ear still ringing from the slap he'd dished out, I sprung up and started raining quick hard punches on him. Down he went like a ton of bricks, crashing backwards into drinkers at the bar.

Then it was Bro's turn. With a bellow, he went for me, but he was big and clumsy, and as I effortlessly heaved him over my shoulder Johnston style, he landed right on top of Bud.

It was over in seconds, and as I nonchalantly headed back to my seat, two security guards appeared and restrained the Americans, who were just about to come back for more. Moments later, the general manager walked briskly in and calmly took control of the situation. 'Joel, Bob—escort our two American guests to their rooms and call the house doctor to check on them, please.'

My father was standing by our armchairs staring at me in disbelief.

'Let's have a seat, shall we, gentlemen?' said the GM, nodding us back to our chairs.

'I'm not finished with you, you little prick,' yelled Bud as he and Bro were led away.

'Go back home to redneck land,' I shouted back, offering him the middle finger.

'Enough!' demanded my father. I don't think I'd ever seen him looking so angry. In fact, I don't think I'd ever seen him looking angry at all.

'My apologies, Mr Black. These things happen so very infrequently,' said the GM as we sat down.

'Don't be sorry, Karsten!' said my father turning and staring at me. 'I don't know what got into my son. I've never been so embarrassed in my whole life. And just wait for tomorrow's papers!'

'I'm sorry, Dad, they—'

He cut me off in a flash. 'I don't care what they might have said or done or how they provoked you. There are simply no excuses for being involved in a fistfight in a civilised five-star London hotel. Others can partake in that behaviour, but not a member of the Black family. Do you hear me?'

He had to give me a dressing down, and I took it on the chin. 'You're right, and I apologise profusely.' Then I turned to the GM. 'Sincere apologies, sir.' He nodded acceptingly.

'I'll try to keep the police out of it, Mr Black. You never can tell with Americans, though. But the fact that they made the first move—pouring a drink over your son—will hopefully keep them at bay.'

'I'll wager we'll have a lawsuit thrown at us by eight in the morning.' My father sighed.

A waiter appeared with a pint for me, another G&T for my father and a small glass of white wine for Karsten, and after a few minutes, my father had cooled from red to amber on the pissed-off scale. I hadn't realised that they'd known one another for years—Karsten had previously run the New York Mandarin, which my father always used on his trips there—and as they reminisced,

I sat reflecting. Why had I been so stupid as to get myself into a fight? What in god's name was I doing?

Half an hour later, Karsten walked us to the lift, and as we were waiting, the young Sikh appeared. As the doors opened, the GM bade us farewell.

On our way down, my father looked at me—thank god—with a touch of humour in his eyes. 'Fancy an early morning run to blow away the cobwebs?'

'Let's see how it goes.' I sighed. 'I suppose it might help me to take my mind off things, though.'

'We'd normally do 6 a.m., but let's try 7 a.m. Just a gentle canter?'

'Done.'

When we got to the ground floor, the Sikh courteously held the lift doors open for us, and as he did so, to my surprise I happened to notice that he wore an identical ring to the one the St Andrews Sikh had been wearing. Weird—both tapped their whisky glasses in the same way and both wore identical rings. It must be a Sikh thing. 'Cheers, mate,' I said to him, and he smiled back.

'It's been one *hell* of a day, Peter,' said my dad as we walked along our corridor. He stopped outside my room and pointed a lecturing finger at me. 'Don't let it become a day that defines your life, son, do you hear me? Just take it in your stride and keep your head screwed on tight. Not easy, but just do it.'

'Go it, Dad, and sorry again for what just happened.'

It was late but, back in my room, the wall-to-wall news coverage of everything that had gone on was enthralling, and I sat up for well over an hour before tiredness finally conquered me.

The individual in orange who had 'so bravely boarded the balloon and thwarted the attempted bombing' was reported to be an off-duty soldier who had paid the ultimate price for his bravery. His name was being withheld for 'security reasons'. George, thankfully, had done his stuff.

As I drifted off to sleep, two images floated off into the ether with me. The first was of me hanging on for dear life as the balloon took off. At the time, I'd just gotten on with it, but the TV footage was utterly scary. Whatever had possessed me to take such an impossible leap?

The second was of Jo standing on the stage overlooking Hyde Park, fist outstretched before her followers. Raw, delicate beauty. Incredible green eyes. A look of utter determination and conviction. She was minutes away from attempting to commit the most atrocious of crimes. She'd wanted me dead. But there had been something uniquely powerful and captivating about her.

Chapter 21

Getting out of bed to go for a run was not what I wanted, but I couldn't go back on my word. Christ, I was tired. I'd fallen asleep as soon as my head had hit the pillow, but by 3.30 a.m. I was wide awake, churning over everything that had happened. My mind seemed to replay events over and over, prime among them those moments when I'd clutched Jo's throat.

Met by a wall of stiffness and pain, I made my way down to the lobby and spotted my dad doing stretches against one of the huge marble columns. 'You look hellish, Peter. Are you sure you still want to go?' Embarrassingly, he was now lying on the floor, stretching his hamstrings.

'The run will do me good. Let's get going, shall we, before they throw us out of here?'

'OK, old son, but we'll take it slowly. Good morning, Jack,' he then said jovially to my friend the doorman as we went out of the main doors.

'Morning, sir,' he replied, looking surprised. 'Goodness, I've just twigged that you are father and son. Thanks to your lad, sir, for helping me out yesterday. It almost came to blows, I tell you.'

'Really?' said my father with a look of surprise. 'Blows? Please fill me in.' But I managed to flash a warning stare at Jack just in time.

'Oh, just some rich kid giving an old geezer a bit of lip. Nothing to worry about, sir. Your son was very supportive in my time of need.'

'Right,' said my father, glancing at me. 'Young Peter seems to make a habit of championing the underdog, it seems ...'

Our route was going to be along Knightsbridge, down Sloane Street, right onto the King's Road, left down Old Church Street, then along the Embankment to Victoria. From there we'd go up to Hyde Park Corner and then back along Knightsbridge to the hotel.

'A lot on your mind?' asked my dad as we headed to Sloane Street.

'Yeah, I suppose so. Sorry I'm so slow. The batteries are a bit flat. I didn't sleep too well last night with all the stuff from yesterday on my mind.'

'Hardly surprising,' he said between breaths. 'But I'm sure everything will settle down in the next few days. Take things in your stride and don't overthink things. Be proud of what you did.'

'I'll try.' It was easy for my dad, though. Nothing ever fazed him, and he never looked back.

It was Sunday and therefore relatively traffic free, but the doorways, bus shelters and gardens were full of marchers sleeping rough—bedraggled bodies strewn everywhere. 'There'll be almighty hangovers today,' said my father. 'Apparently Hyde Park and Green Park are like vast campsites. I'd hate to think how much pot and beer was consumed.'

'I wonder what they'll be thinking about their great leaders, Green and Jo?'

'Interesting question,' he puffed as we approached the old cinema building at the corner of Old Church Street. 'I'd imagine that most of them will be horrified. A small few, though, might see them as martyrs. Now let's take a left here,' he said, picking up the pace a bit.

Halfway down, as we reached the Chelsea Pig—a pub I'd once visited on a rugby tour—we heard a motorbike approaching from behind. Then it suddenly revved loudly, making me jump out of my skin, and it started to belt down the road towards us. But it was short-lived, as about a block ahead, four mounted police were just turning into our street. The idiot braked abruptly, tyres screeching. He then crawled past us, staring anonymously from behind his mirrored helmet. 'Arsehole,' I mouthed to him. Thankfully my father was there, or I'd have shoved him off his bike.

'Couldn't agree more. What a bloody moron,' said my father as we watched him creep gingerly past the horses before turning onto Embankment and roaring off.

As the officers passed by, my dad offered them a hearty 'good morning'. He'd already brushed off the biker incident. I was still fizzing. 'Checking the revellers are behaving themselves down there on the Embankment?' he asked.

'That's it, sir,' said the lady in charge. 'There are hundreds of them sleeping out. We're doing a shift change. The horses need a rest after being up all night.'

We would normally have jogged along the river walk, but with so many drunken bodies lying around and vast amounts of vomit and urine, we opted for the other side of the road. When we reached Vauxhall Bridge Road, we cut left and aimed for Grosvenor Place.

'Dad,' I asked as we ran towards Victoria, 'OK if I ask you a question about your past?'

'If you must,' he panted.

'Did you ever do any work for the Firm?'

'Why do you ask?' he replied, throwing me a glance.

'I guess I was surprised to see you at HQ and the fact that you know the Commander.'

We ran on a full block before he replied. 'Peter, from time to time, in the long distant past, I may have helped here and there. It was minor stuff. I was sort of a mediator where, often knowing both sides quite well, I might try to get the parties to agree on something somewhat tricky or contentious. I'm, of course, signed up to the Secrets Act and have probably already told you more than I should have, but I don't think it's anything more sinister than that.'

'Does Mum know?'

'No, but she's always had suspicions, and, as you know, she's no fool.'

We reached the top of Vauxhall Bridge Road. 'Last question, Dad, if I may?' He pulled up ten metres ahead of me and jogged gently on the spot.

'I know what you're going to ask me, and I'd rather you didn't. I'm not going to tell you, plus I take my oath to my queen and country *very seriously* indeed. I also don't think it's fair for you to ask me something that you know I can't answer.'

'Understood,' I said, realising that I'd cornered him. 'Come on, let's keep running. We've got a breakfast to attend, haven't we?'

'Yes, we have.' And he set off at a blistering pace along Knightsbridge.

I had been wanting to ask him if he'd killed for his country. Something inside me made me think he might have done. Just two days ago the whole idea of it would have been utterly absurd. Now everything was different.

Chapter 22

We got back to the hotel, turned around in fifteen minutes and took a car to Claridge's, where a smartly dressed doorman greeted us on our arrival. A line of Union flags fluttered proudly in the breeze above the entrance. As we entered the lobby, a tanned, mid-height gentleman in his sixties immediately got up from one of the plush chairs. 'James, good morning. Ah, this must be young Peter!' Both of us received a vigorous handshake, and I warmed to Ricardo Guzman immediately.

'Ricardo, it is our great pleasure to join you and your family for breakfast.' My father beamed, and, chatting as we went, we followed him down a thickly carpeted corridor to the opulent dining room.

'They're towards the back somewhere and so looking forward to meeting you both.'

Is that them? I thought, seeing two women sitting together. The younger one was reading the *Financial Times* and the older one—the mother—was sitting patiently. She waved and stood up, and the daughter quickly put her paper down and stood too. I was taken aback. Both were exceptionally attractive and beautifully dressed, and I wished I'd made a bit more of an effort.

'James and Peter, please can I have the great pleasure of introducing you to my wife Marta and daughter Ofelia?' We all shook hands. 'Ofelia, dear, Peter is studying at St Andrews in the north. Peter, Ofelia is in year two at Yale.'

'I hope you're having at much fun at Yale as I'm having at St Andrews. May I ask what you're studying?' I asked politely. She was petite with short sandy blonde hair and green eyes. My father had said that they were South American, but to me she looked more European.

'I'm majoring in Psychology with a minor in Business.' She had a really nice smile and a friendly, relaxed manner. 'It's really fun but quite demanding too!'

'Fabulous,' said my father as we all sat down. 'And are you both having a nice stay here in London while Don Ricardo and I spend endless hours surrounded by accountants and tax advisors?'

As Marta gave a little laugh and started talking, I imagined how she must have looked like the replica of her daughter when she was younger. 'We're having *such* a nice week and doing all sorts of nice mother-daughter things that we haven't done in such a long while. Oh my, we've done so much walking too. It really is a walking city, isn't it—the parks, the museums, the restaurants?'

'It's been wonderful,' chipped in Ofelia, 'although dreadfully sad to see what happened yesterday. I still can't quite believe it. It was like something out of a movie.'

'Utterly tragic,' said my father glancing at me. 'Beyond all comprehension.'

'Truly,' agreed Don Ricardo. 'Thank Dios someone got on that balloon to stop them.' He turned to me. 'What's your reading of what went on, Peter?'

I looked at them, but I wasn't concentrating. My mind was suddenly back up in the air, reliving the moment I'd held down the boxer and Jo. I could feel myself squeezing Jo's neck, tighter and tighter, my face pressed against hers.

'Peter?' My father was nudging me with an elbow. 'Your thoughts on the attempted bombing?'

I quickly zoned back in, embarrassed and feeling uncomfortable as hell. 'Sorry. Excuse me. My mind was elsewhere. My thoughts? Well, I suppose I admire the fact that they were willing to go all the way to make their point. We're flogging the Earth to death, and millions will die in the future because of our failure to act today. They felt compelled to make a statement but didn't manage to pull it off.'

'Thankfully!' chipped in Ofelia. 'But perhaps they've achieved their goal? Today, because of them, every single person around the world is talking about global warming. The media is full of it.'

'Good point, Ofelia.' My father nodded.

Thankfully we moved off the topic and went on to have a very enjoyable breakfast, with the conversation not straying onto the topic of the potential business deal until towards the end. 'James and Peter,' declared Mr Guzman, 'I think there is exceptional chemistry between our two organizations and hopefully a marriage to be done?' Marta and Ofelia were nodding heartily, and I suddenly felt incredibly happy for my father, who responded in kind.

'Don Ricardo, Marta and Ofelia, I sincerely hope that our companies do come together and that our two families forge a lasting partnership. I only wish that my wife, Ann, and Peter's sister, Samantha, were here with us today. However, I'm sure you'll meet them in the fullness of time.'

Marta pitched in. 'Guzman & Co. is Ricardo's pride and joy. He's spent his life building it, and there have been many, many difficult times. To let it go will be *so* difficult for him, but now is the right time.' She turned and put her arm around him. 'I will be able to spend a lot more time with you, my dear.' Ofelia put her hand on her father's shoulder. What a close-knit family they were.

'Yes, indeed,' he sighed with a big smile. 'The business and its staff will be in safe hands, and I'm convinced, James, that Guzman & Co. will be instrumental in helping you to grow in the Americas.'

He and my father shook hands, and the three of them continued chatting while Ofelia and I broke into our own conversation. Interestingly, I found out that while she was Colombian, from

Bogotá, they had moved to the US when she was twelve due to the rise in kidnappings during that period. Going around the city in armoured cars with motorcycle outriders wasn't for them.

As breakfast concluded, ever forthright, my father suggested that I 'show Ofelia and Marta around London' while he and Mr Guzman 'thrashed through the nitty gritty of the merger'. 'That would be … just fine with me,' I stuttered, half in surprise and half in embarrassment.

'Ofelia, wouldn't that be lovely,' replied her mother. 'The two of you can do that while I meet Marjory—my old school friend. You'd find it quite boring compared to a nice afternoon with Peter.'

'Wonderful!' said Ofelia with a big, genuine smile. 'Let's do it, shall we?'

'Great idea!' I laughed. 'I tell you what. We can start at a nice little Arabic café I visited yesterday.'

Chapter 23

The plan was that I'd meet Ofelia outside Harrods at 1 p.m., and after the Claridge's breakfast, I left my father to continue his discussions with Don Ricardo while I headed back to the hotel in a taxi. Halfway there, however, I made an impromptu decision and got the driver to head over to the Cromwell so I could check in on McPherson again.

Breakfast had been a huge success, and I was pleased that I'd been able to help my father. Truthfully, I'd expected the meet-up to be a little staid and boring, but it had turned out to be really enjoyable, and I was totally excited about the prospect of spending some time with Ofelia in the afternoon. I liked her and even felt there had been a bit of chemistry between us. Maybe the tide was finally beginning to turn on the extraordinary run of bad luck I'd had in the last few days!

The Cromwell reception was mobbed—mostly foreigners, probably checking in for procedures to be carried out in the week ahead. The facility hosted some of London's most highly regarded specialists and had a reputation for attracting rich and famous customers from around the world—often from countries with very weak medical systems.

Wait a minute! What on earth? I'd just spotted Bullet sitting patiently in a corner of the reception. It could only be him. He was tethered to a chair, and when he saw me, he started wagging his tail like crazy. 'It *is* you, Bullet, my old dog.' He jumped up and licked my face as we greeted one another like long-lost friends. 'Where's your master, my old friend? Is he upstairs?'

After petting him for a few minutes, I bounded up the back stairs. When I got to McPherson's room, I found both Bob and the Commander, and to my amazement, the patient was sitting up in bed.

'Good morning, Commander. Good morning, Bob,' I whispered, quickly shaking their hands before going over to Christine's bedside. She was on a drip, but other than that, she wasn't connected to anything. What a miracle!

'Hi, Peter,' she whispered in a very faint voice before stopping to give a long swallow. 'It's so good to see you … and are you OK?'

'Christine, I'm fine, but more to the point, how are you?'

'Fucking A,' she whispered with a faint smile, her eyes beginning to close.

'Pardon her language,' said her grandfather with a bit of grumble. 'It must be the medicines.' Both the Commander and I laughed.

'That's great, Christine.' I smiled, ecstatic to hear her being so foul-mouthed. 'It looks like you're getting your old sense of humour back.'

Eyes still closed, she gave a tiny nod. 'I suppose so. But I want to get my hands on whoever did this to me.' Now her eyes were open, and they had a bit of their old sparkle. 'I'm going to track them down … and make them pay.'

'That wouldn't surprise me.' I grinned. 'And I hope I'm there to watch it.' I'd have loved to have told her that I'd thumped one of them in HQ, but I knew I couldn't.

Then she seemed to find a little more energy. 'Peter, what happened to me? And what happened to you? All I remember is meeting you outside the tube station, then we began to walk up Knightsbridge through all those people. After that, I can't for the life of me remember a thing.'

I looked at the Commander and Bob. 'Can I have a go at trying to fill in the pieces?'

'Yes, lad. Please do,' said Bob, going over and squeezing his granddaughter's hand. 'But not for too long. You really need to sleep, dear.'

For the next few minutes, I filled Christine in, telling her that I'd taken her to the march and that sometime after leaving her there to go back to my hotel, she'd taken on the security team and effectively raised the alert. I congratulated her on being the only person to have had any clue about Jo and Green's heinous plans. The Commander then chipped in and talked about the off-duty soldier boarding the balloon and the explosion over the Thames.

'Oh my god,' whispered Christine. 'So they're ...' Her voice began to peter out.

'Yes, Jo and Green are dead, the two pilots and the guards,' I explained.

'*And* the soldier,' remarked the Commander.

'What a bloody waste.' Her eyes filled with tears. 'And so avoidable.' Then she stared ahead as if in a trance, desperately trying to process everything.

'Visiting hours are over, folks. Christine needs to rest,' said a young doctor, sticking his head around the door. She was already fast asleep.

Out in the corridor, Burke and Bob thanked me and asked if I'd like to join them for lunch at the Commander's private club, but I politely declined. We went down to reception before the three of us and Bullet made our way out into the parking lot.

'I was totally out of order yesterday, Peter,' said Bob offering me a gracious hand just before stepping into the Commander's car. 'Please accept my apologies once again.'

'No worries, Mr McPherson.'

'Let's meet up in St Andrews soon, then, shall we?'

'Let's see.' I smiled, hopefully giving him a gentle hint that he should look elsewhere if he had plans to try to sign me up.

'Right, then. Indeed,' he replied, looking slightly uncomfortable.

As they drove away, perhaps a bit of me wished that I'd joined them for lunch just to have another peek into their world. But any thoughts of that soon faded away. Now I was off to see Ofelia, and I felt a tingle of excitement about the prospect of seeing her again.

Chapter 24

Rather than go to the hotel to change, I headed straight to a Ralph Lauren and kitted myself out with jeans and a white shirt, and, for good measure, I splashed on some of the store's cologne. Ofelia had been immaculately dressed, and I was keen to make more of an effort for our afternoon together. Just outside the store, there was a guy sitting on the pavement asking for money, and I politely handed my old clothes to him. 'Fanks, mate! Cheers,' he said, looking completely surprised.

As I approached Harrods, I immediately spotted Ofelia standing midway along the store's stunning frontage, staring into one of the display windows. The tingle of excitement was back again.

'Ofelia, is that you?' I asked, attempting a bit of humour, and in return, I was greeted with an infectious smile and a discreet kiss on each cheek.

'Oh, Peter, don't I love your fragrance!'

'I have to be honest,' I replied, feeling myself blushing, 'I've just bought the shirt and jeans, and I sprayed on some of the house aftershave. Sorry if it's a bit potent!'

'Oh, I see. So you're on a date, are you?' She giggled.

Now I was beetroot red. 'Well ... it's just that I ... erm ... wanted to try to look my best,' I bumbled. 'You dress so nicely, and I felt so scruffy at breakfast in comparison.'

'That's really nice of you,' she said, briefly touching my hand. 'Don't worry, I'm only kidding you about the date stuff. I'm so touched that you made such an effort.'

'Let's go, shall we? It's just around the corner.' As we set off, she slipped her arm casually through mine and we ambled slowly down the little side street towards the café.

'Ooh, this looks interesting,' she said as we walked through the door. 'Doesn't it feel as though we've just been transported to the Middle East?'

'Phew, I'm so glad you like it. I was worried that you might have preferred something a bit more "tea and scones" British.'

'Oh, not at all. Now I can brag to my Arabic friends when I get back to school—the reviews on this place are amazing, did you know?' I didn't, but I wasn't surprised.

I spotted Ahmed, and he immediately came over and ushered us towards a nice table. 'Sir, so nice to see you again so soon. You must have liked our Arabic coffee?'

I laughed. 'I liked it so much that I thought I'd introduce my friend to it as well!'

'Wonderful.' But then his face turned more serious. 'Sir, would you mind if I enquire how Ms McPherson is doing? We're all *dreadfully* concerned about her.'

Before replying to Ahmed, I thought I should fill in Ofelia, and I turned to her. 'I was in here yesterday with the lady in the wheelchair who got into that trouble at the start of the march.'

'Oh my god,' she gasped. 'Peter, I had no idea.'

'Don't worry, she's going to be fine,' I said to both of them. 'I visited her this morning in hospital and she's making a remarkable recovery.'

Ahmed immediately turned to a busy waitress who was passing. 'Noor, I have very good news. Ms McPherson is going to be OK, inshallah. This gentleman knows her and just gave me the good news!'

Noor gasped with relief and put her hand on her heart. 'Oh my god. I was watching it last night on the television and I screamed at my mother when I saw her being attacked. It was so brutal what they did to her. Were you nearby, sir, when it was happening?'

'No, unfortunately I wasn't,' I replied, remembering the Commander's instructions.

'Ms McPherson is so kind,' continued Noor. 'When my mother was desperately ill, she sent flowers and chocolates and a beautifully written card. People think she's unkind, but I tell you she's the nicest person I've ever known. Such a wonderful heart.'

'Sir,' said Ahmed very politely, 'when I saw the footage, I thought for one horrible moment that the brave man who jumped on the balloon might have been your good self. Thank god it wasn't.'

'No, not me, Ahmed.' I squirmed. 'I'm not brave enough to do anything like that. May the chap's brave soul rest in peace.' I hoped I'd come across convincingly despite my discomfort.

'Shall we order?' Ofelia smiled, putting a protective hand on my knee, sensing my uneasiness.

'Leave it with me,' said Ahmed, giving his little bow. 'I think you'll like our Arabic Classic Selection.'

Ofelia looked as though she was about to ask loads of questions, but after a moment's reflection, thankfully she changed the subject. 'I *must* bring my mother here tomorrow. She'll absolutely love it.' We sat a little awkwardly for a few moments until Ahmed arrived with an ornate tray loaded with coffee, dates, sweets and a selection of unusually flavoured ice creams.

After he'd ceremoniously poured the coffee into our quaint little ceramic cups, I watched as Ofelia gently took in the aroma before taking a delicate sip. 'Oh my god …' she sighed, closing her eyes and leaning back in her chair. 'I hereby swear I'll never drink Starbucks again!' Two Arabic ladies sitting at the next table overheard her and giggled in delight.

As we tried the delicacies, I found myself studying her face. Green eyes, delicate little nose, a hint of a dimple in her chin, light freckles sprinkling her cheeks ... but then she caught me looking and blushed ever so slightly as I tried my best to disguise my fascination from her.

'Hey, Mr Black,' she said, taking a date and holding it out to pop in my mouth. 'So, what do you think about our fathers going into business together?'

I offered her one in return, which she dealt with *far* more delicately than I had managed. 'I'm all for it. What about you?'

'Me too, and now I really think it's meant to be.'

We talked for almost two hours, and there were none of those difficult moments when you don't know what to say next. I told her about the fantastic time I was having in St Andrews and about my flatmates. She was fascinated by my upbringing in Hong Kong and the fact that I spoke both Mandarin and Cantonese.

Before leaving Bogotá, the Guzmans had led a privileged life. They'd lived in a massive apartment in the hills overlooking the city, but their departure to America had been prompted by the tragic kidnapping of a close school friend of Ofelia, who was never seen again. Within a few hours of it happening, Don Ricardo had taken his family to the airport and they'd left forever

Ofelia had taken months to settle into her boarding school in upstate New York, but she finally managed to, and in the process learned to become independent and resilient. She explained that the happiest day of her life was when she got accepted to Yale. 'I'm not super smart, Peter, and after working my butt off for two whole years, getting that offer was the most amazing thing ever. My parents were so incredibly proud of me, and I did it all for them.'

As our Arabic experience drew to a close, I found myself beginning to feel sad about the prospect of our afternoon together ending. I'd convinced myself that she'd want to go back to her hotel to meet up with her parents rather than spend more time with me. But I needn't have worried. After signalling to Noor to bring the bill—which she insisted on paying—she turned to me. 'It's a lovely day. Maybe we could take a stroll and end up with a nice glass of wine in a typical English pub?'

'What a great idea. I'd love that.'

Chapter 25

'I know it's terribly touristy,' said Ofelia as we left the café, 'but I've never seen Big Ben and Parliament. If it's not too far away, could we maybe go in that direction?'

I didn't know if I was quite ready to see Parliament again so soon, but how could I refuse? 'It's a bit of a hike, but absolutely. Let's do it.'

'Fabulous,' she said with a big smile, and before long, her arm slipped through mine again. We were deep in discussion, in a world of our own, as we cut through the back streets towards Victoria.

'So, what's the plan after Yale? Do you want to use your psychology degree to practise, or maybe you've thought about going into your father's business?'

'Oh, I'm all over the place on careers.' Ofelia sighed. 'One day I think I want to work with special needs children and add real value to society, the next I'm thinking it might be fun to do a PhD. I've even considered going back to Colombia to work with people displaced by the decades-long civil war. Oh, dear god, so many children need help and support.' She gave another long sigh. 'But in all honesty, I really don't know what I'm going to do.' Then, squeezing my arm, she gave a little giggle. 'Maybe I should just relax and help my father spend his money. What do you think?'

'Sounds like a plan.' I laughed. 'But it's fine to be undecided. I'm exactly the same, and I can't think of one of my friends who has clear sight of what they want to do. With me, I know it'll be *something* to do with business, but within that, it could be a thousand different things. I suppose the positive of joining the family firm is that one could choose to live in an interesting location like Beijing or Sydney or Bangkok.'

'You know what?' she said, stopping in the middle of the pavement. 'I really hope our fathers' deal goes through and maybe, just maybe, I could go work in some of those wonderful places too.'

I stared at her. Was she just an incredibly nice, open person or had she just given me a massive hint that she liked me? Why were women always so darn difficult to understand? 'That would be *really* nice. Visit Hong Kong any time you like—successful deal or not.'

'I'd love that,' she replied, her smile radiating.

Half an hour later, we turned into Parliament Square and the vast parliament complex with Big Ben at its side came into view. 'I simply can't believe we're here,' gasped Ofelia. 'Quick, let's take photos!' She stopped and asked an elderly American couple if they'd take one of the two of us.

'Gee, you two make the most adorable couple,' drawled the lady after a few shots.

'Hear that?' said Ofelia mischievously, digging her elbow into my side. 'Aren't we adorable?'

'Definitely,' I muttered. But I wasn't really listening. A strange sensation had begun to come over me. What was going on? My hands and arms suddenly felt weak, and in fact it was becoming so bad that they felt semi-paralysed. There were pins and needles too, creeping all over my body. Light at first, but now it was intensifying. I took deep breaths and gritted my teeth, trying to ignore it, desperately trying to hide my predicament from Ofelia. Christ. Was this stress—the thing the Commander had warned me about? Or was I about to have a goddamn heart attack?

As we got closer, we saw that there were crowds of people gathered all along the pavement in front of Parliament. 'Let's go closer,' she said, almost dragging me along. God, I felt wretched, but I thought I was managing to control it—just. 'It's kind of like DC where they're always protesting about stuff.'

Pushing through the onlookers, to our astonishment we found literally hundreds of people silently kneeling, shoulder to shoulder, heads bowed. But that was only half it. The railings were festooned with pictures of Jo and Green, including a colossal one of 'that' image of Jo. Her eyes seemed to be drilling right into me. 'My god, Peter. They're mourning their death. Isn't it creepy!'

Peter, why did you kill me? I had to wake the world up, but you stopped me. It was Jo, whispering to me. She was back from the dead.

'But *why*, Jo?' I whispered back. 'You had the whole world eating out of the palm of your hand. You didn't need to bomb and kill.'

But why did you do it to me, Peter, when you find me so attractive? Now her voice was incredibly kind and soothing.

'I don't know ... I really don't know. I hate myself for it.'

I felt someone tugging at my jacket. 'Hey, Peter. Why were you holding me so tightly? And why were you like ... murmuring?'

I stared at her. It was Ofelia. What had I been doing? I felt a rush of embarrassment. She'd think I was mad if I told her. 'Sorry. It was nothing. Daydreaming. Away with the fairies ...'

'Right?' She gave me a 'how weird' look. But then she nodded towards the river and tugged my jacket. 'Come on. Let's walk along past them all. I want to see what kind of people are doing the vigil. Isn't it just so interesting? Kids, students, parents, pensioners. All idolising Jo and Green.'

Shit, now the numbness and pins and needles were back. Worse this time. God, even my face seemed paralysed, and I could barely feel my feet or hands. '*Ofelia. Wait. Please wait.* I need to go.

Now. Away from here. Away from all the crowds. Away from everything to do with yesterday.'

'Sure, Peter. What is it? Are you OK? You look pale.' Hands on my shoulders, she was staring right into my eyes. She was calm, but she looked confused. God, what a mess. I'd blown it.

'That one,' I blurted out, seeing and waving down a passing cab. 'Let's take it.' Thankfully it pulled up and I stumbled towards it, my useless legs barely doing what I was trying to tell them.

Ofelia got in first and, unable to make the step up, I half crawled in after her, then dragged myself up onto the seat beside her. I'd never felt so useless in my whole life.

Chapter 26

'You've gone so, so weird on me, Peter. Talk to me,' she said as the cab took off. 'Did I do something wrong?'

'Anglesey Arms, South Ken,' I gasped to the cabbie. 'I'm fine. Don't worry,' I whispered. 'You'll love this little pub. And I assure you, you've done absolutely nothing wrong.'

I wasn't fine, though, and I closed my eyes and desperately tried to relax, sucking air into my system, hoping that it would settle me and drive away the numbness and pins and needles.

I had surely blown my chances with Ofelia. She'd think I was totally off my head—and just wait, in a moment or two she'd be asking to be taken back to her hotel and that would be that. Eyes still shut, I braced myself for what was sure to come. I cursed Jo for screwing with my life, and, for that matter, I cursed the woman on the golf course too. Both were to blame for my— for my— good god, I could barely face up to the words. For my *breakdown*.

I shouldn't have worried, though. I suddenly felt Ofelia slip her fingers through mine, and when I opened my eyes and looked at her, her eyes were closed too. She certainly didn't look as though she was about to abandon me. Was she mad? What on earth did she see in me?

'We'll be there in five minutes,' I whispered.

'Great,' she whispered back. 'I think I'll try a pint of that black beer stuff. What's its name again?'

'Guinness?'

'Yes, that's the one.'

'I think I'll join you.'

As we approached South Kensington and the pub, my episode of PTSD—probably what it was—began to fade away.

Chapter 27

'Two pints of Guinness, please,' I said to the heavily pierced girl behind the bar, a little taken aback by the sheer quantity of tattoos she was sporting.

As the Guinness was being poured, I looked over at Ofelia. She'd managed to find a small high table in the busy pub and a guy was hovering, chatting to her. More like chatting her up.

I paid and headed over with the pints. 'Lovely talking to you,' said her admirer in a plummy accent. 'So interesting to hear that you are at Yale, and please give me a call if you are ever looking for an internship in private banking. You'd be wonderful, and it's a fascinating career.' He wished us both a pleasant day before heading back to his friends.

'You make friends very quickly,' I said, raising an eyebrow.

'I don't know what it is about the male population.' She laughed, her face going red. 'You all seem to walk around with one and only one thing on your mind.'

I couldn't disagree with her, but soon we were deep in discussion, and before long, we'd finished our drinks. 'Fancy another one?' I asked, praying that she wouldn't pull the plug on everything.

'I shouldn't, but yes, I'd love another one. These stools are so awkward and uncomfortable. Maybe you could find something more cosy while I go to the restroom?'

'That alcove over there is free,' I said, jumping up, and as I went to bag it, I ordered from a passing waiter, then sat down, stretched out my legs and closed my eyes for a few seconds.

'Hey, lazy bones. Wake up.'

I opened my eyes and there was Ofelia sitting opposite me, her second beer already half finished. 'Christ. Tell me I haven't been asleep?'

'I must *really* bore you?' she joked. 'But you looked so cute, so I just let you take a snooze. It's nice that you feel comfortable enough with me that you can just nod off.'

The booze was beginning to take the edge of my inhibitions. 'I have to confess I do feel totally comfortable when I'm with you, even though I've only known you for a few short hours.'

'That's *really* nice,' she replied, taking a little sip. 'Gosh, I hope you don't have to carry me home. This stuff is going straight to my head.' I smiled, amused at seeing such a petite girl drinking a pint.

'What's so funny?'

'Oh, nothing really. You make me happy.'

'Fair enough.' She smiled, taking a longer sip. 'Here's to us.' She touched my glass with hers.

'Listen, Ofelia. I'm … I'm really, really sorry about earlier. I mean, back there at Parliament …' I sat back in my chair, wondering what she'd say.

'Oh, don't worry a bit,' she said, sitting up and gently touching my arm. 'And can I make a confession?'

'Sure. What is it?'

'You've been giving off a weird sort of aura ever since we met at breakfast. I can't put my finger on it, but what happened outside Parliament totally reinforced that feeling I have. I hope I'm not sounding like a psychologist. I absolutely don't mean to.'

I took a long sip, then put my elbows on the table and looked at her. 'I'm feeling sad, Ofelia.'

'Sad. But why? We're having fun, aren't we?'

'Yes, of course. But in an hour's time, or maybe two, we'll probably be going our separate ways. And despite all my weird issues, which I *sincerely* hope you can forgive, I'm really, really enjoying being with you and I don't want it to stop.'

We both sat there quietly, just staring at one another. It wasn't an awkward kind of quiet, just a natural, enjoyable kind of quiet.

'Peter?'

'Yes?'

'Do you think I'm attractive?'

We both sat back in our seats at the same moment, embarrassed, and then we both burst out laughing. 'So, do I think you're attractive?' I said mischievously. 'Why do you want to know?'

'Oh, don't be so mean. I was just sort of wondering.' She twisted her hair nervously as she waited for my reply.

I took a deep breath. 'You know fine well that I find you attractive. My goodness, everyone in this pub can probably see that I've fallen completely head over heels for you.' I'd said my piece, and with that, I grabbed my glass and took a long drink.

'Oh my god,' she said wiping away a tear. 'Since the moment we met this morning, I don't know what it is. I've just felt this incredible connection that I've not felt with *anyone* else, ever. Even my mother picked up on it at breakfast.'

She came round to sit beside me, and as I put my arm around her waist, she put her head gently on my shoulder. After a few moments, she lifted her head and we kissed until we noticed the group opposite staring at us and we pulled back.

'Oh my god, Peter, I don't think I could even have made this up. It's *so* perfect.'

'Let's go, shall we? We can continue our walk and stop off somewhere else.'

As we walked slowly, arm in arm, towards South Kensington station, we stopped from time to time to steal another kiss or two. On the tube, anyone looking would have seen two people captivated with one another, deep in their own little world.

We went just one stop to Knightsbridge and into Harvey Nichols' champagne bar, and there we stayed for the next two hours, talking and talking. The more we talked, the more and more I liked her, and all the trauma of the terrible events of the last few days seemed to fade away.

Chapter 28

After far too much champagne, we made our way out of Harvey Nichols and stood on the pavement on Sloane Street waiting for a taxi.

As one going the opposite way U-turned and came back to pick us up, from the corner of my eye I saw someone in the crowd moving quickly in our direction. As I turned, I saw it was a well-built Asian woman, her stare fixed on me with a determined, angry look. She immediately reminded me of the woman on the golf course. Suddenly, to my horror, she started digging for something in her bag. *What on earth is she doing?* Was it a gun or maybe a knife? I had to do something.

'*Stop,*' I yelled, darting forward, grabbing at her before she could take whatever it was out of her bag. In the scuffle that ensued, we both stumbled, and before I knew it, I'd fallen on top of her. As we lay on the ground, she started screaming, '*Thief, thief, thief.*'

'Peter. Peter. Stop,' screamed Ofelia, and now passers-by were trying to pull me off her. Good god, had I got it wrong? Was she just a normal person?

I jumped up, and as I stood there realising what a terrible mistake I'd made, Ofelia stepped in. 'I'm so sorry,' she said, helping the poor woman to her feet. 'You see, my friend has recently been through a traumatic experience and he sometimes gets panic attacks in busy places. Let's not call the police, shall we? I'm going to take him home right away.'

As I hung my head in shame, I felt the numbness and pins and needles starting up again.

'Don't worry at all. I'm fine,' said the woman, dusting herself down. 'I was in such a terrible rush to get a taxi and my phone was ringing in my bag. I must have frightened him, and I do hope he's OK.' She composed herself, thanked everyone and headed off down Sloane Street.

'I don't know what to say, Ofelia, I really don't. You must think I'm a total nutcase. I thought she might have been ...' I stopped. How could I possibly say that I thought the woman was going to kill me? It would have sounded utterly absurd.

Another taxi drew up and we climbed in. 'We'll go to my hotel,' Ofelia said extremely calmly. 'Please take us to Claridge's,' she instructed the driver.

'Of course you're not a nutcase,' she said as we got going. 'On the contrary, I think something has happened to you, and you're bottling it all up. You're not sharing it with anyone, and you need to.'

'Oh god, Ofelia. You're right, but I can't tell you what it is. I just can't, OK? I wish I could.'

'Don't worry,' she said gently. 'One day, when you feel the time is right, you can tell me, and you'll find that I'm an excellent listener. And I won't judge you either. You're a good, kind, gentle human being, and whatever you've done, it will have been for a very good reason.'

I stared out of the window, confused and frightened. When I'd had to rise to the challenge to stop terrible things from happening, I'd done so without fear. Now I was a wreck, my mind playing terrible games with me. *Gentle.* She'd called me *gentle.* If only she knew what I'd done.

As the taxi was going to pass right in front of my hotel, I asked Ofelia to drop me off so that I could take a quick shower and change my clothes. I also badly needed a few minutes to myself to get my mind in a better place before we went out for dinner.

Forty minutes later, refreshed and feeling more settled, as I waited downstairs in the lobby of her hotel, I gave my dad a quick call—though not really expecting him to pick up. Luckily, he did. 'Peter, I'm in the thick of meetings. Let's make it quick. Now tell me. Did it go well this afternoon?'

'Absolutely fine, Dad. We had a really nice afternoon.' Christ, he'd have flipped if he'd seen what I'd done to the poor woman outside Harvey Nichols. In fact, he'd probably have had me locked up in the Priory if he'd got the slightest whiff of how badly my body and mind were playing up.

'Good—she seems like a super girl. And you're still bearing up after yesterday?'

'Yep, Dad, I'm bearing up really well.' I wasn't going to say a thing about what had been happening. I'd sort it all out myself in my own good time, in my own way.

Just then, Ofelia appeared out of the lift, dressed in casual sports gear—not quite what I had been expecting for a nice dinner out. 'Liar,' she whispered. 'You're not bearing up at all well!'

I stared at her for a second like a lovestruck teenager. Wasn't it incredible how much bad luck I'd had, and then suddenly I'd had the good fortune to meet her? Life was so unpredictable.

'So, what have you got planned for this evening, son?'

'Ofelia and I are going for dinner,' I replied, throwing her a confused look, pointing at her clothes.

'OK, then. So, let's meet again for a drink in the Mandarin. Shall we say 11 p.m.—I'll be finished by then. And let's hope there are no Americans in the bar this evening,' he joked.

'Very funny. See you at eleven.' Thank god he was now joking about my brawl!

I stood up and Ofelia and I gave one another a long, warm embrace. 'I thought we'd have a quiet evening in,' she said. 'Maybe we can order room service and watch a movie.'

Chapter 29

I got back to St. Andrews at 11.30 a.m.—not at all bad considering the 7.45 a.m. pick-up and Monday morning traffic.

It had been midnight when I'd finally made it to the bar to meet my father, and despite a long day coaxing lawyers towards a conclusion, he had been in an ebullient mood. 'Not quite there yet. Just a few more days dotting I's and crossing T's and we'll be done.' I was ecstatically happy for him, but I decided not to let on about my own good news. It didn't seem appropriate.

In the morning, he, Peng and I had a quick breakfast and then, bang on 7.45 a.m., I got into the limo—but not before my father had given me a massive father-son hug. Just before the car took off, he'd signalled to me to wind down the window. 'No more fighting with those lads in town, please! Blacks don't do that kind of stuff, do they?' I put the window up and watched him as he stood casually with his hands in his pockets. But wait—he wanted me to put the window down again!

'What is it, Dad? I need to get going.'

He placed his hand gently on my head. 'I'm so immensely proud of you. Never forget that, will you?' Then he stood aside and waved as the car drove off.

I called him a minute later from the car.

'Hey, Dad, just to let you know I love you and thanks for everything.'

'Thanks, son. And remember. Take all this stuff in your stride. Stuff happens, right?' It was then that I confided in him, whispering so the driver wouldn't hear me.

'Dad. To be honest, my head's not in a good place. Something else happened a few days ago, and I think everything combined is screwing with my mind.'

'Right,' he said, pausing. 'Peng thought you didn't seem quite right. And, on reflection, these brawls aren't really you, are they? A bit of a red flag, eh?'

We agreed that he and my mother would call me when he got back to Hong Kong. 'Don't worry, Peter. I promise we'll get you all fixed up, and remember, no matter how bad things get, your family is always here for you. If it's any consolation, I've been in some rather dark places too, back in those early days. I wish I could tell you more.'

God, it felt good to have confided in him, but I'd only tiptoed to the precipice. I couldn't imagine what he and Mum would think when I told them that I'd killed a woman in St Andrews. Then I'd somehow have to explain to them that there wasn't a body. Christ, the story was so farfetched that maybe they wouldn't even believe me.

When I walked into the flat, Trudy and Shaun were sitting in the kitchen. I joined them for some tea and toast, and naturally the conversation veered towards the Save the Planet march.

'Total and utter nutters, the lot of them,' said Shaun. 'But I suppose you can sort of admire them. While the world is merrily marching towards Armageddon, there are committed people who are willing to give up their lives to give everyone a badly needed wake-up call.'

'Absolute rubbish,' countered Trudy. 'What you're saying is that it's acceptable for people to kill and maim in order to get a point of view across. You should feel ashamed of yourself!'

'Now, now, folks.' I laughed. 'Let's lighten the mood, shall we? I've got some news.'

'Oh, I smell gossip,' said Trudy, jumping up. 'Come on then, what is it?'

'Before I say a thing, you've got to promise you'll keep it within these four walls.'

Trudy squealed in delight. 'Oh god, I think this is going to be big. Just what is it, Peter? Out with it!'

'Do you all promise?'

'Yes,' they both shouted as Trudy sat perched like a dog waiting for a bone.

'OK, here we go. While I was down in London, I ...'

'You what?' shouted Trudy.

'Yes, you what?' said Diti, walking into the kitchen. 'This sounds interesting ...'

And then I hit them straight with it. 'I met someone. And I *really* like her.'

For about the next hour, I went through a deep and meticulous interrogation, and by the end of it, I had pretty much recounted everything that Ofelia and I had done during our day together. 'I'm so happy for you, Peter,' said Diti when it was only her and I left in the kitchen. 'Truly, truly happy.'

Happy that my best friends were happy and with half an hour to kill before going to Economics, I went up and lay on my bed. I took a quick look at my messages. There were two, both from Ofelia.

'Peter, I'm missing you so much and just couldn't bear saying goodbye to you last night, xxx'

'In Windsor with mom and wishing you were here. She keeps asking me why I'm so glum, but while I'm desperately sad, I'm so incredibly happy that we spent our beautiful day together. I pray that there will be many more, xxx'

When we'd said our tearful goodbyes, we'd agreed to look on the bright side. Yes, we'd only had a day together, but if we really wanted, there could be many more in the future. I sent a note back. 'Arrived back at the flat. Missing you terribly but still can't believe we had the amazingly good fortune to meet one another. There will be many happy days and we'll see each other very soon. Peter x. PS—I told my flatmates, and they are incredibly pleased for us.'

My bike was still at the rugby ground, so I grabbed one of the others, and in no time I had reached the busy area around the library and the quad. The country had come perilously close to losing its Parliament over the weekend, but good old St Andrews just went about its business as normal as it had done for centuries. I felt strange. I'd only left on Saturday morning, but such a lot had happened. Now I had a strange feeling inside me as if I somehow didn't belong here anymore.

As I cut down a little footpath connecting North Street and the Scores, I spotted Captain Declan walking to Economics, and I drew up alongside him.

'Hi, Dec, how's it going? Good rugby match at the weekend?'

'Indeed it was,' he bellowed, raising his fist into the air. 'We whipped them 24 to 12!'

I laughed. 'And the piss-up afterwards? A good one?'

'It was indeed very good, but we missed you, of course. And how was your old man?'

'He was in fine form—thanks for asking.'

'Oh boy, you'll have seen the social media chatter doing the rounds?'

'No? I'm a bit out of touch. What's it all about?'

'You're kidding! Apparently those two lads from the other night are out on bail and out for your blood. Don't put it past them to try something.'

Memories of the stupid scuffle came flooding back and I gave a little laugh. 'Oh, let the little fuckers bring it on!' If I could thwart a bombing, I could deal with those two *and* their army of little morons.

'Don't worry. If they mess with you, they'll have the whole 1st team to deal with. If they go for one of us, they go for all of us.'

The class was all about tariff theory, delivered by an uninspiring fill-in for our quite brilliant Professor Wozniak, and within minutes my mind was going round and round in circles as I replayed everything that had happened over the last few days, trying unsuccessfully to make sense of it all.

Management was next, in the quad, but my head wasn't in the right place, and while I hated missing classes, I decided to go for a coffee instead. After that, the plan was to have a rest back at the flat before doing my shift in the pub in the evening.

I got the bike and cycled slowly up the Scores towards the castle and then round to South Street, where I picked a little café with tables out on the pavement. I had a Business Ethics essay due in a few days, and I surprised myself by doing a solid thirty minutes of decent writing until my mind began to wander once again.

This time, I wasn't thinking about the crazy women or the mad Save the Planet people or scrapping with dumbass Americans. Instead, my mind was replaying every moment that I'd spent with Ofelia. I closed my eyes, sat back and tried to make it last for as long as possible. I knew it wouldn't be long before my demons returned.

Chapter 30

When I got back to the flat, Trudy was in the living room in her big armchair reading a book. 'Peter, why don't you lie on that favourite sofa of yours and talk to me? Keep me company.'

'Sounds good, but *please* don't let me fall asleep. I've got my shift at seven.'

'We're all so happy for you, do you know that?' she said as I lay down. 'Ofelia sounds so lovely.'

I put some cushions behind my head and stretched out. 'Thanks, Truds, and I'm so glad I was able to spice up your day with my good news.'

'Are you still having nightmares?' she asked. 'I hope not, for Ofelia's sake. It will scare her to death if you start effing and blinding at 3 a.m., scrunched up beside her in bed.' She burst out laughing and I burst out laughing too, as we so often did. God, I loved her humour.

'Nope, no nightmares. Everything's just fine,' I lied. 'And you. Are you OK, Trudy?'

'Oh, I'm fine. You know me. Happy-go-lucky Trudy. No shortage of gorgeous suitors, grades OK, sport going fine. Yep, everything is hunky dory. My only worry in life is you,' she said half-jokingly.

With that, we heard the front door open, and moments later Shaun appeared, red in the face and out of breath. 'Peter, you'll want to see this.' He was waving his phone.

'Oh no,' said Trudy. 'What in god's name have you been up to now, Peter?'

'You're in the *Evening Standard*, old boy.'

'What!' Shit, I knew exactly what it was.

'A fight in a hotel bar in London?' said Shaun.

There I was, right smack bang in the middle of the front page. 'Billionaire's son fights American tourists in top London hotel.'

I held my head in my hands for a few moments.

'It's a long story, guys. Please don't judge me,' I said quietly, looking at them both.

'Of course not,' said Trudy, coming over to hug me. 'We'll stand by you all the way.'

I stood up. 'Thanks. I'll tell you about it later. I'm going to call my dad.'

Up in my room, after composing myself and taking a deep breath, I called him. 'Hi,' I said as soon as he picked up. 'Where are you?'

'Somewhere over Eastern Europe on our way home. Now, before you ask, yes, I'm aware of the stuff in the press. I'm afraid we're just going to have to take it on the chin and let it blow over. If reporters ask you anything, ignore them. Tell your friends not to talk to them either.'

'I'm so sorry. You really don't need this right now, I know. God, I've been a fool.'

'Son, we all do silly stuff in our lives, so don't worry about it. At least you were standing up for what you believe in. Don't beat yourself up, and for now, take my advice and keep your head down. Now let me go to sleep, will you? We land in Hong Kong at 9 a.m. and I've got a string of meetings from lunchtime onwards and need some shut-eye.' I knew he was *way* more hacked off than he was letting on, but in times of crisis, he would always support me and Sam to the hilt, no matter what.

Just as I'd finished, there was a little knock at my door. It was Shaun seeing if I wanted to talk. 'Mate,' I replied, 'I've got some more calls to make to sort this mess out. Let's catch up later.' I didn't have more calls; I just needed space. I suddenly thought about Ofelia. What on earth would she think of me? Worse, what were her parents going to think? God, I would have done anything just to go back in time. I'd have ignored Biff and Boff and their childish comments and walked away.

Now my phone was ringing. As I reached to switch the thing off, I noticed that it was Christine McPherson and I had to answer it. 'Christine! What a surprise. You must be feeling a bit better?'

'Much, Peter, thank you. Listen, did you know that you—'

'Yes.'

She paused. 'The thing in the *Evening Standard*?'

'Billionaire blah blah blah. Yes, I know.'

'Did you *really* get into a brawl? In the Mandarin Oriental of all places?'

'Guilty,' I said bluntly. But I didn't tell her what had sparked it off. Why upset her?

'Oh, fucking hell,' she replied sympathetically. 'That's not good, Peter, not good *at all*.'

'Yep, but there's squat all I can do about it.'

'I really feel for you. Let me know if there's anything I can do.'

'Any chance you could turn back time?'

'Don't I wish.'

After we'd hung up, I got ready for my shift, and when I went downstairs, all my flatmates were sitting at the kitchen table waiting for me. 'Listen, guys,' I started as I made for the door. 'I owe you an explanation, I know, but could it wait? I just wouldn't know where to begin.'

'At the beginning?' said Diti. 'We've been talking, and we think we deserve to know what happened. We're already getting tons of messages asking what's going on.' She was right, but I kept heading for the door. Whatever story I cooked up would be a lie, and I didn't want to lie to my friends.

I stopped at the door. '*Please* don't speak to the press if they contact you.' They didn't say a word. 'Sorry, guys. I feel awful about all of this. I'm a total and utter dick, I know.'

Chapter 31

The first half of my shift was peaceful and uneventful.

Word was beginning to creep out, though, and then—catastrophe! My bar fight story had made it onto the BBC nine o'clock news—and the TV above my bar station—and at that point, I called the owner and asked if I could be relieved from my shift. 'Wise move, Peter,' he said. Ten minutes later, he'd driven in from his home on the outskirts to take over from me.

Old Jock was the last customer I served. 'Dinny worry, laddie, I'll no judge you,' he said as I tidied up. 'You're a good lad, and if you battered some Yanks, they probably deserved it. In any event, they're all a bunch of tosspots.'

Feeling very sorry for myself, I poured myself a Guinness, left my bike behind the empty kegs and started walking slowly homewards, sipping my beer as I went. I almost called Trudy to ask for a lift, but I wasn't exactly flavour of the month, plus did I really want to face another grilling?

Halfway up a quiet leafy road—home to the town's largest houses—far behind me, I heard a motorbike approaching and watched it purr past. The rider was dressed in black leathers and a mirrored helmet. It reminded me a bit of the bike on Old Church Street, but I didn't give it much more thought. I wondered if Dad had arrived safely. It would be almost 6 a.m. in HK.

What the hell!

It was the biker. He'd turned at the junction and was tearing down the *pavement* towards me.

I heard the scream of another engine. I swung round and behind me, closing in fast, was another biker.

Johnston and Jimmy? It could only be them. *Jesus, what are they trying to do?*

I was frozen with fear.

Chapter 32

I flung my half-empty pint glass into a bush. What the hell was I going to do?

Stand my ground and fight? But they'd have knives.

Run? But there was an enormous wall running the full length of the street, protecting the villas, shutting out any escape.

They were closing in. I only had seconds to act.

Just ahead of me was an overhanging branch. Surely it was too high? But it was my only hope, and I dashed forward, jumping as high as I possibly could, arms stretched upwards.

I got it. Just in no more—one hand only, like with the balloon. But that was enough.

I got the other one on, then began swinging my legs like an acrobat, two, three, four times, until I had enough momentum to get a toe up onto the top of the wall. From there, I shimmied my hands along the branch and got myself lying on top of the wall.

Shaking like a goddamn leaf, I watched as, below me, first one and then the other screeched to a halt. It couldn't be Jimmy and Johnston—these two were shorter, stockier and way more professional.

What the—?

Guns! They were pulling *guns* out of their jackets!

My brain seemed to freeze. Guns? Silencers? *You cannot be serious! What are they doing?* Was this a silly game or something? Was it the rugby team playing a prank?

Tack-tack-tack-tack. They fired.

I launched myself over the wall. *Crash.* I landed in the bushes. No time to fuck about. I fought my way out of the foliage. Ran for my life. Was I hit? I don't think so. No pain. No blood. I must be OK.

Jesus Christ. They'd tried to kill me. The bullets were real. I'd heard branches splintering and I'd even felt one scream past my ear just like on the golf course when the crazy woman had fired at me.

As I charged across someone's back garden, reality hit me. It *must* be connected to what had happened on the golf course. It was clear as day. There were people out there trying to kill me.

Peering back, I saw one of them getting up on top of the wall.

He jumped down. He was after me.

Chapter 33

With the late evening light fading fast and fear driving every stride, I rocketed through the front garden and then across a cul-de-sac into the grounds of the property opposite. It took seconds to cross its front lawn and then I was over the fence into the back garden before vaulting over the high wall at the back into yet another property. This one was an overgrown jungle, and I waded through the undergrowth until I saw a dense patch of brambles, where I dived in and burrowed deep.

I hoped I'd lost him, but after only a few moments of peering out from my hiding place, I watched as he slid quietly over the wall, still helmeted, gun in hand. He stopped where he landed and crouched, scanning the garden with the light from his phone. I was bricking it, but it was impossible to see me, and I stuffed my face in the undergrowth so he couldn't hear me gulping for breath. In the distance, there was the faint sound of a police siren. *Please be coming this way.*

He stayed still, listening and watching, until his mobile rang, and with my breathing thankfully beginning to settle, I watched as he talked. Then, still talking, probably to his biker accomplice, he slowly stood up before randomly firing a frustrated volley into the undergrowth. One, two, three, four shots in a fan across the garden, hoping luck might get his prey. Not even close, thanks god.

Moving quickly, he made his way to the corner of the garden and climbed onto a flat-roofed shed, where he crouched again, watching, looking for me. There were garages close by and probably an access lane from where he'd be picked up. Mercifully, the siren was getting closer.

I felt my anger building as I realised that my would-be assassins were going to get away, leaving me to wonder for evermore who they were. It just wasn't right. I was done with cowering like a dog.

Peter. Please, no. Don't be so bloody reckless, whispered my father's caution in my head. *He'll kill you in seconds.* But I didn't listen.

Puncturing and scratching myself, I eased myself out of the brambles until I was lying in the long grass, watching him, his back towards me. Off to my right, I heard the other bike making its way cautiously up the lane toward him. In the distance, more sirens, but still too far away. *Here goes.*

I took a massive deep breath and took off, silently bounding through the long grass, sprinting when I got to the shorter stuff. Closer and closer I got and still he hadn't heard me. Still his back was turned to me. Now I was the hunter, and my helmeted prey was exposed.

I leapt onto the hut. As I lunged for him, he jumped out of his skin and fell off the roof into the lane. Crawling frantically to the edge, I watched as he threw himself onto the back of the speeding bike. With a cloud of dust and gravel, they tore down the lane towards the garages. I screamed in frustration. Beside me lay his gun where he'd left it.

But wait. They're turning round. They'd hit a dead end, and a second later they were roaring back up the lane towards me.

Hands shaking. Heart pounding. Lying flat on the roof. I took aim. Closer, closer, closer they came.

I fired.

Chapter 34

The gun only allowed me a single shot, but in the light of the lamp in the lane, I saw an enormous cloud of red spray as his helmet exploded.

I'd got the one at the front, not the one who'd chased me.

He slumped forward, and the guy at the back somehow managed to grab the handlebars and continue up the lane before disappearing into the night.

There wasn't a chance that I hadn't killed him.

Now I was a three-time killer.

Chapter 35

I saw the blue flashing light first and then the police car as it pulled to a halt on the quayside. Two officers got out and started half running, half walking up the pier towards me.

The sun was beginning to come up, and the only human life I'd seen had been a small fishing boat chugging out of the harbour an hour earlier. Maybe it had sounded the alarm, or maybe not.

I was coming to terms with what I'd done.

When I'd killed the woman, I'd gone crazy, running around St Andrews like a headless chicken. This time, I'd clinically taken the biker's gun and got rid of it. Then I'd walked to the 24-hour Tesco, bought a bottle of whisky, and headed for the pier, where I'd been for the last six or seven hours.

I was beyond freezing cold, with the beginnings of a raging hangover, but I had worked through things in my mind. I was glad I'd got up off my sorry arse and taken the battle to the enemy, and the fucker with the hole in the head had got what he'd deserved. I only wished I'd got the other one too.

What I just couldn't come to terms with, though, was the fact that I was now a multiple killer. It was a dreadful stain on my life—something that would haunt me forever. I'd never be the same again.

'Good morning. Are you OK?' said one of the approaching officers. It was the plod from the station together with a guy who looked half my age.

'Just grand.'

'Why are you here?'

'To see the sunrise,' I said, pointing towards where the sun was beginning to rise behind dark, angry clouds. 'I had a few things on my mind to work through.'

'Hang on. Aren't you the jogger who came into the station the other day?'

'Hang on. Aren't you the guy who likes reading the sports pages?'

'I beg your pardon?'

I stood up. 'Nothing, sir. I'm just heading home.'

'Your face and hands are all scratched. How did that happen?'

I certainly wasn't about to confide in this useless idiot. I'd made a firm decision that the only person I'd talk to was my father. He would know what to do about the biker and about everything else.

'Can we give you a lift home? You look pretty rough,' said the young one.

I hesitated for a moment. I was absolutely shattered, and a lift would have been good. 'I'm fine, thanks. I need the exercise.' I got up and began walking off down the pier.

'You haven't been having any funny thoughts, have you?' called the useless one. 'There are some good helplines that we can recommend.'

I ignored him and twenty minutes later I was in bed. Despite the madness of what had gone on, or perhaps because of the whisky, I immediately fell asleep until music from downstairs rudely woke me, kicking my mind into overdrive. What time was it? My phone said 8.24 a.m.

I hadn't checked my messages since before going to the pub, and there were four. Two from Ofelia, one from Dad and one from Sam. I read them one by one.

11.30 p.m.: 'Hi Peter. Are you there xxxxx'

12.30 a.m.: 'Peter, I thought you were going to call but I guess you didn't get back till late. My mother and I will be off early to Bath in the morning. Let's talk in the evening. Missing you so much xxx'

01.55 a.m.: 'Peter, just to let you know that we arrived back at 9 am, HK time. It was a smooth flight, your mother and sister say hello, please don't forget to call them from time to time! I'll have a quick rest this morning and will head down to the office at lunchtime. No rest for the wicked!'

06.10 a.m.: 'Call me the minute you wake up. Dad has had an accident.'

Chapter 36

'Sam, what the hell is happening?' I snapped as soon as my sister picked up my call.

'Peter ...' she replied. She was sobbing bitterly. 'Oh, dear god ... it's Dad, he's ...'

'He's *what*, Samantha?' My hands were beginning to shake.

'He's had a terrible accident in the car.'

'Is he in the hospital? How bad is it?'

'No, Peter it's ... it's ...' Her voice tailed off and I suddenly realised the unimaginable.

'Sam, is he *dead*?'

'Yes,' she whispered.

Dead. How can he be dead? Don't be so silly. Dad doesn't do dead!

'You're joking.'

She'd stopped crying. 'No, Peter. Honestly, he's dead. He crashed the Morgan. Coming down Magazine Gap Road.' Suddenly it began to hit home. This was for real. He really was dead.

'Oh, hell, sis, surely not?' I said, the tears beginning to trickle down my face.

She didn't say anything, and a massive, horrible, paralysing sensation flooded my body. 'Give me a moment,' I gasped, and I lay back on my bed.

'It's even worse, Peter. There's Peng. He's dreadfully badly injured and they don't think he'll live.'

'Oh, Jesus. *What the hell happened?* They'd only been back in Hong Kong for a matter of hours.' I was crying my eyes out.

'I know,' she sobbed. 'They'd been home and then they were going to Dad's meetings, and they came off the road on one of the sharp bends.'

'That's ridiculous! He's done that trip tons of times. Hell, he could drive it blindfolded!'

'I know'—she sniffed—'but he always did go very fast and—'

I cut her off, suddenly remembering our mother. 'Where's Mum? Let me speak to her.'

'Right, yes. I'm just going to their room now.' I heard her steps on the wooden stairs, then on the little landing where the oil painting of my father hung. Finally, there was the familiar squeak of the door handle of their bedroom.

'Mum, I've got Peter on the phone ...'

'OK, dear.' I could hear the emotion in her voice. 'And ...'

'Yes, Mum, he knows ...'

I heard the handset being handed over. I was dreading hearing her voice. 'Peter, darling, are you there?'

'Yes, Mum.' I let out a long sigh, not really knowing what to say.

'It's terrible, Peter, and we just don't know what happened.' I noticed how calm she was. 'One moment he was there, getting into the car and making silly jokes. Then, minutes later, he was gone.'

'What have the police said?' Her calmness was calming me too.

But then she started crying. 'They went over the side on the sharp corner. Smashed through the barrier, then the car rolled over and over, nose to tail, as it went down the hillside. And ...' She stopped and I could hear her swallowing hard. 'There's footage out on social media.'

'What the hell? Who in god's name did that?' Then I heard Sam taking back the phone.

'It was some horrible mainland tourists. They were going up the hill in tour buses and caught it on film. I've heard it's horrific, and it's gone all over social media like wildfire, especially in China.'

Then suddenly, it hit me. I realised that I and Mum and Sam would never again see my father. That was it. He was gone. He was dead. We'd never hear his voice again, never have breakfast with him or walk on the Peak with him or hear his silly jokes again or go on holiday with him. Or anything.

'Oh my god, Sam, and what about the company? He *is* the company!'

'I've put you on speaker,' she replied.

'Mum, what about the company?' I asked. 'What will happen? Oh god, and the acquisition of Guzman & Co. Dad was literally inches away from winning it.'

'I informed Chairman Leung about half an hour ago,' said my mum tearfully, 'and he was distraught, as you can imagine. There's a plan to cover this kind of eventuality, and the board will meet with urgency to discuss everything.'

'Where is he now? I mean, where is his ...' but I couldn't bring myself to say the word 'body'.

'HK University Hospital,' said Sam bravely. 'Peng is there too, hanging on by the thinnest of threads, and Pengie is by his side.' Sam had called Mrs Peng 'Pengie' for as long as anyone could remember.

'Listen. I'll get there as soon as I possibly can, OK? I'll book a flight and I'll leave immediately.'

'We love you, Peter, and I just wish you weren't so far away and having to hear all of this by phone,' said my mum, breaking down into tears again.

'I love you both too.' Now my tears were in full flow too. 'Take care of one another till I get there.'

Chapter 37

I had just answered a call from the Commander when the PA system at my gate kicked into life. 'Flight CX 04 to Hong Kong is now ready for boarding.' It had been a frantic dash to Edinburgh airport, but I made the short London flight by the skin of my teeth. Trudy had dropped everything and given me a lift, but it had been a horribly sombre journey down the coast. When we'd arrived, I'd given her a quick hug and then run to check in. 'Be strong, Peter,' she'd called after me.

'I'll keep it brief,' said the Commander. 'Janet and I wanted to pass on our most sincere condolences to you and your mother and sister.'

'Thank you so much, sir.'

'It is the most unbelievably tragic news one could possibly have received.'

'Honestly, sir, my family and I just can't believe it.'

'James was a dear friend to me, Peter. I want you to know that. We go back a long, long way. A story for another day, but he once saved my life—with an act of extraordinary bravery.'

'If you'd told me that a week ago, I would have just laughed. I guess that Official Secrets Act of yours will prevent you from telling me the gory details?'

He gave a little laugh. 'You're probably somewhat wary of me and my organisation, but if there is *anything* I can ever do for you, please just ask. I'm a normal human being, as it happens, and I'll always be here to help. You know the esteem we hold you in— not to mention your father.'

'I might take you up on that one day, sir.' I was so, so close to confiding in him and asking for his help. But now wasn't the time, plus the gate was teeming with travellers.

'Of course, we'll be looking into James's death in parallel to whatever the Hong Kong police might be doing. However, their preliminary findings very clearly point to human error.'

I almost dropped my phone. '*What?* You're serious? Looking into his death to see if there was—what? *Foul play?*' I couldn't believe what I was hearing.

'Standard procedure. High-profile figure. Links with the government. Anyway, we'll put our Analytics unit on it straight away and I'm sure it will come to nothing.'

'Links with the Firm, you mean?'

'As I say, Peter, standard practice for all high-profile British figures. We'll keep it very discreet.'

'OK.' I sighed. 'Listen, I'm about to board.'

'One final thing before I go. You should know that we've offered Christine McPherson a job to recognise the role she played in thwarting the eco-terrorists. She'll start when she's fully fit. She'll be joining Analytics, as it happens—an exceptional bunch, and her brain power and grit will go down extremely well.' He offered his condolences once again and left me to board.

Chapter 38

I had a plan for the flight. Five or six stiff drinks, crash out and hopefully wake up just before landing.

It worked like clockwork, but as soon as I awoke, the empty feeling that I'd taken onto the flight came back again. I wondered if there were any other people on the plane making the horribly sad journey home having just lost a parent.

I was one of the first off, but just before I reached Immigration, a smartly dressed guy in his thirties darted out of a little office. 'Apologies. Are you Mr Peter Black?'

'Yes. What's the matter?'

'I work with airport security, sir, and I'd like to take you out a different way, if that's OK. There's a large press contingent waiting for you in Arrivals.'

That lot badgering and hassling me was the very last thing I needed—I'd probably end up punching the lights out of one of them. 'I appreciate it. Thank you.'

'There will be a car waiting for you courtesy of the airport. Follow me, please.'

Less than five minutes later, after heading down a labyrinth of passageways, we exited a small nondescript door at the side of the terminal and I hopped into a BMW 5 series and headed for the city. The press would find me eventually, though. Of that, I was sure.

On a normal trip from the airport, I'd have been marvelling at the views across the channel to the New Territories or the Lantau Peak. This time, having decided to drop into the hospital on the way home, I was staring into the ether, thinking about Peng. I was dreading seeing the shape he'd be in.

I remembered the day fifteen years ago when my father had come back to our house with Mr and Mrs Peng in his car. He'd gone early morning birdwatching at Mai Po mud flats where, from a rustic hide, he'd spotted the pair paddling their way—lying flat on thin wooden boards—across the vast expanse of mud flats from the Chinese mainland. A border patrol had been close by, and my father had quickly waded into the mud and hauled them to safety before concealing them under a pile of rugs in the hide. If they'd been caught, who knows what might have happened to them?

A short stay had turned into a longer one, and after being legalised, they became our housekeepers, living in the cottage on the grounds of the villa we eventually moved to, high on Victoria Peak.

Over the years, they'd become like family, with Mr Peng more and more becoming an assistant and confidant to my father. Often he'd be asked to give his view or opinion, particularly when my father felt that something needed to be seen from a totally different perspective. 'I need that contrarian mainland view,' my father would often say.

Peng divulged little about his past, but my father's confidential background checks had established that his father had uncovered local government-level corruption in his home province and he and his wife had been brutally murdered as a result. To escape the same fate, the newlywed couple had fled their northern province, making the dangerous journey south to Guangdong before taking on the treacherous mud flats. My father's quick action that day in Mai Po changed their lives forever.

The driver left me outside Hong Kong University Hospital, and I went straight to ICU on the 19th floor, where a nurse escorted me to Peng's room. 'Is Mr Peng's wife with him?' I asked as we went along the squeaky, shiny-floored corridor.

'She's been at this side since he arrived.' I wasn't surprised. They were the most devoted couple.

'And the outlook?' I asked nervously.

'He's in terrible shape, but there may be some signs of stabilisation. The doctor will brief you.'

When Mrs Peng saw me, she jumped up and rushed over to hug me, tears streaming down her cheeks, and after whispered hellos, we sat quietly by his bedside. 'Terrible shape' was an understatement. Legs, arms, ribs and pelvis were broken in multiple places, but most worrying was a blood clot on the brain which they wouldn't be able to tackle until he was strong enough to withstand an operation. He was hooked up to every machine imaginable, just as McPherson had been.

'He'll never recover from this,' she whispered, consumed with grief. 'And if he does, there's a high chance he'll lose his ability to think and function. Isn't it better that they just turn off all these machines?' I really didn't know what to say to that, and the best I could do was to comfort her.

After a while, a doctor came in and introduced himself, and he gave us a faint glimmer of hope. 'Mrs Peng, I've seen many severe trauma patients over the years and while your husband is in the gravest of danger, I hold out hope. His fighting spirit is quite remarkable.'

'There is no stronger person on the planet,' I chipped in. 'Let's be strong, shall we, Mrs Peng?'

She nodded her head and managed a tiny smile, but I knew fine well that she held out little hope.

'Visiting time is over,' announced the ward sister a little later. 'Mrs Peng is free to stay, of course.'

Before leaving, I gave her another long hug and reminded her about that perilous journey they'd made years ago. 'He will make this journey too, Mrs Peng.' Deep inside, though, I wasn't so sure.

'Wait, Peter,' she said just as I was leaving, and she went to her bag and pulled out a small Chinese-style envelope with a large red seal on it. She then hung her head and burst into tears. 'Peng told me to give it to you—and nobody else—if ever something happened to him.'

How strange. Peng had often written to me over the years to help me improve my Mandarin, but I had no clue what the letter would be about. 'No, Mrs Peng,' I said, offering her back the letter. 'There's no need for me to take this. He's going to recover. Just you watch.'

'No, Peter,' she demanded, pushing my hand away. 'You *must* take it. It's what he would want.'

I slipped it into my jacket pocket, and as I left, I was struck by how her eyes had lost their old sparkle. And while she'd always seemed ageless, now she appeared old and frail.

Chapter 39

With our parting conversation playing heavily on my mind, I took the lift down. But as I got out into the lobby—*oh shit!*

Just my luck. The press was standing right there by the doors—ten or more of them with their cameras and microphones. Who in hell's name had tipped them off?

As they swarmed towards me, there was only one thing to do. *I legged it.*

I darted left and tanked it down a long corridor, and when I looked back, they were belting after me, jostling and shouting. But I didn't get very far. After crashing through the first set of swing doors, when I got to the next lot, they were keypad locked and all I could do was duck into the ladies' toilet beside them. Fortunately it was empty, and in no time I'd managed to squeeze out of a partially open window and drop down into an alleyway. From there, it was a brisk walk to the rear of the hospital, where I jumped into a red Hong Kong taxi. I'd outwitted them, but only just.

'Magazine Gap Road, please,' I yelled to the ancient driver in Cantonese. 'Halfway up.'

As we pulled away, four or five of them burst out of the alleyway and threw their hands up in despair as they saw me disappear. I hated the miserable little parasites.

It didn't take long to forget them, though. In no time, we were climbing Cotton Tree Drive and from there onto Magazine Gap Road. As the old taxi groaned up the ultra-steep road, the knot in my stomach grew tighter and tighter. Normally I wouldn't have given the dense, lush undergrowth and steep slopes a second glance, but things were different now. Desperately holding back tears, I imagined the Morgan crashing down the mountainside with its two precious passengers inside.

Peering ahead as we approached the fifth or sixth bend, I spotted a solitary police van parked in the tiny layby on the cliff side of the bend. 'Pull in by the police van, please.'

'Can't stop. Police give ticket,' he mumbled.

'Please, it's important,' I implored, and with a scowl, he pulled in for a second. 'Keep the change,' I said, pushing him a HK$100 note, but without thanks, he U-turned and tore off down the hill with a screech. I was too sad to be bothered about it.

Ducking under the blue and white police tape, I walked over to the edge. The metal crash barrier had been obliterated, and as I peered over the side, I gulped at the sheer drop and the sea of dense, impenetrable semi-rainforest.

'You'll not see a thing, sir,' came a voice and when I looked around, a young officer was getting out of the van. 'Can I help you? You shouldn't really be here. It's the scene of a fatal accident.'

I peered back over the wall, straining my eyes, trying to catch a glimpse of the Morgan's white chassis. Not a chance. The foliage was just too thick and dense. 'I'm James Black's son,' I said, still staring down the mountain. 'I just wanted to see where it happened.'

'Yes, sir, of course. I'm very sorry for your loss. Such a tragic accident.' When I turned to thank him, his head was slightly bowed, Peng style. My father had sat on the Police Department board for many years, his work highly regarded, and the news would have caused quite a ripple.

I looked back over the side. 'Not easy to get down. How did they manage it?'

'Two by helicopter winch, the rest on abseil ropes. One of the team even got bitten by a bamboo viper. But he'll be OK,' he said hastily, seeing the look of shock on my face.

Just as I was about to ask him where the car had ended up, my phone rang. It was McPherson, and I signalled to the officer that I'd be a few moments. 'Hi, Christine. How are you?' I walked slowly up to the top of the layby and sat down on a still-intact part of the crash barrier.

'Oh, my dear Peter,' she said. 'I'm so, so sorry to hear your tragic news.'

She was tough, opinionated, and sometimes crude, but in the next few minutes, she was the kindest and gentlest of souls, and my estimation of her went up even more. She knew what it was like to lose a parent—in her case two—in tragic circumstances, and she counselled me to take things slowly and to let time heal the pain. As she talked, I stared down the mountain, picturing again the car crashing through the trees, and once again, I fought to hold back my tears.

'Thanks for being so kind to me, McPherson. What you've said has really helped.'

'Not at all. I really can't explain how terribly sad I feel for you.' But then I felt her tone toughen a little. 'I do, though, have two important things I need to discuss with you. Normally they could wait, but they're just too important. Would you mind?'

'I'm fine. Get on with it.' I stood up. Something big was coming.

'Right, here we go.' She took a deep intake of air.

Chapter 40

'It was you, Peter, wasn't it? Admit it.'

'What do you mean?' Shit, how had she found out?

'You know fine well what I mean.'

'You mean the—' but before I could answer, another call came in, this time Sam. 'Wait a minute, would you, Christine? My sis is calling.'

'God, OK! I'll wait. But don't dare try and dodge the issue, OK?' I put her on hold.

'Sam, I'm on another call, and I'll call you straight back. I'm at the crash site and I'll be home soon.'

'At the crash site! We'll be down in five minutes to pick you up. Just wait there.' She hung up.

'I'm back, McPherson. Now what is it you're accusing me of?'

'The fucking hot air balloon, you idiot. My mind is fuzzy, and I'm probably slightly brain-damaged, but I remember you being there, running towards the balloon. I've also analysed the pictures of that man and of course it's you. *Duh.* You were even wearing my rain mac! You must think I'm stupid.'

'No one is supposed to know,' I whispered, checking that the police officer wasn't listening. 'It's top secret. The Commander said I couldn't tell a soul.'

'Fucking hell, Peter. What on earth happened up there? It's unbelievable. Unfathomable.'

'Wrong place at the wrong time, McPherson.'

She snorted. 'Right place at the right time, you mean. Without you, Parliament would be in ruins and countless lives would have been lost. You thwarted them, Peter. Can't you see that? It's a huge, huge deal. Now tell me the whole thing from start to finish.'

Pacing up and down in the layby, feet away from where my father had lost his life, I told McPherson *everything*. Well, almost everything. She was utterly stunned into silence. 'What's the second thing on your mind?' I asked her.

'In a minute,' she replied. 'God, I'm in total and utter shock. It's just so unbelievable that Green and Jo really were going to do it. *She* messed with all those poor people, twisting them to her way of thinking. It's really frightening.'

I hadn't told her I'd killed 'she' with my bare hands and that it was doing my head in. Damn it, why was I so upset about killing her when 'she' would gladly have killed me and hundreds more?

'Peter, before I talk about the other thing,' she said, softening her voice, 'are you OK? Like, mentally OK. You sounded so unfazed and *normal* when you visited me in the hospital. But are you sure everything's OK? The Commander's really worried about you.'

'I'm bearing up fine, McPherson. No need for anyone to worry.'

Chapter 41

My 'I'm bearing up ... no need for anyone to worry' response was met with a moment's disbelieving silence, but she didn't press the point.

'I've still got thousands of questions about what happened up there on the balloon, but let me get on to the other matter. It's important.'

'I'm curious to know what it is.'

'OK, so I think you know that I'm going to begin work with the Firm, right?' she started.

'Yes, and congratulations. You thoroughly deserve it.'

'Thanks. OK, so the Commander told me that my first assignment is to check into your father's death—to rule out foul play. He told you, I think. So last night I got my colleague, Charles, from Imperial, to come to the Cromwell with some IT kit and we stayed up all night looking into things.'

'*McPherson*. You're supposed to be recovering! It was just a few days ago that those wankers kicked the daylights out of you and put you in a coma. You shouldn't be playing detective.'

'Thanks for looking out for me, but trust me, I can't lie around in bed feeling sorry for myself.'

'McPherson. Dad's death was an *accident*. It must have been. He was jet-lagged, driving too fast, lost control ...'

'Peter. *Stop!*' Her voice was kind but firm. 'We've found something, so please hear me out.'

I felt a shiver go up my spine. What had she uncovered?

She explained how she and Charles had hacked into every conceivable CCTV, home security, and bus and taxi surveillance system in the vicinity of Victoria Peak, the area near my home and the crash site. Having got the reams of footage, they'd then shot AI smart worms through it to try to identify if there had been any unusual activity at the house. 'We were getting zilch until Charles—who you *really* must meet—spotted something.'

'Spotted what, exactly?'

'A street sweeper. Specifically, a Sikh street sweeper.'

'*A Sikh*! Go on.' Images of the Sikhs from St Andrews and the Mandarin flashed through my mind.

'We think he was more than just a lowly street sweeper,' she explained. 'Highway Department records show he switched to the Victoria Peak roster just two weeks ago, but it is the footage that is key. He spent lots of time in the close vicinity of your house, sometimes well after his shift should have finished. But listen to this! Shortly after the crash, we can see him rushing up to the crash scene from lower down on Magazine Gap Road. Now, that doesn't make him guilty, but then we see that he sends a message on his phone, and with a bit of hacking into PCCW Telecommunications, we found that it was a two-word text message in a weird language.'

'Christ. We need to get it translated.'

'Already done. Charles was on it straight away.'

'Come on! What in god's name did it say?' I shouted at her.

'*Job completed.*'

My mind flipped into overdrive. Asian woman on the golf course. Sikh in the pub. Another in the Mandarin. The bikers—maybe Sikhs too? And now a Sikh loitering around the house and sending texts from the crash scene. 'Jesus, McPherson. Oh my god, we need to talk. There's so much stuff to tell you. Stuff you don't know about. It's all linked.'

Her voice quickened. 'Peter, we need to move *fast*. The sweeper's on a flight to Delhi at 9 a.m. tomorrow. We know where he lives. *We need to do something.*' But before I could reply, I heard the toot of a horn and pulling into the layby was Sam, driving, and my mother in our old Range Rover.

'Listen, Mum and Sam have just pulled up to collect me from the crash site. Give me a bit of time and I'll call you later, OK? And I *must* tell you about all this stuff that's happened.'

'Sure.'

'And ... McPherson ...'

'What?'

'Thanks for everything. You're amazing.'

'No, Peter, I'm the one who wants to thank you. For being so brave to stop Jo and Green and for believing in me when everyone else thought I was crazy. And oh my god, for thumping that man in HQ! The Commander told me about it. Did you really do that right in front of their noses?'

'I didn't hit him nearly hard enough. Now I've got to go.'

I watched as Mum and Sam got out of the car, my mother's face blotched from crying, Sam white as a sheet. Then I looked down the mountainside beyond the mangled crash barrier. Somewhere down there he'd taken his last breath, and now I knew that *someone* out there had ordered his murder.

'Christine, are you still there?'

'Yes, of course.'

'Send me the sweeper's photo and address, will you?'

'I'll do it straight away, and I'll get the Commander to contact the Hong Kong police.'

'*No, McPherson.* This is something I'm going to do myself. Don't breathe a word. Promise?'

'You can't be serious. It's too dangerous.'

I was deadly serious.

Chapter 42

Sam and my mum rushed over to me, and we stood silently in the layby embracing one another. There really was nothing to say.

'Oh, it's all *so* dreadful,' said my mother finally, wiping away her tears. 'I just never expected it to end this way. I was convinced that James and I would grow old together, that he'd hand the company on to both of you and then there'd be grandkids and all those nice things to look forward to. But now he's gone. Just like that!' She snapped her fingers. 'Literally five minutes after he'd left the house, he was dead. It's all just so unbelievable. Like an awful dream.'

I went over and thanked the officer, then the three of us walked arm in arm to the car. 'I stopped off to see Peng on the way in from the airport,' I said quietly. 'My *god*, he's in terrible shape, and Mrs Peng looks utterly dreadful.'

'Let's hope he makes it.' Sam sighed, starting up the car. 'I don't know if I can take a second death.' Then she shook her head. 'Oh, Christ! Now we've got to get back through those journalists camped outside the front gate. You'll hate it, Peter. It's a total invasion of our privacy.'

She wasn't wrong. As we pulled into the narrow lane shared with five other neighbours, I saw them up ahead, congregated around our front gate. 'For fuck's sake, there's like fifty of them. Haven't they got better stuff to be doing than annoying us?'

'They must have heard you were coming,' said Sam, turning to look at me in the back. 'After all that nonsense in the London Mandarin, there's twice as many as there were.'

'We'll talk about that later,' said my mother sternly before I could defend myself. 'Firstly, let's get through them as best we can.'

Sam pressed the gate opener and started to flash the lights and honk the horn, but they didn't budge an inch, and soon they swarmed around us, blinding us with a volley of camera flashes.

'Let me have a civil talk with them,' said my mother, winding down the window. But no sooner had she done it then three or four cameras and microphones were stuffed through the window, one of them bumping her solidly on the forehead. 'It's OK. It's OK,' she shouted as Sam went nuts.

It wasn't OK, and I swung open the door, bashing a few of them with it in the process, then jumped out. *'Bloody ridiculous,'* I screamed.

I hauled two of them away from the car and shoved a few more out of the way, and Sam began to inch forward. But it was clear it was going to turn ugly and when a big fat guy put his hands on the front of the car to try to stop it and wouldn't budge. I ploughed into him rugby-tackle style, bulldozing him—and me— off the path until the two of us crashed down a bank into the shrubbery. Seconds later, with his buddies yanking me off him, I started throwing punches at anyone within range.

'Enough!' came a loud shout. *'Enough!'*

Everyone suddenly went quiet. It was my mother. She was out of the car, climbing down the bank towards us. Scarlet faced. Pissed off like I'd never seen her before.

'Go to the house *now*, you idiot,' she said, pointing at me. 'And you, miserable inconsiderate lot,' she said, pointing at the press, 'I'll give you all a five-minute briefing right now, but only if you get back outside the gate where you belong.'

Tamed, they began to move back outside the gate while I hoofed it up to the house, fists clenched and ready to beat up anyone who came anywhere near me. 'Nice one, little brother,' scoffed Sam, who'd parked the car and was walking back to give our mum moral support.

'Useless little parasites they are,' I shouted back at her, 'and I don't know why Mum is giving them the time of day. Plus the fat boy got what he deserved.'

'You just can't help yourself, can you?' she snapped back. She was right, of course.

I went straight upstairs to my room, threw myself on the bed and lay there trying to simmer down. But to be honest, it didn't take too long at all. I really didn't give a stuff about the press or what trouble my ugly temper might have got me into. All that was important now was to focus, go find the sweeper and get him to talk. Someone must have been pulling his strings, and it was my job to find out who.

I looked at my phone, hoping that McPherson had sent the address and his photo. If she hadn't, I'd be calling her to give her hell. Thankfully she had.

There, staring at me, was a mug shot of a Sikh along with an address in Mong Kok, a zone over on the Kowloon side of Hong Kong. Other than his orange turban, there was nothing particularly distinctive about him. He looked well built, wore a beard, and looked like he was in his late twenties.

I typed her a message. 'I'm going to Mong Kok now. Will call you when I arrive.'

As I went down to the basement garage, I heard Mum and Sam coming into the house above and heading for the kitchen. By the time I got back, hopefully my mother would be in a more forgiving mood, and with luck I'd know a lot more about my father's death.

In the garage, I stopped for a moment. Maybe I should be calling the police? Wasn't it their job to find out who had murdered my father? But then I saw the empty space where the Morgan would usually have sat, and I thought about the many happy hours that

Dad had spent down here tinkering around, happily going about his business.

I took a long metal wrench from his toolbox, pushed it into my waistband and put a roll of duct tape in my jacket pocket.

'Are you down there, Peter?' came my mother's voice. 'Isn't it time we had a talk?'

I slipped the cover off my father's old Royal Enfield motorbike, turned the key and it roared into life.

'I'm going to find out who did it, Dad,' I whispered as I raced up the ramp into the drive, scattering my friends the press as I sped past them.

Chapter 43

After purring down Stubbs Road, I passed the Jockey Club—where race evening would soon kick off—and from there, I took the Cross Harbour Tunnel under Victoria Harbour towards Kowloon. Inside, my emotions were all over the place, a strange mix of sadness, loneliness, anger and excitement

Less than half an hour after leaving the house, with the sun going down, I arrived in Mong Kok, the edgy district famous for its inexpensive outdoor markets, fake designer goods and cheap eateries. As always, it was teeming with people—tourists and locals alike.

I pulled into a side street and called McPherson as I parked the bike. She picked up immediately. 'Christine, I'm—'

'I know. You're there already. I'm tracking your mobile and I've got visuals on you from CCTV. You're on a bike wearing blue jeans and a brown leather jacket.' Despite the tension building inside me, I couldn't help but laugh.

'God. No wonder Burke hired you.' I hadn't laughed since those happy times with Ofelia in London. That seemed like an age ago, and I hadn't even called Ofelia since my father's death.

'I'll be with you the whole way, Peter, OK? You can think of me as your eyes and ears. I'm really pretty good at this kind of stuff too, so trust me and make use of me.'

I didn't doubt her one bit. In fact, it felt incrediblyreassuring to have her there by my side. To anyone looking on, I might have appeared confident and in control. On the inside, however, I was scared as hell, and being honest, I didn't really have much of a plan. 'His apartment building is three blocks up the street. Now, are you sure you want to do this? We can still call in the police.'

'No police. They'll screw it up and there's no time.' I was walking and had almost reached the main street.

'OK, but before you go any further, don't you have something important to tell me? Maybe it's time to get it off your chest.'

She was right, I did, and I about turned and went back to the bike and sat on the saddle. 'I warn you, McPherson, it's bad. Are you ready for bad?'

'As it happens, there's been rather a lot of bad in my life. I'm sure I can take it.'

'Here we go, then. But you promise not to tell anyone? Not a soul. Ever.'

'I promise.'

It took me ten minutes. First the attack by the crazy woman. Then the story of the bikers. Then, finally, I fully fessed up to killing Jo.

She didn't say a single word throughout, and when I'd finished, there was a long, deathly silence.

'Please say something, would you, Christine? I know it's utterly awful. I've killed three people.'

'It's just *unbelievable*, Peter. I don't know what to say. It's all so shocking. With Jo, I had no idea and just assumed she died in the blast. And that woman and those bikers, out to kill you in cold blood. But why? Why would anyone try to kill you? What have you done to deserve that?

'And it looks like they wanted my father dead too ... and they succeeded.' As I said it, I felt my anger rise again at the sheer unfairness of it all.

'We *have* to call the police, Peter. It's way too big for us—we're total amateurs.'

'Let's not go through that again. Let's just do what we agreed.' I got off the bike and started walking up to the main street again. 'If you don't want to be a part of it, I'll understand, but right now, I'm going to visit the sweeper, and if needs be, I'll beat the truth out of him.'

'But what if he's armed or with his criminal friends? They'll do away with you. What will that achieve?' I could feel her anger and frustration.

'*Come on.* He *killed* my father. There's no way in hell I'm going to sit back. I barely know you, but I think I've got the measure of you, and I know that if it was your father who'd been killed, you'd go straight in there, no questions asked. Admit it!'

'*Asshole!*' she yelled down the phone.

'Yes, I am an asshole, and you'd better get used to it.'

By now I was up on the main street and heading towards where he lived. 'But I need to know. Right now. Are you in or are you out?'

'How do you keep going?' she replied more calmly. 'You've knifed a woman in the throat. Strangled Jo. Blown someone's brains out. And on top of that, you've just lost your father. Most people would be in therapy and taking pills.'

I ignored her. 'Now, where the hell is the apartment block, McPherson? You're supposed to be my eyes and ears.'

A switch had flicked inside me, and no matter what, I was going to find out who was behind it all and no one was going to stop me. I'd never felt so determined about anything in my entire life.

Chapter 44

Thankfully McPherson was in and not out. I wouldn't have wanted to take on the Sikh without her.

From the opposite side of the road, I approached the decrepit twenty-storey block where he supposedly lived. It was shrouded in bamboo scaffolding, the odd man out in a street where most of the buildings had either been renovated or replaced by tall residential towers. Mong Kok, like other up-and-coming areas of Hong Kong, was changing, with the poor being pushed out into the New Territories while smart young accountants, lawyers and tech geeks took their place.

'Charles found the building plans,' said McPherson sternly. 'There are four tiny apartments per floor, two at the front and two at the back. The numbering is all screwy, though, and we can't work out if he's at the front or the back. It's on the fifth floor, though.'

'There are lights on in the front two,' I whispered, counting the floors. 'I'll check out the rear.' I began sauntering across the street and down a narrow side lane, following it until the back of the sweeper's building came into view. 'Rear two units don't have lights on.'

'Back on the main street, in the block facing, there are restaurants, and I think some of them look over into his apartment block. Might be worth checking out?'

'That's a good idea.' As I got back to the main street, I saw two eateries which might give me a view. 'It's Wuhan Hotpot or Cantonese Lucky. What do you fancy this evening?'

'I'm not in the mood for humour,' came the snappy reply.

'Just trying to break the tension. Let's go with Hotpot.'

The lift up to Wuhan Hotpot was incredibly small, and just as the doors were closing, an ancient Chinese lady dressed in a grey

Mao-style tunic and black Chinese slippers stuck her stick in. The doors automatically slammed open again and she waddled in.

'Good evening,' I said to her in Cantonese. I asked her if she'd been out for an evening walk, to which she replied in English, 'Not many gweilo'—foreigners—'speak Cantonese. Yes, I've been out sitting with old friends in park.' She then stared and pointed her stick at me. 'Watch out. Hotpot place, no good. The pork very bad. Make sure you don't get ill. The owner also very mean.'

'Thank you kindly,' I replied as the lift stopped at my floor. 'Maybe I'll stick to noodles with vegetables,' and I wished her a good night's sleep.

Inside, I took a window seat, ordered a hot tea and sat studying the menu, occasionally glancing across the street at the block opposite. The view into the two 5th-floor apartments was perfect. In the one to the left, I saw a young Chinese couple sitting on a sofa watching television. The other was lit but there was no sign of life.

My tea arrived, and as I stirred the rather greasy-looking stuff, I noticed that the couple were becoming quite affectionate with one another, and after a few minutes, the guy got up and closed the curtains. I felt a bit like a peeping Tom.

A few minutes later, an elderly Chinese man with a Zimmer frame appeared in the other flat, slowly shuffling towards his chair, a helper dutifully walking behind him carrying a tray with some food on it. 'No luck, McPherson,' I said, blowing gently on my tea. 'Young amorous couple in one. Pensioner in the other. Our friend must live at the rear.'

Shit. Wait. I'd just seen him. It was the orange turban I'd seen first, and there he was, coming out of the 7-Eleven just up the street from his block. He must be heading for home.

'*McPherson!* I've got a sighting. He's walking to his building.'

'Got him. *That's him.*' Now there was raw excitement in her voice, and I could feel my own adrenaline kicking in. I left a twenty on the table and raced down the stairwell until I got out into the street.

'I'm going round the back again to see which apartment he goes into.'

'Wait,' she suddenly shouted. But she didn't need to say anything, because I'd seen him too. I quickly turned my back and looked in a shop window. He'd come back out of his apartment block and was walking slowly up the pavement, tapping something into his mobile phone.

I began following him on my side of the street. 'Looks like he's going back into the 7-Eleven.' I watched as he slid open the door of a tall fridge and pulled out what looked like a pack of beer. 'Buying booze. Looks relaxed.'

'Don't let him see you!'

'I'm not completely stupid,' I whispered back.

'Sorry. Of course.'

Instead of heading back to his flat, he continued up the road. After only fifty metres or so, he cut into a tiny park and sat on a small stone bench underneath a huge old tree. There he lit up a cigarette and pulled out a beer. He'd probably done this many times before.

'Beer and a smoke. Glued to his phone.'

'Is there anyone else around?' asked McPherson.

'Not a soul. The street's busy, but he's the only one in the park, and half the world probably doesn't even know it exists.'

'So what's the plan?'

'I either take him there or in his flat.'

'No, Peter! It's far too public.'

But he made my decision for me as I watched him drain his can, chuck it in the bushes, then pick up the bag and begin heading slowly back towards the apartment block.

'He's headed for home. Not a care in the world.'

'Take care. I'm feeling *really* nervous about this.'

About a minute after he'd gone into his block, I crossed the street and gingerly entered the filthy lobby. There was no lift, and somewhere above me I could hear him singing to himself as he climbed the stairs, flip-flops scuffing with each step that he took.

'I'm going up the stairs after him.'

'Are you sure?' She sounded terrified.

'It's fine. His guard is down.'

Keeping to the outside in case he peered down the stairwell, I crept up the first flight of stairs. Somewhere above me I heard a door unlock, then a loud squeak as it opened and again as it closed.

'He's gone in,' I whispered.

Hardly daring to breathe, I kept going until just before his landing, I peeked round the stairwell. His was the first door—the scuff marks in the dust gave it away, plus from the little gap at the base of the door I could see that a light was on inside.

I tiptoed past and on up the stairs, then stopped just round the corner on a little half landing.

What was I going to do? Go down, knock on the door and clobber him with the wrench? But what if he had company or if he was armed?

I had an idea. The landing window was slightly open. If I could climb out onto the scaffolding, then down a few feet and along, I'd be able to look into his window and see if he was alone. It was getting dark outside, and it wouldn't be easy for him to see me looking in.

'I'm going to hang up,' I whispered. 'I need full concentration. I'll call you as soon as I can.'

'Wait ...' I heard her shout as I cut the call and put my pods in my jeans pocket.

Chapter 45

Other than the creaking sound that bamboo makes, the climb down was more straightforward than I'd thought it would be, and soon I was standing about two metres from his apartment window. My feet were perched on a horizontal pole while my hands held the one above. For a moment, my legs trembled as I thought about the thousands of labourers who must have fallen to their deaths over the years on rickety bamboo scaffolding in Hong Kong.

Part—perhaps a third—of his window was obscured by an ancient whining aircon unit, and I sidled along my pole, then took my hands off the one above, grabbed the unit and crouched behind it. Once I was happy with my balance, I took a deep breath and poked my head around the side, hoping and praying that he wouldn't be right at the window looking out.

I saw him, looked for a second or two, then ducked my head behind the unit again.

I'd seen an ultra-messy, tiny apartment, and he'd been lying flat out on what looked like a camp bed just a few metres from where I was precariously crouched. He was playing a game on his mobile, beers by his side, and I hadn't seen anyone else in there. His window had been ever so slightly ajar.

I took a second look—this time longer—and tried to visualise how I might take him on.

Clobbering him at the door using the element of surprise was still an option, but what if he didn't open it or if the neighbours were alerted? With the benefit of hindsight, I should have taken my chances in the park when there hadn't been anyone around. I could have just beaten the truth out of him right there and then and it would all have been done by now.

I peeked again. Now he was levering himself out of bed. *Crap, he's coming to the window.*

I quickly pulled back and crouched as low as I possibly could. If he could see the top of my head, I was dead.

The window gave a loud groan as he pushed it wide open.

I held my breath and prayed to God.

Chapter 46

I gripped the unit for dear life, every part of me trembling. If he saw me, I was going to have to jump down onto the lower struts—nigh on impossible in the dark. Or fight him from where I was.

I heard him clear his throat, then snort, and then he gobbed out of the window, some of the spray hitting me. It stank of beer and cigarettes. He did it a second time, then I heard him light a cigarette and I caught a whiff of the smoke before the window—thank god—closed again with a groan.

After a few seconds, I quickly peeked round the corner. He was back, sitting on his bed. The window was still open a tiny bit—it probably didn't close any further—and over the din of the aircon unit, I could hear music from the game he was playing on his phone as he puffed his ciggy.

I'd seen enough. With a plan forming in my mind, I climbed carefully back up the way I'd come, and two minutes later I was back out in the street. I called McPherson. 'Hey, it's me.'

'*Oh my god*, Peter. I've been so beside myself with worry.' As I walked slowly down the main street, I gave her chapter and verse before telling her my plan.

Chapter 47

Killing two hours wasn't easy, and as well as stopping for a McDonald's, I ended up riding the Enfield twice around Hong Kong island. My father would have frowned at the speed I got up to on the quieter south side.

I almost called Ofelia, but something stopped me. Of course, I should have, but I had that ever-growing feeling inside of me that I simply wasn't good enough for her. I was a three-time killer. Damaged goods. Didn't such a nice, kind, beautiful person deserve so much better?

After parking the bike and reconnecting to McPherson, I went and checked the rear of the building. Sure enough, his apartment lights were off. So far, so good. I just hoped he hadn't gone out.

'Someone just switched off all the CCTV in the district,' whispered McPherson with a hint of mischief.

'Nice! Always one step ahead of the game, aren't you?' I laughed, liking her humour. There was a bit of the Trudy in her. Then, as she listened in, I retraced my steps to the upper stairwell, eased my way out onto the scaffolding and lowered myself into position behind the aircon unit.

It seemed much darker this time, and I crouched for a few moments, letting my eyes adjust and my nerves settle—breaking into flats to go after people wasn't something I did every day. Then, vision improving, I sidled towards the window. Thank god! It was still slightly open.

I could just about make him out, stretched out on his bed, and above the din of the aircon, I could hear spluttered—probably beer-induced—snoring.

It was time, and I took a few long, deep breaths just as I would have done before going into a judo bout. Peng, my ringside mentor, had always insisted on it in the same way that he'd always drilled into me that bouts are won by taking immediate and early control.

'I'm going in, McPherson.'

'Take care,' she whispered. 'And don't be afraid to run if you have to.'

Very gently, I tried pulling the window towards me. It didn't budge. I tried a little harder. Still nothing until finally I gave it a big old yank, and with that same horrendous groan, it swung wide open. Like a frightened roach, I scuttled back along my pole to my hiding place. Surely he'd heard me. Half of Hong Kong certainly had.

But no. Seconds ticked by and miraculously, he didn't appear. The noisy air conditioning—or more likely the alcohol—must have saved my bacon.

I squeezed in through the window and slowly tiptoed across the room to his bed, making sure I didn't kick any of the trash on the floor. His snoring was like nothing I'd ever heard before.

I stood over him. Was this simple labourer really involved in my father's death?

Without warning, the snoring suddenly stopped, and he began to stir.

Chapter 48

As he came to, with the full might of my weight behind it, I drove a fist straight into his Adam's apple. It was crude, but I didn't feel comfortable using the wrench. What if I killed him?

For a second there was silence. No movement. Then, all of a sudden, with an almighty squeal, I watched his body vault into the air. He landed face first on the floor beside his bunk.

He was clutching his throat with his hands, heaving, desperately trying to suck air into his system. None was going in. Panic. Wheezing. Convulsing.

He tried to get onto his knees, but I stamped on his back, slamming him onto his stomach.

'Peter, Peter,' yelled McPherson into my ear. 'What's happening? Tell me you're OK!'

'I'm fine,' I whispered. I'd had major jitters at first, but now I was calm. In control.

It was time to fully immobilise him. As he lay face down, gasping like a fish out of water, I wrapped him in duct tape—ankles first, then knees and finally arms to his sides. It was all done in less than a minute and I'd got him where I wanted him. Or had I?

Suddenly the little bastard let out a raging bellow, and I furiously started wrapping tape around his head and mouth, leaving only his nose free to breathe through. That'd soon shut him up.

'Are you OK?' whispered McPherson, still with panic in her voice. 'Tell me what's going on.'

I stood up and walked over to the window. 'Overpowered. Taped up.' I whispered.

'Has he seen you?'

'Negative.'

'Get moving, Peter, in case someone heard him. Get him talking.'

'Yep.'

As I walked over to him, I walloped him in the guts with a kick, then knelt and whispered in his ear. 'Nod your head if you work as a road sweeper on the Peak.'

He didn't nod. Three more kicks and still no movement.

'You will *fucking* well tell me what I need to know, you little shit. You've got three seconds.'

I counted to three, then squeezed his Adam's apple tight. But still nothing.

'Your choice, mate.'

'Peter, what are going to do to him?' yelled McPherson. 'Don't go too far.'

'Why?' I snapped back at her.

Pulling him over onto his back, I grabbed one of the cans beside his bed, opened it and with a knee wedged into his neck I held his head back and began slowly pouring the beer down his nostrils.

'When you're ready to talk, just let me know,' I hissed in his ear.

Ten seconds later, after snorting, spluttering and writhing like a deranged animal, he nodded his head furiously, desperate to talk.

'Did you work as a street cleaner on the Peak?' He nodded immediately.

'Did you tamper with James Black's sports car?' He suddenly went very still. I had the right man.

'Did you tamper with the car?' I said again, this time grabbing his nuts and twisting hard, holding my hand over his mouth and nose to muffle his cries.

'What in god's name are you doing? You can't. There are rules against this kind of thing.'

'He's a murdering son of a bitch, Christine. If you don't like it, go join Amnesty for all I care.'

I ripped the tape from his mouth and grabbed his nuts again. 'You're not going to make another sound, are you?'

'No, no, no ... I won't make a sound.'

'Why did you do it? Who paid you?'

'I don't know,' he gasped. 'I was made to do it.' It was ugly and barbaric, but finally, I was getting somewhere.

'What do you mean? *Who* made you do it?'

'I didn't meet anyone. It's all by text. You do a job, they give you money. I think they're from Delhi.'

'Who is "they"?'

'I don't know. I met someone at the Sikh temple three years ago. I think he was from Delhi, and he got me started. The first time I got a text instructing me to break someone's leg with a metal bar, and after I'd done it, they left me cash. Then every few weeks they'd send a message and I'd do more jobs. Later, when I wanted to stop, they sent me a photo of my dear mother back in my village and threatened to kill her. Bless her soul, she passed last month, and now they can't harm her.' I rolled him onto his side so he could breathe more easily. 'Now I'll join my mother too,' he said miserably.

'Tell me about the James Black job from start to finish.' I began opening another can.

'No, no. I'll talk. Please, please. They told me to switch my shift to the Peak and to watch the big house and wait. Someone called every few days for information, but I don't know who. I spent some evenings hiding in the bushes and I went into the house and parking garage when no one was around. Then the sports car arrived, and I sent them photos. Then they told me to—'

'Peter, Peter, Peter,' shouted McPherson frantically. 'I think someone's coming. I've got an eye on the entrance from a street camera and a motorbike just pulled up and the rider has sprinted into the building. Get out *now*. *Now*, I tell you.'

I twisted his nuts again. 'They told you to do what?'

But it was too late. I could hear someone at the door. They were unlocking it!

I bolted.

'Help me. They'll kill me,' I heard my captive squeal as I squeezed out of the window.

As I looked back, the door burst open and a guy in a helmet rushed in. I launched myself out onto the scaffolding and started throwing myself down from pole to pole. Seconds later, bamboo splintered in all directions as shots rained down, and with three levels to go, I jumped for it.

I don't know what I landed in, trash or contractor debris, but I crawled out alive, picked myself up and sprinted for my life. I was hurting all over, but I was in one piece and everything was working.

'McPherson?' I gasped as I slowed to a jog out in the relative safety of the main street. 'I'm OK, but the maniac fired a ton of shots at me.' But wait. Where was she? 'McPherson, are you there? *McPherson?*'

The line was dead.

Fuck, fuck, fuck. Stupid damn idiot! There was no McPherson because I'd gone and left my phone on the floor beside the Sikh.

I'd have to go back for it. There was no choice. If the guy with the gun got hold of it with all my contacts and photos, the consequences would be unimaginable.

Chapter 49

In no time, I was back at the front of the block of flats. The bike was sitting outside, its engine still running, and I pulled out the keys and flung them into a rubble-filled skip.

With no time to lose, I bounded up the first flight of stairs, then stopped and listened. *Crap.* He was already on his way, moving fast, his steps clattering down the staircase somewhere above me. He'd get to me in no time.

Was I going to confront him right there on the stairs? Maybe I should be smart for once in my life and play the long game—I wasn't going to find my father's killer if I was dead. Now he was just one floor up. Run? Stay?

But no. I wasn't for running.

Heart pounding, I pulled the wrench out and crouched low, just round the corner, a few steps down from the landing. He wouldn't be expecting me, and no matter what, I was going to have to capitalise on my advantage and win the battle before it even got going.

I counted *five, four, three, two,* and on one, just as he turned the corner, I sprang up and clubbed the helmeted thug in the kneecap again and again. His gun went flying. Without mercy, I battered him relentlessly five, six, seven times or more, anywhere and everywhere. Neck, knees, chest, shins, arms … whatever I could reach. I wasn't going to give him one shred of a chance.

It had worked. I'd got him, and as he lay paralysed in pain, groaning, I rifled through his pockets. But there was no money. No ID. No wallet. No nothing. And then, to my relief, just as I was about to give up, I pulled down the zip of his jacket and there was my phone in the inside pocket. 'No way I was going to let you get this, you piece of shit,' I said to him, flipping up his visor.

He was Indian—no big surprise—but if I thought I was going to get any information out of him, it wasn't going to happen. Such was the beating I'd given him that he was barely conscious.

All of a sudden, there was a screech of tyres in the street below. First one car, then another, then more. Doors were opening. People were shouting. The sound of running footsteps. Was it more Sikhs? Or maybe it was the police? Whoever it was, I wasn't going to wait to find out, and I knew that my only route to safety was up and then out onto the back scaffolding again.

In making a dash for it, I stumbled—the groaning biker had got a hand onto my trouser ankle and was holding on for dear life. Desperately trying to kick myself free, I suddenly saw the ring on his finger. It was the same as the others. Same finger. Same knuckle. Same everything. 'All you little fuckers have them, don't you?' I snarled as I finally got myself free, and with time fast running out, I spent a second or two unsuccessfully trying to prise it off his finger before bolting off up the stairs.

I was out and back round onto the main street in a matter of minutes, and from a distance, as I walked casually away, I saw that it was the police, not the Sikhs. Five or more unmarked cars were now pulled up outside.

When I called McPherson, she was in floods of tears. 'Is that you? Peter, is it really you? I was sure you were dead.'

'It's me, and I'm safely out. Don't worry, Christine. I lost my phone and had to go back in.'

'Oh my god, you fucking bastard,' she sobbed. 'I was just so sure that he'd got you. I heard the shots. I heard everything. It was horrible, and I just knew in my heart of hearts that you were gone.'

I walked for almost a full hour, initially calming her—and myself—down and then talking through everything with her.

While our latest discovery was horrific, it was incredible what we'd achieved in such a short period of time. When I'd landed earlier in the day, I'd fully believed that my father had died in an accident. Then, in just a few hours, thanks to McPherson and Charles we'd worked out that Dad had been murdered by a Sikh gang with a connection to Delhi. It was chilling and horrible, but it could so easily have never been discovered.

'I want to thank you, Christine,' I told her as I got back to my bike.

'What on earth for? And by the way, I think I prefer it when you call me McPherson.'

'OK, *McPherson*. Not only did you identify the sweeper, but you saved my life tonight. Without you and your crazy tech stuff, the biker would have walked into the flat and put a bullet in my head.'

'That's what "eyes and ears" do, Peter. But thank you, and I forgive you for your nasty little Amnesty moment.'

'Apologies for that, McPherson. It was in the heat of the moment, and I'm sorry too that—' I stopped and decided not to say what I was going to say. It was over now.

'Sorry that what?'

'OK ... I just wanted to say that I'm sorry that you had to listen in on some of the stuff I did to the Sikh. I'm not proud of what I had to do. I had to get results.'

'Yes, but at what cost?' she replied. 'Beating. Torturing. It's not you, and I can only imagine that one day it will come back to haunt you.'

'No need to worry, I'll be fine,' I said defiantly.

I didn't believe for one minute that I'd be fine, but what I did know was that a long journey lay ahead, and I was going to have to get a grip on myself if we were to have any chance of finding my father's killer.

Chapter 50

I headed slowly back towards HK island on the bike, replaying over and over in my mind what had happened.

Why would a bunch of killers from Delhi want my father or me dead? What had we done? Had Dad crossed someone? Had something come back to bite him from the past—maybe something to do with the shadowy stuff that he couldn't talk about? Or maybe it was to do with Black & Co.? One thing was for sure, though; whoever was behind it all was powerful as hell. They could strike in Hong Kong or the UK, and they were well organised, with both women and men on their payroll.

Powerful or not, dangerous or not, I wasn't going to run. On the contrary, they'd killed my father and I was going to hunt down the ringleader even if it took me the rest of my life.

Rather than take the eastern tunnel, this time I took the western, surfacing near Central, and instead of going straight home, I headed towards Hollywood Road to see if there were any bars open. My mind was buzzing, and I needed a beer or two to settle myself down if I was to have any chance of getting some sleep tonight.

Near the walking elevator which carried people from the city up to the many residential towers sprawling the Peak, as I was parking the bike, my phone rang.

What did *he* want?

'Commander?'

'Evening.' He didn't sound happy. 'What in *god's* name have you been up to over there, Black?'

'What do you mean, sir?'

'Two dead bodies in Hong Kong, that's what I mean!'

My blood ran cold. 'Sir, I don't understand. What do you mean, two dead bodies?'

'One heavily bound apartment dweller with bullets to the head. One apparently badly beaten biker who took a deadly poison concealed in a ring as the police approached him on a stairwell.'

'OK, I was there, but …' In my mind, I was desperately trying to process what had happened. The biker had put a bullet in the guy in the apartment and then he'd killed himself. The ring I'd been trying to get off him had had poison in it!

'I know you were there,' he snapped. 'We've been keeping an eye on you.'

My anger kicked in. 'Keeping an eye on me? Your damn people have been *following* me?'

'For your own safety,' he fired back. 'Not that they were able to do anything to stop you.'

We were both quiet for a moment in our separate corners.

'I didn't kill the guy in the flat, sir,' I said quietly. 'The biker must have killed him.'

'I believe you, Peter'—he sighed—'but please, tell me everything. Start to finish.'

I started, and on mentioning McPherson's involvement, he immediately patched her in. After he'd given her a stinging rebuke for not having told him about our 'operation', he told her to 'sit quietly' before telling me to 'get on with the debrief'.

I continued to the point where I'd left the biker in the stairwell. 'That's the whole story, sir. We got the sweeper talking and we know that the order to kill my father came from Delhi.'

'Please tell him about the other stuff too, Peter. He needs to know.'

'Other stuff. What other stuff?' he barked.

I hesitated for a moment. 'I don't know if—'

'Out with it,' he bellowed. 'The body count is rising. I need to know *everything*.'

So, after warning him, as I'd done McPherson, I told him about the crazy woman and the bikers and braced myself for his onslaught.

But it didn't come.

'Thanks for confiding in me.' His tone had moderated. 'This is very important indeed. My god, you've been through a lot.'

'Yes, I suppose I have, sir,' I replied cautiously.

'Ms McPherson,' he said calmly, 'find the Sikh from the bar in St Andrews. He's key. I'll connect you up to Border Control. He'll have left the country, and we need to find out his exit airport and where he was going. Find the one from the Mandarin Oriental too. And scour CCTV in St Andrews—if the godforsaken village has any—to try to find out what they did with the bodies.'

'Will do,' she replied. 'By the way, Charles is already looking at Border Control data.'

'Right,' he murmured. 'And who the hell might Charles be?'

'A teenage genius,' she snapped, and he backed off.

We heard ringing in the background. 'I need to take another call. I'll call you back, Peter.' He hung up.

'Fuck,' said McPherson.

'Fuck indeed,' I replied. 'The biker killed the sweeper and then he took his own life. Christ, these people are tough fuckers.'

'I'd imagine the Commander's going to want to put you into protection or maybe a safe house until we work out what's going on.'

I laughed. 'I'd like to see him try.'

'Listen, Peter, don't go against him. Believe it or not, he's firmly on your side. He speaks so fondly of your father and would do anything for you. If Parliament had gone down, he'd have been toast.'

'McPherson?' I said, changing the subject. 'I'm going to need your help.'

'Oh, dear god. *Please* don't say what I'm thinking you're going to say.'

'I have to do it. But without you, I can't. Eyes and ears and all that.'

'Oh god. He'll never allow it.'

'He can't stop me, and I'll just tell him where to go.'

'*No, Peter.* I won't allow it either. I can't let you get yourself killed.'

'Let's chat tomorrow, shall we? And please just think about it.'

Chapter 51

At a pavement bar on Hollywood Road, in a big armchair, I'd sunk four beers before he called back. In the meantime, I'd also worked out who'd been spying on me—a mid-thirties couple sitting in the Pacific Coffee café across the road from me. They just didn't look quite right. Awkward. A little too distant from one another and, generally, not very convincing.

'Ms McPherson tells me you're going to Delhi?'

'Ms McPherson would be correct. And—'

'I know,' he cut in. 'We can't stop you. It's a free world and so on and so forth.'

'What would you do in my shoes? Go to ground?'

'Most certainly not. I'd be doing exactly the same. I'd go after my father's killers with a vengeance.'

'So you'll let me go?'

'I'll deny all knowledge of it, but yes, I'll let you go. However, there are two conditions. First, Christine McPherson needs to be part of the mission. Secondly, you need to work with one of my team members in Delhi. His name is Nilay and he's one of our best.'

'McPherson, sure, but not the other guy. I don't need him.'

There was a pause at the other end of the line. 'Peter. Before he left for Hong Kong, your father called me. He made it clear that he didn't want you to … how shall we say … work for your country in the way that he may have done in the past. I agreed; however, he also asked that I look out for you should anything ever happen to him. Assigning Nilay to you is essentially me honouring his request.'

I thought for a moment or two. 'OK, Commander, I agree. I'll work with this guy Nilay.'

'Good. Anything else before we go?'

'Please can you get the couple that is tailing me to stop? I can see them from where I'm sitting.'

'I'll do that for you,' he said rather grimly. 'And Peter, one more thing.'

'Sir?'

'How are you doing? I mean mentally. I got wind of an incident outside Harvey Nichols.'

'None of your damn business, sir,' I snapped. 'And please stop snooping on me once and for all.'

'OK, son, have it your way. But remember I'm here if you need me. Good night.' He hung up.

His use of 'son' reminded me of Dad, who'd used the term a lot, and as I drank another beer, I sat quietly, reminiscing about what a wonderful father he'd been to me and Sam. Life without him was going to be unimaginable.

It was a lonely ride back up the Peak to the house.

Chapter 52

It was past 10 a.m. by the time I was awoken by Sam with a gentle shake. 'Wake up, Peter! We're all going to have to go down to Dad's office this afternoon for a special board meeting.'

'Right,' I mumbled from under my covers. 'Down in fifteen minutes.' Going to India to hunt down my father's killer was my top priority, but I had to play my part in helping the company to overcome this monumental shock. I'd probably have to vote on a resolution or something like that.

'I didn't hear you come back last night. Were you late?'

'A bit.'

'You just left?'

'Cruised around a bit on the bike, that's all. Just needed to get my head together after that nonsense at the gate.'

'Don't worry, Mum's not going to say anything about it. Sleeping dogs and all that.'

'How are you both doing?' I asked, sitting up.

'Another day into it, I suppose. But it doesn't feel any easier. See you downstairs in a bit.'

After she'd gone, I checked my messages, which were numerous. Trudy, Shaun, Diti and Declan all wished me well and hoped I'd arrived safely. There were three from Ofelia and four missed calls from her as well. I'd absolutely *have* to call her today. It was only fair, and despite all my paranoia about what she might think of me, I missed her like hell and needed to hear her voice.

But it was the last message, sent just forty minutes earlier from McPherson—at about 1.30 a.m. UK time—that got me out of bed and onto my feet. Did she ever sleep?

'You're not going to believe it!' said her message. 'We traced your Sikh. He went Birmingham-London-Tehran-Ahmedabad-Delhi using multiple passports. Call me at 8 a.m. UK time—need to sleep.'

You bloody genius, McPherson.

Before going downstairs, I logged onto India's website for immigration, and no more than ten minutes later I'd paid eighty US dollars and applied for a thirty-day tourist visa which would—all going well—be processed within twelve to twenty-four hours. I had heard that Modi was trying to shake things up and break India's long-held reputation for bureaucracy. On this measure, it was working.

My mother and Sam were in the kitchen having a cup of tea, and while I put some toast on, my mother told me about the special board meeting. 'The three of us are significant shareholders, and the meeting is to discuss your dad's death and to read out a sealed "in the event of my death" letter that he always had ready,' she said dejectedly. We'd then need to vote through his wishes.

'What do you think it will say?' asked Sam.

'I don't know, dear, but whatever it is, I'm sure that your dad will have thought it through and whatever the decision, it will be what's best for Black & Co. Appointing a new CEO is the most pressing item on the agenda.'

'I can't imagine anyone doing the job even half as well as he did,' I chipped in.

'Quite,' said my mother with a long sigh.

Now was the time to break the news and as I took my seat at the huge table with my plate of toast, I went for it. 'Mum and Sam. As part of my course, I've to do a project about Indian business practices. I'm going to go there for a day or two before the funeral.' God, I hated lying to them.

'You're going to *India*?' said my mother, putting her cup of tea down and staring at me as if I was totally mad. When I looked at Sam, she was staring at me too, equally perplexed.

'It's got to get done, and it'll take my mind off things. I'd have done it in Reading Week in a couple of weeks, but it makes more sense to do it now while I'm here. Delhi's just a short hop, and I decided when I was out on the bike last night. I've already ordered the visit visa and now all I need to do is contact Black & Co. India and ask them if I can interview a few of the execs in the Delhi office.'

'The funeral is on *Monday* and then there's a memorial service in London on Wednesday. Do you really need to be dashing off before then? Goodness gracious, it's already Thursday.'

'Yes, I do. It's a great project, and my prof thought Black & Co. India would be a great case study. It's a comparison of Indian business practices with those in the west. Fascinating.'

'I don't doubt that at all,' she replied sternly. 'But are you sure you want to go *now*?' I could see that she was beginning to concede.

'If the visa arrives today, I'll take this evening's flight and I'll be back on Saturday—or latest Sunday. Piece of cake.' I glanced over at my sister. Was she on to me?

'Oh, just let him go, Mum. If he doesn't do it now, he'll have to do it another time, and it's better just to get it over and done with. I wish I was going too. Anything to take my mind off things!'

'Thanks, sis,' I said, giving her a little smile. Christ, to have managed to pull the wool over her eyes had taken some doing. I must have been convincing.

She was about to say something when the landline phone rang, and Mum answered it.

'Yes, this is Mrs Black ... you're calling from the hospital ... is Mr Peng all right?' Both Sam and I watched as our mother went visibly pale. 'Oh, dear god. That's the worst news imaginable.' She sat slowly down in her chair.

I looked over at Sam. Tears were already running down her face.

Chapter 53

'Ladies and gentlemen, this special meeting is now in session,' announced Chairman Leung, the smartly dressed mid-seventies gentleman who had chaired Black & Co. for the last thirty years. I counted fourteen people around the huge boardroom table.

We had almost asked for the meeting to be cancelled, so distraught were we at the news of Peng's death. However, the longer Black & Co. carried on in a 'void', the more damaging it would be, and my mother, after sobbing bitterly for half an hour or more, had finally said, 'We must soldier on, no matter how difficult it is.' She and Sam had dashed down to the hospital to collect and console Mrs Peng, while our GP, Dr Wong, was summoned to the house to attend to her on her arrival.

The tension around the table mounted as Leung got ready to speak, but, while I was keen to know my father's instructions, India was my absolute priority, and all the more so now that Peng had passed away. As the old man tapped his cup with a spoon, I pressed send on a text to McPherson.

'Peng's dead. He couldn't be saved. I'm booked on the 7.30 p.m. to Delhi. Please can you try your hardest to find out where the Sikh lives. Everything is cleared with the Commander—no police, just you and me and his man in Delhi. Dear god, Christine, help me to find the truth.'

After an eloquent and moving tribute from the chairman, he sat back and slowly opened the sealed envelope with a paper knife and began reading.

Dearest Executive Board,

If you have cause to open this letter, it is because I am no longer with you. The plans for my succession are as follows:

I would like my wife, if she agrees, to take over the chairmanship of the company on a full-time basis, following Edwin Leung's planned retirement. Gavin should become the Group CEO, reporting to my wife, and should hold this position until Peter's 29th birthday, at which point Peter will become CEO and Gavin is to assume the chairmanship. Sam, I would like you to run the to-be-formed Black Foundation. Please talk to our lawyers, Yeung & Associates, who have details of how that should be set up and its mission. My wife should chair this foundation indefinitely.

*In the event that my demise takes place before the conclusion of the Guzman & Co. acquisition, the company should press ahead with it. Under **no** circumstances should we pull back from our mission. The future of our company depends on us acquiring Guzman and the digital dimension that it will offer us.*

I thank you all profoundly for your friendship and, of course, for the unstinting dedication that you have shown to Black & Co. It has been the most amazing journey. Whether my ending was illness, accident or even, God forbid, a crime, the show goes on. Onwards and upwards!

Peter, you have all the attributes required to make a fantastic CEO. Prepare yourself— either within or outside Black—over the coming years. Follow your instinct! I cannot say enough how immensely proud of you I am.

Yours sincerely and forever, James P. Black

'There we have James's wishes,' said Leung solemnly, waving the letter before everyone when he'd finished. He then asked each of us—my mother, Sam, myself and Gavin—in turn if we were happy to proceed with what Dad had instructed. Each of us solemnly replied with a simple 'yes, Chairman'.

The idea of becoming CEO at 29 had hardly registered, and I wasn't giving it the slightest thought. All I was thinking about was India—packing and getting going. 'Now let's go down to reception,' said Leung, 'where we'll hold a minute's silence with Black & Co. staff.'

As we made our way out of the boardroom, Gavin came up to me with a friendly smile and shook my hand. 'Congratulations, Gavin,' I said to him. 'When I met my father at the weekend, he spoke very highly of you indeed.'

'I sincerely hope I can live up to his expectations,' he replied. 'And do accept my condolences, Peter. I can only imagine how you are feeling.'

'Many thanks,' I said. He was tall and intelligent looking and seemed very genuine, and I didn't doubt one bit that my father had chosen well.

'Shall we talk about the future another time?' he suggested. I nodded, my mind already back into India planning mode.

Following the minute's silence, my mother gave a short speech to the tearful audience, followed by Gavin, who did his very best to try and rally the overall morale. Not an easy job. My father was the company, and deep down, everyone was worried about the future.

As soon as I could, I snuck out and headed back to the house, leaving Mum and Sam in the office.

On the way, I stopped off at the bank and got myself five thousand US dollars in cash. I was sure that McPherson would try her best to locate the gang in Delhi but, equally, if it came down to it, I'd happily grease palms to get what I needed.

Chapter 54

Staring into space, I sat in the lobby of my hotel in Aerocity, about five kilometres from Delhi airport. It was 10.45 p.m. and I had arranged to meet up with Nilay Kumar in the hotel.

The flight had been uneventful, and despite the horror stories I'd heard about four-hour queues and missing luggage, I'd got through the airport without any problems. In fact, Delhi airport was easily on a par with Hong Kong and a million times nicer than Heathrow or Gatwick. The taxi services were excellent too, and within two minutes of getting out of the Arrivals hall, I had been sitting in a Meru cab—like a cheap Uber—on my way to the hotel.

As I sat there waiting for Nilay, my mind was all over the place. I was imagining the sweeper taking a series of bullets to the head as he lay bound where I'd left him. He probably deserved it, but what a way to go. The fact that his killer had ultimately taken a poison pill as the police moved in on him was equally frightening and like something out of a movie. My thoughts then jumped to Gavin and my mother. Yes, Gavin would make a good CEO, but I wasn't so sure about my mum as chair. She was a wonderful kind mother, but I just didn't see her as a cut-and-thrust businesswoman. Saying that, surely my father wouldn't have given her something that would make her unhappy or that was beyond her capabilities? Only time would tell.

Just as I'd been sneaking out of the office, Gavin had briefly pulled me aside again and asked for my help. My father must have told him that I'd been at the Claridge's breakfast, and he asked if I'd join a meeting that he was planning with Don Ricardo immediately after the London memorial service. 'He might be getting cold feet without your father at the helm,' he'd said to me, 'and we're going to have to pedal hard to convince them. You and I both being there may help.' I'd promised Gavin that I'd do everything in my power to help but hadn't let on about the thing I had going with Ofelia—not that I felt there was any hope for the two of us after what I'd done.

Before leaving the house, with little time to spare, I'd rushed out to the cottage to say goodbye to Mrs Peng. She'd been sitting out on the veranda staring out across the valley towards Lamma Island and it had taken quite some coaxing to get a few words out of her. 'Dear Peng is now with the gods,' was all she'd managed, and when I'd hugged her, her embrace had been limp and lifeless. How I wanted to get those little bastards who had done this to us.

'Peter Black? Are you Peter?' came a voice, and, snapping out of my thoughts, I saw a mid-thirties Indian guy standing looking down at me. I quickly jumped to my feet.

'Nilay Kumar?'

'It is,' he replied as he formally shook my hand while looking me up and down. 'You're ... hem ... how should I say ... quite young, aren't you?'

'I'm a student, if that's what you mean, and if you don't like it, feel free to take a hike. I told Burke that I don't need any help.' He took a step backwards.

'The Commander briefed me. More or less.' He smiled. 'And there's no need for any hiking. The report gave the impression of someone a little older, that's all.'

'Right,' I grunted, not sure at all if I liked the thought of Burke briefing people or of there being a report. 'A rosy narrative, I hope?' I said cynically.

'Quite impressive, as it happens.' He nodded.

I shrugged, not really believing it.

'You weren't followed. I've tailed you since the moment you got out of Arrivals.'

I looked at him. '*Followed?* What do you mean?'

'You can never be too sure. You are high profile, and the Indian Secret Service will likely know you're here. Like everything else in India, they're corrupt, and there is always a chance that they'll be in with the bad guys. India is a web of deceit and corruption even though it may not seem that way.'

'That's why we need to move fast,' I replied, masking my nervousness. 'The very last thing the gang will expect is me turning up on their doorstep looking for answers.'

'I see ...' he murmured. 'The bit in the report about the impetuous streak wasn't wrong.'

I ignored his comment. 'Do we know where the Sikh lives? Christine McPherson, on the Commander's team, has been trying to find out.' I checked my phone to see if she'd sent a message.

'I understand they were making some progress,' he replied, 'and I was to call her once we met up.'

Seconds later I'd got her on the line. 'McPherson. I'm in Delhi. Have you found him?'

'Where's Mr Kumar?'

'*Christ.* He's here with me. Come on. Hurry. Have you found the Sikh?'

'I'll patch Nilay in,' she said very calmly, and seconds later both of us were standing there with our pods in, listening to her news.

'We've tracked him to a villa in the Embassy district and I'm sending you both the locator *now*. Looks like he lives there with his family and has owned the place for years. It's a very expensive part of the city.' Our phones pinged in unison as the locator arrived.

'The Embassy district certainly is very expensive. Good work, Ms McPherson' said Nilay. 'We'll go do reconnaissance in the morning once Peter has had a good rest after his long journey.'

'No, we do this *now*.' I pointed to the doorway. 'Come on, let's get moving.'

'No, Peter,' replied Nilay calmly, staring at me patiently. 'We'll look at it in the morning with fresh eyes. We need to build a plan which carefully considers all the eventualities. It would be—'

'Are you coming?' I was already heading for the entrance. 'A cab or your car?'

'Please just go with him, Nilay,' intervened McPherson. 'There's not a thing you'll be able to do to change his mind when he's in this mood. I apologise on his behalf. He gets like this.'

Chapter 55

With McPherson still on the line and doing her tech stuff as we talked, we made our way through the dimly lit streets of Delhi in Nilay's car, heading towards Chanakyapuri—the Embassy district. As we approached, the place was eerily quiet.

'I have the villa in my sights,' she said confidently. 'From the heat imaging, I can see one, two, three ... six people in six separate rooms. Five seem motionless, probably sleeping, and the sixth is moving around towards the back of the house. From what I can see, there are also what are probably guard huts—one at the front, on the street, and another at the foot of what looks like a large back garden. The thermals show two people in each.'

'Security, if you can call it that, is normal in Delhi,' commented Nilay. 'Especially with villas. Labour is dirt cheap, and the rich fear being robbed.'

'So, what's the plan?' asked McPherson.

I replied before Nilay did. 'Quite simple. We break in and I beat the crap out of my whisky-drinking friend until he tells us what's going on.'

'Oh god,' sighed Nilay, navigating a roundabout and almost taking out a tuk-tuk rider who was weaving all over the place, talking on his mobile. 'I *really* don't like the sound of this *at all*.'

'It's crude, but it's about striking fast while their guard is down. Plus we've got a special weapon.'

'And what's that?'

'McPherson and her tech.'

He shook his head in dismay but didn't seem to be calling a halt to what we were doing. 'Listen,' he said. 'If anything, god forbid, goes wrong tonight and we get separated, go straight to the

British High Commission. You'll be safe there. It's a huge plot of land, one kilometre by one kilometre, with heavily guarded entrances on each side. Any tuk-tuk will take you there, or it's even walkable from here.'

'Thanks, mate.' Although I didn't know him, I was beginning to get a bit of a good feeling about him. Plus the Commander rated him. 'Apologies for being a bit pushy back there, Nilay.'

'He warned me about you,' he said, turning to me with a bit of a smile. 'He said once you get the bit between your teeth, there's no stopping you.' I heard McPherson give a little chortle.

'Total rubbish. The man doesn't know the first thing about me.'

'That's not the Commander I know!' He laughed. 'He knows things about people that they don't even know about themselves! Never, ever underestimate Burke would be my advice.'

'You're getting close to the house,' cut in our eyes and ears.

Chapter 56

We parked on a side street about one kilometre away from where the villa was located, but just before we got out, my new friend dug around under his seat. 'Weapons,' he said, turning to me. 'Just in case.'

'Weapons? I don't really do weapons.' The bloody image of the biker taking the headshot flashed through my mind.

'Just a precaution,' he replied, handing me two small ankle holsters, one holding a small gun and the other a short stumpy knife. He had a set for himself too. 'I don't go anywhere without them when I'm on a project.' He took his gun out and showed me how to unlock it. 'If you need to use them,' he said sternly, 'no pissing around. Go for the kill. Shots to the upper torso. Blade in the gut.' As he said it, he poked a finger in my chest and then in my guts. 'Upper torso. Gut. Got it.'

'Got it.' I nodded, the words 'torso' and 'gut' lingering with me. McPherson didn't make a sound, but I knew she was listening, and I knew she'd be mortified. 'Have you ever used them?'

'From time to time,' he said, getting out of the car. 'It's been a couple of months, though. Here, take the tape and plastic cuffs too.' He tossed them at me. 'Useful kit on any operation.'

I stuffed them inside my jacket and we set off on foot, Nilay taking the lead. When we'd left the hotel, it was me leading him, now it was the other way around. But I was fine with it—he clearly knew what he was doing. In fact, I was very glad he was with me.

'Don't worry, we don't look out of place. Every night there are a few boozed-up diplomats staggering home from events. You can pretty much party every night once you get on the circuit. One night it'll be the Swedish embassy, then the Russian, then the British, and so on. The diplomatic world is just a massive piss-up!'

'You are about seven-fifty metres out,' said McPherson. 'Keep going, then take your first left.'

As we walked, a white 4 × 4 police vehicle approached on the other side of the avenue and then passed us. 'There are police patrols all the time in this neighbourhood but nothing to worry about.' However, when I glanced back, I saw it had turned and was coming slowly up the road behind us.

'They're on to us,' I whispered nervously to Nilay.

'Don't worry, they rarely stop,' he whispered. But as we kept walking, the vehicle began to crawl behind us until, after about half a minute, it accelerated and pulled up alongside. In the back, a grey-haired man in uniform rolled down his window.

'It's late to be out, gentlemen. Is everything OK?'

'Everything is just fine, sir,' replied Nilay jovially. 'We're just heading back to the British High Commission compound.' He flashed his diplomatic pass.

'Isn't the Commission back that way?' said the officer, pointing towards where we'd come from.

'Indeed it is, sir. We'll be turning around up ahead. We're taking a walk while we rehearse a sales pitch that we're due to give tomorrow. I work in the Commission's trade department and my friend here works for a UK company that we're helping to promote in India. He only arrived this evening, and we thought we'd grab some fresh air.'

'Understood,' said the officer.

'You are quite a high-ranking officer to be out so late,' said Nilay, pointing towards the multiple stripes on the officer's shoulder.

'Very perceptive,' he replied, looking carefully at both of us. 'I'm the chief of police for Delhi South Side. From time to time, I like to get out in the field to support my officers.'

'It's a pleasure to meet you, sir, and so nice to see you setting an excellent example to your team.'

'Have a good evening, and I wish you luck with tomorrow's endeavours. You Britishers have had a lot of experience in India,' he said with a hint of irony, 'and I'm sure you'll do well.' With that, the car moved off, and after we'd walked a little further, we turned and headed back the way we'd come.

'Best we go all the way to the High Commission just in case they swing back round,' said Nilay.

'He seemed pleasant enough,' said McPherson quietly. 'Wait—hang on. His car has just cut down the side street that you'd have taken to the Sikh's place. I'll keep an eye on it for you, but I do agree, I think you should walk all the way to the High Commission.'

It took just ten minutes and just as we got there, the police car passed by again. We gave it a friendly salute. 'Track it, please, Ms McPherson, and let us know where it's going,' instructed Nilay as we ducked into the guardhouse at the main gate.

'They're heading back into Delhi city centre,' she said after a few moments. 'I've hacked into their comms and they're heading into their HQ.' The mention of HQ made me think of Burke's HQ and the moment I'd gone for McPherson's attacker. Green and Jo and that incredible Saturday afternoon seemed like an eternity ago, and it was incredible to think that the feisty woman I'd met in the Arabic Café was now helping me find my father's killer. The whole thing was scarcely believable.

A three-wheeler came slowly down the road. Nilay waved it down and we jumped in. 'Drive. I'll direct you,' he barked at the barefooted driver, who nodded obediently, and we sped off. Before we'd even reached the first roundabout, he turned to us. 'Shopping? I take you to good shopping, sirs?'

'Just drive,' replied Nilay dismissively, and with an obedient nod, our driver gave the machine an extra burst of acceleration.

'What's he going on about? Shopping at this time of night?' I whispered.

'He'll be on commission. Shops, bars, restaurants, seedy joints, drug dens, anything. If he takes foreigners and they buy stuff, he'll get a cut,' explained Nilay. 'And why not? The poor guy probably lives in this tuk-tuk, he's so poor.'

When Nilay said the word, the driver pulled up and we jumped out. 'McPherson, can you guide us from here?' he said as he handed the now-beaming driver a wad of notes.

'Take the first left ahead, then walk up to the T-junction. There you'll see a row of twenty villas facing you—ten to the left, ten to the right. The Sikh's is fourth down on the left, but I think it's best if you go to the right, all the way to the end, then cut around the back of the villas. You'll find a path that runs all the way along the rear of the twenty properties. Watch out, though—there are strange heat images in some of the gardens and I think there might be dogs.'

'Dogs! There are always bloody dogs.' Nilay sighed. 'Gazillions of them, flea-infested and most of them rabid. But don't worry, Peter, I carry a high-pitched emitter and they run a country mile the minute they hear it. My son, Ravi, is absolutely petrified of them.' I liked this guy more and more.

Before long, in the dim light of the back streets, we found the road with the twenty villas—all of them enormous—and, taking McPherson's suggestion, we cut right.

'These must be worth a bit?'

'Ten to fifteen million dollars a pop,' replied Nilay. 'Delhi real estate is some of the most expensive in the world—which is ridiculous when you see the state of some of it.'

'You should find a little lane cutting down the side of the last house,' advised our guide.

She was right, and, helped by the light of a tiny thin torch that Nilay produced, we made our way to the end and found—just as McPherson had described—a narrow dirt path leading all the way along the rear of the properties. Each villa was protected by towering walls, and on the other side of the path, to our right, there was a canal and beyond that, dense woodland.

'You're a genius, McPherson. We've found the track,' I whispered to her.

'Wheelchair-bound but not completely useless,' she replied.

'When we get to our Sikh's villa, how the hell will we get over the wall?' murmured Nilay.

'We'll find a way,' I replied.

'I admire your confidence,' he said as he switched off the torch. We stood for a few moments, letting our eyes grow accustomed to the darkness, although dotted along the rear walls was the occasional dim light—just enough to help us.

What was that? Nilay grabbed my shoulder. From just over the wall to our left came a deep growling. Nilay immediately dropped to his knees and started frantically digging around in his pack for the emitter.

The growling grew louder and louder, and we could hear claws scraping furiously at the wall. The growling became snarling. It was about to bark the place down. We were only at the first house and already screwed. *'Nilay. Let's go back,'* I whispered frantically.

Chapter 57

'Ah, got it,' he whispered with a huge sigh. We heard an agonised yelp from over the wall and the sound of the dog thundering up the garden towards the house. 'Damn mutt. Now let's go.'

We started running up the path before taking shelter in some bushes beside the canal. 'I'm a fool,' he whispered, breathing loudly. 'Should have had the thing ready right from the start. I'll leave it on full blast from now. It'll be good for thirty to forty minutes.'

The pathway smelled disgusting and was clearly a dumping ground for trash, garden cuttings, dog shite and pretty much anything else that could be heaved over the walls. Even worse was the filthy expanse of water, which smelled rank and must have doubled as a sewer. 'Watch out for rats,' whispered Nilay. 'If I were a rat, I'd love to live in there.'

'There's a guard hut coming up at the fourth house,' warned McPherson. 'There's someone in it, but I don't detect much movement. Maybe asleep?'

As we got closer, we saw that the hut formed part of the wall itself. Glancing through a little window as we snuck past, we saw an elderly uniformed man fixated on an old black-and-white TV. 'They love their Bollywood,' whispered Nilay.

Two houses up, there was another hut, but this time the guards—two of them—were sitting outside by our path, one smoking, the other playing on his phone.

'What do you think we should do?' I asked Nilay as we lay on our chests on the track about twenty metres away from them. 'If we can't get by them, we'll have to go all the way round.'

'No time. Only one thing to do,' he replied. 'I'll create a diversion. You sneak past them. I'll catch you up. It's not perfect, but I can't think of anything else. Stay where you are.'

'Wait, no ...' I whispered, but he was already up on his feet, heading towards the guards. 'He's off, McPherson. Couldn't stop him.'

Nilay let out a loud groan and I watched him stagger, then fall and start crawling towards the guards, who immediately sprang to life, pulling out their guns.

'Stop. Who is it?' shouted one of them, but Nilay just kept groaning. He rolled onto his side, clutching his stomach. 'Help me. Help me. I'm lost and terribly ill. *Please* help me.'

One of the guards immediately ran to his aid, while the other hung back, gun at the ready. 'Who are you? What's wrong with you?' he said in English.

'Please call an ambulance,' groaned Nilay. 'And maybe help me call my wife?' he gasped. 'No, no, wait,' he said, changing his mind. 'Not my wife. She'll kill me if she finds out.'

The one who'd hung back let out a laugh. 'Hey, you've been up to no good, man!'

'Don't worry, sir, we'll help you,' said the other, helping him up into a sitting position. 'Our sir and madam are both out, but we'll take you through house and get driver to take you to clinic.'

'Oh, dear god, thank you, thank you. I'll make sure that you're both rewarded for your kindness. We good honest Hindus look after one another, don't we? Oh god, my stomach hurts ...'

As they half carried, half dragged him through the hut into the garden, I took my chance and pelted up the path past the hut.

'An Oscar-winning performance,' whispered McPherson. Through our pods, we could still hear him retching and groaning and talking about what his wife would do to him if ever she found out.

'I'm past the hut, Nilay,' I whispered, hoping he could still hear me.

'Dear friends,' we heard him theatrically announce, 'I think I'm beginning to feel a little better. It may be beginning to pass through, whatever it is.' He let out a long 'Aaaaaaaaaaaaaah' as if to indicate that whatever nasty thing was in his system was finally managing to escape. 'I don't want to leave a mess on this nice car,' he said. 'Let me sit quietly on the kerb for a few moments and maybe you could pass me a small cup of water to revive me?'

'Yes, sir. Of, course, sir,' came the reply.

'Let me find a few rupees for both of you.'

'I'll keep going, Nilay,' I whispered. 'Catch me up when you can.' So close to the Sikh's house, I knew I had to get on with the job I'd come to do.

There were two more guard huts between me and the Sikh's villa, but I managed to creep by both undetected. At the first, the guard was out by the path, fast asleep. At the next, the guard had disappeared into a rickety tin hut toilet, and I snuck easily by. Their lords and masters were clearly not getting good value for money, but then again, what a job it must be, working all night long stuck at the end of the garden, earning pennies.

'Yours is the next villa,' said McPherson. 'There are two guards at the rear, and it's still all quiet in the house except for that one person. He or she is in the back room facing onto the back garden.'

'Thanks, McPherson.' I didn't like not having Nilay with me, but it was comforting to know she was there, almost looking down on me. I simply couldn't have done this without her.

I crept up to the guard post and snatched a peek through the window. My heart missed a beat. I took a second quick look before retreating into the undergrowth.

'Jesus, McPherson!'

'What is it?'

'For one, the guards areSikhs. But more worrying is their machine guns and fancy computer screens with multiple CCTV feeds.'

'You *must* stay where you are until Nilay gets there. *Do you hear me?*'

'Where the hell is he?' I whispered as I stared up at the thick razor wire running along the top of the immense wall. The place was a fortress compared to the other villas. 'Nilay. Are you there?'

'Have to go,' blurted out Nilay. 'Police chief's back. Keep going, Peter. See it all the way through.' There was a click and he'd gone.

'McPherson, what's happening? Can you see him?' *What a total disaster.*

'They're putting him in a car. Wait. The screen's gone blurry. There's like a scuffle or something.'

Christ. What was I going to do? Should I just get the hell out of there?

'The car is driving off. They've taken him,' she reported. 'He's left his phone on the street. You've got to get out of there while you still can. What if they come looking for you?'

I lay down in the dirt and took long deep breaths, trying desperately to get myself thinking straight. This whole thing was beginning to turn into a car crash. But I was *so* close. The Sikh, who held the key to what had been going on, was just metres from me on the other side of the wall.

'Peter. What are you doing? Get going. Get out of there. We'll regroup and maybe try again later. The Commander will know what to do.'

No. Nilay was right, I *had* to keep going. I'd come this far and there was no turning back.

'I can't leave, Christine,' I said quietly. 'You're probably completely right, but no, let's just get on with it. And *please* don't try to change my mind.'

'Hell,' she snapped, 'I think—' But then she shut up, probably knowing resistance was futile.

My mind now 110 per cent on the job, I'd worked out a way of getting over the wall. Nigh on impossible, but if I stayed focused and applied myself, maybe I could do it.

'Come on, Peter,' I whispered to myself. 'Get it done. Get it done for James Black. *For Dad.*'

Chapter 58

There was a towering tree on the far side of the canal, and one of its huge branches arched over the path and the garden. If I could climb up it and get along the branch, I could drop into the garden. The problem, though, was the fifteen feet or more of bare trunk to get up before reaching the branches. And there was the stinking cesspool to cross before even getting to the tree.

Whispering my plan to McPherson as I went, I slid slowly down the bank into the water. Ten or so quick strokes later, I was through the stinking soup and pulling myself out on the far side. I was close to puking, it was so disgusting.

Quietly I picked my way through the dense undergrowth towards the sapling I'd targeted. Tall, skinny, fragile, dwarfed by the huge tree beside it, it was my only chance.

Like a fireman I started shinning up and up. Near the top, I leaned ever so slightly to my left and the sapling started to bend, carrying me towards its towering brother, and in a few seconds I'd clambered into the thick branches. 'Made it,' I whispered. I sat for a moment gathering my strength, sizing up the huge branch that I'd now have to crawl along in the darkness.

As kids, Sam and I spent many happy hours shinning up 'bendy' saplings in the woods at our Scottish summer house. When close to the top, the saplings bend with your weight, carrying you to the ground before whipping back to the vertical. I'd never in a million Sundays have believed that I'd be using my sapling-climbing skills to try to get to my father's murderer.

'Any chance you can create a diversion?' I whispered to McPherson as I crawled on my front along the branch. 'They'll hear me when I drop down into the garden. I'll land with a hell of a thump.'

'Let me think.'

I gave her a moment or two. 'Come on, hurry up. Have you—'

'Got it,' she snapped back. 'I'll set off car alarms out in the street at the front. Best I can do.' By now, I was nicely out over the garden, and one final shuffle would get me perfectly into position.

God! What was that?

The tree suddenly came to life, black shapes darting everywhere.

I lost my balance.

I was falling.

Chapter 59

Flailing wildly as I fell, I snatched at branches and got one, just, with a single finger. It wouldn't last long. It didn't.

I'm slipping. I just can't hold on.

'McPherson,' I gasped. *'Alarms!'*

The alarms went off just as I hit the ground, and as I scuttled under a bush, the guards' door suddenly burst open and the two Sikhs ran the length of the lawn up to the house.

That was my chance, and no sooner had they gone in than I followed them, diving into a heap of foliage by the back gable wall. How on earth they hadn't heard me, I'll never know, but McPherson had saved the day once again, and we were another step closer.

As I lay there catching my breath, figuring out what to do next, I saw an enormous black cloud of what could only be bats circle the house and then flock back into my tree. They'd given me the biggest fright of my life.

'You're beside the house?' whispered McPherson. 'What on earth happened?'

'There was a freaking swarm of—' But before I could finish, the back door burst open and the two security guards started walking back towards their hut, cursing loudly about the car alarms.

'Never mind, I'll tell you another time. I'm going to climb onto the small annexe roof. From there up the foliage on the gable wall. Can you cut the power to the house?'

'Give me a minute.' I could hear her typing like mad on her keyboard.

'Anything on Nilay?' I asked her.

'Nothing. I'm *really* worried about him.'

'Me too. The inspector looked like a real snake.'

'I'm into the electrical distribution system. It's quite clunky and it looks like I'll have to take down the whole district. Hospitals and the like can't be without power for long, so I'm only going to do it for two minutes, right?'

'Two minutes will do it.' I rolled silently out onto the lawn and stared up at my challenge. 'Ready when you are.'

'Three, two, one,' she counted. 'Go!'

The whole place suddenly went pitch black, and before I knew it, I was on the annexe roof and scrambling up the gable creeper. *But not so fast.* The guards were out of their hut again, and as I buried my face and body in the thick foliage, I could feel my heart blasting in my chest.

'Shit, the whole place is down,' I heard one of them say. 'Backward, shit-ass country. One minute it's the alarms, next we're out of power. Son of a bitch Modi.'

They went in the back door of the house again. The moment it closed, I resumed my climb until I reached the tiny window I'd been aiming for. To my massive relief, it opened, and after checking that no one was inside, I wriggled headfirst into a tiny bathroom.

'Power going back on,' barked McPherson, sergeant major style.

'Go for it,' I whispered as I lay on the tiled floor. Finally, I was in.

Lights immediately came on in the house. Crawling to the doorway, I peered out onto the landing, hoping and praying that no one was coming my way.

'Guards have gone back to their hut,' said McPherson. 'Five still sleeping. The sixth is still in the room directly below you, moving occasionally. Let's hope it's him.'

'Let's drop the call. I need my wits about me. I'll call you just as soon as I can, OK?'

'Okay, but *please* take care, Peter. And I know you can do it.'

I tiptoed out onto the tiled landing, along to the top of the stairs and peered down into the hallway. A door leading into the room directly below me was ajar and a light was on. I desperately wanted to know if it was him in there.

Very slowly, I went down one step and then another before stopping and listening. Then two more.

My heart missed a beat. There was a noise. A cough. A man's cough.

Footsteps!

He was coming to the door.

Chapter 60

As I cowered on the staircase, not daring to move, I didn't manage to catch a glimpse of him, but I heard him go down the hallway to another part of the house.

Taking my chance, I bolted down the rest of the stairs and crept into the room he'd come out of. He'd left the light, on so most likely he'd be back.

It was a sitting room-cum study with two enormous sofas and a bunch of armchairs, and down at the end, by the bay window, there was a huge writing desk. Beside it was a smaller table hosting a wide array of whiskies and other liquors. On the main desk, along with a pile of books and papers, sat a half-consumed glass of whisky. My Sikh was a whisky man. Surely this had to be him?

I heard his footsteps coming back. *Where am I going to go?* Hide behind the door and take him from there? Lie behind one of the sofas? Neither. Seeing the huge curtains, I darted down to the bay window and slipped in between the thick velvet layers, desperately trying not to move them.

I'd hardly got in before I heard his short, purposeful steps as he entered the room and made his way back toward his desk. He'd surely smell me. I stank like a sewer. Whatever I was going to do, it had better be quick.

I got a sudden whiff of coffee and heard his big desk chair creak as it took his weight. My Sikh had been heavyset. Surely it had to be him—McPherson never made mistakes.

I heard ice cubes being stirred around in a glass. Then a little slurp.

I'd recognise that slurp anywhere. Bullseye! We'd found him, one hundred per cent.

He moved some papers around and then started drumming his fingers gently on his desk—car alarms and power outages clearly hadn't fazed him a bit.

Was it from here, in Delhi, in this nice big house, at this big desk that he'd given the order to tamper with Dad's car? Why had he done it? Was it his decision and his alone, or was he part of a wider conspiracy, a pawn in a much bigger game?

There were so many questions, and now it was time to get the answers.

Chapter 61

Very slowly I eased out from behind the curtains and stood still for the briefest of moments, staring. He was less than a metre from me. Dark blue turban. Wispy grey hair on the neck. A familiar hunch. Then, as he reached for his glass, I got my confirmation. The ring on his massive knuckle.

I made my move. *Bang. Bang. Bang.* No holding back. All the strength I could muster. Three ferocious slams, smashing his head into the corner of the solid teak desk.

A second later he was splayed face first on the floor, out cold, blood gushing from his nose and mouth. His glasses lay beside him in little pieces.

Then I was sprinting for the door and wedged myself behind it. Someone must surely have heard the banging, and with the little gun ripped from its ankle holster, I waited, all the time watching him as he groaned. *Torso and gut*, I kept saying to myself. If anyone came, I knew exactly what to do.

But no one did come, and soon I was taping him up, seeing up close just how much damage I'd done. Four or five front teeth lay in a pool of blood and gunk on the floor, and his nose was totally busted. Worse was the massive lump going from the bridge of his nose all the way up his forehead. I must have fractured his skull, and the lump was steadily growing as the fluids built up.

I dialled McPherson and propped the phone on his desk, ready to film his confession.

'Peter, what did you do him?' she gasped when she saw him. But I didn't answer her. She wouldn't understand, plus he'd come round and was lying there looking surprisingly calm and composed.

'I want information,' I said to him quietly, out of his view. 'You'll tell me what I need to know.'

Breathing slowly and calmly, he ignored me, and I knew immediately he was going to be way tougher than the sweeper. 'Going to talk?' I said, raising my voice, but again I got no response. He almost seemed to be meditating. 'I'll cut to the chase,' I said, moving close and shoving the stubby knife to within a millimetre of his left eye. 'Talk or I take out an eye. Understood?'

'Peter, *no*,' yelled McPherson in my ear. But there was only one way to deal with hardened killers, and the one lying before me was the one who'd set the dogs on me and orchestrated my dad's death. I'd hack out his eyes *and his balls* if that was what it took.

'Final chance,' I whispered in his ear. 'Tell me what I need to know. Tell me why you had James Black killed. Who paid you to do it? I'll carve you up unless you tell me.'

'Walk away, Peter' said McPherson more calmly. '*Please.* You know this isn't your way. It's their way, and you can't stoop to their level. Let the police deal with it. *Please* just get out of there.'

'Final chance,' I said calmly. 'You've got three seconds.' As I counted down, he gave a long deep sigh and closed his eyes, mentally preparing himself for whatever I was going to do. Answering my questions just wasn't something he was going to do.

I couldn't bring myself to do an eye. Instead, I drove the blade deep into his left thigh and held it there for a few seconds before ripping it out. Then I drove it in again. 'No, Peter,' wept my partner back in London. *'You're insane.'*

The Sikh recoiled and froze but didn't make a sound, using every ounce of inner strength to absorb what must have been the most excruciating pain. Then, after about a minute, his body slowly began to relax, and soon he was lying there exactly as he had done before.

It was then that I realised that even if I did it again, or even twenty more times, he wouldn't talk. Eyes, balls, fingers, whatever—I wouldn't be getting a squeak out of him. Jock had said they were hard as nails, and this one was the hardest of all of them.

Suddenly there was a little knock at the door.

I was up like a shot, sprinting to my spot behind the door again just as it began to open. Why the hell hadn't McPherson warned me? She was probably too damn preoccupied with human rights.

'Gurmi, are you there?' came an old croaking voice. 'Why are you not in bed? It's late?'

It must be the father. What the hell was I going to do now?

Down at the other end of the room, my hostage had become animated and was straining and groaning, desperately trying to free himself.

Had I found his Achilles heel?

Chapter 62

Part of me felt bad for the old man, but I had no choice. As I grabbed him from behind, I covered his mouth with my hand and bundled him to the ground. 'Your murdering son needs to answer my questions,' I whispered in his ear before taping him up like his son.

Even with his mouth taped, he whined like a pig—probably trying to get the attention of the guards—and it took a solid punch in the guts to get him to shut up. His son wriggled and writhed in desperation to help his old man.

'OK, Singh,' I said dragging the winded old man by his feet over to where his son was. 'Give me the information I need or the old man loses his eyes. Are we clear?'

'Jesus, Peter,' yelled McPherson. 'You can't. He's innocent.'

'I doubt it,' I said quietly, and grabbed the son by the scruff of the neck and pulled him to within an inch of his father's face. 'Tell me what I need to know.'

He wasn't there yet. I just knew it.

I sank the blade into the old man's thigh. The son recoiled in utter shock as the old man let out a horrific muffled squeal before passing out.

'Fucking hell, Peter,' whispered McPherson. 'You'll go to prison for this.'

But I wasn't done yet. With the thumb and forefinger of my left hand, I prised open the lids of one of the old man's eyes and put the bloodied tip of the knife against the flesh by the base of the eyeball. McPherson gasped and went silent.

'Talk,' I said very quietly to the son. 'This is only going to get worse.'

Chapter 63

He nodded his head ferociously in compliance. I'd finally conquered him. 'I'm going to take the tape off, but if you yell, I swear I will kill your old man, then you. *Understood?*'

In the background, I could hear McPherson's terrified breathing, but deep down in the trenches, there in the Sikh's lair, I felt extremely calm. Maybe she was right. Maybe I was insane.

When I ripped off the tape, blood spewed from his mouth, and after he'd spat out more gunk, he raised his head, straining his eyes. 'Who are you?' he garbled. 'I can't see without my spectacles.'

I pushed my face up close to his. 'Who do think it is, you blind twat? It's your St Andrews bartender Peter Black, here to find out why you had my father killed.'

He took it in for a moment. 'I thought you might come.' More gunk oozed out of his mouth.

'Hurry up. You need to get out of there,' whispered McPherson, sounding more composed.

'Why did you kill him?'

'It was a simple contract.' He spat a tooth onto the floor. 'Someone wanted him dead.'

'*Who* wanted him dead? Now get on with it.' I moved the knife towards his father again.

'I don't know,' he said, resting his weary head on the floor. 'We only met an intermediary. There is often a chain, so nobody ever finds out who is really behind these things. It was nothing personal, it was just a money matter.'

Just a money matter. Fury seared through me, and in my rage, I sank the blade back into his thigh and left it there. McPherson shrieked but didn't utter a word. 'A name!' I said quietly, ramming his face into the floor. 'And it *is* personal. *Very* personal.' I ripped the knife out.

'I don't have a name, I really don't,' he snorted through gritted teeth. 'We met in a bar near London. We got half a million in cash. A million afterwards. We were told to kill father or son.'

I sat back on the floor, staring at him. Both targets! Who in hell's name would want to do that to us? What had we done?

'Find out which bar, Peter. If we know, I can find him. Date as well if you can.'

'Which bar? When? What time?' I spluttered.

'About one month ago in Richmond, near London. A bar down by the riverside just after noon.'

'That'll do it,' said McPherson. 'Now get out while you can.'

'You outwitted my people,' he said, lifting his weary head. 'I told them not to underestimate you, but they did. And I'm sorry about your father, but if we hadn't done it, another group would have. There are many out there who offer these services.'

I couldn't take it anymore and got the phone from the desk. 'I'm switching it off. I'll call you later,' I said to McPherson. This next bit was just going to be between me and my two dishevelled captives. After switching it off, I pulled the little gun out of its ankle holster.

'*Wait.* I have something for moments like this. But please let my father live. He's an innocent man. I'm the bad one.'

I saw him glance at his ring.

'James Black was an innocent father too, but you chose to take his life.'

Tears were now rolling down his face, the strong man well and truly broken. 'Please! For the sake of his grandchildren and my frail mother. I beg you, Peter Black. Let him live.'

He lowered his head to his hand and started trying to get at the ring with his mangled mouth. 'Help me open it,' he cried. 'Let me take my own life in return for my father's.'

I knelt beside him. 'What do I do? How do I get at the poison?'

'Press the two tiny diamonds on either side of the cap, then turn it clockwise.'

I did as he said and sure enough, the cap detached from the ring, revealing a tiny black pill in the cavity below. 'Will you spare him?' he begged.

'I have another question for you.'

'Yes. Anything. Just spare him.'

'Did you send a woman to kill me on the golf course? Was she part of everything?'

He nodded. 'You should be careful. Her brother and sister will not rest until they avenge what you did to her.'

'Take it now,' I snapped. 'The coward's way out like the scumbag did in Hong Kong.'

'My father. Do you give me your word?'

'He'll live,' I replied. 'Now *do it.*'

In a matter of seconds after taking it, the convulsions kicked in, and by the time I'd got to the door, he was dead.

Chapter 64

After slipping past the guards in the front yard and jogging, I got onto the main avenue heading towards the British High Commission, then called McPherson.

'I'm out. On my way to the Commission.'

'I'm glad,' she replied coldly. 'Mission accomplished.'

'Christine, I know you're pissed at me, but I didn't—' But before I could finish, I saw a vehicle approaching at great speed. I dived off the pavement and took cover behind a low hedge, only lifting my head a fraction as the car roared past. It was the same one! The inspector was in the back, pointing ahead, yelling instructions to his driver.

'They're going to the Sikh's place,' barked McPherson. 'And watch, there's another one on its way too.'

Sure enough, in the distance, I saw another set of headlights approaching, and half a minute later, a dark sedan screamed past with five or more Sikhs in it. I started sprinting. They'd soon be after me, and if I didn't get to the safety of the Commission, I'd be a dead man. 'Two kilometres to go, Peter.'

'Fuck,' I screamed at her, willing myself to move up to a gear I didn't know I had until I was literally flying down the road, pumped up with fear and adrenaline.

Ahead, I saw a tuk-tuk idling at the side of the road, the driver squatting in the dust nearby. 'They're coming back,' shouted McPherson.

'Sorry,' I shouted at the man as I jumped into the tuk-tuk. 'You'll find it at the British High Commission.' I twisted the throttle as far as it could possibly go and took off.

'How far?' I shouted, peering into the tiny wing mirrors and seeing the headlights getting nearer and nearer. They were driving like lunatics.

'Another kilometre. Can you see it? It's up on the left.'

I could, but only just. 'If I don't make it,' I shouted breathlessly, 'find my father's killers. Do you promise? Do whatever it takes. *You bring them to justice.*'

By now I could hear the scream of the engines behind me. *'You can make it,'* she yelled back. 'You've got to. Head for the security post.'

The security post was too far away. I'd never make it. Instead, I aimed for the nearest corner. The tuk-tuk smashed over the kerb before ploughing through bushes and over a stretch of grass until it shuddered to a halt beside the enormous security wall. In a flash, I was up on the vehicle's roof and hauling my terrified self onto the top of the barbed wire-covered wall.

By now the saloon was tearing across the grass. As the Sikhs unleashed the might of their machine guns, I threw myself into the darkness of the British High Commission's grounds.

Chapter 65

I awoke in the morning to the sound of my metal prison door opening, and a short Westerner in a suit peered in with two Gurkha guards by his side.

All hell had broken loose when I'd landed face-first in the British High Commission rose garden. In a matter of seconds, a team of Gurkha guards with their Alsatian dogs had 'arrested me' and flung me into the Commission's small, very basic jail. Their 'superiors' were to deal with me in the morning.

'Rob Knot, Head of British High Commission security. Who are you?' said the short man bluntly and expressionlessly. *Officious little bastard*, I thought to myself.

'I'm Peter Black. I was with your colleague Nilay Kumar last night. Can you tell me if he's OK?'

'What were you doing last night?' he said even more bluntly, completely avoiding my question.

'I'd rather not say anything, and I urgently need to speak to Commander Burke of the security services back in London. Do you know of him?' Still no reply. 'Or maybe I could see the High Commissioner instead? He knew my father—James Black—really quite well. You've maybe heard of him? He died earlier this week in Hong Kong in a car crash.'

Knot nodded to the two guards and the three of them left, closing the door with a loud bang.

'Fuck you, you useless officious bastard,' I screamed after them in exasperation, jumping up and pounding the door with my fists. 'I'm not a fucking terrorist!'

It was another two hours before I heard the door open again. This time a tall man in a well-cut suit accompanied Knot, minus Gurkhas. I got to my feet.

'Peter, please accept my apologies for keeping you in here. I'm Richard White, Deputy High Commissioner. I do apologise, but John Sergeant, the Commissioner, is out of station, otherwise he would have come to see you personally. Please follow me. We'll hightail it across to my house here on the campus and Cook will rustle you up something tasty. You must be famished!'

'Thanks, Mr White. Much appreciated.' Christ, the guy seemed from a different era.

'Mr Knot has briefed me, but perhaps you can tell me what's been going on?'

'Is Nilay Kumar OK?'

'He turned up this morning in one of the public hospitals. He's sporting a bad head wound, but he's going to be fine. Maybe you can shed some light on what's been going on, Peter?'

'First I need to talk to Commander Burke. I also need my phone and pods—I lost them when I came over the wall.'

'Indeed. And quite an arrival.' White smiled tensely. 'Most of our visitors come in the main gate and often give a little knock, you know?'

'And without a carload of gun-wielding lunatics chasing them and firing into British sovereign territory.' Knot snorted.

'Quite,' said White, shaking his head. 'We've never seen anything quite like it. Anyway, I'm sure it can all be explained.'

Once we got outside, Knot parted company with us and we headed towards a row of villas overlooking a large swimming pool. 'Hopefully, Cook will have something ready, eh?'

I stopped for a moment, staring after Knot. Not many people riled me quite as much as he had. 'That man is a total idiot. Does he treat everyone he meets like shit?'

'Oh, I see,' replied White stiffly. 'I'll have a quiet word, shall I? Customer feedback and all that.'

'Maybe better not to bother.' I sighed. 'It's unlikely to do any good.'

As we went into his villa, a smartly dressed young guy—no older than me—appeared from nowhere, holding a phone. 'Deputy High Commissioner White, there is a Commander Burke on the phone for Mr Peter Black.'

I snatched the phone. 'Let's leave Mr Black in peace, shall we?' said White, forcing a smile.

'Peter, is that you?' came the now-familiar voice.

'Sir,' I replied.

'Patching in McPherson—hang on a second.'

'God, Peter, I'm so glad you're safe,' said McPherson immediately. 'I watched it all on the satellite and I thought you'd made it but couldn't be sure. I tried calling the British High Commission, but they refused to speak to me.'

'All fine, McPherson. I think the Hindu gods were looking down on me last night.'

'Yes, good to hear you're safe,' cut in the Commander. 'However, before we go on, I have some …' He gave a little pause. 'I have some very bad news for you.'

A dark feeling of dread swept over me. Someone was dead. I just knew it.

Chapter 66

'Commander. Tell me it's not my mum or Sam.' I could barely contain myself.

'Don't worry, they're fine,' he assured me. 'It's your housekeeper, Mrs Peng.' He paused again. 'Very sadly, she was found dead at dawn this morning in Hong Kong.'

'What?'

I heard him take a deep breath. 'Yes, I'm terribly sorry, Peter. It's dreadful news. Very unfortunately ... it looks as though ...'

'She killed herself,' I cut in, suddenly seeing it all very clearly. Of course, she had. She'd been in terrible shape when I'd left. Totally and utterly depressed. And I'd done *nothing* to help her.

'Yes, Peter. Very sadly you're correct.'

There was a deathly silence as they gave me a bit of time to take it all in. 'I should have seen it coming. I shouldn't have come here. I should have stayed with Sam and Mum and tried to support and take care of her. God, I'm such a useless, self-obsessed arsehole.'

'I don't think you could ever have guessed this would happen,' said McPherson gently.

'Indeed,' said the Commander quietly.

'Who found her, sir? How did she do it?'

'I don't have a lot of details, son,' he replied, 'but I understand it was death by hanging.'

'Oh Jesus. Do you know where?'

'I believe she was found hanging from an upper window of a property at the rear of the main house.'

'Christ.' I sighed. 'That was where the two of them lived. In the cottage at the back. The upstairs bedroom has the window.'

'Do you mind very much if we talk about last night, Peter?' asked the Commander delicately. 'If you're not ready, then of course it can wait, but I do need to know what happened. We also have to get you out of India as soon as we can. I've got someone looking at that as we speak, in fact.'

With McPherson listening in, I gave him a five-minute debrief, starting with the key information that we'd found, and I worked back from there. I didn't say what had happened to the Sikh.

'Excellent summary,' he said. 'And first-class work by the pair of you, if I may say so.'

'I'm already trawling through CCTV footage in Richmond,' cut in McPherson. 'Nothing to report yet, but I'll find something. It's only a matter of time.'

'We couldn't have done it without Nilay, sir.'

'He's top-notch, isn't he?' replied the Commander. 'Thank god he's OK. But we're going to have to get him out of India fast too. Just one further thing, Peter.'

I knew what was coming. 'Yes, sir?'

'What happened to the Sikh?'

I had already prepared my answer. 'I had to rough him up a bit to get him talking, sir. The father too.'

'And ...?' asked the Commander. 'Dead or alive?'

'The son took poison, just like his operative in Hong Kong. The old man is still alive.'

'Interesting. And McPherson,' he asked, 'is that the way you see it?'

'It is, sir,' she said with conviction. My god. Despite our differences, she was loyal to the end.

'Why would someone want me or my father dead, Commander?' I asked.

'That's a really good question, Peter, but I don't have the answer. We're just going to have to keep working at it and in time the truth will come out, as it always does.'

'Are you sure there's nothing from my dad's past, sir?' I asked bluntly. 'It doesn't take an idiot to work out that he was once one of you lot, and maybe something has come back to bite him. If there was something, you'd say, wouldn't you?'

'I can't comment on your father's past exploits, and I could only tell you something if it wasn't classified. You know how it works.'

'Listen, mate,' I said, raising my voice. 'You better not be hiding something. All this cloak-and-dagger bull is beginning to annoy me. Can't you just be honest for once in your life?'

'Peter,' cut in McPherson. 'Don't speak to Commander Burke like that. It doesn't achieve anything.'

'It's all right,' he cut in. 'I can fight my own battles, Christine. Peter, I can understand your frustration, but let's leave it at that for now, and I'll be back in touch very shortly, once I've worked out how to get you out of Delhi.' He hung up.

'Idiot,' said McPherson, staying on the line. 'You need to learn to control your temper. He's on our side, you know, and you need him. Especially right now.'

'I'll call you when I get back to Hong Kong. If I get back,' I replied obtusely and hung up.

I sat contemplating for a few minutes. I was annoyed with the Commander. I was annoyed with McPherson. I was annoyed with myself. McPherson was right, he was a hugely important ally, but at the same time, he probably knew all sorts of stuff that might be important, and not revealing it just wasn't on. Still, at least he knew my views, and I really didn't care if he was Joe Bloggs or the King of England. He didn't own me. Nobody did.

Chapter 67

Less than five minutes later, just as I was finishing sending a message to Mum and Sam letting them know I'd heard the news, the Commander was back on the line telling me I'd be picked up in less than an hour.

'Sanjay Sharma is an old India State Security friend of mine and totally trustworthy. His son, also in ISS, will take you to the airport and you'll be on your way back to Hong Kong before anyone realises you've gone. Sanjay is with Modi today otherwise he'd have done it himself.'

'Thanks, Commander … and I apologise for what I said. I was out of order.'

'Let's forget about it,' he replied. 'Anyway, it's water under the bridge. But rest assured, if I do think of something important or relevant from the past, I'll let you know. I have skin in the game too—he was your father, but he was my best friend.'

'Thanks, sir.'

Fifteen minutes later, White walked me through the compound to the front gate, where an official-looking white car with a small Indian flag fluttering at the front was waiting. A tall young man in uniform stepped out from the back and walked over to me.

'Hari Sharma. A pleasure to meet you. My father sends his sincere apologies—the PM summoned him, and as you can imagine, you drop everything. Come, let's get going. The roads can be awful.'

I thanked White for his kindness. 'Do visit again sometime.' He smiled.

'Wait,' I said, seeing the badly damaged tuk-tuk parked near the main gate. I dug around in my pockets and pulled out a thousand-dollar bill, which I handed to White. 'See that the poor guy gets this, would you?'

'I certainly will. What a noble gesture.'

We set off, and soon Hari was enthusiastically telling me about the year he'd spent in the UK at Sandhurst. He adored all things English and told me about all the places he had visited and how he'd love to do a stint at the Indian Embassy in London in the future. Then, very quietly and out of earshot of his driver, he told me about falling madly in love with a local girl from one of the villages near Sandhurst and how he used to sneak out to see her late at night. He was now married to an Indian lady, but one got the impression he'd much rather have married the English girl. Poor chap!

Although there was tons of afternoon traffic, it kept flowing surprisingly well, and when we arrived at the airport, Hari took me to the front of the long queue waiting to get into the terminal. With a flick of his ISS badge, we were waved through.

'Right, Peter, I'll leave you here,' he said as we got to the Cathay Pacific counter. 'I'm sure you'll be perfectly safe here in the terminal, but I'd be happy to take you through Security as well if you wish?' As he said it, he glanced at his watch. He was clearly pressed for time.

'Not at all,' I lied. 'I'll be fine from here.' We gave one another a friendly fist bump. 'Make sure you get in touch if you ever do that stint in London,' I called after him.

'I most certainly will!' he replied with a little salute.

Feeling a bit on edge, I took my place in the check-in queue. After about ten minutes I got my boarding pass, then went to a pharmacy on the way to Security. I had a headache coming on, which paracetamol would hopefully fix, and then I'd go and relax in a coffee shop after immigration.

As I was paying, the sight of my tired, haggard self in the mirror behind the counter gave me quite a shock. But then the mirror gave me an even bigger shock. Back in the heart of the terminal building, I saw a policeman peering at me from behind a pillar. Then I saw another one. Then, to my utter dismay, I saw that the inspector was with them. Panic struck.

Outnumbered. Trapped. They'd arrest me. Gift me to the Sikhs. I'd be dead within the hour.

Trying desperately to calm myself and think, I walked out of the pharmacy, pretending I hadn't seen them. When I glanced at them, I saw that they were moving through the crowds towards me, most likely aiming to cut me off before Security. What the hell was I going to do?

My only option was the toilets off to my right, and as I half ran there, I could hear the commotion behind as my pursuers jostled with the crowd. There had to be an exit—a window, a fire escape or something—but if there wasn't, that would be it for me.

I sprinted past the urinals, then down the long line of stalls, but there was nothing. No open window, no fire escape exit, no nothing. Screwed and panicking, all I could do was duck into the last cubicle and shut the door.

'This is the police,' came a voice from the entrance. 'Please would everyone come out of the restrooms, as we believe there is a dangerous criminal in there. We need everyone to come out with their hands above their heads. This is an order from the Delhi Police Department.'

I jumped up on the toilet seat, then on the cistern itself and just managed to touch the ceiling with my fingertips, thinking I might be able to go up through the ceiling. But no. The panels were fixed tight. There was no way out. I was well and truly done for.

I jumped back down again and in desperation, I called Nilay. 'What's up, Peter? Are you already at the airport? You'd gone by the time I got back to the BHC.'

'I'm screwed, Nilay. Totally fucked.'

'What do you mean?'

'I'm in the toilets. The inspector and his men are about to take me.' As I whispered, the stall doors were being bashed open one by one.

'*Do not* go down without one hell of a fight, do you hear me, Peter? Use the gun and the knife. Remember everything I told you.'

'Right, yes, right,' I stuttered. Like an idiot, in the frenzy, I'd totally forgotten about the ankle holsters.

'Wait, sir. I'm sitting here shitting,' came an elderly voice from the fourth or fifth cubicle up from mine as the police hammered on the door.

'Get out. Go and shit somewhere else,' bawled the officer.

'That's no way to treat a senior citizen,' came the response. With that there was a huge crash as his door was forced open, and I heard the man being dragged out, screaming in protest.

Holding the tiny gun between my teeth, I climbed up on the cistern again. I squeezed myself onto the top of the cubicle partition and lay along it.

Slowly, I slid forward to look at what was going on. *There they were!* Two of them. No sign of the inspector. They were about to kick open the cubicle next to mine, and their guns were drawn.

Chapter 68

I shrank back and just as they kicked in the door, I pointed the tiny gun at them from above. 'Move an inch and I'll kill you.'

Skinny, moustachioed and barely older than me, they froze and stared up at me, wondering whether the puny little gun was a serious threat.

'Want to try me?'

Both shook their heads. 'Guns on the floor,' I snapped. 'Down on your fronts. Hands behind your head. Eyes shut. *Now.*' Both immediately did exactly as I'd instructed.

'What's happening, officers? Have you found him?' came a shout from outside. It was him.

'Not a word,' I whispered to the two of them, sticking the gun butt in the taller one's neck, then I darted back into the stall and took the cistern lid off.

From outside there was suddenly the crackle of a walkie-talkie. 'Why haven't you brought him to me?' demanded an ancient voice. I should have taken care of the old weasel when I had the chance.

The inspector started spewing out excuses. 'Don't worry, we're on our way. My men are ...'

I took my chance. *Crack.* First I knocked one out cold with the cistern, then the other. Then I leathered it past the urinals towards the entrance.

I skidded round the corner into the passageway between the male and the female toilets and there he was, out in the open, busy clipping his walkie-talkie to his belt. He hadn't even seen me. *Bang.* I floored him, and before he knew it, he was being hauled ferociously back into the toilets by his trouser ankles.

'You're dead, you're dead,' he screamed, writhing and kicking the length of the place until I finally booted him in the nuts and flung the wiry little shit on top of his two men.

'We can sort things,' he groaned, doubled up in agony. 'A deal. I'll help you.'

'Like hell. If you'd got me, you'd have fed me to the wolves.'

'We have no choice. The Sikhs own us. *All of us.*'

'Bullshit. It's greed that owns you, and it's time to pay for your greed.'

I grabbed him, shoved him onto his front and pinned his back with my foot. There was no Christine preaching her moral code. Just me and him, and he was going to pay. For what he'd done to Nilay. For protecting the Sikhs who'd murdered my dad. For the countless other terrible things, he'd undoubtedly done. 'This country will be a much better place without you,' I whispered in his ear, and he suddenly went rigid as he felt the gun barrel touch the back of his head.

'God, no. Please spare me. I'm sorry for what I've done, I'm really sorry,' he wailed.

It was too late.

Chapter 69

I pulled the trigger three times, but each time, nothing happened. God himself, or maybe even McPherson, must have intervened.

My moment of madness was thankfully over. He got the cistern lid treatment instead, then I dragged the three of them into the attendant's storeroom, stuffed their mouths with floor cloths, bound them with electric cord, locked the door and got out of there. As soon as I was back out in the terminal, I called McPherson.

'McPherson, it's me.'

'I've been trying to find you everywhere on CCTV. Are you OK?'

'No, I'm not.' I quickly took her through what had happened, bar my failed attempt at murder. 'If they get me, I'm dead. I've got to get through Immigration, onto the plane and out of this godforsaken place. Who knows what else the evil old bastard has got up his sleeve for me.'

'Go hide till I call you,' she said calmly. 'I'm going to get you out of India. Trust me.' At that moment, there was no one in the world that I trusted more than McPherson.

Less than ten minutes later, she was back. 'Good news. You're not tagged in the Security or Immigration systems, and no chatter on police comms, so I think you'll get through OK. I'll keep an eye on things, of course. As far as the old Sikh is concerned, Charles has been working his magic again, you'll be pleased to know. He's hacked the inspector's mobile and sent the Sikh a text saying that you're on the run, having escaped from the airport. As we speak, the Sikh is sitting outside the airport building in his convoy of cars spitting venom that you got away.'

'I'll owe you and Charles forever, McPherson. The pair of you just never fail.'

'Yes, you will,' she replied, 'but let's not get ahead of ourselves. We've still got to get you out.'

After going through Immigration, I had the most anxious ninety-minute wait of my life. Finally, I boarded the plane, but it wasn't until it was a good hour out of Delhi that I began to relax. But it was short-lived. As we landed late at night in Hong Kong and taxied towards the gate, I switched on my phone to check my messages and found three in quick succession from McPherson.

'You lied to me, Peter.'

'How could you have done it?'

'They'll extradite you back to India for this.'

Chapter 70

Before we'd reached the gate, I sent her a message. 'What on earth do you mean?'

'Three police found dead in Delhi airport toilets,' came the reply. 'Gunshots to the head. Foreigner in his early twenties the primary suspect.'

'No, no, no, no. *Not me. Absolutely not me.* Please believe me.'

'Call me when you get into the terminal. I want to believe you.'

When I got off the plane, I'd barely started talking to McPherson before the Hong Kong police swooped. 'I'm being arrested. Call Burke. I'm bloody well innocent,' was all I could say to her as they took my phone away.

Three hours later—as the sun was coming up—I was released and told to report to Central Station at 3 p.m. 'You've got friends in high places,' commented the senior officer on my release. He and his colleagues had asked me lots of questions, but I'd decided not to answer any of them for fear of incriminating myself. 'I'm innocent,' was my response to every question, and on several occasions I was directly asked if I'd been involved in the murder of three men at Indira Gandhi International Airport. I felt utterly wretched throughout it all and scared out of my wits.

I was also deeply unhappy with myself for what I'd tried to do to the inspector back in Delhi. Yes, he was a murderer. Yes, he was complicit in my father's death. Yes, I'd been in an unbelievably stressful situation. But I shouldn't have done it. I shouldn't have crossed the line and pulled the trigger, and I felt sick to the stomach about what I'd become.

I turned off my phone so that I didn't have to confront McPherson and the Commander.

It was a lonely ride from the airport to the house. By the time the taxi rolled down the drive through a spattering of the press, I was feeling worse than I'd ever felt in my whole life. I quietly went up to my bedroom and locked the door.

In my state of distress and despair, I just knew that I had to call Ofelia. I deserved her even less than I did before, but she'd been there for me when I'd had my Parliament and Sloane Street meltdowns, and now I needed her more than ever. But that's if she'd answer my call. I hadn't replied to any of her messages since Dad's death.

I turned my phone back on and nervously called her.

'Peter! What a lovely surprise. It's quite early there, isn't it?' *God*, it was good to hear her voice, and she didn't sound angry or distant at all. I felt my whole tensed-up body suddenly relax.

'Eight in the morning here, so it must be late with you?'

'I'm just turning in, my love. My mother and I have been all over London today.' Hearing her say 'my love' sent a shot of emotion through me.

'Please accept my apologies, Ofelia,' I began. 'I should have called you, but ...'

'I understand. Honestly, no need to apologise.' Her voice was so incredibly soothing and relaxing. 'But I want you to know that I— and my parents—have been thinking about you a lot. I can't imagine what you're going through, but I know you'll get through it in time. You're strong.'

'I wish.' I laughed, tears welling up in my eyes.

'I hope you haven't been bashing anyone?' she said with a little giggle.

I laughed again. 'If only you knew. You know me.'

'Oh god, I don't like the sound of that. Will we be seeing you in the press again?'

'Very possibly.'

'Should I believe what I read?'

'No, not this time. Sure, I bashed those two big morons in the hotel, and I apologise that you had to read about it, but this next thing—if it surfaces—is pure fabrication. I hope you'll believe me.'

'Let's see, shall we?' she said jokingly.

As we were speaking, a message flashed up on my screen from McPherson. 'Get off the phone. I've got news about Richmond.' I sat up.

'Ofelia. I hope you don't mind, but could you excuse me? A really important call has come in. I can't elaborate, but …'

'Of course. But *wait*. When am I going to see you again? I don't care about all these stories and stuff. All I want is to see you again.'

I sent McPherson a quick message saying I'd be with her in a moment. It was time to be straight with Ofelia.

'Listen. I love you to death, but isn't it better that you forget about me? All this stuff I've done—lots of it you don't even know about … I'm not worthy of you. It's what I honestly feel.'

'Let *me* be the judge of that,' she replied in a firm tone. 'Now, why don't I stay here a few more days so I can come to your father's service with you? Would that be OK? My father will be staying too. And we can go through all this "worthy or not" stuff when we meet.'

'I don't know. If you knew everything, you'd—'

'No, Peter. *Enough.* Stop talking like that. You're a good man. Do you hear me?'

'OK. OK. I've got the point.' I laughed before pausing. 'Ofelia?'

'What?' she said softly.

'I miss you like crazy.'

'Me too.'

After hanging up, I sat quietly on my bed for a moment. Yes, I felt ecstatic about the thought of seeing her again and about how close I felt to her, but at the same time, I had this horrible feeling in the pit of my stomach. Surely it could never work out. Not now.

'What have you found?' I asked when McPherson picked up. It was time to forget Ofelia and to refocus.

'I've just sent you a photo of someone standing by the River Thames at Richmond. Tell me if you recognise him.'

As soon as I opened it, I recognised the young Sikh from the Mandarin. 'Jesus, it's the one from the hotel. You're a certified genius, do you know that?'

'It was quite easy. We hacked into the Mandarin's system. Got ourselves images of this guy and then did a matching search through Richmond's CCTV archives and *bingo*, we got a hit. He and Singh met up at the bus station and then walked down to the river together. Singh went into the pub while this guy loitered outside keeping watch.'

'And the money man who Singh supposedly met in the pub?'

'Invisible so far,' she replied, 'but we're working on it. Both Charles and I get the feeling that he's cunning and we're going to have to work hard to find him and identify him.'

'I have every faith in the two of you.'

'More good news, by the way,' she then said. 'You'll be owing Charles a big thank you for it.'

'God, McPherson, let it be Delhi! The whole thing is killing me. I swear I didn't shoot them, but I'm already feeling like a convicted murderer.'

'No need to feel like that anymore, Peter. We've got footage of two thugs leaving the old man's convoy and going into the airport about half an hour after you went through Immigration. They went straight into the gents, came out thirty seconds later, then disappeared back out of the airport.'

'Good god. A hit squad—probably the nutters who chased me to the Commission.' I suddenly felt the most colossal weight lift off my shoulders, and I could have hugged McPherson and Charles.

'Correct. Both are wanted for a litany of crimes in India and beyond. The Commander has the information and is talking to the Hong Kong Police Commissioner on your behalf to get you fully exonerated. Oh, and by the way, when you were being held earlier, he put his neck on the line for you by telling them that Peter Black is no killer and should be released immediately.'

'Very noble of him indeed.'

'Come on, Peter. Don't be like that—you're not exactly a saint,' she said angrily before quickly apologising.

I didn't rise to the bait. She knew damn well that I'd crossed the line, but for now, it was time to push my demons deep into the back of my mind and move on.

Chapter 71

Feeling much better, I took a quick nap, showered and headed downstairs, where I found Sam in the kitchen. Mum was in town meeting a few friends.

After giving Sam a glossed-over update about my trip, all of it lies, the subject moved on to Mrs Peng.

'Do you mind if we go take a look at where she did it?' I asked her, and she led me out of the back door and down the red-tiled path.

'We think she took the tow rope from the garage,' she said emotionally as we stood staring at the cottage, 'then went upstairs to their bedroom, tied one end around the rosewood wardrobe, the other round her neck, and then jumped out the window. The doctor said that her neck would have snapped instantaneously. How on earth she had the guts to do it I'll never know.'

'Who cut her down?'

'Mum and I did,' she replied, the tears beginning to flow.

'Come on, Sam,' I said to her, putting my arm around her, and we went and sat on the little wooden bench where Mr and Mrs Peng would sit each evening looking out over the South China Sea.

'It was honestly the most awful thing I've ever had to do in my life,' she said, wiping her tears away. 'Good lord, Peter,' she said, staring out into the distance, 'it's just one horror after another, isn't it? I just hope and pray that's the end of it.'

'You've been very brave, sis, and I'm so sorry that I wasn't here to play my part.'

She turned and glared at me. 'Mum and I are *extremely* concerned about you. Did you know that? You've been acting so strangely, and to be frank, we want to know what's going on. Why don't you tell me? I promise I won't say a word to Mum if you don't want me to.'

'Everything is fine, sis,' I replied, dodging her stare and looking at two dragonflies which had parked themselves on the arm of the bench. 'Nothing's going on and there's nothing to worry about.'

'I don't believe you one bit,' she replied with a snort, and she pointed at me. 'I'm not daft, you know. I can read you like a book. You're hiding something, and I very much hope it's not something that's a concern to us all.'

'As I said, everything is fine.'

Even if I had been willing to tell her something, where on earth would I have begun? The woman in St Andrews? The bikers? Mong Kok? The Sikhs in Delhi? It was all just so completely screwed up and complicated.

Back in the house, up in my room, I gave Mum a quick call and got her while she was in the Conrad Hotel having morning coffee with one of her old friends.

'Just wanted to let you know I'm back. I'll see you when you get back to the house.'

'Oh, Peter, I'm so pleased,' she said quite formally, her friend obviously in earshot. 'Why don't we all meet for lunch at our favourite place? We all need a break, I think.'

'Great idea, Mum.' As soon as I was off the phone, I yelled down the stairs to Sam. 'Lunch with Mum at Lo's in an hour. Let's take the bike.'

'Excellent,' she shouted back. 'Anything to break the misery!' Then a minute later I heard her shout, 'I'm driving. You're on the back.'

'Fine,' I shouted back.

Just before 11.30 a.m., I heard the Enfield roar into life and when I looked out of my window, there was Sam out in the drive revving the engine and beckoning me to shift it. A few minutes later, we went flying past the press as we set off into town.

I half expected her to go the long way round, avoiding the crash site, but she didn't, and as we approached the bend, she slowed and began to pull over into the little layby. 'What are you doing, Sam?' I said, taking off my helmet as she walked over to the edge.

'Tell me what the *hell* is going on, Peter. I want to know, and I *deserve* to know.'

'It's nothing—nothing at all,' I said quietly, staring down the slope.

'Bull, little brother.' She was inches from me, staring angrily into my eyes. 'Mr Nice Guy Peter Black beating up Americans, scrapping with the press, flying off to India at the drop of a hat. I tell you it doesn't stack up. Plus you look like absolute crap, as if you're carrying the weight of the world on your shoulders. Peter, I want to know everything *now*, before we go on.'

I had to tell her. It just wasn't fair otherwise. 'All right, all right.' I sighed.

'Thank you, dear Lord,' she said, clasping her hands together and looking up to the heavens.

Anxiously running my hand through my hair, I took a deep breath. This wasn't going to be easy. 'Sam, yes, there is something going on. One hell of a lot, as it happens.' I paused and thought about where the hell to begin. 'It's a long and complex story, and I don't know where to start, but maybe I should sit you and Mum down when we get home after lunch. I promise I'll tell you everything from start to finish. Would that be OK?'

'I would much prefer you—' She stopped. 'OK, let's do it that way. It's only fair that Mum should hear it too at the same time.' Then she came and gave me a long hug. 'I know that what you're going to say will be quite devastating,' she whispered, 'but I'm prepared for it.'

'Yes. I'm afraid it will be, Sam. In fact, it's awful.'

Chapter 72

Sam rode carefully down the rest of Magazine Gap Road, but on Cotton Tree Drive, she let rip, and by the time we'd got down to Central, we must have been doing over eighty. She occasionally had 'crazy' moments, and this was one of them—probably triggered by my partial confession.

'Christ, Sam,' I shouted in her ear, 'you'll get us pulled over.' She just waved me off, and soon we were flying past Pacific Place along Queensway. But then, just after we'd crossed the tram tracks onto Queens Road East and as we went down a side street towards Johnston Road, I heard a police siren. 'It's the police. Now you've done it.'

'Almost there,' she yelled, and thirty seconds later we pulled up at the tall corner building where Lo's was located just as our mother arrived in the Black & Co. chauffeur-driven car.

'Sam and Peter, how nice that you're on James's bike,' she said, stepping out and walking over to us. 'He would have loved to have seen this.'

However, at that moment, our cop in pursuit—a motorcycle cop—came tearing up the street and screeched to a halt, lights blazing and siren blaring.

'What on earth?' said my mother, looking at both of us.

'Don't worry, Mum' said Sam confidently. 'I may possibly have skipped a red light. Why don't you both go up and I'll follow on in a minute?' Sam winked and pulled a silly face at me when Mum wasn't watching, loving the thrill of her brush with the law.

'Fine,' replied my mother, scowling at a group of nosey onlookers. 'Come on, Peter, let's go.' As we got into the lift, I heard her mutter 'My kids are going off the rails and it isn't at all dignified.' It was a glass lift facing out onto the street, and as we went up, I smiled to myself as I caught a glimpse of Sam trying to blag her way out of her predicament. God, I loved her to bits!

Ten minutes later and HK$2,500 and three points poorer, Sam joined us in our usual spot, up a little flight of stairs on a private balcony overlooking the thirty-plus round tables in the main restaurant. 'Yes, little brother. You're not the only rebel in the family.' She smiled proudly, throwing the keys over to me. 'You can drive home. I've had enough for today.'

'*Samantha.*' My mother sighed with a look of utter despair on her face.

As he always did, Chef Lo himself came to greet us. He was carrying the same ancient rolling pin that he'd used for years and gave his usual little bow before offering us his deepest condolences. My father had always had a soft spot for Lo and over the years had often got him to chef at the house for important guests. He was a reserved man of very few words, but he quickly brought us to tears. 'Mr Black was a most honourable man, and while I have few friends, I always counted Mr Black as a true and honest friend. Mrs Lo and I went straight to the temple when we heard the terrible news and lit candles and gave prayers for all of you. It is very difficult to get over his passing.' My mother got up and gave him a warm hug, then Sam and I stood up and shook his hand eagerly.

We never ordered in Lo's, with today being no different, and after ten minutes, a steady procession of little bamboo baskets was brought to us up the fifteen steep steps (I used to count them as a boy). There really was nothing better than Chef Lo's dumplings washed down with his fine jasmine tea, and, as was his custom, Lo would visit each table throughout, checking that his clientele was happy. I doubt he'd ever received a negative comment in all his years.

As we ate, we talked through the details of Monday's ceremony. There was going to be a massive turnout, with all 750 seats likely to be filled, and there would standing room for a further 200 at the back. It was invitation only, and the list, which my mother produced from her bag, was an incredible collection of the great and the good of Hong Kong, plus numerous Black & Co. staff. There would also be ordinary people whom father had got to know over the years. If you had seen my father walking down the street or sitting in a café, you wouldn't have twigged he was one of Asia's most successful businessmen. He treated all people, rich or poor, with tremendous respect, and he had close friends from all echelons of society.

After about an hour, as I sat sipping tea—feeling as though I had eaten one dumpling too many—a waitress came up the stairs holding a phone. 'It's an urgent call for Mr Peter Black.'

'I guess that's me.' I laughed. 'I wonder what could be so urgent.' As my mother and sister looked on, I took the handset and put it to my ear. 'Hello, Peter Black speaking.'

'Get out of there now!' screamed McPherson. 'There are two men on their way into the restaurant and another waiting outside in a car. They have instructions to kill you and your family.'

Chapter 73

Still holding the phone, I looked across to the entrance just as two men in balaclavas barged into the restaurant and grabbed the receptionist by the throat.

'What is it, dear?' I heard my mother say.

Now I was up on my feet. The receptionist had pointed at our balcony and the two men—guns in hand—were pacing through the busy restaurant towards our balcony.

'They've got guns,' screamed Sam amidst shouts from other diners. 'Are they coming for *us*?'

'Get down *now*,' I yelled, and as the three of us hit the floor in a huddle, bullets rained down on us, sending food and shattered crockery showering all over us. They'd be up the stairs in seconds. We'd be dead. *What do I do?* I couldn't think.

The table. There was nothing else. I flipped it on its side. Grabbed its stem. Rammed my shoulder under its struts. Drove forward. Launched myself down the steps like a battering ram.

Ploughing into them, the whole thing went smashing down the stairs, stopping abruptly at the bottom. I felt myself somersault over the top, landing on my back on the floor of the main restaurant, the pain searing. Winded, I staggered to my feet.

One man, gun still in hand, was lying close to me, disoriented. The other, yelling and struggling, was wedged out of sight under the table. In the background I heard screaming and the crashing of chairs as diners fled for the exit.

I dived on the first man, held down his shooting arm and, using my only weapon, started headbutting him in the face over and over and over until his arm went limp and he passed out.

Drenched in his blood, my ears ringing with the pain in my forehead, I ripped the gun from his hand and swung round just in time to see the other one crawling out from under the table. He was looking right at me, gun raised. I knew I was done for.

Instinct kicked in. I threw myself to my right and fired, but not before I'd seen the flash from his gun.

Chapter 74

As if in slow motion, I saw his forehead take my bullet just as I slammed into a table of cowering diners. Surely I'd been hit too? It was impossible for him to have missed. As I slumped to the floor, gasping for air, I waited for the pain and for death to set in.

But it didn't seem to be happening. I was still breathing. Still alert. No pain. Had I defied the odds?

The whole place had descended into pandemonium. As I got up, people were gathering around an elderly Chinese man who was gripping a bloodied shoulder. He'd taken the bullet meant for me.

I was back up the fifteen stairs in a flash to check on Mum and Sam. Thank god they were safe. 'Do *not* go back to the house,' I shouted. 'There could be others. I'm going after the third one.'

'No, Peter,' gasped my sister, who was shaking like a leaf.

'They're part of a gang that killed Dad,' I whispered to her, helping her up. 'I *have* to get him.'

'Yes, yes … OK,' she stuttered, her face literally grey with shock.

'I'll explain everything later, like I promised, sis. OK?'

My mother looked more together, and after getting her to comfort Sam, I grabbed the handset from the floor and headed for the entrance, stopping momentarily to pull the ring off the finger of the man I'd headbutted. There was no way he was going to avoid justice. 'Keep an eye on him until the police come,' I shouted to a shell-shocked Lo. 'Club him with the rolling pin if he tries anything.'

As I got to the lift, I spoke into the handset. 'Christine? You still there?'

'Yes, I'm here. Tell me you're all OK!'

'Two gunmen down. One diner is injured. Just getting in the lift to go after the driver.'

'Twenty cars up on the right,' she shouted as the phone faded. 'He's out on the pavement.'

Lying on the lift floor so I couldn't be seen from the street, I peeked for a second and spotted a stocky Indian guy, no turban, some way up the street, pacing up and down. It had to be him.

At the bottom, I grabbed a huge bouquet of flowers from the lobby florist and walked casually out of the building, shielding my face with the blooms, and made my way slowly up the street.

Everything was going well until, midway to the car, a girl let out a scream. 'Mummy! Look! He's all covered in blood.' My cover was blown, and before I knew it, I was pinned behind a parked van with yet another volley of bullets coming in my direction.

Seconds later, there was a screech of tyres and he sped off.

Without giving it a second thought, I was sprinting back to the Enfield so I could go after him.

Chapter 75

A minute later I was on the Enfield, screaming off after him, wobbling wildly as I fumbled around trying to call McPherson on my mobile, stuffing my pods in my ears. 'You there?' I shouted. 'Goddamn it, tell me where the hell he is!'

'Yes, yes, yes,' she shouted back. 'I can see you. His car is moving fast, skipping red lights. He's heading towards the main highway hugging the island, going east.'

'He'll take the eastern crossing to Kowloon or he'll keep going to North Point.'

Driving straight through a main junction on red, narrowly missing a bus and another motorbike, I made it onto the main highway and spotted him way ahead. He was weaving wildly in and out of traffic, and I pushed the Enfield as far as it could possibly go.

Suddenly I saw him veer sharply into the lane for Cross Harbour Tunnel, but then, at the very last moment, he swerved back onto the main highway, causing a fuel lorry to do an emergency stop, narrowly missing a pair of red taxis. *Crazy damn lunatic.*

Suddenly, he began to slow down. 'He's phoning India,' shouted my eyes and ears. 'Charles is hacked in. It's foreign language gibberish, but he's on it with translation software. By the way, he's the one who worked out that they were coming to try to take you and your family out.'

'I owe him big time,' I yelled.

By now, he'd slowed down even more, and I imagined him frantically weighing up his options. 'Translated,' blurted out McPherson. 'He's to kill you at any cost. If he doesn't, all his relatives will be slaughtered back in northern India.'

'Fucking animals.'

By now I wasn't far behind him, and at that moment, his car swerved dangerously again, and I watched him accelerate and shoot down a slip road towards an industrial part of North Point. He slowed as he approached an ageing multistorey car park, and after a bit of hesitation, he drove up the entry ramp. I saw him peering back to make sure I was following. He was luring me in, and one way or another, this whole thing was going to be settled in there.

'Peter. *Don't go in.* He's too dangerous. And I don't know if I can track him well in there.'

'No way. I'm going in.' With McPherson trying her level best to dissuade me, I rode the bike cautiously up the ramp and parked just by the entrance. 'I'm going on foot.'

'Why not take the lift up to the top and work down?' she suggested. Liking the idea, I sprinted silently across the tarmac straight into the open cabin, where I hit the button for the eighth and top floor. Creaking and shuddering, the contraption began its climb. When it finally arrived, the doors clunked open and I dashed for the cover of an abandoned van sitting up on blocks.

'The police are on their way, Peter. The first car is four minutes out.' I could hear sirens in the distance. He'd hear them too.

'I'm on eight and I'll start going down,' I whispered to McPherson. I took the gun out of my waistband.

'He's cornered. Take care.'

Crouching low, I began to creep down the ramp towards seven, every few seconds peering over the ramp wall to check if I could see him below.

There was no sign of him on seven or six, and just as I started going down to five, I heard a helicopter hovering somewhere above. His options were closing by the second, and I could only imagine what thoughts of self-preservation were going through his mind.

I heard a noise below. Footsteps. Voices.

Crouching low, I peered over and below me, to my horror, I watched as he marched a young mother and her child at gunpoint towards a parked car. I whispered an update to McPherson.

'I'll let the police know there are hostages,' she said calmly, the word 'hostages' sending a shiver down my spine. The stakes were now sky-high.

'Don't worry, Jay,' I heard the lady say bravely to the child. 'This nice man is just playing a really fun game with us.' Then in a cheery voice, she asked him, 'What would you like us to do, sir? Do you want some money, or do you want the keys to our car?'

'Get in the car,' I heard him snap. 'Strap up the kid and drive me out of here. I'll be in the back, and if you don't do what I say, I'll shoot him in the head.'

'Oh, dear god,' she said, putting her hand up to her mouth. 'Please don't hurt us.' Then she just lost it, bursting into tears, completely consumed with shock and fear.

'*Shut up!*' he screamed, and he shoved her against the car, causing the boy to start howling. Then, without warning, the kid bolted across the tarmac towards a row of parked cars.

'McPherson, it's spiralling out of control. The kid's on the run.'

'*No, Jay!*' shrieked the woman. 'Come back. *Come back.*' She started lashing out at the Indian, who flung her to the ground and slowly raised the gun. He was going to shoot her. For sure.

'It's me you want,' I yelled, standing up on the ramp and waving my arms in the air. 'Just let her go and you can have me.' I started walking down the ramp towards them.

'No. He'll kill you!' shouted McPherson in my ear. She wasn't wrong. Without a moment of hesitation, he started running at me, firing as he went. With bullets ricocheting around the parking lot, I ran for my life back up the ramp.

Close to the top, heart pounding, I looked back, expecting he'd be at the bottom but, holy Christ, he was much, much closer, and as I tore round the corner, he let loose another volley.

I'd never felt terror like this. He was so damned fast. And armed. And I had nothing.

Hiding was my only option. In the precious seconds I had until he'd get to the top, I scrambled like a madman up the back of a tall parked lorry, crawled onto its blue tarpaulin roof and lay flat, bricking myself with fear. All I could do was hope and pray that he hadn't seen me and that I'd bought enough time for the police to get there and save me.

'What's happening?' whispered McPherson. 'I keep hearing gunshots.'

'Can't talk,' I whispered. I could hear him. He was very, very close.

In fact, he was just down below at the front of the lorry, talking on his phone. I could even hear the other person giving him what sounded like a tirade of abuse. Very quietly I slid forward on my front, inch by inch, and when I got up to the lip, I looked over.

There he was. Phone in hand. Saying nothing, just listening, taking the flak. All the while, he was scouring around looking for me, and now he was moving between my lorry and the one alongside, towards the rear. What if he'd seen me climb onto the roof? I'd thought he hadn't, but if I was wrong and he had, that would be me. He'd climb up and gun me down like a sitting duck.

I was about to explode with the tension.

Do something, Peter, I screamed at myself.

Chapter 76

A millisecond before I landed on him, he looked up. But he was too late. He had been crouching, looking under the lorry, when I'd jumped.

The full force of my body hit the base of his neck and as I hit the ground, I was on him, wrapping my legs around his head. With an almighty wrench and twist of my body, I broke his neck. It was over in seconds with a sickening sound like a whip cracking. A sound I'd never forget.

'Peter!' gasped McPherson. 'What was that?'

'He's dead. It's over.' I released my leg hold and sat and stared at my latest victim while the gory details of all my kills and near kills flashed before me. Knife in throat. Asphyxiation. Blood-sprayed headshot. Waterboarding. Knifings. Forehead shot. Snapped neck.

'Another two today and it's still only mid-afternoon. Why me? Why?'

'You had no choice. It was them or you.' She was calm now and reassuring. 'You survived, and that's all that matters. You did brilliantly.'

The police arrived a few minutes later. After I'd told them what had happened, they took me down to where an ambulance was waiting, but I refused their suggestion that I go to HK University Hospital for a thorough check-up. My father's body was there in the morgue, and probably Mr and Mrs Peng's too, and I didn't want to go anywhere near the place. Plus I just needed to be alone.

As I was climbing out of the ambulance, a senior officer in full uniform was waiting for me. 'I'm Commander Ng, today's officer in charge. You're not going, are you?' he said calmly, shaking my hand. 'It would be good if you could take me through what happened.'

'If I'm not under arrest, can it wait? I've briefed your guys already and I need some head space.'

'No arrest, Mr Peter.' He smiled. 'In fact, quite the opposite. We've been liaising with your Commander Burke throughout the afternoon as everything unfolded. He sends his regards.'

'He's not *my* Commander,' I said quietly, barely hearing him, consumed by my latest killings.

'He said you wouldn't fail and that you'd do everything you could to save the woman and her child.'

'Well done to Mr Burke.' I sighed. 'It's good to know that he knows me so well.'

'Indeed?' he replied, picking up on my sarcasm, and he handed me his card. 'Call me later when you're ready and I'll come to see you for a statement.'

'Of course,' I murmured, feeling the beginnings of dark clouds descending on me once again.

As I started the Enfield, I thought about the old Sikh. He'd so nearly wiped out the entire Black family, and he was still out there. If he'd been in Hong Kong, I'd have gone right now, found him and pulled his limbs off one by one.

Chapter 77

Leaving North Point on the bike, I called the Commander. 'Peter. First-class job. Are you OK?'

'I'm fine, but I need something from you. You owe me one for Parliament and I want to call it in.'

'Go on ...' he said a little nervously. 'Ask away.'

I didn't beat about the bush. 'I want him dead. Either your team does it or I'll do it myself.'

There was a moment of silence from the Commander before he replied. 'I'm sending you footage from an Indian news channel from earlier today. Rest up and I'll see you in London at the Service.' Then he was gone. Maybe he knew he was going to get an earful for what he'd said to Ng.

It took some time for the Commander's link to arrive. When it did, I pulled into a side street in Tin Hau, and as I walked up a steep set of steps towards a tiny Chinese temple overlooking the harbour, I began to watch the clip. Any feelings of depression quickly lifted.

It was a scene of total carnage—four burned-out vehicles sitting at the side of a busy highway and a commentator describing the convoy having been ambushed and attacked by grenade launchers. The report went on to say that the deceased were believed to be members of a Sikh-run international crime syndicate and the gang's octogenarian patriarch was believed to be one of the dead. The convoy had been returning from the funeral of its leader.

I couldn't believe what I was seeing. Someone very powerful had taken the decision to wipe out the gang, and they'd hit hard and decisively. I tried calling the Commander again, but he didn't pick up. He'd of course deny any responsibility, but surely he must have had a hand in it, and maybe even Nilay had been involved or perhaps Burke's pals from ISS. Whoever it was, I owed them big time.

I tried McPherson and when she picked up, I asked her if she'd seen the footage. She hadn't, and when I forwarded it on to her, I heard her gasp as she watched it. 'Justice served,' she said quietly when it had finished. 'The question is, by whom? Although I guess we'll never know for sure. But the most important thing is that you and your family hopefully don't need to worry about them anymore and we can get on with the job of finding out who contracted them in the first place.'

'Will you thank Charles unreservedly?' I said, changing the subject. 'He pulled out all the stops today.'

'Of course. And what now? Where are you?'

'I'm sitting at a temple about to pray for forgiveness,' I said half-jokingly. 'The fact that I've killed five people in ten days isn't resting well with me one bit.'

'I don't know what to say, Peter, but I wish I was there with you to help you to make sense of it all. You sound very lonely.'

'I *am* lonely, McPherson, and I'm—' But I stopped, not wanting to sound weak.

'You're what, Peter? Come on. You can tell me. I'm your eyes and ears, after all.'

'It's embarrassing, but I'm getting, like, these waves of darkness flooding over me. It must be depression or PTSD or something.'

'Of course you are, and you wouldn't be human if you weren't.' She was back in kind, compassionate McPherson mode. 'You shouldn't beat yourself up, you know. You're a wonderful kind human being who just happens to have become mixed up in the most awful situation, and you should feel proud of the way you've gone about everything.'

'I've convinced myself that when all the news finally leaks out, my friends, flatmates and probably even my family will never treat me the same again.' It was only as I said the words that I realised just how afraid I was of this. 'Forevermore I'll be known as the guy who killed a bunch of people, and it's as if I've lost my innocence. Then there's Ofelia. She's been incredibly understanding, but what on earth is she—never mind her parents—going to think after everything that's happened today? If she has any sense, she'll run as far from me as she possibly can.'

'Rubbish, Peter. That's nonsense. I can't believe that anyone will hold it against you, and in any case, once the whole thing has blown over, things will soon get back to normal. Trust me, everything is going to be fine, and in fact, I think people will see you as being brave and noble.'

'When it's all over, I'm going to have to get help. I'm resigned to that.'

'Yes, just like I had to and still do, and you'll find that it helps enormously.'

I gave a long sigh, then started thinking ahead. 'Any progress yet on finding the paymaster?'

'Not yet. We'll get there.'

'I'm going to fly to London on Monday afternoon straight after the Hong Kong ceremony. I'll get in very early on Tuesday morning. I'm really hoping that you and Charles will have something by then. You'll really try, won't you?'

'Leave it with us, Peter.' She hated people nagging her and telling her what to do.

After finishing our call, I headed home. In theory, I was supposed to be joining Mum and Sam in a safe house, but there wasn't a hope in hell that anyone would get me to do that. My home was my home.

As I climbed Victoria Peak on the Enfield, the gruesome images from India played vividly in my mind and I wondered if Nilay really had been involved. Could I imagine him going into attack mode and firing grenade launchers at the Sikhs? Yes, I probably could, and a part of me wished that I'd been there too, helping to rid the world of my father's murderers.

Chapter 78

The next twenty-four hours spiralled into a total disaster that I wished I could have erased.

Mum and Sam returned home late in the evening, and as we sat in the kitchen, stress levels began to rise as I told them about what had been going on. I didn't even tell them about the two attacks on me in St Andrews or anything about Jo and Green. But when I told them about confronting the sweeper in Mong Kok and then the Sikhs in Delhi, my mother went off at the deep end. As a family, we never fought, but there in the kitchen, all three of us exchanged extremely harsh words. By the end of it, I ended up storming out and disappearing off on the Enfield. 'You'll not see me at the fucking funeral tomorrow,' were my parting words as I slammed the back door off its hinges.

I spent the night in a cheap hotel way up in the New Territories, licking my wounds, wishing that I hadn't said all that I'd said and wishing that my mum and sister hadn't said what they'd said. My mother had accused me of putting everyone in danger and I'd accused her of not being grateful for all that I had done. Poor Sam had been caught in the middle, and she'd lashed out at both of us. The wounds were open and raw, and I wasn't going to be the one trying to seek rapprochement. Fuck, if only they knew what I'd done in London. I'd saved countless lives and all my mother could say was that I was a 'stupid child running around trying to set the world to rights'.

More wound up than I'd ever been in my life and drinking heavily, it wasn't until 5 a.m. that I fell asleep, but not before I'd thrown a whisky glass straight through the TV screen. The channels were wall to wall with what had happened, but it was the reporting on Ofelia and her description as 'Peter Black's secret lover' that made me hurl the glass in rage.

The service was at 10 a.m., but I didn't even wake up until 9.30. Of course I was going to go to my father's funeral, and after a suicidal dash on the Enfield, I walked down the aisle at 10.20 and took my place beside my mother and sister. Anyone could see that we'd had an almighty bust-up, and sure enough, by lunchtime the news channels were all over it and, of course, the good name of Black & Co. was taking a beating when it least needed it. My father would have been beyond livid.

If he had been looking down, however, he would have seen old friends paying their final respects to a fine and super-talented human being. The minister presided over it all wonderfully, and his précis of my father's life couldn't have been more perfectly delivered. As I sat there in my own little world, with a shiver running down my spine, I wondered how my own life story might end up being written. On its current trajectory, it was likely to be an extremely short one.

During the final hymn, amidst stares of shock and surprise from the congregation, I left and headed to the house to pack my bag for London. I didn't give a flying fuck what they all thought. There was only one thing on my mind, and that was to find the people who'd ordered the killing. They had murdered my father. Wrecked my life. I was going to hunt them to the end.

As I boarded my flight that evening, hiding behind sunglasses and an oversized hoodie, I got the text I'd been waiting for. 'Finally identified him. Lives in West London. Meet me at my flat when you arrive. Safe flight. Really hope you are OK?'

Chapter 79

I made it swiftly through Heathrow Arrivals, jumped in a cab and headed straight to the Mandarin, where the GM, Karsten, personally met me as the taxi drew up.

'Welcome back, Mr Black, and so good to see you again,' he said in his very Austrian way, and he courteously let me know how sorry he was to have heard the tragic news about my father. He would be attending the service on Wednesday.

I dumped my bag, freshened up a bit and slipped quietly out of the hotel. After a refreshing ten-minute walk, I found McPherson's apartment block, which was halfway down Sloane Street and a couple of streets to the west. As I stood outside the elegant red brick building, I called her from my mobile.

'Hey, McPherson! It's me. I'm standing down in the street!'

'I'll buzz you in.'

The tiny lift reminded me of the one the ancient Chinese lady and I had shared in Mong Kok, and as it climbed, I began to get a strange feeling—a weird sort of apprehension—about meeting McPherson. I was totally excited to be seeing her again, but it occurred to me that I'd only actually spent two or three hours in her (physical) company despite the huge amount we'd been through together. It all felt rather weird, but I guessed that she might be feeling a little strange too.

As the lift doors opened, I walked out onto the small landing and there she was, sitting in her chair in her entranceway with a huge smile on her face. 'Wow, McPherson does smile after all,' I said jokingly as I walked towards her.

'Only on special occasions.' She laughed, putting her arms out, and I knelt down and we hugged as though we'd known one another for years. 'You look pretty awful, Peter, but all things considered, I was expecting a little worse.'

'I'm feeling pretty weird, to be honest,' I said, standing again and smiling at her awkwardly. 'I feel as though I've known you for years, but I also feel as though I don't know the first thing about you.'

'Me too, solider,' she said jokingly, beckoning me into her hallway. 'Let me give you the grand tour and then we can have some breakfast in the living room. I agree it's strange. A bit like internet dating, I guess—not that that's my kind of thing!' she said hastily, blushing.

Her apartment was stunning, a treasure trove of antiquities from all over the world, and most especially the Middle East. 'This was Mum and Dad's London pad,' she said with a distant smile. 'They collected wherever they went. When I moved in, I hated it all at first—it brought back memories—but as time has gone on, I've learned to appreciate everything. There's an interesting little story behind each trinket.'

'It's spectacular,' I said, browsing around the living room, stopping momentarily to pick up an Aladdin-style ornate curved dagger that was lying on top of a pile of letters.

'That's my oversized letter opener,' she said with an ironic little laugh, but then her voice wavered. 'The old man in the souk said it was a lucky dagger, then three days later ... my parents were dead.'

I put a hand on her shoulder. 'I'm so sorry, Christine.' She gave my hand a little pat and regained her cheer.

'Such is life.'

We had breakfast and started talking about general stuff—her apartment, her neighbours, how her grandfather was doing—and soon she was telling me about Michael Bailey, the person she'd identified as the man the Sikhs had met at the pub at Richmond riverside.

'He works in the city as Chief Information Officer for a large American IT company. But on the day that your Sikh friends met him in Richmond, he was anything but a CIO,' she explained. 'It took Charles and me forever to work it out—he's a master of disguise—but finally, we did. To cut a long story short, he arrived by tube at Richmond as a vagrant, and ten minutes after going into the public toilets carrying his life in filthy polythene bags, he reappeared as a respectable country gent carrying a small suitcase, no doubt full of money. After doing a few circuits around town, he headed down to the river for the meet.'

'Wow, amazing detective work!'

'At first, we couldn't find any trace of him going into or leaving the pub, but eventually, we, or rather Charles, had the brainwave of hacking into the CCTV system of the Thames Pleasure Boat Company, which has boats passing by the pub every fifteen minutes.'

'Charles strikes again!'

'A regular genius.'

'We caught him darting in the side entrance, and while we have no footage from inside the pub, we know the Sikh from St Andrews had been inside for quite some time while the younger one hung around outside on watch.'

McPherson then described how Bailey, minus suitcase, made his way back to the tube station and went into the toilets again before re-emerging as the vagrant. He'd then hopped on the District Line, getting off a few stops down the line at Turnham Green, where he'd backtracked on foot towards Kew, where it transpired he lived.

'He has a wife, four children and a whacking great salary, and Charles managed to hack into his home computer system and found traces of him having been on the dark web. And ...' she said with a worried look on her face.

'And what?'

'It turns out that our Mr Bailey has a military background.'

'*Really?* What kind of military? Air or sea or land?'

'He went straight from undergrad at Durham University into military intelligence, and then it looks like he went into combat roles, seeing action in Serbia, the Middle East, Africa and other places. It's really difficult to get detailed info on him, which suggests he may have been Special Forces. Then, aged 35, he left the military and rose through the ranks in a series of different companies selling IT hardware and software. The wifey,' McPherson went on, 'is a *very* successful architect who designs fancy shopping malls all over the world. The kids are 5, 11, 13 and 15 and attend private schools in West London. She's in the United States this week on business.'

'Right. So what's our plan?' I said, standing up. 'I need to question him.'

'Steady. Special Forces are lethal. We must leave him to Burke's people.'

'Garbage. Special Forces or no Special Forces, he's mine. If we ask for help, they'll either take too long or they'll screw it up, and they most certainly won't let me be involved. It was my father he killed and my life that's been screwed up. I *need* to do this.'

'No, Peter,' she said firmly. 'I won't allow it. This time is different, and I'll not let you go and get killed. Plus it's clear that you're not in a fit emotional state. You're all over the news and—'

'*Fit emotional state!* Let me be the judge of that. Yes, I'm angry. Yes, I'm tired. Yes, I'm plastered all over the press. Yes, my life's gone to fuck. But I get things done and I'll keep going until we get to the end of this whole thing. Whatever it takes to get to the truth, right?'

'Peter, I genuinely believe that you're out of control,' she said gently, coming over to me in her chair and clasping my hand. 'Come on. Please. Let's call in help. You've done amazingly, amazingly well and you've got us this far, but *please* let's call in the Commander and the might of his team.'

'McPherson, *please*,' I sighed, relaxing a bit. 'I just *have* to get on with this. If you don't want to join me, I'll completely understand, but *please* just give me the address in Kew.'

She leaned back in her chair, stared up at the ceiling and, in a fit of resignation and frustration, gave a long, low dog-like growl before looking at me and pointing a finger at me. 'On one condition!'

'That depends on what it is.' I smiled.

'Nilay is here in London. Will you take him with you?'

'He's here? My god, of course I'll take him. Christ, we couldn't have done Delhi without him.'

'Stubbornness will get you killed one day. Do you know that?'

'Rubbish. Let's get moving. All systems go. We do it this morning.' My adrenaline was kicking in.

After a long sigh, she picked up the phone to call Nilay. 'Are you *sure*?' she said, checking one last time. 'I've got such an ominous feeling about all of this.' A solitary tear rolled down her cheek.

'Everything will be fine,' I said, gently wiping away the tear with my shirt sleeve.

I had an ominous feeling too, but I was beyond caring.

Chapter 80

Nilay had only arrived from Delhi in the small hours and despite his head wound, didn't give it a second thought when asked for help. Within an hour, we'd hatched a simple plan.

McPherson was to call Bailey at his office in the city pretending to be from the friendly estate agent located in Kew Village. She'd tell him that while passing his house that morning, she'd spotted a burst pipe which was causing significant damage to the property. The hope was that he'd come back from the city to deal with it and Nilay and I would confront him. McPherson would make the call at about 10 a.m. and Nilay and I would meet up in Kew village at about 10.45 to wait for Bailey.

From McPherson's, I went back to the Mandarin for a shower and change of clothes, but as I approached the building, I saw the now-familiar press beginning to gather outside. They must have been tipped off, so I snuck around to the back and got security to call Karsten. A few minutes later I was back in my room.

Before I jumped into the shower, I noticed that Trudy had sent me a WhatsApp, and rather than message her back, I gave her a call. I'd received hundreds of messages over the last few days—including quite a few from my flatmates—and hadn't replied to any of them. I simply couldn't put her off anymore.

'Peter, thank god you called,' she said as soon as she picked up. 'We can't believe what happened to you in Hong Kong. It's horrible. Is your family OK? It's all over the news and the whole town is talking about it.'

'I bet they are,' I replied, my anger tickled. 'And yes, Sam and Mum are fine.'

'Thank goodness. And are you yourself OK? I mean, the news is saying that you *killed* two people. Is that true? I mean, did you really do it? Are you hurt?'

'There's a damn good reason for all of it,' I lashed out. 'Now why don't you—'

'Stop,' she cut in. 'I'm so sorry. I really am. I shouldn't have said anything. It's all still so raw.'

I felt awful. We'd never had a moment like that before. 'Listen, I'm truly sorry. Really, I am. It's … it's the situation. It's … it's sort of out of control. Please forgive me.'

'No, no, not at all. Don't worry, I'm fine. *We're* fine.'

As I sat there on the end of my bed, it really hit me that nothing would ever be the same again. It would be impossible to fit back into university life after everything that had happened. Impossible to get my old life back with my friends. There was no way I could go back.

'Hey, are you still there?' she called with a nervous little laugh.

'I'm here. I was just thinking about how difficult it's going to be to come back to uni after all this stuff. I'm not sure I'll be able to fit in again.'

'No, Peter. We'll help,' she said positively. 'It'll be tough, but we'll all rally round and we'll *make* it work. I promise you.'

'Let's see.' I wasn't so sure. 'And sorry again, Trudy. I didn't mean to hurt your feelings.'

'Will you call me again, maybe tomorrow?' she asked. 'It's important to talk. Don't go MIA on me again, please.'

'Of course.'

After my shower, as I was getting ready, there was a little knock at the door. It was Karsten again, warning me that both front and rear were now mobbed by the press. However, like all good hotel GMs, he had a plan, and ten minutes later I was being ferried in the hotel's laundry van and dropped at South Kensington tube station. From there I'd take the District Line to Kew.

As I stood on the platform waiting, McPherson called and patched in Nilay. 'Good news. Bailey fell for it "hook, line", and he's just left his office. I'm guessing it will take him just under an hour to get back. I'm tracking his journey.'

'Great work. I'm just getting on a tube at South Ken. What about you, Nilay?'

'I'm on a bus due to reach Kew in thirty minutes. We'll get there more or less at the same time.'

My journey out to Kew was fine. To be on the safe side, I sat in the last carriage with my sunglasses on and hood up, my face buried in one of the free dailies. When the train arrived, I walked out into beautiful Kew Village, found a corner café and called Nilay again.

'I'm arriving in a few minutes. You?'

I explained where I was, then patched in McPherson. 'What's the latest on Bailey?'

'He's seventeen minutes out, five trains behind the one you took. I can see that you're in a coffee shop just down from Kew Gardens and Nilay, you're just about to arrive on your bus?'

'Nilay, I suggest you go to the Starbucks a few doors up from me, take a window seat and once he's passed by, we can follow him to his house.'

'Sounds good except for the Starbucks part. I hate that dishwater!' he joked, trying to ease the growing tension.

'That's why I opted for the café with the Illy sign.' I laughed.

'My god,' exclaimed McPherson. 'What's with all the silly banter? This is serious stuff. Anyway, whatever!' She sighed. 'I'll call you both as his train approaches.' And she hung up.

Still hiding beneath my hoodie and glasses, I ordered an espresso from the Polish girl at the counter, then took a spot by the window and browsed through the café's *Telegraph*. Christ! The first three pages were devoted to my exploits in Hong Kong, the funeral, my father's life, the damage done to Black & Co., and more. The only thing it didn't mention was my family's monumental bust-up—one for the *Sun* and the *Star* no doubt.

McPherson called as Bailey arrived, and with Nilay in position in Starbucks, my adrenaline began to kick in. I'd been waiting for it, hoping it would come, almost craving it. I loved that feeling of alertness. The sharpened vision. The strength and speed. Was it becoming my drug? My addiction?

'He's off the train and walking towards you both. Nilay, can you see him? Blue suit, open-neck white shirt, brown shoes, red socks. He's walking past Starbucks right ... *now*.'

'Roger that. He's just passed by. Seems relaxed and confident. Fit. Mid to late forties.'

'*Fuck,*' cursed McPherson.

'What is it?' I whispered.

'He might be heading for your café.'

Chapter 81

I kept my head down, reading my paper, and the bell jangled as the door opened. I glanced up—as naturally as possible—and the tall man in the blue suit gave me and the one other customer a friendly little nod. 'Good morning, Agnieszka,' he bellowed, striding up to the counter. He didn't strike me as a person who might have a sideline engaging with hit squads. Was McPherson's intel wrong?

'Hello, Mr Michael, what can I get for you? This isn't your usual time.' The corner café I'd chosen must have been his local, probably where he'd pick up a morning coffee on his way to the tube.

'A single espresso please, my darling. It seems I have to check on the house—but there's always time for a shot of caffeine in my favourite café served by my favourite Polish lady. Could you take it over there?' he said, pointing towards the table beside mine.

'That's fine, Mr Michael. I'll bring it in a moment.' As I remained buried in my paper, I heard his footsteps approaching.

'Excuse me, lad,' he said as he sat down. 'Would you mind if I read the business section?' He nodded towards the supplement sitting on the corner of my table.

'All yours,' I replied, my heart beating like mad. I didn't even dare look up.

'Quite dramatic, that whole affair over in Hong Kong,' he said, pointing at my open paper. My whole body tensed up. God. Was he on to me, or was he just making small talk? I *had* to keep my nerve.

'Sure,' I replied as calmly as possible but without making eye contact. That was all I was giving him. Hopefully, he'd get the message that I didn't want to talk to him.

'The *Telegraph* is *such* a good read, isn't it?' he went on. 'Far better than the *Guardian*, which always manages to bore me to tears.' The waitress appeared and put his coffee down.

'Anything else, Mr Michael?' she asked before turning to me. 'Another coffee, sir?'

'No thanks, Agnieszka darling, the espresso is just fine. I'm not sure about my friend?'

'Thank you, no,' I replied, and she stared at me for a moment before going back to her coffee station. *Shit*, had she recognised me? I glanced over at her and caught her staring again, then she started tapping into her phone, probably searching for my photo.

He continued talking. 'You have a bit of an unusual accent, if you don't mind me saying. Very subtle but perhaps with a bit of a Scottish tinge. Am I close?' My adrenaline hit was rapidly being replaced with a surge of fear. He must be on to me—but I couldn't be sure. Maybe he was just one of those chatterboxes who talked to everyone. He seemed reasonably likeable.

'Nope,' I replied bluntly, draining my espresso.

'I could have sworn there was a little something in there.' He sighed. 'Oh, by the way, I do like those shoes of yours. Really quite snazzy. I'd love to know where you got them.'

I looked down at the leather shoes that my father's cobbler in Hong Kong had handmade in his little shack on Pedder Street. 'Oh, these are great, aren't they? An old geezer up in Camden makes them, and I swear by them.' If he could talk utter nonsense to me, I could do the same to him.

'Careful,' whispered McPherson in my ear.

'Two more espressos, please, Agnieszka,' he called over to her before turning to me. 'Allow me to shout you one. And apologies, I'm notorious for chatting to people.' He stood up. 'Anyway, back in a jiffy. Nature calls.' He strode across the café towards the toilets at the back.

'He's playing you, Peter. Isn't he, Nilay?' said McPherson worriedly.

'I don't like the sound of him one bit. I'm on my way,' cut in Nilay.

'Ah, that's much better,' said Bailey, returning far more quickly than I thought he would. 'I find I'm having to take a micro wizz rather a lot these days. Must be these new meds.'

With that, the door opened and Nilay walked in and wandered casually up to the counter. 'An americano, please, love, and a piece of that nice-looking gingerbread. What about a nice dollop of fresh cream on top too?' It reminded me of his famous acting routine on the dirt track in Delhi.

'I used to be in the military, years ago,' Bailey said suddenly, looking straight at me as if trying to get the measure of me. Thank fuck I had my shades on.

'Active duty?' I replied, staring back at him. Inside I was trying hard to get a grip on myself.

'Lots of it, I'm afraid. Battles, skirmishes, hand-to-hand combat, death, lost colleagues, the lot. It all takes its toll, and it just sort of sits there in the background, always there and always happy to come back to haunt you if you're one of the unlucky ones. You know, I used to be able to look in my soldiers' eyes and spot the ones that were going to crack with PTSD. I was right every time.'

I felt myself squirm and looked away.

'Such a talent must have been in Special Forces?' I countered. I was beginning to detest him.

'I couldn't possibly say,' he replied, sitting back in his seat and stretching his legs out as our espressos arrived. 'But I miss it, to be honest. The camaraderie. The friendship. It's so different to the day-in, day-out snipping and backstabbing that you get in a big corporation.'

'This is too weird for me,' whispered McPherson. 'I don't like it one bit. Isn't it time to get out?'

At that moment, a blushing Agnieszka arrived with our espressos, and I had a sense of what was coming. 'Excuse me, sir. Can I ask? It's been frustrating me so much. Aren't you that guy from Hong Kong who fought off those armed criminals?'

'Not me,' I said calmly, shaking my head. 'You're not the first to ask, though.' After apologising profusely, she scurried off into the back.

'Looks like you're busted, Peter.' Bailey smirked, picking up his espresso and taking a sip. 'God, this stuff is good,' he said, licking the foam from his top lip. 'Only Arabic coffee comes anywhere close.'

'Jesus,' whispered McPherson. 'The egotistical prick has been spying on us.'

Keeping my cool, as Nilay pulled up a chair, I slipped off my hood and my glasses.

'Why have my father killed, Bailey? Let's stop the fucking around.'

'So good you could join us, Mr Kumar,' he said, smiling at Nilay, 'and especially after all your fun and games in India. The last time I saw anything like that was in Serbia. And so nice to see you up close, Peter. Aren't those eyes of yours just fascinating? I'm sure I've seen that haunted, troubled look somewhere before.'

'Don't rise to the bait,' said McPherson sternly. 'He's trying to mess with your mind.' She was dam, right and, close to launching myself at him, I took a long deep breath and went to take another sip of my espresso.

'*Stop. Wait a second.* Don't drink it,' he said abruptly.

'What's going on?' whispered McPherson. I froze, the tiny cup inches away from my mouth.

'Can you be sure that I didn't spike your coffee? Maybe when you were looking at your shoes? Or when you looked up at your cake-loving friend Nilay as he walked in? Maybe you've already ingested it and your airways are about to start to contract. Maybe you're already dying.' He laughed.

'Maybe I could blow your bollocks off with the gun I'm pointing at you,' growled Nilay.

I started sweating. *Had* the nutter poisoned me?

'You could do, my British Indian friend. But if you did, you'd never find out who ordered the death of Peter's father. What a wasted journey you'd both have had!'

'Have you poisoned me?' I said quietly.

'That's better, Peter. A little less excited,' he said condescendingly. 'No, I haven't, but I could have if I'd wanted to.' He put his hand inside his jacket and pulled out a see-through bag full of tiny white pills and waved them in front of me. 'Or I could have snapped your neck. I was a bit of an expert neck breaker back in the day. Maybe we should compare notes on technique? That little boy and his mother were very lucky that it was you in that car park and not some run-of-the-mill bloke.'

'Go fuck yourself, freak,' I yelled, jumping to my feet.

But just as I was about to go for him, the café door burst open.

Jesus, what's he doing here?

Chapter 82

'Oh my, if it isn't Mr Burke,' said Bailey slowly, clapping his hands as the Commander walked in, flanked by two of his men. 'What a wonderful surprise. I had no idea that my new friends Peter and Nilay moved in such illustrious circles.'

'Three snipers have you in their cross hairs, Bailey,' said the Commander, sitting down opposite him, 'so don't try anything silly or you're a dead man.'

'Ah, I thought I saw some movement up on the hotel roof up there.' Bailey nodded to the street. 'But I sincerely hope you wouldn't authorise the shooting one of your own, Commander Burke.'

'You stopped being one of us long ago.' The Commander chuckled as two more of his men appeared from the back and led the one other customer and Agnieszka away. 'OK, Bailey, it's time to talk. You can either do it here, freely, or we can always take you to one of our little warehouses down by the Thames. I think you know the drill?'

'I know the drill well.' Bailey nodded, looking completely unfazed.

'Yes, you do, but we both know that no matter how hard we squeeze, you'll never talk.' He turned to me. 'Peter, if I were to tell you that no amount of torture could get this man to speak, what would you do to him to get him to tell you who'd paid him to kill your father?'

Before I could say anything, Bailey sat up pertly and started mimicking my accent. 'Oh, Commander, I'd torture one of his children or his wife until he spilled the beans.' Then he turned to me. 'Pray tell, Peter, is that what you'd have said?'

'No need to respond,' said the Commander. 'He's famous for his psychological mind games and, if I'm not mistaken, his comrades used to call him Psycho Bailey. Am I correct, Bailey?'

'No comment,' he replied with a tinge of annoyance in his voice before putting his hands behind his head and leaning back in his chair again, ultra-relaxed. 'Allow me to congratulate you on spotting such a winner in Black. I see a young lad prepared to go all the way to get the job done, just the way you like them. I'd imagine uni recruitment has had him in its sights for quite a while. Remind me of the name of that old fart up there in St Andrews. It's Bob McPherson, if I recall?'

I couldn't contain myself and lunged at him, aiming for the base of his nose with my palm. Do it right, driving the nose bone up through the brain, and it's deadly.

I'd moved fast, but he was faster. He grabbed my arm, twisted me around and put me in a headlock, and I suddenly felt the most agonising pain in my neck. He was pressing something into my neck harder and harder, and I could feel myself losing consciousness. I couldn't hold on. He was going to kill me.

'Not even your snipers can stop me from killing him, can they, Commander?'

'No, they can't,' said a totally unflustered Commander. 'Now, get on with it if you have to.'

'I can see why you got all the way to the top, you cold-hearted bastard.' Bailey laughed sardonically, releasing his finger and shoving me to the floor. 'Now, be a good boy, Peter, and go sit back down where you belong, or I really will kill you.'

Close to puking, gasping for oxygen, I crawled back to my chair and pulled myself up onto it. I'd never felt so useless and humiliated in my entire life.

'Don't worry,' whispered McPherson. 'Special Forces. That's what they're trained to do.'

'I'll do a deal,' said Bailey out of the blue.

'A deal?' The Commander smiled, raising an eyebrow. 'Murderers don't usually have a great deal of bargaining power.'

'Let me explain ...'

'We're listening,' said the Commander, glancing over at Nilay and me, 'and it had better be good.'

'Why would I do a deal?' he continued. 'It's quite simple, really. A few days ago, my kind doctor told me I've got stage four cancer eating away at my guts and I'll be dead before the month is out. I may look fighting fit, but as one would say, I'm right royally screwed.'

'That's very sad,' said the Commander, not sounding at all sad. 'What's the deal, Bailey?'

'Allow me to die in peace at home with my family and in return, I'll try to help you find the people who wanted James Black dead.' He glanced over at me as he said my father's name.

'You'll *try*,' replied the Commander. 'It'll have to be a lot more than try.'

'Listen, Burke. Everything is done on the dark web, and I've never met these people in my life. But there was a development yesterday which may present an opportunity.'

'What development?' said the Commander, becoming visibly frustrated. 'Get on with it. We don't have all day.'

Bailey continued. 'The proponent put out a fresh hit on the dark web yesterday. I happen to be the preferred contractor, and the final negotiations take place this evening at 8 p.m. It's maybe an opportunity to try to flush them out of the shadows—assuming you agree to my terms.'

'A new bounty. Who is the target?' asked Nilay.

But before he could answer, a little girl and an older boy, both in school uniform, walked past the window. The girl, catching sight of Bailey, suddenly stopped and hammered on the glass. 'God, it's my youngest with my son,' he said, jumping up and beckoning them towards the door. 'Ask the chap at the door to let them in, will you, Commander?'

'Daddy, Daddy. You're home early!' yelled the little girl, bursting into the café past the bouncer.

'Yes, Poppet,' he said, scooping her into his arms, and she immediately clung to his neck and burst into tears. 'Timmy, what's going on with Poppet?' he said to his son as he walked in.

'Emelia has been poorly, Dad, and she wanted to go home to bed. She came to my class, so I decided just to bring her myself. I have prep all afternoon and can do it from home.'

'Good thinking,' said Bailey, putting his hand affectionately on his son's head. 'She does look a bit green and pasty, doesn't she?'

'Who are your friends, Daddy?' asked Emelia, lifting her head weakly from his shoulder.

'Oh, this is my old friend Mr Burke. We used to work together, and we were meeting for a quick coffee to catch up on old times. These are his two friends Peter and Mr Kumar.'

'Daddy, please, please don't go on that long adventure that you talked about last night. I think it's the thought of it that's making me feel poorly.'

'Oh, dear Poppet.' He pulled her close to his chest and I looked on in astonishment at how he'd just morphed from mental case to kind, loving father. 'Don't worry, tiny thing. We'll talk about that later, darling, but now it's time to get you to bed.' He then turned to the Commander. 'With your permission, sir, I'll take her home. We can meet later, and I promise I'll try my level best to help.' As he said it, he glanced briefly at me, almost seeking my blessing. I shook my head in astonishment.

'Let's do that,' replied the Commander. 'A car and a couple of my lads will collect you at 6 p.m. and we'll meet at HQ for seven. No funny games, of course.'

Bailey nodded.

'One last thing before you go. The bounty. Whom does it pertain to?'

'My friend over here,' he said, nodding toward me. 'And it's to be carried out by 3 p.m. tomorrow.'

'What the hell? Why me?' I wheezed, my neck and throat still in agony.

Nilay put a hand on my shoulder. 'Don't worry, mate. We'll sort it out.'

'I'm fine,' I replied, angrily pushing his hand away. Who the hell out there wanted me dead?

'Peter, Nilay,' said McPherson quietly in our ears. 'I've checked his medical records and it's true. He's got aggressive stage four bowel cancer. He's already booked in for palliative care.'

'Christine has confirmed his condition,' whispered Nilay to the Commander, pointing at his ear pod.

'On you go, then, Bailey' said the Commander, and the three of us watched as he disappeared off up the street with his kids.

'So we let the fucking psycho schizophrenic murderer get off scot-free, do we?' I raged. 'See out his days cosied up with his family? While Dad spent his last moments on an insect-infested hillside?'

'Calm down,' whispered McPherson.

'I'll drop you off at your hotel on the way back to HQ,' replied the Commander grimly. 'We'll talk about it as we go. Nilay and Christine, meet us at HQ at 7 p.m.'

Chapter 83

I sat in the back of the car with one of Burke's team while he sat up front with the driver. Neither of us said a word until we were close to the hotel.

'I just don't understand, Peter,' he suddenly said angrily. 'Whatever possessed you to go for him? He was dying for the chance to show his superiority, and you fell for it hook, line and sinker. You've got one hell of a lot to learn.'

'What do you mean, I've got a lot to learn?' I shot back. 'It's not in my career plan to be like one of these dumbass goons of yours. Plus you didn't seem particularly bothered if he killed me or not.'

'Don't answer back to the guv like that,' snarled the red-bearded guy beside me in a thick Liverpudlian accent. The one driving let out a condescending chortle.

'Idiots,' I rebuffed.

'Enough,' barked the Commander. 'Now get your head down while we get through the press, and once you get into the hotel, for your own safety, *don't leave* until the car picks you up at six. Don't forget you're the target.'

'I'll do whatever the hell I want to. And if someone kills me, so be it.'

My doorman friend, Jack, opened the car door as we drew up. 'Welcome back, Mr Black.' But in my anger, I ignored him and stomped into the hotel lobby, where I immediately called McPherson.

We both blew off steam for a few minutes. She was licking wounds too, Burke's sidekick George having just called her to give her a verbal dressing down and a final warning for her part in 'Operation Bailey'. 'It might be one of the shortest careers ever in the Firm,' she said with an ironic little laugh.

'Screw them *all*. We've driven everything from the word go, and we'll keep going all the way until we get to the bottom of this whole thing. Agreed?'

'OK, partner,' she replied nervously. 'My god, you're such a bad influence on me.'

We agreed that she'd come to the hotel at 4 p.m.—it was now 2 p.m.—so we could spend some time strategising and then we'd go together to HQ. In the meantime, she and Charles would keep trying to work out who the mastermind was. Neither of us truly believed in Psycho Bailey's offer of help.

'I want his head on a plate,' was my parting comment to McPherson.

Up in my room, I ordered some room service, and as I was waiting for it, I got a text message from Gavin. 'Just left HK on the jet with your mother and sister. Disturbing news. A company called CB today made a knockout offer to acquire Guzman & Co. Our talks with R. Guzman after tomorrow's service, therefore, take on new urgency, and I'll need your help and support. We'll be staying in the Ritz. Let's meet there tonight at 10.45 for a nightcap?'

I opened my laptop and started searching for CB. Who the hell was muscling in on Dad's deal? This was all we needed.

It only took a matter of minutes to find out that CB was in fact a large company called Craven Barns. The news about its offer for Guzman & Co. was all over the business wires. On Reuters it was 'Craven Barns & Sons has made an unsolicited offer for Guzman & Co., which, if successful, would create an international player in logistics, property, and insurance.' Meanwhile, the *Wall Street Journal* talked about Guzman & Co. as being a 'key missing piece in CB's growing overseas portfolio' and something it was willing to pay a significant market premium for. Another article gave some background to Craven Wood, the Craven Barns CEO, describing him as 'a highly driven businessman of humble origins who defied the odds to build a thriving and highly profitable empire after starting his career aged 16 in a small factory in Doncaster'.

I sent Gavin a quick reply. 'Terrible news. I'm ready to help if I can. See you at the Ritz bar.'

Next I went onto the Craven Barns website to see who and what we were up against. I was immediately struck by how slick the site looked. CB claimed to have market leading positions in the UK and Europe and over the last decade had been aggressively buying up small and medium-sized companies in North and South America, all with a digital slant to them. On the press release section was a copy of an article issued less than an hour ago.

'Craven Barns is pleased to announce that it has made an all shares offer for Guzman & Co., valuing the company at a 60% premium to its 300-day average. We do not believe that this offer will be matched or that any other company can provide Guzman & Co. with such a platform for growth and success, and we look forward to notification of acceptance. Our board believes that the combined organisation will rapidly become the leading global force in logistics, insurance and property, with digital platforms and enablement unmatched by its competitors.'

I forwarded it to Gavin, who replied almost instantaneously. 'Unlikely CB would issue this unless it felt sure that it had Don Ricardo's acceptance. This is extremely bad news. However, let's keep pressing on. As your father used to say, "It's not over till it's over."' I admired his tenacity and positivity, but clearly Don Ricardo was concluding that Black & Co. was a far less attractive option without my father at the helm. It was slipping from our grasp.

I wasn't sure that there was much more I could do to help Gavin, but the thought of losing the deal made me even more determined to find out who'd ordered my father's death. Not that I needed any more incentive. Finding him or her or them was consuming my life.

Too wound up to eat, I abandoned my lunch, hit the gym and took my aggression out on the rowing machine before heading back to my room for a nap. It was going to be a long evening.

As I lay there thinking about what had happened in Kew, I realised how stupid I'd been. Bailey had effortlessly wound me up, then humiliated me, and I'd been a total idiot to take on an SAS veteran in the first place. Then, in the car, I'd acted like a 2-year-old with the Commander in front of his men and made an utter fool of myself. Burke may have had regard for me after what I'd done to thwart Green and Jo, but now he probably thought I was a fool and a liability.

But what was done was done. I was still in the game. I had McPherson. And I had a burning desire to find the truth. *Watch out, whoever you are. I'm coming for you.*

Chapter 84

From my quiet corner in the lobby bar, I watched as Jack helped McPherson out of her cab and in through the huge front door of the hotel. People looking on might have seen a fragile soul in a wheelchair, but I saw strength, smarts and perseverance. If the Firm did ever fire her, they'd be completely mad—she was without doubt an incredible human being. If it hadn't been for her, my father's death would still be an 'accident' and a bunch of ruthless killers would have got away unpunished. Instead, the sweeper was dead, the Sikh gang in Delhi was decimated, we'd found Psycho Bailey and there was only one more rung on the ladder to go.

'Here she is, young man,' said Jack, kindly pushing McPherson to my table.

'Thank you, Jack, and sorry for not saying hello earlier. I was in a hell of a grump.'

'Not a problem, sir, and very understandable considering everything.'

'No more trouble from the boy racer?' I asked, smiling.

'Funny you should say that,' he said, lowering his voice and looking nervously over towards reception. 'The little so-and-so has cruised by two or three times in the last day or two.' He then spotted a guest struggling with a large case. 'Excuse me, sir,' and he dashed off.

'Boy racer?' asked McPherson.

'Oh, it's nothing. Long story …'

'So, how are you bearing up after this morning?' she asked.

'Pissed off as usual, but it's in the past, so no point dwelling on it. Take a look at this,' I said, handing her my phone. 'It's a Reuters news flash. Have a read.'

'Is that the big deal that your father was hoping to do?' she asked, carefully reading through it. 'And can I take it that the Guzman referred to is related to Ms Ofelia Guzman?'

'Correct on both counts, and it looks like the deal's slipping. My father would be utterly pissed if he were still around. He had his heart and soul set on winning Guzman & Co.'

'That's the world of big business for you. It's a mucky old game, and if CB has a pot of money to throw away, Guzman will likely gladly take it. That's just the way these things work.'

'I suppose so, but I just kind of thought ...'

'That because you were shagging the daughter, the deal would be safe?'

I almost got angry with her, but maybe there was a grain of truth in what she had said. 'Nice one, Christine.' I smiled. 'You have such a way with words.'

'I've been giving the Bailey matter some thought,' she said, changing the subject. 'He's "preferred bidder," but there's still some negotiation to take place, and we have to hope that he can persuade the client to pay in cash, person to person. If it's all done on the dark web with crypto or whatever, we haven't got a chance.'

'Let's hope he can do it, but I wouldn't trust him as far as I could throw him.'

'I don't disagree with you.' She sighed. 'Anyway, come on—we should use our time productively. Let's stand back from things and brainstorm why someone might want your father dead. We've surely got to be missing something.' I agreed, and after beckoning a waiter, we ordered some coffee and cakes and set about going through the possibilities, with McPherson firing ideas at me.

'Could it have been someone in Black and Co.? A disgruntled employee?'

I laughed. 'Everyone—literally *everyone*—adored him, so I don't think so.'

'What about Gavin, the new CEO? With your dad out of the picture, he's progressed through to the top job. Could he have orchestrated the murder?'

'I don't know him very well, but I really don't think so. Incredibly loyal, highly intelligent, Oxbridge educated and already my father's top pick for a successor. Possible, but highly unlikely.'

'Nevertheless, I'll get Charles to dig around in his past to see if there are any red flags.'

'Sounds good, but I doubt you'll find anything.'

'What about some random person in Hong Kong who has an axe to grind with billionaire tycoons? There are always a few loons out there.'

'There's never been a hint of anything. No prowlers or stalkers, no funny Chinese-style poison pen letters, no restraining orders. There was an elderly HK Chinese tycoon a few years back who had a demented woman chasing after him, but that's about the only story I've ever heard.'

'I'll get Charles to check where that woman is now and what she's been up to, plus any other restraining order or complaints, etc.'

'You're right, and it's worth checking, but I doubt it will throw up anything.'

'Mr and Mrs Peng?'

I laughed. 'Never in a month of Sundays.'

'Why do you say that? How can you be so sure?' I knew she was being deliberately provocative.

'Because he rescued them. Gave them a life. Gave them a home.'

'Servants can often be bitter souls. The cases are numerous of longstanding hired help doing nasty or strange things to their employers. They're often named in the will—sometimes massively—and try to find ways to accelerate the ageing process! Or they're not named and have a grudge to bear.'

'McPherson. *They are both dead!* Plus they wouldn't have had the resources to pay Bailey. Plus why would Mr Peng put himself in a car that he knew had been tampered with?'

'True, but mistakes can happen.'

'Come on. Next crazy idea, please!'

'What about people from your dad's past?'

'This is where Burke comes in. Only he and your new employer know what shadowy stuff my father may have been involved in, but I think it's entirely possible that he might have made enemies. They could have been individuals or possibly even states.'

'I agree with you, and there are highly confidential files that can be accessed, but I don't have the authorisation. It's possible to hack them, but if they ever found out, I'd end up in the Tower!'

'Let's see how this evening goes with Bailey. If it all goes to shit, I'll tackle Burke again on Dad's past. He *has* to know more than he's letting on.'

'Might I suggest finesse and diplomacy ... rather than attack dog?'

'Yeah, yeah, point taken.' Thank god she hadn't seen me in toddler mode in the Commander's car.

'And please try not to go off the deep end with Bailey this evening. He's utterly vile and horrible but, ultimately, he'll get his comeuppance courtesy of his cancer.'

'That I can't promise, McPherson, but for what it's worth, I admit that I screwed up this morning.'

'My lord!' She stared at me in disbelief. 'Did Mr Black just concede having made a mistake?'

'I may have done.'

We spent the next hour going through a myriad more scenarios, many of them outlandish. Just before 6 p.m. my bearded Liverpudlian friend appeared and we set off for headquarters. It had been important to consider all the possibilities, but we weren't really any further ahead, and Bailey's help to tease the mastermind out of the virtual world was going to be critical.

As we drove through the streets of London, a message arrived on my phone from Ofelia. 'Fuck,' I cursed, turning it off.

'Problems in your love life?'

'She wants me to call her—she'll have seen the news from Hong Kong. I don't know what the hell I'm going to say to her, and I can imagine how thrilled her parents will be to know that the guy she's dating shot a guy between the eyes and snapped another's neck. My life is screwed. Forever.'

I saw Scouse glance at me—did I detect a sympathetic look?—in the rear-view mirror.

McPherson said nothing, then a few moments later she turned to me. 'You can never turn the clock back, Peter,' she whispered, 'but you can adapt and still live a good life. We all have our cross to bear, but you can't let it break you.'

As we drove along Embankment, I texted her. 'Arrived in London. Will try to pass by late evening.'

Chapter 85

'It's far quicker coming in the back door via the river,' I joked with McPherson as we spent almost half an hour going through a series of security checks to get into HQ. But finally we got through, and after waiting in a nondescript meeting room just like the one I'd been in before, Nilay, Burke and George arrived. Bailey followed, escorted and in chains.

'We've taken the precaution of demobilising him,' said George. 'We don't need one of our most talented ex-operatives running amok in HQ, do we, Bailey?' I remembered my attack on boiler suit and wondered if he was still in the building. It seemed like a lifetime ago.

'Let's get started,' said the Commander. 'Bailey, I'm assuming that you're going to try to arrange a face-to-face meet-up with the proponent, correct? And for the avoidance of any doubt, if we don't get anywhere with this, you'll not be going home to your family again. Do you understand?'

'No, Burke,' he replied menacingly, slamming his shackled hands on the table. 'For the avoidance of any doubt, I'm not going to do squat unless I get a cast-iron guarantee that, success or failure, I get to go back to my family to see out my last few days. That was the deal. *Are we clear?*'

I stared at him—the man who'd got the Sikhs to murder my father—loathing everything about him.

The Commander pondered for a moment or two and looked across at George, who shrugged his shoulders. 'We'll work on that basis,' said the Commander grimly, knowing that we wouldn't be going much further unless we agreed to the demands. George stood up and put a laptop in front of Bailey, who started to bash in all sorts of letters and numbers. After a minute or two, he confirmed that he'd logged into the dark web.

McPherson, who was sitting alongside him, let out a mutter. 'God, you're good, aren't you?' She was clearly impressed with his skills.

'They've updated the contract conditions,' he said after fiddling around for a few moments, and he began reading them out. 'Bounty three million US dollars. A hundred per cent on completion in crypto. Must deliver by Wednesday 3 p.m. Final clarifications are to be registered by 8 p.m. today. Contract award 8.30 p.m. today.' He looked at his watch. 'That gives us twenty minutes.'

'Ask for 50 per cent to be handed over face to face, cash, tonight as a condition,' said the Commander.

'Better go with 20 per cent,' said Bailey, 'but there's still a risk they say no, or worst case, walk away.'

'Twenty it is. Now do it, Bailey,' snapped the Commander.

'Crossing our fingers,' mumbled Bailey, and he started bashing stuff into the computer. 'It's done,' he said a few minutes later. 'I asked that due to the extraordinary timeline and to cover exceptional expenses, an upfront cash payment of 20 per cent be made at a location of their choosing.'

'Good,' said Burke with a nod.

Bailey sat back. 'They tend to be punctual and businesslike. We'll not need to wait long.'

'I'll get some teas while we wait,' said George, calmly standing up. 'Milk and two sugars all round?'

The tension was almost too much to bear, and after excusing myself, I took myself down the corridor to the gents to kill time. When I came out, McPherson was pacing up and down the corridor in her wheelchair. 'McPherson, I've got one hell of a bad feeling about all of this.'

'Hold your nerve,' she counselled. 'Whoever these people are, they want you dead and they want it fast. Desperate people do desperate things, so don't be surprised if they agree with what he's proposed. If they do, the Commander's elite units will nail them—they're the very best in the world. Failing that, we'll just have to put our thinking hats on.'

'I guess.' I sighed

'Whatever happens, we'll find a way,' she said, taking my hand and giving it a firm squeeze. 'We've faced countless challenges and if another comes our way, so be it.'

George appeared, walking carefully down the corridor with the tray of teas, and I held the door open for him and McPherson to go through. 'Let me help you hand out the teas, George.'

'Very kind of you.'

'Here we go,' said Bailey suddenly, sitting up, looking at his screen. 'They're online.'

Everyone stopped talking, and as my heart pounded in anticipation, I slid the teas across the table to everyone. Except Bailey's, which I left on the tray—I wasn't going to waiter for the scum.

'Oh my god,' exclaimed McPherson, peering at the screen.

'Fuck, fuck, fuck,' shouted Bailey, and I watched as the colour drained from his face.

'*Explain,*' barked Burke, staring at Bailey and McPherson.

'They must have smelled a rat,' said McPherson quietly. 'They've aborted ...'

'Shit,' yelled Nilay, punching the wall behind him with his bare fist while I put my head in my hands.

'Do something, Bailey,' yelled the Commander. 'Get talking to them. *Whatever it goddamn takes!*'

'They've closed the link. They've closed everything,' he replied, frantically typing on his keyboard, trying to rescue the situation.

Nobody said a word for two minutes or more, and then the Commander stood up and went over to the phone on the wall and pressed some numbers. 'Take prisoner Bailey to Belmarsh,' he said coldly. Then he turned to him. 'Peter's right—it just wouldn't be right to let you go home after what you've done. I consider myself to be a man of my word, but there are always exceptions.'

'Little wanker,' he said quietly, glaring at me. 'I should have killed you when I had the chance.' He leaned forward and calmly took the solitary mug of tea from the tray before sitting back in his chair and taking a long sip. 'Still, at least we got your old man and the old Chinese cunt!'

I didn't say a word.

'Let me at him,' screamed Nilay, going for him, but George, with surprising speed and agility, held him back. Moments later, four men appeared to take Bailey away.

'Wait, guards,' I said, standing up as Bailey began shuffling out in his chains.

'Leave him,' warned the Commander. 'He's going to get what he deserves.'

'Rest assured, Bailey, I'll find out who paid you and I'll make them pay.'

'Like hell you will, you useless little crap.'

'Be sure to enjoy the rest of your life.' I smiled.

'Be sure to enjoy yours too! Don't think they've abandoned. They'll retender before the hour's out. That's the way it works.' He pointed his index finger to his heart and pulled it trigger fashion. 'Bang, bang. By 3 p.m. tomorrow, you'll be in the hands of the undertakers.'

'Take him,' shouted the Commander, and he was dragged off down the corridor, laughing loudly as he went.

I was positive nobody had seen what I'd done.

Chapter 86

We all sat back down, and McPherson immediately made a call to Charles to get him to watch out on the dark web for any new tender.

'Bailey's right,' said the Commander to me. 'Odds are they'll go out to the market again. We'll need to put a security detail in your hotel.' He turned to George. 'Sort it out, please, and fast.'

George whipped out his phone. 'Immediately, Commander.'

'What'll happen to him now?' asked McPherson.

'We'll see,' replied the Commander, his mind clearly elsewhere. Then he turned to me. 'I'm surprised you didn't have a go at him. Common sense finally prevailing?'

'Just showing some respect to the institution, Commander Burke,' I replied as calmly as possible, but inside my stomach was churning.

'I see,' he replied, staring at me. Why was he looking at me like that? Did he smell a rat?

'Shall we go, Peter?' asked McPherson. 'Let's share a taxi to the West End.'

'Sure.'

Just then, there was a sharp knock at the door and one of the four men who had taken Bailey away stuck his head in, looking flustered, 'Commander. It's the prisoner, sir. He's collapsed.'

'What the hell?' he said, jumping up. We all followed him out of the room and down the corridor to where Bailey was slumped against a wall by the lift, surrounded by the guards.

Foam was oozing out of his mouth and nose. He saw me, tried to mutter something and then his head dropped, his expression in death one of resignation. He knew what I'd done. But did anyone else?

'He must have been carrying poison,' snorted the Commander with utter disdain. 'Chose not to die like a man, facing up to what he'd done.'

'Indeed,' chimed in George. 'A damn coward.'

'Man, I didn't see him as being a bloke who'd take his own life,' chimed in Nilay.

Seeing McPherson pale and clinging to her chair in shock, I pressed the lift button. 'Come on. I'll get you out of here.'

'Peter. One moment,' called the Commander as we got into the lift.

I froze. 'Sir?'

For a second, he said nothing, thinking deeply. 'Remember you're a target. Lie low. Understood?'

'Understood, sir.'

Chapter 87

McPherson was deeply shaken, and we sat outside HQ for almost an hour, going over what had just happened, until finally she felt strong enough to get in a taxi. It was the first time I'd seen my tough, resilient partner showing her vulnerabilities.

She hadn't cottoned on to the fact that I'd spiked Bailey's tea, but I didn't doubt that one day she'd work it out and confront me, just as she'd done with the Green and Jo episode. The Commander, I'm sure, had his suspicions, and if he did, I hoped he'd never use it against me. I made a promise to myself that I'd never admit to or tell a living soul about what I'd done.

'Drop me home first, please,' asked McPherson. 'I want to get on with following up on the things we talked about earlier and to make sure Charles is up and running on the dark web.' She sounded tense and frustrated, but Bailey's death was in the past and she had the bit between her teeth.

'Thanks, McPherson. I don't know what I'd do without you.'

'Just take care, would you?' she replied angrily. 'You need to assume that there are killers out there looking for you, so just get back to the hotel and lie low as my boss told you. Will you listen for once in your life? You need to rub off that stubborn "no one tells me what to do" edge of yours.'

'I will, McPherson. Chill.' It was good to see her getting back to her old argumentative self.

'Of course I worry,' she said.

As the taxi pulled up outside her flat, despite my offers to help her, in typical McPherson style she shooed me away. 'I've done this every day for the last ten years. Don't mollycoddle me!'

'Not one to argue with,' joked the cabbie as we drove off.

'Too right. She can be a little feisty at times.' I laughed.

Back at the hotel, before going to my room, I went to the gents in the lobby and flushed the ring away, still not quite believing that I'd had the guts to go through with what I'd done. And in HQ of all places!

Going up in the lift, I got thinking about Mum and Sam and our ridiculous fight, and I made a commitment to myself to make it up with them. Hopefully they'd have checked in okay at the Ritz, and after my 10.45 with Gavin I'd have a go at clearing the air.

As I got out on my floor, on the landing there was an old man sitting on a mobility scooter with what must have been a private nurse kneeling by his side. 'Don't worry,' I overheard her say, 'I'll make sure you're nice and warm, dear.' He was wrapped up like a parcel in a huge winter coat, a scarf, a thick woollen hat and mittens. Christ, he must have been sweltering under all of that!

As I made my way to my room at the far end of the corridor, my mind shifted to Ofelia, and I decided that I'd go on to her hotel after the Ritz. It would be very late, but we absolutely had to talk. It would break my heart, but after what had happened in Hong Kong, I just knew that our embryonic relationship *had* to finish. I was no longer the decent, normal human being that she'd met just over a week ago, and she deserved better. On top of everything else, there was a bounty on my head. I didn't doubt that the coming days would involve more bloodshed and misery, and I needed to protect her from all of that … protect her from me.

I took three cold Asahis into the shower with me and soaked myself for ten minutes, and with each slug, I felt the day's tensions ebb away. When I'd finished, towel around me, I scuttled out of the bathroom to put the TV on so I could catch the news. *'What the hell!'* I nearly had a heart attack.

'Not a word,' said a woman from behind me. 'Raise your hands.' I felt something solid pressed against the side of my head. It could only be a gun.

I dared not turn to see who it was, but I didn't need to. Sitting in the corner of the room was the red scooter, and the old man was in the process of taking off his layers. Then, before my eyes, he tore off a false beard and a wig. *It was the Sikh from the Mandarin.*

'Sit,' instructed the woman, walking into view, and she pulled a chair into the middle of the room.

'Tie him to it and remove the towel,' instructed the man, and before I knew it, I was sitting there completely naked, my ankles and wrists bound tightly to the solid chair.

'It was your sister, wasn't it? She attacked me,' I said quietly, my voice quivering. 'It was dark. We fought, then fell and the knife stuck in her throat. I was defending myself.' They weren't listening.

'Set it up,' said the man, and as my whole body began to tremble, I watched the woman take a video recorder out of the scooter basket and set it up on the side table. 'Press record, sister.'

'Let's talk about this, shall we? I know some very influential people and—'

The woman slapped me across the face. *'Quiet. No more talking.'*

'Dear family,' he started. 'You are going to see what we do to those who spill our family blood. This coward killed our sister, then tortured Uncle and Great-Uncle, and for this, we'll exact the ultimate punishment.' As he spoke, I watched the woman lift the scooter seat and from the compartment beneath, take out the most enormous knife I'd ever seen.

Heartbeat going haywire, frantically gasping for air, I knew this was it. Loved ones and friends flashed through my mind—Mum, Dad, Sam, Ofelia, the Pengs, Trudy, Diti, Shaun, McPherson. I began weeping and I begged them to spare me. My body lost control of itself.

'Black isn't the brave soldier after all,' shouted the man to the camera. 'Look how he shits and pisses in the face of death. Look at how his tears flow like a river down his terrified face. Sister, Uncle and Great-Uncle showed only courage and strength in the face of adversity.'

'Please stop!' I screamed. 'They'll hunt you down. You'll go to jail for the rest of your lives.'

'Remove his balls one by one. Then his eyes. Then the heart. *Make him pay.*'

As she moved towards me, wielding the knife, I frantically rocked the chair, trying desperately to get away from her. Just as she got to me, it toppled over with me still attached. As I lay helplessly on my side, she prised open my thighs, wrenched my penis aside and swung the blade.

Chapter 88

I came to. I must have passed out.

Was I still alive? Yes, I definitely was. I was on my back, still wedged in the chair, and she was slumped over me, lifeless, blood gushing out of her head onto my chest. What on earth had happened?

I caught sight of my privates, and everything was still attached. Whoever had stopped her had stopped her just in time. What about the man? I strained to look at where the scooter was. There he was, lying beside it, motionless, with half his head missing, blood and gore all over the carpet. The curtains were flapping in the wind and there was glass everywhere. Wriggling, I tried to push the woman off, but I couldn't. Who the hell had done this? It could only have been the Commander's men.

Bang, bang, bang. I jumped out of my skin, sending the woman sliding off me. Smoke began to fill the room. My eyes went to shit.

I heard pounding footsteps and my chair, with me still on it, was suddenly hoisted up and I was being carried at great speed out of the room and down the corridor. I couldn't see, but I could hear grunting and heavy—oxygen-assisted—breathing.

'Got him, guv,' gasped a voice. 'Alive and well. Two perps down. Head shots.' It was Scouse. I'd know that accent anywhere.

'You OK, lad?' said one of the others. We'd stopped, and they were cutting me free and dousing my eyes with liquid.

'I *think* so,' I replied shakily, trying to focus. I was beside the lift. 'You guys saved my life.'

'Saved your nuts, more like.' He laughed, and I managed a little laugh too.

'Thanks, mate,' I said to Scouser as he tore his breathing kit off his massive head. 'And sorry for all that nonsense I came out with in the Commander's car. I was fuming. I didn't mean it.'

'No worries, and don't tell anyone, but it was pretty funny hearing the guv taking a bit of lip. Nobody, I mean *nobody*, normally gets away with that kind of stuff.'

'Guv's on his way right now,' said the other. 'You should go and get cleaned up, and you'll need a cup of tea to stop that shaking.' I stared at my hands and arms. They were quivering uncontrollably.

'How did you know they had me?'

'Talk about lucky,' replied Scouser. 'We'd only been in station two minutes, in the building opposite, when we saw the female with the knife through the gap in the curtains.'

A wave of emotion hit me. 'Christ, I don't know how much more of this I can take. I've had enough of all this stupidity and killing.'

Scouse gripped my shoulder and pointed an angry finger at me. 'We all get bad days, but you never, *ever* give up. *Do you hear me?* Think about what they did to your father and go find them and make them pay.' A pep talk from Scouse was the last thing I was expecting, but it gave me the kick up the backside I needed.

A few moments later, Karsten appeared, unflappable as always. He moved me to a room on another floor and soon I was having my second shower of the evening, this time scraping blood and brains and who knows what else off myself.

I was still in the game.

Chapter 89

I'd barely got changed into fresh clothes when there was a knock at my door. It was Commander Burke and George.

'Good to see that our goons were of some use.' The Commander smiled, walking straight over to the mini bar and helping himself to a whisky miniature. 'Your usual, George?' he said, tossing him a Martell. 'A beer, Peter?'

'Yes please.'

'So, who were they?' said George.

'Brother and sister of the crazy woman who tried to kill me on the golf course. Singh warned me that siblings would be out for blood.'

'A close call,' remarked George, struggling to get the cap off the little bottle.

'Profoundly,' said the Commander. 'However, hopefully that'll be the end of it as far as the Sikhs are concerned. Now let's call Christine McPherson, shall we, to see what's been happening on the dark web.' He took a long sip straight from the bottle and laid the phone on the coffee table with the speakerphone on.

'Commander? It's late. Is there a problem?' she answered.

'Christine, I'm here with George and your good friend, Peter. Have you got any more news for us?'

She gave a little pause. 'Bailey was tricking us,' she said angrily. 'One of his associates—someone called Trig—has quite possibly taken on the job. As we feared, it was re-advertised just before 9 p.m. and stayed up for less than ten minutes.'

'How do you know this Trig person knew Bailey?'

'Charles hacked into Bailey's encrypted email account and found a message sent this afternoon—shortly after he'd have got home to his kids—encouraging Trig to look out for the reposted job. He described it as a "nice little pension booster" and said that he'd be "doing a dying friend a favour".'

'No clues as to who the proponent is?' asked the Commander.

'Nothing.' McPherson sighed. 'Zero traceability and the job's still all crypto.'

'Do the following,' he instructed. 'Go into Bailey's military files, all the way back to the very first day he joined up, and search for this Trig character. I wager he'll be there somewhere. Get on it right away.' Then he turned to George. 'Does the name Trig ring any bells with you?'

George rubbed his chin for a few moments, deep in thought, then took out his phone and made a call. 'Rod, it's George. What was the name of that sniper who made a name for himself in Afghanistan saving countless from our side? Wasn't it Tim or Jim or Trig or Greg or something?'

We heard a voice on the other end, then George hung up without a word of thanks.

'And?' snapped the Commander.

'There's a man who goes by the name of Trigger Tristan,' replied George, unflappable, 'and we should check if he and Bailey served together. I seem to remember hearing that he'd become a hired gun and may have taken out a senior Mafioso in Sicily. Legend has it that he shot the old guy through the heart in a busy market square from a country mile away, high in the surrounding hills.'

'Already got it,' said McPherson, the excitement back in her voice. 'They served in the same elite forces team on multiple tours. It *must* be him. He's rated the SAS's best sniper ever!'

'Alert the Met and Scotland Yard, George. Find him, and find him fast.' Then he turned to me. 'I'm going to arrange a safe house for you. Not what you might want, I know, but entirely necessary.'

'I'll be fine, sir. It's appreciated—but it won't be needed. I don't hide, not from anyone.'

'Quelle surprise,' said George under his breath.

'On your own head be it, son,' said the Commander calmly. He stood up, nodded to George and the two of them headed for the door. 'Hope you live to attend the service tomorrow.'

'I'll be there, sir,' I replied, brushing off his comment. And sir, before you go, I *sincerely* thank you for what your men did today. Without their fast thinking and incredible skill, I'd be dead.'

'Your thanks are accepted,' replied the Commander brusquely, but he didn't look at me and was already striding off down the corridor with George close behind. Once again, I'd stepped out of line.

Christine immediately called me back. 'What happened? What did his men do for you today?'

As I headed down the back fire escape, I ran through what had happened. Towards the end, to my great surprise, she burst into floods of tears. 'Oh, good grief,' she wailed. 'Hasn't this all gone *too* far? You *will* get yourself killed, you know. But if we stop now and you go into hiding, at least you'll live, and once this Trig and the mastermind are apprehended and locked up, you can go back to your old life and I to mine. I wasn't the greatest fan of my boring old existence at Imperial, but it was way, way better than what we're living now. We *have* to stop, Peter. *Please.*'

'Christine,' I replied bluntly as I made my way out into a side street, 'don't do this to me yet again. You *can't* stop now, and you'd better not even dare. I can't do this without you, do you hear me?'

'But Peter, I really *can't*,' she said quietly, the tears stopping. 'Can't you see? I've reached the end.'

'Bullshit,' I said as I flagged down a cab heading towards Piccadilly. 'We carry on regardless, no matter the danger. That's who we are. Now let's talk first thing in the morning, and in the meantime, *please* help me find this guy Trig before he puts a bullet in me. *And help me find the son of a bitch who's bankrolling him.*'

'No,' she screamed back at me.

'If you can get through Kabul, you can get through this,' I shouted back, immediately regretting what I'd said.

'Go fuck yourself,' was what I got in return as she hung up on me.

Chapter 90

Despite everything that had happened, I arrived just ten minutes late to the Ritz and found my mother, my sister and Gavin having a drink in the lobby bar.

'The past is the past,' said my mother, getting up to give me an embrace, 'and we'll not say anything more about Monday.'

'Definitely,' I replied, 'but I'm really, really sorry for everything. Things just sort of spiralled.'

'I'm sorry for how I reacted,' she said, giving me another hug. 'I'd like to take back everything. It was all said in anger, and I didn't mean a word of it. And I want you to know, from the bottom of my heart, that I'm enormously grateful for everything that you've done.'

'You look dreadful,' said my sister, also giving me a hug.

'Thanks. I wish I could say the same about you.'

Gavin gave me a formal handshake. 'I simply can't believe everything you went through on Sunday. It was phenomenally brave of you, and I hope you're managing to put it all behind you.'

'Wrong place at the wrong time. What more can I say? Anyway, let's talk about that Craven Barns company, shall we?' I didn't want to dwell on the Hong Kong thing, plus I was in a hurry to get across to Claridge's.

'We cannot and will not let CB win,' said my mother emphatically. 'This was the acquisition that James wanted, and we need to do whatever it takes to win. In confidence, James told me that without Guzman & Co., he feared for the long-term survival of Black & Co., such is the pace of change in our markets. We need its digital skills, not to mention America's footprint, to give us badly needed economies of scale.'

'I'd agree,' said Gavin bleakly. 'The world has moved on very quickly in recent years and we're quite vulnerable. We might even be at risk of takeover ourselves if we don't secure Guzman.'

Sam jumped up out of her chair. 'What can we do? Haven't we got to fight back? What would Father have done in this situation?'

'He'd have gone to Ricardo Guzman and he'd have talked through all the merits of joining Black & Co.,' said my mother, 'and they are numerous. He'd have talked about our culture and the way Guzman employees will thrive in Black & Co. He'd have talked about making Guzman's leadership part of our leadership. He'd have made sure that our success was their success.'

'The chairman—your mother—is right,' said Gavin, smiling. 'That's exactly what he would have done and exactly what we must do.'

'So why not take the chair*lady* with you both tomorrow?' suggested Sam, to which we all agreed.

'We should also go back to the board to seek approval to raise our offer,' said my mother. 'We won't be able to go all the way to CB's figure, but I think we can go a little further.'

Sam and I looked at one another and I'm sure we were both thinking the same thing. Our mother was stepping up admirably and confidently to the challenge of being chair, and it was our astute father who'd seen her incredible potential.

We then spent some time talking about the service. The PM himself was going to be there, along with half the cabinet and a string of industrialists, philanthropists, old school friends and many more. 'I'm surprised the queen herself isn't going to be there,' commented Sam. There was also going to be an array of speeches, including both my mother and Sam, but it was felt that I was too much of a 'hot potato' to be going up into the pulpit. I was absolutely fine with that.

'You look shattered,' announced my mother, seeing me nodding off in my seat. 'I'll order a car.'

'I accept.' I yawned, and as we walked to reception, we all agreed that we'd do breakfast in the Ritz at 8.30 before heading on to the memorial service.

'It's going to be such a very sad day,' said my mother as we parted, 'but we must put a brave face on it.' The three of us embraced, our ugly spat now a distant memory.

Trigger Tristan may have been out there plotting to kill me, but it was Ofelia who was on my mind. 'A detour to Claridge's, please, guv,' I said to the driver as we pulled into Piccadilly.

As we drove the short distance to Claridge's, my anxiety levels began to climb at the thought of seeing her again and what I knew I had to say to her.

Chapter 91

'Peter, is that you?' she answered. She sounded excited, or maybe just surprised? I wasn't sure which.

'Hi, Ofelia.'

'It's quite late—I'm in bed.' Now she sounded cool towards me. 'Where are you?'

'In London.'

'Well, I knew that!' She laughed.

'I'm standing right outside your hotel. I've just hopped out of a taxi.'

There was a pause for a moment or two. 'Come on up.'

'We can leave it until tomorrow if you prefer. It's probably too late?'

'Don't be so stupid, Peter. I want to see you.' Her voice had softened.

'We need to talk about what I did in Hong Kong and a whole bunch of other stuff. It's—'

'I'd rather we didn't,' she interrupted. 'What you did to those terrible men doesn't matter to me—not in the slightest. I know you'll be beating yourself up about it, but honestly, it doesn't change how I feel about you.'

'But—'

She cut in again. 'No buts. In fact, we're not even going to talk about it. Let's just talk about normal everyday stuff like normal people would do.'

Instead of going straight up to her room, I headed to the gents and stood there for a moment looking in the mirror, psyching myself up, lecturing myself to just be the simple, happy person I used to be. Then I took some long deep breaths and headed for the exit.

Just as I got to the door, it opened and a silver-haired man in his early sixties walked in. I stood to one side. 'Pardon me.'

He nodded, looked away, glanced at me again with a bit of a 'do I know you?' kind of look on his face, then kept going to the cubicles. After Hong Kong, half the world seemed to be doing double takes at me, but this guy freaked me out. I don't think I'd ever seen such cold, almost evil-looking eyes on a person, and I felt a shiver run up my spine as I walked out into the lobby.

The shiver quickly turned to embarrassment, however, as standing in front of me in the middle of the lobby was Ofelia's father, Don Ricardo. How awkward. It was well past midnight.

'Peter! What a surprise!' he said, immediately shaking my hand. 'What brings you here so late?'

'I'm, erm ...'

'Ah, I guess you're here to see my daughter.' He smiled, quickly glancing at his watch.

'Correct, sir,' I replied. 'I got in today from Hong Kong and, what with one thing and another, I just hadn't managed to pass by any earlier. I'll just be saying a quick hello, then I'll head back to my hotel.'

'Not an issue. I know how keen Ofelia is to talk to you after everything that has happened.' Thankfully he didn't open the conversation any further.

'Thank you, sir.'

'And Peter, please accept my and Marta's profound condolences. Your father's death has deeply shocked us. Such a wonderful, talented gentleman, and we'd only just begun to get to know him. Ofelia and I will be at the service tomorrow, of course.'

'Thank you *so* much, Don Ricardo. Very kind words indeed and much appreciated.'

'Right, I'll leave you to go up, then,' he said, nodding towards the lift. 'I'm just waiting for a business associate. Until tomorrow, then.'

Breathing a sigh of relief but still red with embarrassment, I went over to the lift and pressed the button. As it arrived, I watched as the man with the evil eyes came out of the toilets. He and Don Ricardo headed off towards the bar.

I kicked myself for not having said something to Mr Guzman about the acquisition. Shouldn't I have pressed the case for Black & Co. just a little bit? Anyway, I hadn't, and it was all going to have to wait until our business meeting tomorrow afternoon.

As I walked down the corridor towards Ofelia's room, the feeling of anticipation began to build, and I didn't think I'd ever felt more nervous in my whole life.

Chapter 92

The moment she opened the door, I knew that I wouldn't be able to break up with her.

She looked utterly beautiful, and despite all the dreadful things that had happened since our Sunday together, nothing had changed between us. We both felt it instantly.

'Don't say anything,' she whispered, pulling me close. 'Just hold me and don't ever let go.'

It was a long, silent, deeply emotional embrace, after which we simply ended up sitting on the floor of her room with a bottle of wine, watching an old black and white movie. There was no talk—at all—about all the stuff that had been going on. No stress. No need to explain myself. No anger. No nothing. It was perfect. We were perfect.

At 4.30 a.m. I left her, but we'd be meeting at the Ritz for breakfast, and I was totally psyched that Mum and Sam would get to meet her.

I fell asleep the moment I crawled, fully clothed, onto my bed back at the Mandarin, but less than two hours after my head had hit the pillow, McPherson was calling me.

'Did I wake you? By the way, you sound dreadful.'

'I'm dog tired. What have you got?' I sat up on my bed—she'd only have called if it was something important.

'I've *got* some news. But first, an apology would be appreciated.'

I'd completely forgotten about my awful Kabul comment. 'I'm so sorry. God, it was massively below the belt, and I do feel dreadful. You know I wouldn't do anything to hurt you.'

'Thank you, and I apologise for my little wobble too. Anyway, enough of that. You'll want to know what I've been finding out about Trigger Tristan.'

'Oh god. On you go, then. Tell me the bad news.'

'It isn't good,' she replied. 'On the battlefield, he's exemplary. Off it, he's a bit of a nutcase. He's from a good family but got expelled from private school. After spells in a youth institute for stealing and fighting, he joined up, and from that moment on, he soared. It's like he found his calling in life. He quickly progressed into the SAS and operated in those eight-man squads as the eighth man, sitting back behind the action taking long-range potshots at anyone or anything that threatened the other seven. The stories of his heroism are numerous. He's highly decorated and everyone speaks incredibly highly of him, and he apparently never, ever misses a shot. However, whenever he'd go on leave, things would go haywire. He'd drink himself silly, get into all sorts of bother and spend rather too much time in military detention. He also acquired some notoriety for bedding the wives of his comrades! So, in summary,' she said with an ironic little laugh, 'if you weren't feeling nervous, I guess you are now.'

She was right. I hadn't been giving this guy Trig much thought—maybe I'd been assuming that the Commander and his boys or the police would sort it out—but now I was beginning to feel distinctly uncomfortable and vulnerable. The clock was ticking too, with only eight hours until the deadline.

'And what about that whole Sicily thing? Was it him?'

'There was never any concrete evidence that he took the shot or that he was in the country, but the distance of the shot from high up in the surrounding hills and the fact that the bullet pierced the Mafia guy's left ventricle indicated that it had to have been him. There are only a handful of people in the world skilled enough to succeed with such a shot, and Trig's trademark, as it happens, is to aim for the left ventricle. These weirdoes all seem to have their own little peculiarity—there's one, for example, who likes to shoot his victims through the ear.'

'Weird indeed. And how much was the bounty?'

'Two point five million euros, according to hearsay.'

'I suppose I should feel honoured to be valued up there with a top Mafioso.' I laughed, my nervousness building.

'Very funny.' McPherson didn't sound amused at all. 'You know fine well the Commander's entirely right to try to keep you out of harm's way.'

'Rubbish. Today's deadline is 3 p.m., but if they don't get me, it'll probably extend to tomorrow or next week or something like that. I tell you, McPherson, I refuse to go into hiding, and you and I both know that the only way to stop this whole thing is for us to find the mastermind pulling the purse strings. I'm certainly not going to do that if I'm cowering in the corner of some safe house.'

'Fine. I disagree with you as usual, but let's do it your way. And *yes*, before you ask, I will do everything in my power to help you. No wobbling. No leaving you in the lurch.'

'Thanks. You're a star. And you're still coming to the service, aren't you? It would mean such a lot to me.'

'I'll be there, but leave me in peace for now, would you? Charles and I and the team continue to dig, and we've tons of leads and theories to follow up on. Your life might just depend on it.'

I showered and got into my best clothes. As I headed out of my room and up the corridor, the events of the previous evening came flooding back to me, and it took all my mental strength to push my dark thoughts into the deep recesses of my mind. I knew the time would come when I'd have to deal with it all, but it absolutely couldn't be now. Not on the day of my father's service.

Just before I got to the lift, to my surprise, I spotted a familiar face on the little sofa by the lift doors. 'Morning, Scouse!'

'Guv's out the back in the car,' he said, standing up to his full enormous height. 'You're getting a free ride to the Ritz, and he won't take no for an answer.'

'OK, fine. Let's do it.' I sighed. If I'd resisted, he'd probably have put me under his arm and carried me.

I followed him down in the service lift and in no time at all, I was climbing into a blacked-out van parked in the deliveries bay. 'Me and my team will be with you everywhere you go until 3 p.m.,' said the Commander as I got in. 'No discussion.' He was impeccably dressed in a morning suit and black tie. 'If you don't like it, I'll have you restrained and taken to a safe house.'

'Is this really necessary, Commander? Your concern is appreciated, but—'

'Enough. The more I've been briefed, the more concerned I've become. He's exceptional, and he'll take you down unless we look after you. Now,' he said, throwing a bag at me, 'put this bulletproof vest on under your shirt. It's plated front and back to protect the heart. I'm wearing one too, and so is the team. *Aren't you?*' he commented loudly to Scouse, who gave a little nod.

'Can we pass by Claridge's to pick up a friend?' I asked, taking my shirt off to put on the vest.

'Denied. Call Ms Guzman and tell her to make her own way to the Ritz.'

'The hell ...'

'Do it,' he said firmly, 'or there will be no service for you.'

'OK, OK, OK.' I sighed, slumping back in my seat and sending Ofelia a quick message.

'And don't worry, I won't be joining you for breakfast. I've got calls to make. The lads will be keeping an eye on you all, though.'

'Commander,' I asked, 'is there any way we can do all of this without letting my family or Ofelia know that someone's out to gun me down? Let's not burden them with that, today of all days, and especially after what happened in Lo's in Hong Kong.'

He nodded. 'We'll keep it as subtle as we can, but *please* do as I and my men instruct. *At all times.*'

As we made our way to the Ritz, it became clear to me that the Commander, Scouse and the driver were massively on edge, constantly scanning the rooftops and listening in on their comms. Burke caught me observing them. 'I hope you realise just how deadly serious this all is, Peter. We have close to *five thousand* officers scouring all possible vantage points, public transport and more, and even with all of that, I'm still bloody nervous. This man is highly dangerous. Do you get it?'

'I get it, sir,' I said humbly. 'Up until Christine briefed me earlier this morning, maybe I hadn't, but now I really do, and I hugely appreciate everything you're doing to ensure my safety.'

'Duly noted,' he replied, still scanning the rooftops.

When we got to the Ritz, the van drew up millimetres from the revolving doors, leaving little chance for a sniper to get a shot in, and I scurried into the lobby with my head well down.

Two minutes later Ofelia arrived, looking absolutely stunning.

Chapter 93

I'd sent Sam a message about Ofelia joining us for breakfast and she and my mother gave her an incredibly warm reception, not batting an eyelid when we walked into the room arm in arm. In a few short minutes the three of them were deep in conversation, and a little smile from my mother gave me the reassurance that I needed. She liked her—but then again, why wouldn't she?

Gavin was there too and must have been dying to quiz Ofelia about her father's intentions, but being the diplomat, he didn't go there. It was a topic that would have to wait until the afternoon. He was, though, clearly preoccupied with everything and certainly not his usual friendly, talkative self.

'Gavin,' I whispered, making sure the others weren't listening, 'has there been anything more on the Craven Barns situation?'

He screwed up his face in despair and replied under his breath. 'There's a rumour that old man Guzman might have met Craven Wood, CB's chief executive, yesterday evening.'

'You're joking! Is he silver-haired, in his early sixties?'

'That's him! Have you seen him?'

'I don't believe this,' I whispered, looking at Ofelia to make sure she wasn't listening. 'I saw them by chance last night meeting up for a drink in Claridge's.'

'Goddamn it!' cursed Gavin. It was the first time I'd seen him losing his cool. 'We're done for.'

At that moment, the Commander—his usual formidable self—approached our table and suddenly everyone stopped talking and looked up at him. My mother stood up. 'Commander Burke, how nice to see you. It's been such a long time. Won't you join us?'

'Indeed, Mrs Black,' he replied, giving her a courteous handshake and taking a seat at the table.

'Your letter was so wonderfully written.'

'From the heart.' He smiled. 'My wife and I were, and are, completely devastated.'

'Let me introduce you to Gavin, who has stepped into James's shoes, my daughter Samantha and lastly Peter—who, I believe, you may be familiar with?'

'Indeed, and good morning, everyone,' he said courteously, shaking everyone's hand. 'Perhaps I'll join you for a quick coffee before the service. And I've got room for one more if anyone would like a lift?'

That was my cue, but before I could answer, Ofelia put our hand up. 'Peter and I can come with you—we can squeeze up. Sam, Mrs Black and Gavin in one car, the three of us in the other?'

'Yes, that'll work well,' he replied a little hesitantly, probably calculating the risks as he spoke. However, I knew he'd be far from pleased about having an extra passenger.

After chatting for half an hour, it was time to go, and the Commander led Ofelia, with me in tow, through the kitchens to the rear of the hotel, where we climbed into the back of the van. 'Sorry about using the back door, Ms Guzman. It's the nature of the job,' he said from up front, smiling. Just before we pulled off, an angry-looking Scouse squeezed into the back beside us. 'Morning, ma'am,' he said curtly firing me a 'what the hell's she doing here?' look when she wasn't looking.

'I'm so glad that I'm here with you,' she whispered in my ear as we drove off. 'I can't imagine how awful you're feeling.' Nodding, I slipped my hand into hers, but like the Commander and his two men, my thoughts were elsewhere as I scanned the streets and the rooftops and peered into passing cars. Was Trig out there? Of course he was, but where and when he'd make his move, we didn't know. I could feel the sweat beginning to run down my back.

It took less than ten minutes to get to the church, and when the car pulled up close to a secluded side entrance, I darted out into the safety of the church hallway. 'Hey, slow down! Whatever happened to chivalry?' Ofelia laughed, dashing in after me. I'd been feeling guilty about not telling her about the danger she might be in, and now I felt twice as bad.

Inside, sniffer dogs were doing a final review of the place and police were stationing themselves one at the end of each pew. 'I've never seen anything like it,' said Ofelia, looking quite alarmed, 'but I guess there aren't many occasions when so many dignitaries congregate together in one place.'

Sam and Mum soon arrived, and we took our seats facing the pulpit and a large framed photograph of my father. It was one of his best, perfectly capturing his kindly smile and his good looks, and when I looked to my right, I saw that Sam and my mum were fixated on him, deep in thought.

In all the fuss of getting to the church, the Bailey madness and last night's attack, I'd almost forgotten about *why* I was in London. We and all his old friends and acquaintances congregated behind us were here because of my dad, the remarkable James Black—to celebrate his most astonishing life and to say a final goodbye. 'I love you, Dad,' I whispered to him, 'and I'm going to get the person who did this to you. I promise you that.'

By 9.50 a.m., as stipulated, everyone took their seats, and then, from a door at the rear, the PM appeared, accompanied by the Chancellor, the Home Secretary and a variety of other cabinet members. It was almost surreal to see them all file in together.

The PM made a beeline for us, speaking first to my mother, then to Sam and Ofelia. I'd met a few important people before, but he was in a different league altogether, and as I waited my turn, I felt my nerves tingling and prayed that I wouldn't make an ass of myself.

'I played rugby with your old man at Oxford,' said the PM as he firmly shook my hand, 'and there wasn't a better human being on this planet, Peter, I can assure you. Everyone in this church today, to a T, will only have kind words to say about him. It's an absolute tragedy what happened.'

'Thank you, Prime Minister,' I replied, wishing I could have mustered something a little more interesting than a simple thank you, but it was all I had in the heat of the moment.

'Come on, follow me, so we can have a more private chat,' he said, taking my arm and gently leading me over towards a little alcove beside the pulpit. Two plain-clothed officers flanked us.

'Yes, sir?' I asked when we stopped.

'Peter,' he said shaking my hand again, 'your country owes you an *enormous* debt of gratitude for what you did up on that damn balloon. I was utterly astounded to hear what had happened, but when I heard that it was a Black who had saved our Parliament, I was not at all surprised. Your father was so proud of what you did, do you know that?'

I was suddenly lost for words and felt myself blushing. 'Thank ... thank you, sir. It's very kind of you and I'm not sure what to say, although I'm sure that anyone would have done the same.'

'Rubbish. Don't be so humble. Most people—including myself—would have run a mile or gone and got themselves killed. But not you. Then, on top of everything, you went on to prove yourself again in India and once again in Hong Kong. What you have done is simply beyond courageous.'

'I really don't know about that, Prime Minister.'

'Humble to the end, just like your father! Listen, Peter, I'd better be going to find my seat, but I want you to know that if you ever need anything from me or your country, just call me at number 10, or, indeed, Commander Burke. Your country owes you a favour or two, of that there is no doubt!'

'Hugely appreciated, sir.'

'One last thing,' he whispered turning his back on his escort and pulling me close. 'I know you're on it, but let's find the murdering son a bitch who did this to your father and let's take him down. Do whatever it takes.' On that note, as the head of the Church of England arrived and walked up to the pulpit, the PM took his seat with his colleagues and I snuck back to the front row.

'What did he say?' whispered Ofelia excitedly.

'Yes, what was it?' whispered Sam with my mother listening in intently.

'Just some nice stories about Dad at Oxford. Nothing else.' I certainly wasn't about to tell them that the PM had just encouraged me to track down and kill whoever had killed Dad.

'Would you vote for him?' joked Sam.

'I suspect I might.' I smiled.

The service, like the one in Hong Kong, was a celebration, and my new friend the PM gave an amazing speech followed by an equally powerful one by my mum, who once again managed to lighten the mood. Though not planned, I had my chance to say a few impromptu words, and while I wasn't a patch on those who had spoken before me, I managed not to disgrace myself. As I stood at the pulpit, the Commander gave me a thumbs up from the congregation to let me know that I'd be safe. Not even the acclaimed Trig Tristan would be able to see me through the thick stained glass.

The service ended at 11 a.m. and then followed almost an hour of chatting with people until everyone began to leave to make their way to the Mandarin for the post-service luncheon. As the final stragglers departed, leaving just the four of us and the Commander, I noticed McPherson sitting alone in a corner, head down with her tablet. 'Christine, let me introduce you to my family.'

'Far too busy,' she replied, not even looking up. 'Need to go and spend time with Charles. We're getting closer but still not close enough, and it's driving me insane. I see you're still alive, though.'

'Just a quick introduction to Ofelia and my sister.' I chuckled. 'They'd love to meet you.'

'Another time,' she said, flustered, and was already pushing herself towards the exit, lost in thought.

'She's on a mission,' the Commander remarked, and after he'd commented on how nicely done the service was, it was back to business. 'The next three hours will be crucial. We're going to get you out of here and back to the hotel. We've got the place like a fortress, and you'll be safe.' He called for the car.

'Want to see him?' he said as we waited, and he produced a photo revealing a weather-beaten, handsome guy in army gear who must have been in his thirties. Slung over his shoulder was a rifle with a long butt. 'Ten years ago. We haven't anything more recent. A shame to see such talent go to waste, but I tell you, when we find him, we'll show not an ounce of mercy.'

'*If* we ever find him' I replied, staring at the photo, thinking about the Sicilian story.

'You look a bit pale, son. No need to worry. You're in safe hands.'

'I'm fine, Commander.' But I wasn't. Seeing his photo and the long rifle had freaked me out and made me think about the left ventricle story, plus I'd just remembered the way Bailey had pointed his trigger finger at my heart. The prick had known full well what was coming down the line. If Trig really was as good as everyone was saying, he'd for sure get a shot in. In his shoes, I would.

The car drew up close, and as soon as we got in, Ofelia started talking about the service—the beautiful picture, the minister's wonderful walk-through of my father's life, the PM's brilliant speech and so on. But though I nodded politely, I wasn't listening. As I stared out of the window, I felt my anxiety levels building and building. When was he going to fire? It was only a matter of time. Jesus, what if he killed Ofelia? As we passed Victoria heading towards Hyde Park corner, I felt my panic beginning to boil over. 'Commander, I *really* don't like this. He's close. He's going to shoot. I feel it.'

'Calm down,' he snapped. 'You're losing it. Just settle down and hold tight.'

'Peter, darling,' whispered Ofelia loudly, 'what's wrong? You're sweating like mad.' She was right. It was pouring off me, and then suddenly I heard a horn and our driver hit the brakes.

'Get down on the floor *now*!' I screamed, and I shoved Ofelia down into the space behind the driver's seat and threw myself on top of her. 'There's someone out there. I'll protect you.'

'Get off me,' she screamed. 'You're hurting me.'

'Move it, Bill!' I heard the Commander shout to the driver. 'Get us to the hotel as fast as you can. He's totally lost it.'

Chapter 94

As I lay on top of her, desperately trying to cover her body, the car engine screamed and we raced towards the hotel. 'It can't be far now. Don't worry, we're almost there,' I yelled.

'Get him off her,' I heard the Commander shout. 'But carefully. This is his PTSD talking.'

Someone began to pull me off Ofelia. 'Come on, lad. Slowly now. We're all fine, no worries.' It was Scouse. Thank God it was Scouse —we must be safe! 'We're arriving at the Oriental, buddy.'

'Don't worry, Ms Guzman. Just a misunderstanding,' said the Commander, stretching around from the front seat to help her up. 'We've been on high alert, and everyone's a bit wound up.'

'Yes, right. I understand,' said Ofelia, clutching at my hand. 'Peter, are you OK? Don't worry.'

What had happened? I sat for a moment, head in my hands, trying to work it out—trying to come to my senses. 'Jesus. What the hell have I done? I really thought Trig was about to attack.'

'Trig?' said Ofelia. 'Attack? What do you mean?'

'It's a long story, Ms Guzman, best told over a glass of wine. Let's go in, shall we?' said the Commander very calmly. The car had pulled to a halt close to the huge doors.

God, I needed fresh air *quick*, and as Jack opened the door, I piled out into the sunshine in a daze.

'No! Not that side!' screamed the Commander.

THUD. Something smashed into me. Heavy. Powerful. Its force slammed me into the car, and I fell to the ground. Oh god. The pain in my chest. It was excruciating.

THUD. THUD. THUD.

Ofelia was screaming.

'Mr Black, Mr Black ...' shouted Jack

Scouse started yelling. 'The guv's down! The guv's been shot!'

McPherson's 'he apparently never, ever misses a shot' commentflickered through my mind as I desperately fought to get air into my system and the pain became too much to bear.

Chapter 95

I must have been out for a few moments, and when I opened my eyes, I saw the Commander lying unconscious on the ground beside me, blood trickling out of his mouth. Jack and Scouse were on the other side of the forecourt crouching low behind a wall, Scouse looking as though he'd been hit too. The driver was still in the car, frantically talking into his walkie-talkie.

The pain was unbearable, like a truck had hit me, but the vest had done its job, and as I desperately sucked in air, I scanned the rooftops until, far off in the direction of Harrods, I saw a glint from a rooftop. *Shit!* More bullets were on their way. As I frantically crawled under the car, I heard more thuds as shots slammed into the chassis. A tyre exploded, then another, shaking the vehicle violently.

Crawling all the way under to the hotel side, I lay there for a second, trying to look through the windows. Where was Ofelia? Has she got herself into the building to safety? I could see people lying on the lobby floor taking cover, others crouching behind chairs and tables.

'You OK?' I called to the driver above me.

'Yes. You?'

'Go help the Commander. The shooter will be on the run by now.'

'Sure.'

He slid down out of the car and crouched beside me.

'Where's the girl?'

'I told her to take cover in there,' he said, pointing to the hotel.

'Are the keys in the ignition?' He nodded, and I pushed him out of the way and started climbing up into the driver's seat.

'Where the hell are you going?'

'After the fucking shooter.'

'Negative, negative,' he yelled, grabbing my collar. 'Are you mad? Get into the hotel *immediately*.'

'The Commander!' I said firmly, ripping his hands off me. 'He's in real bad shape. Get to it.'

'Crazy dumb idiot!' he yelled before dashing to the shelter of one of the forecourt pillars.

Keeping my head down, I turned the key in the ignition and floored it.

Chapter 96

After ploughing through the exit barriers, the car almost rolled as I took a hard right and tore out onto Knightsbridge. My chances of finding Trig were surely zero, but something inside me was telling me that I had to give it a shot.

No sooner had I got going, I was hitting the brakes as the traffic ground to a total standstill. 'No, no, no!' I yelled, slamming the steering wheel with my fist, but seeing that the oncoming lane was relatively clear, horn blaring, I went for it.

Cars scattered, a bus veered and slammed into a parked car, an elderly cyclist fell, and pedestrians screamed, but I just kept forging ahead until a kilometre up the road, I finally got past the blockage and screeched back into the correct lane. They'd put me away for this for sure, but I didn't care.

It was going to be like looking for a needle in a haystack, but as I approached the area from where I thought he'd taken the shot, I frantically filtered out women, children, couples, families and non-Caucasians, desperately looking for a mid-forties man who might be acting suspiciously. But what chance did I have? The pavements on either side were teeming with people.

The traffic began to grind to a halt again, and to add my woes, I could hear the all-too-familiar sound of sirens echoing across the city, heading in only one direction. I opened the door and stood perched on the running board, staring into the hordes of people. *Look for something strange. Different. Out of the ordinary*, I said to myself. *There has to be something.*

I saw someone dressed as a clown. Blue wig, red nose, funny jacket, walking down the street juggling a load of red balls. No, it couldn't be him. I kept scanning. A man in his forties in a suit, but he looked as though he might be of Arabic descent—couldn't be Trig. Two guys walking along together, arm in arm. Nope.

Wait—hang on a minute. Had the clown been wearing combat-style boots? I looked again. There he was, still juggling. Yes, he did have combat boots on, and they looked a bit out of place. Maybe nothing, but worth a closer look? Abandoning the car, I started walking across the lanes just as the traffic started moving again. A horn went off, then another, and shouts of abuse started raining down. But they were just going to have to be patient.

The clown, seemingly oblivious to the commotion, kept walking, still juggling, until I lost sight of him as a red bus passed in front of me. *Probably not him anyway*, I said to myself, darting around it.

Wait. Where is he? The pavement was back in view, but he was gone, and as I sprinted along, I saw his red juggling balls rolling into the gutter. *He's done a runner! I've spooked him. It must be Trig!*

'Where did the juggler go?' I yelled, but everyone ignored me—I was just another London weirdo to be given a wide berth. 'I'm a plainclothes officer, damn it. Where did the juggler go? This is important. He's a dangerous criminal.'

'He ran into Harvey Nichols,' shouted a woman, pointing to the store. Another quickly confirmed it.

'Took the wig off as he went in,' shouted another as I legged it in through the store entrance.

I leapt up onto one of the display counters and quickly scanned the entire ground floor. *Where the fuck are you?* Nothing, but off to my right, two security guards were racing towards me. Then it dawned on me what he might have done—what I'd have done. He'd probably cut diagonally across the store, out the side exit, and jumped onto a bus or dived into the tube station.

With the guards closing in, I sprinted along the top of the row of display counters, leapt across onto another row, dashed along them, then jumped down and shot out of the exit into Sloane Street. There, I stopped for a second. But no sign of him. No cars racing away. No buses. He must have gone into Knightsbridge underground. If he hadn't, I was screwed, but I had nothing to lose.

Almost stumbling down the steep steps, I pulled to a halt in the packed ticket hall. There were deep queues at the barriers, queues at the ticket machines, tons of people milling around and—hell!—armed police officers beside the barriers. *Shit, shit, shit.* What was I going to do? He'd be through the gates and heading down to the platforms. Time was running out.

Nothing to lose. Before the police knew what had happened, I'd hurdled the disabled barrier, shot past them and was rushing down the fast lane of the long escalator. 'Police. Police. Out the way,' I shouted at the hordes ahead, while behind, the real police were hot on my heels.

Just then, way down ahead of me near the bottom, I spotted a commotion as a man pushed people out of the way. Could that be him? I kept going, watching, and when he got off and swung left, he turned and looked up at me. *It's him!* No wig or red nose or multi-coloured jacket, but without doubt an older version of the man I'd seen in the photograph. My adrenaline shot through the roof.

Tearing down the remaining steps, I turned at the bottom and charged along the passageway, then down a short flight of steps until I could see the platform ahead of me. But the train doors were closing, and just as sprinted onto the platform, it began to pull away.

Desperately trying to spot him, I ran along beside the carriages, faster and faster, desperately peering in until finally my legs could no longer keep up and *crash*, I sprawled face first on the platform. I watched the train disappear as my phone skidded off the platform onto the tracks.

A split second later there was a shout. 'This is the police. Stay down.' I turned to see two officers, both kneeling with weapons raised. 'Hands behind your head, face to the ground. *Now.*'

Why hadn't I seen Trig? I'd managed to look in a bunch of carriages, but he wasn't there. Maybe I'd missed him or perhaps he'd been down on the floor, but on the other hand, what if he'd never got on the train in the first place? What if he'd dashed up the platform and cut through to the adjoining platform? He was smart, and maybe he'd tried to give me the slip.

With my hands behind my head and the police running at me, I suddenly heard the rumble of a train arriving at the other platform. I *had* to check. I'd come this far. After three deep breaths, I was up and sprinting for my life, praying they wouldn't shoot. But just as I skidded round the corner into the interconnecting tunnel, the bullets came, ricocheting in all directions, shattering wall tiles. I fell and picked myself up, then—*fuck*—I slipped and fell again before lunging the final few metres, throwing myself full length through the doors just as they closed. I was up in a second, ready for the fight of my life.

But he wasn't there. As the train took off, all I could see were bemused faces, a dozen or more, looking at the maniacal thing that had hurled itself into the carriage. *Where the hell has he gone?* But then, as the train gathered speed, I saw him. Walking calmly along the platform. And as our eyes met, he smiled and made an 'I take my hat off to you' gesture. Then he was gone.

I sank to the floor in total despair. I'd come *so* close, and he'd known it and had even shown me his respect. But close *absolutely* wasn't good enough, and I knew that I'd probably never get another chance. Within a couple of hours, he'd sneak out of the country and disappear forever. Having shot the boss of the Firm, he'd have to be on the run for the rest of his days.

At the next station, seconds after the doors opened, I was dragged out, cuffed, frogmarched through the station and flung unceremoniously into a police van.

Chapter 97

Sitting quietly in the van outside Hyde Park tube station brought back memories of the moment the police van had screeched to a halt outside the pub in St Andrews. That was the night I'd come across the tough Sikh from Delhi who—unbeknown to me at the time—had sent the crazy woman to kill me on the golf course. From that moment on the eighteenth hole, my whole world had imploded.

What the hell was going on? Why didn't they just take me to the police station? There was a huddle of them out on the pavement, but nothing seemed to be happening. 'Hey! What's happening?' I shouted. But they just ignored me, and no amount of banging my feet on the van floor or yelling seemed to attract their attention.

After about twenty minutes, a blacked-out BMW 5 series drew up. Two plain-clothes guys got out and after a conversation with the huddle, one of them came over to the van. 'You're free to go, Peter,' he said, 'and I have a message for you from Commander Burke.'

'He's *alive*?'

'Punctured lung and some busted ribs, but he's fine.'

'Thank god for that.' I sighed. 'And Scouse, the red-haired guy on the Commander's team?'

'He'll live too.' But then he became more serious. 'Commander Burke also told me to tell you that you are, quote, "a goddamn liability".'

'Well, you can tell him to *piss off* from me,' I shot back, stopping the guy in his tracks. 'I went after the guy who shot him, so what's the problem with that?'

'I'll pretend I didn't hear that,' he replied coolly, beginning to unlock my cuffs. 'You need to learn how to control yourself and your emotions. In our game, it's that kind of thing that gets you killed.'

'I'm not in your game or Scouse's game or even George's fucking game,' I yelled at him, jumping down from the back of the van. 'Can't you idiots understand that? I'm not—I repeat *not*—one of you. Remind your boss again about that when he gets his arse out of the hospital.'

'All right, mate,' he said, putting his arms up in surrender as I stomped off. 'Didn't mean to offend you, honest, mate.'

My stomp took me into Hyde Park, where I headed west towards the Serpentine, using the walk to try to clear my head and think through what to do next. I was desperate to call McPherson, but that would have to wait until I got my backup phone—stuffed somewhere in one of my bags back at the hotel. She'd better have made some progress.

Seeing one of the park's dark green cafés and realizing I was ravenous, I grabbed a hot dog, a cheese sandwich and a drink and sat for a few moments at one of the outside tables, flicking through the *City AM* freebie paper. How surreal. Half an hour ago I'd been chasing an assassin who'd gunned me down from two kilometres away, and now I was sitting out with the blackbirds, chaffinches and crows having a picnic and browsing the business headlines.

Finished with the hot dog and halfway through the sandwich, a headline suddenly caught my attention, but it was the photograph below it that made my jaw drop.

The article was about Craven Barns' mega bid for Guzman & Co., and the photo showed the silver-haired, evil-eyed Craven Wood standing alongside his board of directors. To my utter astonishment, the director on the far right was the boy racer who'd taunted Jack, and the caption below the picture revealed exactly who he was. 'CEO Craven Wood pictured with fellow

Craven Barns directors, including son Bradley Wood, last from left.'

My mind started racing, and I just knew that I had to go and find McPherson. What had Craven's son been doing hanging around my hotel? Surely he must have known who I was if his father's company—that he himself was a director of—was going after Guzman & Co. Was it possible that this Bradley guy might be part of what was going on? Maybe his father too? It seemed totally absurd, but then again, *someone* had to be orchestrating the whole thing, and it was clear that with my father out of the way, Craven Black had a clear shot at Guzman & Co.

Throwing the rest of my sandwich to the birds, I set off. The adrenaline, the sharpened vision and the feeling of strength were back, and my jog soon became a sprint as I headed for McPherson's place.

Chapter 98

It took me about fifteen minutes to get there, and after I'd repeatedly pressed the bell, a ferocious-sounding McPherson answered. 'This'd better be good. Now, who the *hell* is it?'

'Sorry, Christine, it's me,' I panted.

'You! Come in, come in,' she said, pressing the buzzer. When I got up to her floor, there she was, waiting by the lift doors armed with a barrage of questions.

'What on earth happened after the service? Were you hit? Is it true that you went after the gunman? Tell me, please. I only know the half of it. Oh, and the powers that be are raging about what you've done. They want your guts for garters.'

'Let them rage, and I'll answer all your questions in good time, but first we need to talk about the Wood family. I think I've found something.'

'*Really?* Charles thinks there's an odour about them too, and he's burrowing, trying to piece things together. First, though, tell me what you've found.'

'It's not a lot, to be honest, but I just know there's something.' As she listened intently, I told her about Bradley's exploits at the Mandarin, my chance encounter with Craven Wood in Claridge's and the *City AM* photo linking the two of them.

'Not enough to convince a court of law, but I agree there's something fishy about them.'

'And from your side? What have you found?'

'First thing is Craven Wood's father. He was brutally murdered twenty-odd years ago and it was never solved. Secondly, Charles has been looking at how CB has grown and prospered over the years and has been looking into some of the companies that it has bought. A possible red flag is the fact that two of the companies in question suffered tragedies shortly before CB took them over.'

'What do you mean? What sort of tragedies?'

'Well, in the case of one in Brazil, the owner's wife was gunned down in Sao Paolo in an apparent drive-by shooting, and in another—a Miami-based company—the son of the owner died of a drug overdose even though he had zero history of substance abuse.'

'How many acquisitions has CB done over the years and how many has Charles looked at?'

'Close to twenty, but he's only looked at three so far. Oh, and there's one more interesting piece of information.'

'Which is?'

'Bradley's wife of two years died in a tragic drowning accident in Mallorca eight years ago.'

I'd heard enough. Perhaps they were entirely innocent, but as far as I was concerned, there was more than enough in it for me to take a closer look.

'You'll probably stand in my way, McPherson, and I understand, but I'm going to have to go and talk to the Woods, starting with the son. Will you help me?'

I was expecting fireworks and excuses, but her answer surprised me. 'I agree—let's get on with it. No Commander—he'll only block it—but let's ask Nilay again if he'll help us.'

Before calling Nilay, McPherson went to the loo, but not before tossing me the control for the TV. 'You've been breaking news all afternoon. Why not take a look? It's probably better to know what everyone's saying about you rather than trying to avoid it.'

'I'll avoid it. I've got more important things to think about.'

'You know the Firm is beginning to think you're completely nuts,' she shouted from the bathroom. 'They're wrong, of course, but that's what they're beginning to say. The Commander's convinced you've got PTSD and are heading for a breakdown.'

'Maybe he's right'—I laughed—'but my meltdown is going to have to wait.'

I heard a little laugh and a groan of exasperation and when she came back, she asked, 'Whatever possessed you to go after Trig? It's possibly the looniest thing I've ever heard, not to mention the fact you caused utter chaos and put countless lives in danger.'

I told her about the chase and how close I'd come. 'I had him, I tell you. I second-guessed him every step of the way, and if he'd been on that train, who knows?'

'I'm glad he wasn't there,' she scoffed. 'The Blacks would have been planning another funeral!'

Ten minutes later, Nilay was on board and briefed. I was to meet him on the hour at Carluccio's café, opposite South Kensington station. Just before setting off, my spare phone arrived, hand-delivered direct to McPherson's by the ever-reliable Karsten.

'There are guests back at the hotel who would love to see you,' he said discreetly as he handed me the phone in a brown envelope. 'The luncheon was cancelled, and your mother, sister and Ms Ofelia are waiting for you. Is there a message you would care to pass to them?'

'Please just tell them that I'm fine and that I'll see them when this is all over. Please could you also apologise on my behalf to Jack, who should never have had to go through what he went through.'

'Yes, sir,' he said with a little nod. 'And I wish you luck, Peter. The truth deserves to be told.'

Chapter 99

By the time Nilay and I met up, McPherson had found Bradley's address. As it turned out, both he and his father lived in the same opulent Thames-side development in Battersea. There were two river-facing towers, with Bradley occupying the east tower penthouse while his father had the one in the west tower. Such properties typically sold for a cool £15m.

'McPherson warned me to not ask too much about what happened this morning, so I'll only say one thing,' he said when we met. 'Well bloody done! They'll be on your back about it, giving you an incredibly hard time, but trust me, deep down they'll be impressed as hell. I certainly am!'

'Kind words, Nilay, but it's history, and now we've got our next assignment to focus on.'

Briefing him as we went, we set off and took a short taxi ride to the Chelsea side of Battersea Bridge. From there we crossed on foot and off to the right, about a kilometre upriver, we could see the two elegant towers gracing the riverbank.

'I'm not sure I buy the whole idea about the Wood duo killing people—I just don't think respectable businessmen go around doing stuff like that. But let's wait and see. If we get it wrong and cause a bit of a rumpus, we'll just take the flak on the chin.' I loved my friend's approach!

As we came off the bridge onto the busy street leading towards the rear of the towers, we patched in McPherson, who, as we'd become accustomed to, was one step ahead of us. 'I'm watching both of you approaching from the east,' she said. 'Luckily the south bank is infested with CCTV. Oh, by the way, I love the bright yellow shirt, Nilay,' she joked.

'Good to see you're keeping an eye on us, and it's unlike you to be cracking jokes. What's the latest on Bradley? Are you able to see if he's home?' I asked her.

'He's on his roof terrace drinking with two friends—champagne and beers, by the looks of things. Not, I should say, the kind of thing someone does if one's plot to kill someone has just failed.'

'True,' I replied, 'or maybe he's simply basking in the glory of having helped take the family firm into the global league. Now listen—I've got a plan, so let me take you through it.'

My plan was simple. McPherson was to hack into the building management system and set off the fire alarm. While the occupants vacated the building, Nilay and I would break into Bradley's apartment and await his return.

'And if his friends come back too?' asked McPherson. 'What will you do then? Bash them up?'

'We'll hide until they've gone,' chipped in Nilay. 'I guess a big fancy pad like that will have plenty of places to hide.' I gave him a big thumbs-up.

'Understood,' said McPherson 'Give me some time—ten to fifteen minutes should do it—to work out how to trigger the fire alarm.'

While she did her figuring out, Nilay and I went into a small park, and we'd done a dozen or so loops of the circumference track before McPherson came back to us. 'I'm ready. After you give me the green light, the alarm will go off thirty seconds later.'

From the park, we crossed the road, then cut up through the development's neatly landscaped gardens until we got to the east tower, where we took a seat in the lobby. 'Just waiting for our friend to come down,' I called over to the front desk security guy, who was watching us. 'He'll be a couple of minutes,' I said, pointing at my watch. He gave a little nod and a thumbs-up.

'Go, McPherson,' whispered Nilay

'Thirty seconds, starting three, two, one, now,' she replied.

Nilay had set the timer on his phone and placed it on the coffee table in front of us. Sure enough, as the ticker hit thirty, a deafening siren rang out. The poor security guard was up in a flash and running around like a headless chicken. It must have been his first ever fire alarm.

'Left,' shouted McPherson above the din. 'The doors should be open.' As we looked over, the lift door magically opened in front of our eyes. 'Bradley and co. have started walking down the fire escape, drinks in hand,' she added, 'so get moving. They're on seventeen, moving to sixteen.'

With the guard still flapping around and beginning to direct some of the first 'evacuees' to muster stations, he didn't see us casually board the lift, and moments later we were on our way up. The plan was to go to the 23rd floor, two below Bradley's, and walk up from there.

The lift was silent and rapid, and when we snuck out into the stairwell, far below we could hear footsteps and chatter as residents made the long walk down. 'I've deactivated the security system,' whispered McPherson, 'and it's telling me the front door's been left unlocked, so no need for you to bash the door down.'

'Very kind of him,' whispered Nilay. Moments later, as we got up to the 25th-floor landing, both of us had a gobsmacked moment as we stared in awe at the stunning views up and down the Thames from the arched windows at either end of the corridor.

The front door was indeed unlocked, and our awe didn't diminish one bit as we walked into a gargantuan living room with panoramic views of the river and the city. In the background, opera music wafted gently through the place, although boy racer Bradley hadn't struck me as an opera buff. Perhaps he'd been trying to impress his friends or maybe I'd just read him incorrectly.

'Just like my mum and dad's two up, two down in Southall,' murmured Nilay.

'Let's familiarise ourselves with the place, shall we, in case we have to hide out?'

'Man, the place lacks warmth,' commented Nilay, and he was right. While the apartment was breathtaking, it was missing something. The living room had two massive L-shaped sofas, four huge armchairs, a long dining table and an even longer sideboard, plus the biggest TV I'd ever seen. But there were no pictures on the walls, no cushions, no knickknacks, no rugs or anything that made the place feel lived in and homely. The open-plan kitchen within the living room looked as though it had never been used.

'McPherson, are they at their muster station yet?' I asked.

'They walked straight past it and have just arrived at the pub down at the water's edge. Looks like the party's going to continue there.'

'Smart move,' said Nilay. 'Hanging out until the fire brigade gives the all-clear, I'd imagine?'

'Keep an eye on them, McPherson.'

'Will do. By the way, I've got bad news. I've got five missed calls from the Commander.'

'Don't answer him, whatever you do,' I implored her.

'I know,' she replied angrily. 'I get it. Now put your phone camera on so I can see what's going on.'

'Who is in the photos?' whispered Nilay, walking over to three framed photographs sitting all on their own at the end of the long sideboard.

'One is his father.' I pointed at a much younger version of Craven Barns posing in a pinstripe suit. 'The woman will be Bradley's mother, Craven's ex-wife?' She looked like a gentle soul, sitting there on a park bench. The third photo was one of Bradley on what must have been his wedding day, his arm around a buxom young lady with a kindly smile dressed in a flowing white dress.

'The one who drowned,' said Nilay. 'I'd be in pieces forever if I lost my Mrs. You've got to feel a bit for the guy.'

'Let's hold judgement,' I said quietly. 'Come on, let's check the bedrooms, shall we?'

There was a master plus three guest bedrooms, but only one of the guest rooms had a bed in it, and even that was still in its wrapping. The master with its east-facing views was vast and stunning, and as the river snaked towards the estuary, one could quite clearly see Parliament, the Shard, the London Eye and many other landmarks. However, like the living room, other than the biggest bed I'd ever seen and an almighty TV screen stuck on the wall, there was nothing. No pictures, no books, no ornaments, no slippers, no mess, no nothing. It was downright strange.

I swept the camera around so McPherson could see. 'Creepy, eh? Almost antiseptic,' she commented. 'Try the walk-in closet. Clothes always say such a lot about a person.'

'Locked,' said Nilay, trying the handle before whipping out his trusted lock pick. A few seconds later, he'd opened it. 'After you.' He smiled, holding open the door and flicking the light switch on.

As I poked my nose in, I expected to see neat rows of shoes, shirts and suits, but instead I got one *hell* of a shock.

Chapter 100

Bradley's closet was a shrine to his deceased wife. Literally every inch of wall space was covered in framed photographs of her. Evenmore strangely, there was a single bed in there, and it looked as though he slept in it rather than out in the master bedroom.

'How weird is this?' said Nilay, staring in disbelief.

'He's leaving the pub,' cut in McPherson suddenly, 'and it looks like he's on his own. You've got about seven or eight minutes until he gets back.'

We inspected the framed photos for a minute or two—some of which went all the way back to when they must have been fourteen or fifteen and high school sweethearts. 'He's got to be ill,' said McPherson. 'She died nine, almost ten years ago and yes, it must have been completely wretched for him, but don't most people somehow come to terms with these things and move on?' It crossed my mind that she might have been comparing his to her own tragedy.

'Yep, not in the slightest bit healthy,' said Nilay, pulling a box out from under the bed. 'Wonder what's in here?' He slipped off the elastic band that kept the lid on.

'Where's Bradley now?' I asked.

'God, he's jogging. About to enter the building. Get moving.'

'It's newspaper clippings,' said Nilay, tipping them out onto the floor. 'Lots and lots of them and from different places—Miami, Houston, Madrid, Brussels ...'

I peered over his shoulder and read some of the headlines. 'Christ, they're all about murders and disappearances.' A hit-and-run in Detroit. A drive-by in Sao Paolo. The disappearance of a young girl in Dallas. A robbery and killing in Mexico City. And many, many more.

'Doesn't look good, Peter, does it?' he replied, staring up at me. 'Worst case scenario, he's involved in these. Best case, he's a weirdo who collects crime clippings.' As we looked at one another, I noticed him subconsciously put his hand into his jacket to check his gun was there.

'Armed?'

'Yep. Got the ankle holsters too. You can never be too sure.'

'Hurry up,' shouted McPherson. 'Send me photos of some clippings, then lock up the closet.'

'Photos on their way,' replied Nilay, frantically clicking and firing them to her.

'He's getting into the lift. *Hurry.*'

As we locked the closet and headed for the living room, Nilay, just as he'd done in Mumbai, began to take charge. 'Stay in the living room. I'll hide behind the main door, and I'll bring him through for a chat. Don't *whatever you do* do a Bailey and let him rile you— you just never know what he's about. And should anything go wrong, get the hell out of this place. Understood?'

Chapter 101

Hiding behind one of the columns in the living room, I heard footsteps out on the landing, then the front door opening. 'Hands high,' barked Nilay.

'Mate. Take it easy.' Bradley sounded confident and unfazed.

'Through to the living room. Slowly. Don't do anything stupid.'

Seconds later, Bradley appeared, his hands in the air, with Nilay walking a few feet behind him, gun pointed at his head. It *was* the guy who'd threatened Jack the doorman, but when he saw me, he didn't show the slightest sign of knowing me. 'Hello there.' He smiled. 'Are there more of you?' And he gazed around the apartment, trying to see if there was anyone else. He then nodded towards one of the huge sofas. 'Mind if I take a seat? Knackered. I've just run back from the pub.'

'Sit,' barked Nilay waving the gun at him. 'Keep your hands on your head.'

'So I guess this is a hold-up, is it?' he said as he sat. 'But listen, there's no need for any violence. I'll give you whatever you want. Cash, credit cards, passports, the whole lot if you want it. I think there are even a couple of gold ingots. Safe's in the master bedroom—I give you the passcode, you take what you want, then we go our separate ways? I'll not even report it to the police.'

I walked over and sat down on one of the huge armchairs. Meanwhile, Nilay had moved in front of the TV and was standing facing him, gun still raised. 'You know fine well this isn't a robbery, Bradley. We've got questions for you.'

'So nice that you know my name.'

'Do you know who I am?' I continued, and he shrugged his shoulders and stared at both of us with a look of confusion on his face. Quite the accomplished actor.

'I don't believe we've met before. Is there any reason that I *should* know you?'

'Listen, you little shit,' blurted out Nilay. 'You know fine well why we're here, and you're going to tell us everything you know about the death of James Black.'

He sat back, looking extremely puzzled. 'Listen, gents, sorry, but I don't understand *what on earth* you are talking about. You've totally lost me, but now you're making me hellish nervous.'

I'd had enough. Without saying a word, I stood up and made my way over to the kitchen, where I'd spotted a large wooden block with an assortment of knives sticking into it.

'Now, take it easy, matey. No need to do anything drastic.' His confidence was beginning to wobble.

'Reminds me a bit of the pork stalls back in the wet markets in Hong Kong,' I said, pulling out the biggest knife, an enormous cleaver. 'Do you know Hong Kong, Bradley?'

He gave a nervous little laugh. 'Come on, let's talk about this rationally, shall we?'

'You'll have read about Peter in the press, Bradley,' barked Nilay. 'He doesn't suffer fools.'

'I really don't know what you mean.'

'Don't you *dare* do anything to him,' whispered McPherson in my ear. 'You'd better just be doing this to worry him.'

'Right, Bradley,' I said, walking towards him brandishing the chopper. 'I'm going to count to three and if you don't—'

There was an almighty crash out in the hallway. Seconds later, two burly men came charging into the living room with guns drawn. I froze. One was aiming at me. One at Nilay. And Nilay was aiming at the one aiming at me.

We heard quick, short footsteps in the hallway.

It was him. Craven Wood.

'Good afternoon,' he said, walking into the room with an air of confidence. 'Looks like I got here just in fucking time, Bradley,' he said, firing his son a withering look. 'You damn moron!' He looked Nilay up and down and walked straight up to him. 'Give me the gun or Simon will shoot Black in the head. I suggest you hurry. I'm not going to wait forever.'

Nilay gave a long exhale, then turned the gun around and handed it to Wood. 'Really sorry, mate,' he said, glancing over at me. It was the first time I'd seen him looking scared.

'Should I call the Commander?' whispered McPherson.

Before I could even think about answering, out of the corner of my eye, I saw Bradley leap up from the sofa. Jesus Christ, he had a gun. Where did that come from? *God.* There was a flash and a bang and Nilay crumpled to the floor clutching his chest.

I stood stunned, trying to process what had just happened. Then I was dashing to his side as I saw the entire front of his yellow shirt turn deep crimson as blood gushed from the wound. 'I'm sorry, Peter,' he gasped. But his eyes were already glazing over and in a matter of seconds, he was gone.

Numb, I looked up. The two goons, open-mouthed in shock, were staring at Craven, awaiting his reaction. Bradley, his eyes out on stalks, was breathing heavily and staring intently at Nilay's body, while his father could only shake his head in disbelief.

'*Do you know who I am?*' screamed Bradley, trying to mimic me. 'Of course I know who you are! You're that little gallivanting cunt Peter Black,' and with that, he started launching kicks into me as I knelt beside Nilay's body. Head. Ribs. Groin. Backside. Everywhere. 'Come on, you two, help me,' he yelled, and as I curled up in a tiny ball, his thugs joined in the beating. But I didn't feel any pain. I didn't feel anything. All I could think about was Nilay. It stopped the instant Craven shouted *'Enough.'* A minute more and I'd have been dead.

Still in the foetal position, I heard him issue instructions. 'Simon and Turk. Take Black to Epsom woods, kill him and bury him with the Indian. Get a move on before the cops turn up, then go to ground for the rest of your fucking lives.'

He then tore into Bradley, slapping him repeatedly in the face and accusing him of being stupid, dense, thick, an idiot and everything else under the sun. Then, as his men yanked me to my feet, I got the confirmation I'd been looking for. 'If you'd only gone with the one who'd got his old man,' yelled Craven, 'instead of the sniper, we wouldn't be in this fucking mess. This little shit should have been dead hours ago instead of turning up in your own bloody apartment. *Yes, your own fucking apartment!*'

'You killed my father—' I started.

'Shut it, Black,' he yelled, lashing out and landing a punch in my face as his two men held me. 'Make sure his death is horrible, slow and painful, and be sure to call me the minute it's done.'

'You can kill me, Wood, but I guarantee you justice will be served,' I said quietly.

'Wait,' he said, ignoring me. He had my phone and was looking at my call history. 'Black's last call—ending just a few minutes ago—was with Christine McPherson, who, if I'm not mistaken, is the woman who got beaten at that eco march. Turk,' he growled, 'leave Simon to take care of Black while you go and find and kill her. *Do it now!*'

'My pleasure, sir.' Turk smiled.

'But we're stuffed, Dad, aren't we?' shouted Bradley to his father. 'Totally stuffed. We've lost the business, haven't we? We've lost everything!'

'Shut up, you imbecile,' he roared. 'Let's get the hell out of here.'

Simon flung me to the ground, gagged me, tied me up and as I lay there, hardly able to move a muscle, I watched him roll Nilay's body up in a bed sheet. He then grabbed each of us by an ankle and dragged us out of the living room, along the hallway and out to the lift.

It was finally hitting home. I'd totally screwed up. Failed. I hadn't listened to or heeded McPherson's pleas or the Commander's instructions or my mother's blunt but accurate criticism. This was the end of the road, and it was the end of the road for McPherson too. And it was all my fault. I wasn't stubborn. I was stupid to the core.

Chapter 102

Fruitless though it was, I tried everything I could to free myself, and as I lay there at the point of passing out, my ankles and wrists torn to pieces, all I could do was cry and whisper apologies to Sam and Mum and Ofelia. With luck, they'd never discover my body—I knew that Simon would be true to Craven's instructions to make my death a slow and painful one.

We were off the main road now—moving more slowly and less traffic—and I had another frantic go at trying to tear myself free, almost popping the blood vessels in my head in the process. But it wasn't going to happen, and I decided to conserve energy ready for the final battle I'd never win.

Wait! I remembered the ankle holsters. *The knife. Get to it and maybe I can cut myself free.* I wriggled, twisted and pushed with my feet until I got myself to the side of the boot, and with the tips of my fingers, I felt around for Nilay's feet and ankles. First a shoe. Then, walking my fingertips up a cold ankle, I felt leather. But which one was it? Knife or gun? My lucky day—it was the knife. I slipped my index finger through the loop and began easing it slowly out of the sheath. If it slipped off my finger, I'd never get it back, but I'd got it firmly, and from my wretchedly contorted position, I began slowly rubbing the ties against the blade.

It took forever, but eventually I felt the plastic break. Seconds later I'd freed my legs and began composing myself, getting ready for imminent battle. The car was already crawling along what felt like a bumpy track, probably in the woods; then it turned sharply and came to a halt. My heart, already in overdrive, started thumping with fear and anticipation. I thought about McPherson and what Turk might be doing to her. I had to take him fast, then get back into London.

I heard his door open. Cocky whistling. Heavy footsteps. I gripped the solid metal wheel jack I'd found. The boot opened and I felt the rug with my friend's body in it being yanked off me.

His hands occupied, I took my chance. As the rug fell to the ground, I jumped out and got him square in the face. Then, as he fell screaming on his back in the dirt, I clubbed him over and over until his face was a mangled mess. He might live, but his face would remember this day forever.

I couldn't leave Nilay there in the woods, so, as fast as I could, I half lifted, half dragged him into the back seat and gently placed my sweater over his head. 'I know I can't bring you back, my friend,' I said to him as I drove out of the woods, 'but I'll see to it that your family never has to worry about money for schooling or a nice house or anything. It's the very least I can do.' Then I told him all about how I'd freed myself and that I couldn't have done it without him. He'd saved me again.

Seeing him lying there was almost too much for me, though, and as I battled the traffic—skipping red lights, undertaking, overtaking, cutting onto pavements, pinging speed cameras—tears streamed down my face. 'If they kill Christine too, Nilay,' I sobbed, 'I don't think I'll be able to live with myself. What if I'm too late? What will I say to her grandfather? And to Burke?'

Frantic and distressed though I was, it was strangely comforting having him there with me, and before long I was hammering up the King's Road towards Sloane Square and McPherson's flat. 'Wish me luck,' I said to him as I jumped out of the car in front of her gate. 'I promise I'll try my best, and if I succeed, then it's on to Bradley and Craven. I'll make the bastards pay.'

Chapter 103

I pushed two or three entry buzzers but purposefully not hers—if someone was already there, I didn't want to alert them. 'Yes. This is Mrs Philipps. Who is it?' came a frail voice.

'Thank you kindly, Mrs Philipps. It's a delivery for Ms McPherson on the top floor. She's out, but it's perishable, and I'd rather leave it by her front door if possible. Would you be so kind as to buzz me in?' To my surprise, she did, and seconds later I was going up in the tiny lift. *God, am I too late?* Creeping out onto her landing and tiptoeing up to the entrance, I saw that her door was slightly ajar.

Now on all fours, I nudged the door open just wide enough to crawl through, then crept silently, cat-like, to the living room entrance. *What was that?* In the faint glow of the streetlamps outside, I could make out something—no, someone—lying in the middle of the living room. Was it her? My eyes growing more accustomed to the dark, I made out her empty wheelchair in the corner.

All of a sudden, with a deep moan, the body began to move. But it wasn't a woman's moan.

He was trying to get up. 'I'm going to kill you, you bitch,' he gasped, his silhouetted image swaying as he got to his knees, and he let out a terrifying groan as he pulled something out of his stomach. Was that a knife? Good grief! Was it the Arabic knife she used to open letters? Where was she? But it didn't take long to find out. Over in the corner I heard whimpering as Turk began lurching towards her, wielding the knife.

I was across the room in a second and ploughed into him, bulldozing him into a cabinet. As he collapsed on the floor, just like I'd done with the boxer on the balloon, I wrapped myself around him and put him in a chokehold. He was big and strong, but McPherson had done the heavy lifting, and it took no more than a minute to squeeze the remaining life out of him.

'What kept you, Peter?' whispered McPherson as I gently lifted her in my arms and placed her on the sofa. Battered and bruised and concussed, she'd had the fight of her life with Craven's thug.

'Very long story.'

She gave a faint little chuckle. 'Looks like I'll be checking into the Cromwell again.'

'Looks like it. But you'll be out again in no time.'

'I told you that knife was a lucky one, didn't I?' I could hardly hear her faint voice.

'No more talking. It's time to rest.'

Waiting for the ambulance to arrive, I called Charles on McPherson's phone, but before I could tell him what had happened, he gave me some startling news.

Chapter 104

'Mr Black. It's Bradley Wood. He's up on Tower Bridge. I'm hacked into police comms and they're saying that he's demanding to talk to Peter Black or else he's going to jump.'

'Tower Bridge! Is his father there too?'

'I don't think so. But are you going to go? Are you going to talk to him?'

'Of course—just as soon as the ambulance arrives.' I gently filled him in on what had happened to his mentor and assured him that she was going to be fine.

It took about ten minutes for the crew to arrive, and after making McPherson as comfortable as possible, they took her down to the ambulance. 'Where's Nilay?' she whispered as they began hooking her up to monitors, but thankfully George called her phone before I could start to fumble a reply. I quickly picked it up.

'Peter here. I'm with Christine.'

'Ah, it's you I was trying to find anyway,' he said hurriedly. 'There's been an important development.'

'I know. Bradley's out at Tower Bridge.'

'News travels fast. I take it you'll be going?'

'I'm just on my way there now from South Ken.'

'Meet me there. Twenty minutes. North side entrance.'

'George, before you go'—I took a long, deep breath—'can I ... can I talk to you about something?'

'What is it? It sounds like bad news?'

I climbed down from the ambulance, out of earshot of McPherson. 'It's about Nilay Kumar, sir.'

'Right. I see. Just tell me straight. It's always the best way. Is he dead?'

I could barely get my words out. 'Yes ... yes ... he is, and I'm so sorry. B-b-b-b ... Bradley ... sh-sh-shot him. His body's in a car outside Christine's flat.'

There was a long pause before he spoke. 'These things happen, and it's never easy. He was a fine man—one of our very best. Now, let's talk about it after we're done at Tower Bridge.'

'Yes, sir. He really was a fine human being.'

Chapter 105

I wanted to take a taxi to Tower Bridge, but being late evening and with the rain beginning to pitch down, there were none to be found, and I had to resort to the car again.

'Sorry, old friend,' I said to Nilay as I got in. 'Not the way I would have wanted it.'

As I raced eastwards through the city, I told him what had happened in McPherson's apartment. 'You'd have been so proud of her, I tell you. The big bastard thought she'd be a pushover and then she goes and sticks the dagger in his fat gut.'

I told him too that I'd broken the news to George. 'He rated you as one of their best, you know. And I'd like to second that—you are utterly fantastic.' Then I remembered my father's view about a career with the Firm. *Sounds glamorous ... but it's a mug's game.* God, how right he was. Countless people in the Firm had probably lost their lives over the years.

Seeing Tower Bridge approaching, I wondered why Bradley wanted to talk to me, and I wondered if I could trust him. Was I really going to go up there on top of the bridge to talk to him?

'Of course I'm going to talk to him,' I said to Nilay. 'There's so much we don't know. We need to find out why they killed Dad. What really drove them? Then there's all the stuff in those newspaper clippings. Were the Woods *really* involved in all of that? Think about all the people—families and friends—affected by it, none of them knowing the full story. If he jumps, it all goes with him.'

As I pulled up at the north entrance, the rain teeming down, I dashed down to the riverside walkway and searched for him high up above me on the bridge. It took some time, but finally I saw him—a tiny speck occasionally lit up by a searchlight trained on him from the far bank. Down below, in the fast-flowing waters, three police boats and a RIB worked hard to hold their positions. Maybe the RIB was the one that had fished me out of the river on that fateful Saturday.

'Peter!'

I turned and there was George, accompanied by a man dressed like Scouse.

'Sir.'

'Let's get going. This is Jez, and he's commanding two teams of eight—a green team and a blue.' Jez gave me a nod. 'We're going to go up the north tower, so please brief me as we go. Everything you know.' He listened intently as I gave him a rapid-fire synopsis of everything that had happened since Trig had taken his potshots. 'Good work,' he said when I had finished. 'We've got to do everything in our power to stop him jumping.'

As we waited for the lift at the foot of the north tower, George then briefed *me*. Bradley had been up there for almost an hour, and whenever anyone had tried to set foot on the walkway, he'd stuck a gun in his mouth and threatened to kill himself. He'd been drinking heavily too, and the police were worried that he might lose his balance and fall over the edge—he'd already stumbled and fallen half a dozen times. Whenever anyone had tried to get him talking, he'd repeated over and over again that he'd only talk to Peter Black or he'd jump.

'Peter,' he finally said, 'there's no way we'll be sending you out along the walkway. It's too risky and he'll probably try to take you out. But having you close by will be useful, and we'll rig up a comms line so you can speak to him. A professional suicide prevention negotiator is also on the way.' He looked at his watch. 'She'll be here any moment.'

'Sir, I think I know him, and I doubt he'll talk to a negotiator. If he's asking for me to go out there to talk to him, I'd better just do it.'

He gave me a hard stare. 'Is this another "Peter's way or no way" conversation?'

'It's just my view, sir. I've met him. You haven't.'

He raised his voice. 'That may well be, but neither you nor any more of my men are dying today, is that crystal clear? Goddamn it, Peter. The Commander took a bullet today and Kumar is *dead*. The Home Secretary is on the warpath and the Firm's reputation is in tatters, so hear me loud and clear. *You will toe the line and do exactly what you're told.*' He then told Jez not to let me out of his sight. I let him deliver his speech and didn't reply.

We reached the top, and from our position in a turret-like room, I could see Bradley way out on the walkway. He was sitting facing upriver, legs dangling over the edge, and, ominously, he was just staring down at the river far below, a bottle by his side. Far away to our right, towards Heathrow, lightning was flickering across the sky. We watched as he picked up something sitting beside him. 'Gun,' said Jez. 'Let's hope he's not going to use it.'

'*George.* Let me go talk to him,' I implored. But before he could answer me, Bradley took a long swig of whisky, then lay back flat and started firing the gun into the air. *Bang, bang, bang.*

'Jez. Prepare your men to shoot on my command. If he hits someone, we're done for.'

'Yes, sir,' replied Jez. 'Ready on your command.'

'Bradley!' I shouted at the top of my voice into the wind. 'Bradley. It's me—Peter Black.'

'Stop it, Black' snapped George. 'We wait for the negotiator.'

Bradley had heard me, though, and he immediately sat up and looked towards me and took another long swig. 'Come over here,' he yelled back, beckoning me with the bottle. 'Come drink with me so we can talk. I've got so much that I want to tell you—so much to get off my chest. Tell those fools that I won't hurt you.'

I looked at George. '*Not a chance.* You can speak to him from here, but the moment he starts firing the weapon again, we're taking him down.'

'They won't let me come to you,' I shouted. 'Let's talk from here. We can set up a communications line.'

'No, Peter. No.' Now he was up on his feet, shouting and pointing the bottle at us. 'What I have to say, I can only say to you and nobody else! Do you hear me?' Then, as he slugged more whisky, he pointed the gun at us.

'On my command,' said George.

'*No! Don't shoot him!*' I screamed.

I had to stop them.

I shoved George into Jez and then I was out of the turret window, jumping down onto the walkway, and from there I started sprinting towards Bradley. '*Drop the gun, Bradley. They'll shoot. Drop the gun,*' I screamed at him.

A second later he'd thrown it at his feet, and as I charged towards him, he started cheering and waving the bottle in the air. '*Don't shoot him!*' I screamed back at George, and as I got closer, I spread my arms try to block Bradley from their sights.

But to my horror, when I was no more than twenty metres from him, as he pumped his fists in the air and chanted my name, he lost his footing and disappeared over the side. '*No, no, no!*' I screamed.

I stopped for a moment in disbelief, then ran the final few metres to the edge. Wait. Was that a hand? It was! Miraculously he was clinging on.

Without a second thought, I dived and grabbed his hand with both of mine just as he lost his grip. I'd got him, but now I was slipping, and I dug my toes into the girders, holding on to him for dear life. 'Fuck, you're heavy,' I yelled, closing my eyes and gritting my teeth. Then, when I looked down, there he was, eyes almost popping out of his head.

'Too much grain,' he gasped, staring back at me, then he glanced down before looking up again. 'Let me go. I deserve it. I'm dead anyway.'

No way! Digging deeper and summoning every ounce of my strength, I started to pull him, slowly, inch by inch, towards safety, yelling to the heavens as I went. It was working, and finally having got his elbows over the lip, I dragged the rest of him to safety before both of us collapsed on our backs beside one another. It was a good minute before either of us could muster the energy to speak.

'Have some whisky, brother,' he said, putting his hand inside his jacket and pulling out an unopened half-sized bottle. But there was no way I going to share a drink with him.

'Why did you do it, Bradley? Tell me why the *hell* you did it. He was my father. A husband. A son. Everyone loved him, but you took him away from us. I need to know why!'

He didn't answer my question. 'He's gone,' he said quietly, sitting up and staring between his legs.

'Who?' I said. 'Do you mean your father?'

He nodded.

'Where's he gone to?'

'He's a total psycho motherfucker, you know?' he said, beginning to sob. 'He always has been and always will be. And you know,' he said, turning to me, 'he even battered his own father to death.' With those vicious grey eyes, nothing surprised me—he'd looked capable of absolutely anything. 'Once, when he was very drunk, he told me the old man had abused him as a child, and that when he'd killed him with a baseball bat, he'd given him one in the face for each time he'd done it. The old deviant's head was pulp by the time he'd finished. He built a monument to the old paedo up at the cemetery in Donny and told me he'd done it so that there would always be something there as a reminder to him to never trust a living soul other than himself.'

'So where's your dad? Where is he now?'

'Gone,' he said, twisting the cap off. 'Nobody will have a cat in hell's chance of ever finding him. He'll sneak out of the country to Europe or Asia, and he'll probably get his face changed. He's got passports and money—literally millions—stashed all over the place. He knew it might end one day and I've zero clue where he'll go. "The less you know, the better," he always used to say.'

'Tell me more about what's been going on.'

Wiping the tears from his face, he put his head in his hands. 'After we left my place, we went to his and he went completely spare. He blamed me for everything under the sun, and he even stuck a gun at my head and threatened to kill me for being so stupid. Then he packed a bag, and before he left, he told me that he hoped me and my mother would rot in hell.'

He stopped for another swig, then continued. 'When I think about all the fucking horrible things I did to help him, and all to help CB grow and be successful', he said ruefully. 'In return, his final farewell was to accuse me of being "fucking dense as shit". Fuck me,' he said, his sobbing starting up again and his voice getting louder. 'All I wanted was his goddamn respect, but he only ever saw me as an incompetent fool.' He pulled himself to his feet and roared in rage, *'Does anyone out there know what it's like to have your father think you're useless?'*

Feeling scared of him, I got to my feet too. 'Other than my father and Nilay Kumar, have you killed anyone else?' I asked calmly.

'You total *twat*,' he said, turning to me with a look of scorn on his face. 'Don't you know that I'm a mass bloody murderer?'

'What do you mean?'

He started reeling them off. A woman in Brussels whose father owned a business that Craven had wanted. The wife of a businessman in Sao Paulo—Bradley had shot her in the face and stolen her car to make it look like a carjacking. Again, Craven had wanted the man's business. He went on and on. Miami, New York, Costa Rica, Mexico City and so on. The model was simple—kill someone dear to the owner, then offer to acquire their company at the height of their sorrow and sadness. 'There must have been eight, maybe nine that I did myself,' went on Bradley, 'but then I discovered the dark web, and I began to get others to do it for me. What an amazing invention that dark web is,' he said, his eyes out on stalks again. 'Buy anything you want and it's totally fucking untraceable.'

It was unbelievable what he was telling me, and I kept going, trying to squeeze as much out of him as I could. 'You had my father killed to stop Black & Co. winning Guzman. Was that it?'

'We couldn't let you lot get Guzman & Co. Kill you or your father and your deal was always going to die,' he said bluntly. Then he smiled. 'But the plan was way more audacious than that.'

'Audacious in what way?' I asked, fighting to contain the rage beginning to build inside me.

'You still don't get it, do you, Peter?' He laughed condescendingly. 'After taking over Guzman, with Black & Co. leaderless and in strategic chaos, we were going to take you over too.'

'Now I get it,' I replied, my fists silently clenching with fury. But I needed one last piece of information. 'There was a young girl in

Dallas. Did you kill her too?' I pictured the clipping of the happy little girl standing beside her mother. 'She disappeared near some lakes, never to be seen again.'

He looked surprised. 'I won't talk about that,' he snapped. 'That was different. It was a terrible mistake and I swear I'm ... I'm ... I'm not like that,' he stuttered. The look of guilt and shame on his face, however, suggested otherwise. Good god, he was every bit the monster his father was and more. A killer. A child rapist. I hated to think what else.

Suddenly his disposition seemed to change and, smiling, he looked into the distance as if reminiscing. 'The journey has been amazing. We were invincible. We grew profits, employed thousands, acquired, won "most admired company" status and we interviewed on CNBC, CNN, BBC and the rest. The adrenaline rush was *amazing*, and yes, my father is nasty and screwed up, but my god, he's good at what he does. You just kind of get drawn in, and you end up wanting more and more and more.'

'But you and your father killed people to get ahead,' I yelled at him. 'Where's the skill and acumen in doing that? Your fucking corporate strategy was—what? Kill to grow?'

'It's a brutal world and you do whatever it takes to get ahead, whenever you must. That's what my father used to tell me,' he yelled back. 'And he was *right*.'

I'd heard enough and now there was only one thing on my mind. *Kill the son of a bitch.*

But he hadn't finished. 'I loved Georgina, my wife. I really did.'

'Was it her tragic death that ended up screwing you up so badly?' I shouted at him.

'My father never liked her. He said I could have done better, and when she started putting weight on, he was objectionable to her and told me that she was bad for our image. "Executives need beautiful wives if they're to succeed," he once said. So, Peter, what did smart, compliant, keep-my-old-man-happy Bradley go and do?' he said, coming closer and pointing the bottle at me. *Jesus. Surely to god he didn't kill her? His own wife?*

What's he doing? He'd snatched at me. Grabbed my windpipe. Iron tight. I was gasping for air. *Wait! What?* Was that a pistol?

He rammed it into my mouth. His strength was unreal. I was powerless. I couldn't get the gun out. I couldn't stop him. The maniac was dragging me to the edge by my throat.

He'd lured me in. Tricked me. He'd won.

We went over the side.

Chapter 106

I just couldn't let him win.

As we fell, locked tightly together, through sheer force of will I prised the gun out of my mouth just as he pulled the trigger.

Had I heard him shriek? Had the bullet got him instead of me? I couldn't be sure, but I hoped and prayed that it had.

Surviving the dive out of Jo and Green's balloon had been a near impossibility, but somehow I'd managed to do it again. Maybe Bradley had hit the water before me and broken my fall? Perhaps finally he had done something good for me after all the bad?

As I came to, well downstream of Tower Bridge, the prospect of death reared its head again as a massive river barge bore down on me. Somehow, though, I managed to dodge its thunderous bow and grab one of the huge tyres tethered to its port side.

Curled up within the tyre itself and shivering with cold, I watched Tower Bridge and London fade into the distance. It was then that I realised that my journey was finally over. McPherson and I had gone in search of the truth, and despite everything that had been thrown at us, we'd prevailed.

When the barge docked later that night near Tilbury, I didn't head back into London. I simply couldn't. The black cloud was back again, heavier than ever before, and I just couldn't face seeing or speaking with anyone. Finding the truth had come at a terrible price for my state of mind, and I knew that my next journey—to recovery—would be long and hard.

Head for the hills was what my inner voice was telling me, and that's exactly what I did.

Chapter 107

PETER BLACK MISSING, PRESUMED DEAD

SEARCH FOR FATHER'S MURDERER ENDS IN TRAGEDY

THE BEGINNING OF THE END OF A DYNASTY?

By mid-morning the following day, I was in Llanberis in North Wales. I'd hitched through the night but remembered little of it, such was my state of mind. By mid-afternoon I was high in the Snowdonia mountains in a remote bothy I'd discovered years before when hiking with my father.

The press headlines outside the local newsagents in Llanberis had kicked me out of my dark misery just long enough for me to call Black & Co. in Hong Kong, and I'd asked to be put through to outgoing Chairman Leung. I'd let my father's faithful old friend know that I'd survived but that I desperately needed time alone. 'Wherever you are, take as long as you need,' he had said. 'It's been a harrowing time, and now you need to begin to make sense of it all—and I'm sure you will. I'll let your family and the authorities know you're safe.'

Rather than feeling so wretchedly miserable, should I not have been feeling at least a little bit good about myself? Saving Parliament, taking on the Sikhs, saving my family in Lo's, taking down Bailey, almost outwitting Trig, exposing Bradley and Craven … the list was endless, and … well, what more could I have done? But no, I just couldn't find any positives, only depression and loneliness.

And what was my body doing? For two days I didn't even manage to crawl out of my bunk. All throughout, I had severe shooting pains down my arms and legs, my chest felt like it was going to explode and sweat oozed out of every pore of my body.

But my mind was a hundred times worse, as it replayed endless loops of all the brutal things I'd done. Killing the crazy woman, asphyxiating Jo, shooting the biker, torturing the sweeper, stabbing the Sikhs, the shot to the head in Lo's, snapping the getaway driver's neck, Bailey's poison and more. Sometimes it was in sequence, other times jumbled, but always horribly detailed.

Night-time was a million times worse—so much so that midway through the second night, I crawled outside into the darkness and just lay there in the howling wind, praying that my life would end. Thank god I'd used the poison pill on Bailey, or I'd gladly have rammed it down my throat.

In the morning, however, surrounded by mountain goats grazing lazily on the plateau as an eagle soared high overhead, I watched the sun come up over Mount Snowdon and things seemed a little better. Perhaps it was the fresh air and closeness to nature, or perhaps I had simply exhausted all my misery. But whatever it was, deep inside I began to feel more positive, and as I went for a gentle walk, I began to reconcile everything within myself.

Sure, people back at uni would stare at me and judge me, but surely I could overcome that. I'd overcome far worse. Plus while I might be a 'celebrity' now, in time everyone would just get on with their lives and Peter Black's wild, crazy stuff would fade into memories. And my close friends and family, the ones who really cared about me, would surely stand by me through good times and bad. And then there was Ofelia. Hadn't I been so incredibly lucky to stumble across her?

I could see now that I'd really let the Firm get to me. I'd been paranoid that they were trying to recruit me when maybe I should have just taken it in my stride and as a compliment. Without a doubt, I'd treated the Commander—one of my father's closest friends—very poorly, and I hoped I'd be able to patch it up with him one day. But one thing was for sure: I'd never, ever join the Firm, and I vowed I'd never get involved in any kind of crazy stuff again.

I'd always be intrigued to know whether Bob McPherson had known that I was going to be out running on the sands that day. Maybe one day I'd just plain ask him—although Bullet would probably give me a straighter answer. Of course, without having met Bob, there would have been no Arabic coffee, no Christine and no one to help me find my father's murderers. I wished, though, that I'd never agreed to take her to the Save the Planet march. Of all the terrible things I'd done, it was killing Jo that had affected me most. Just what was it about her that had driven so many to madness?

In the late morning, having set myself the goal of climbing up to the peak high above the bothy, as I made my way along mountain tracks, my energy and happiness levels began to steadily improve. It shouldn't really have been that way. On the entire climb I was thinking about my father and Mr and Mrs Peng, but, strangely, all my thoughts were positive ones. Kind and humble, our housekeepers had overcome incredible adversity to build a new life for themselves, and I realised up there in the hills that I too would overcome my own adversity. The way my father had helped them said a huge amount about him, and I knew that if I tried hard, I could live my life in the way that he had lived his.

As I approached the summit and looked out across the magnificent mountain range, I don't know why, but I suddenly started speaking out loud to my father. 'My meltdown is over with, Dad. It's time to pick myself up and start rebuilding my life. What's more, I'm going to make it one hell of a successful life, just like yours.'

You'll look after Sam and your mother along the way, won't you? I seemed to hear him say.

'You know I will, Dad, just like I did in Lo's.'

No more bust-ups, eh, Peter? It wasn't a very Black thing to do, to leave my funeral early.

'Never, ever again, Dad.' I laughed, embarrassed. 'It was just a one-off. The pressure, I guess.'

CEO on your 29th birthday? Of course you're up for it, and I wouldn't have suggested it otherwise, he said with his usual conviction. *But it will be up to you at the end of the day.*

'I trust you, Dad, all the way'—I laughed—'and you were so right to make Mum chairman.'

I'm so proud of you, son, he said, *and I'm here if you ever need me. Now, do something for me, will you? Please remember to read Peng's letter.* And with that, as I watched the clouds race across the blue sky, his presence was gone.

Chapter 108

I'd forgotten about the letter, and as I approached the summit, I pulled the water-damaged envelope from my jacket and took shelter in the lee of a large boulder. The neat little red seal was still intact, and as I scraped it off and saw the yellowish parchment paper, my heart began to race. Why would my father have been so keen for me to read it?

Dear Peter,

This is a short letter, and I'm sorry to burden you with what I am about to request. If you feel that you can't carry out the difficult and dangerous task, I will understand. You are, though, the only person I feel I can trust to carry out it out. The only one with the necessary skill and resolve.

Many years ago, I and Mrs Peng had to flee China. My father—who was a good, hardworking and honest man and my mentor and guide in life—discovered that a man at his place of work was being very dishonest. This person discovered that my father knew his secret and then killed him and my mother in the most terrible way. To escape his further wrath, Mrs Peng and I had to flee, and you know our story after that. The killing of my parents was inexplicably savage, and the man who did this has caused death, heartache and suffering to many more families. I always vowed that I would right the wrong by taking this man's life.

If you are reading this letter, it is because I am no longer living, and I therefore must ask you to carry out this difficult task on my behalf. My mother was sexually abused by this man as my father looked on, and after her throat was slit, my father suffered a slow and excruciatingly painful death. This man is smart and cunning and now lives in luxury and beyond the law. He cannot be underestimated, but YOUcan defeat him.

Your father, your mother, and you and your sister became our new family, and I and Mrs Peng are forever grateful for the way that you took us in. You will go very far in life, young Peter.

Please accept my apologies again for burdening you with this most difficult of requests,

Your humble servant and friend, Peng

I leant back against the boulder, stunned. Horrified at what had happened to Peng's parents but also amazed—and, to be frank, angry—that Peng could have made such a request.

Near the end of his letter, I'd been distracted by a faint humming sound, and now, as I sat there shaking my head in disbelief, the humming grew louder. In the distance I spotted a helicopter coming up the valley far below me. It was probably on training exercises from RAF Anglesey.

'Thanks, Peng,' I said out loud as I watched the thing bank and head off towards Mount Snowdon. 'Thanks for asking me to go and bump someone off.' It was so outlandish an idea that I roared with laughter and then crumpled up the letter and stuffed it back in my pocket.

Now the helicopter, still way below me, had turned again and seemed to be heading this way.

Instinctively I got down on my front amongst the rocks. Maybe it was Search and Rescue looking for me? Maybe Craven had hired yet another assassin? Maybe it was neither and nothing to worry about? It steadied its course and headed straight for the bothy.

My adrenaline began to kick in.

Chapter 109

I watched from my hiding place high above as the helicopter landed. Two people climbed out and sprinted low towards the bothy. Who the hell were they? Friend or foe?

As they disappeared into the tiny stone building, two more began to get out of the helicopter. *Oh my god. What on earth? Unbelievable.* They were lifting a person in a wheelchair out of the helicopter cabin. *My eyes and ears!*

I pulled myself to my feet.

The other two had come back out of my safe house onto the porch and were scanning the horizon—looking for me—as McPherson was carried towards them.

Suddenly it clicked, and I felt a bolt of emotion shoot through me. My sister and Ofelia! I *thought* I'd recognised that familiar running style of my sister's. McPherson was beside them now, and the three of them and the two wheelchair bearers—soldiers—were all staring up into the hills.

One of the soldiers had binoculars—I saw the glint of the lens just like with Trig—and in no time he'd clocked me. I watched as he pointed and handed them to McPherson.

I stood still, waiting until she found me. 'Hi, McPherson,' I whispered, and I gave her a little wave as I wiped away some tears. She paused, putting the lenses down, and gave me one back, and then I saw the other two rush to her.

My sister took the binocs first and after a bit of guidance from McPherson, she clocked me too. Then it was Ofelia's turn. What on earth had ever possessed her to come back for me?

Ofelia and my sister left McPherson and the soldiers and started half running, half walking in my direction. I set off down the long, winding goat path towards them, bursting with emotion.

Chapter 110

'She's going to kill you, by the way,' said Sam, nodding towards McPherson, after the three of us had pulled ourselves together and started walking, arm in arm, down the hill towards her. 'We're all furious with you, but Christine's fury is in a different league altogether.'

At about fifty metres out, I let go of Ofelia and Sam and jogged down to McPherson. After a brief barrage of abuse, I knelt and we hugged one another. 'I just knew you couldn't be dead,' she said emotionally. 'You're a total and utter bastard, Peter Black, but I just knew you were alive, and then I found you up here on this bloody Welsh mountain.' I didn't ask her how she'd found me, but knowing her, she'd probably hijacked a North Korean satellite!

'Before the other two catch up, quickly brief me, would you, McPherson?' I asked her, nodding towards Sam and Ofelia. 'What about Bradley? Alive or dead?'

'His body was picked up in the Thames by the SBS. He'd died from a bullet wound to the head.'

'*I knew it, goddamn it* ... and Craven? Has he disappeared?'

'Vanished,' she replied bitterly. 'But we hope to get him eventually.'

'I'm not so sure. And what about Trig?'

'We think he's headed for Latin America, but we'll get him. The Commander wants his guts!'

'I wish.' I laughed. 'But I fear he's too good for all of us.' I remembered his gesture to me as he'd strolled off down the platform. 'McPherson,' I then said, staring at her firmly. 'All this stuff we've done. I'm finished with it. It's history and I'm not going to talk about it again to anyone *ever*, all right?'

She nodded. 'I understand completely, Peter, and I *desperately* hope you get your old life back.'

'I'll get it back,' I said firmly, but the hint of scepticism in her voice hadn't escaped me.

Chapter 111

'Your flatmates are cooking dinner for you this evening to welcome you home,' was the way Sam had described it, and so, after almost two hours in the helicopter, we touched down at Leuchars airbase. From there, a military car took us on the short drive to St Andrews. I deliberately looked away as we drove past the golf course and the spot on the eighteenth where it had all started.

'Nervous?' said my sister as we drew up outside the flat.

'Beside myself.' I laughed anxiously. 'But it'd have been so much more difficult if the three of you hadn't come to fetch me.' I felt Ofelia squeeze my hand and I squeezed hers back. I was the luckiest guy in the whole world to have met such an amazing woman, but I also knew that there wouldn't be any more chances.

On the mountain, she'd given me the amazing news that Gavin had done the deal with her father. Finally my dad's dream of Guzman and Black being united was going to become reality. Before we'd taken off, I'd stolen a few minutes for myself and told my father how proud I was of him. He'd initiated the deal and made it all possible. He was a genius.

Sam and Ofelia went on ahead up the path to the flat while I pushed McPherson. 'That one's a keeper,' she said, turning to me with a little smile, and I smiled back and nodded. Of course, she was right, but how was I going to handle a serious relationship after everything that had happened?

'McPherson,' I said, suddenly remembering Bob and Bullet, 'we need to meet your grandfather.'

'Knowing him, he probably knew we were coming before we did'—she laughed—'but yes, I'll call him and we can go and say hello. Maybe tomorrow?' Talking of him made me wonder again if our encounter on the beach that day had been by chance or by design.

'It's quiet in here,' said Sam, poking her head into the kitchen from the utility room.

'Go straight through to the lounge all the way at the back,' I suggested. 'They sometimes crack open a bottle of wine through there when we're doing a house dinner.'

'You go first,' she said, coming back and swapping chair duties with me. 'You know the way.'

The hallway was eerily quiet, and I stopped for a moment, beginning to get that feeling that I got when I sensed danger. My adrenaline began to pump. My heart rate was going up. Something about the house just didn't feel right. Not a bit.

'Stay back in the kitchen,' I mouthed to the three of them, waving them back.

I crept towards the closed door at the end of the corridor, scenarios flashing through my mind. More Sikhs? Trig—unfinished business? Craven—retribution for Bradley? Were my flatmates in grave danger?

Whatever it was, no matter how bad, I was there and I'd give everything to save them—to the death if need be. Fuck. It was all my fault. I was stupid to have believed that the danger had gone.

Storm the fucking place, I said to myself. *Three, two, one. Now GO.*

Chapter 112

Just as I was about to kick in the door, I heard a dog bark from inside. Didn't I know that bark?

Heart still thumping, I stopped and put my ear to the door. There was a muffled giggle. Then another. *'Shush,'* hissed someone.

I took a huge deep breath and stood myself down. The dog could only be Bullet. One of the gigglers was, without doubt, Trudy—I'd know that infectious little giggle anywhere. 'It's OK,' I sighed, looking back at the others. Sam and Ofelia were smiling obliviously, but McPherson was looking at me as though I was deranged. 'Give me a break, would you McPherson?' I laughed. 'Just being cautious.'

As I gently pushed open the living room door, all hell let loose. There must have been well over a hundred people jam-packed in there. Flatmates, classmates, friends from the pub, the golf team, the rugby team, Bob, Bullet and tons of booze.

It was all done in the most amazing way. Not a single person talked about the events of the last two weeks—the closest anyone got to it was when Trudy got up to say a few words. It was brief and from the heart, and the whole place fell deathly silent. 'Peter, on behalf of all of us, we welcome you back with open arms. We missed you enormously and we hope you'll never leave us again. For all of us here today, you are the same kind, wonderful Peter that left for Hong Kong, and I can assure you that you'll have our full support in the days to come.' She came over and planted a huge kiss on me and a massive cheer went up. In response, all I said was a quiet and appreciative thank you to Trudy and to everyone else. I absolutely didn't want the limelight.

I enjoyed the party and company enormously, but at one point in the evening, I found myself sitting alone in a huge chair in the corner, looking in on the proceedings. Ofelia was chatting to McPherson to my left. Sam was standing with a glass of red wine being wooed by one of the rugby crew. A bunch of people were dancing to '80s music; Bullet lay fast asleep by the fire; the place was alive with chatter and happiness.

It was a typical happy university party but, deep down, I wasn't at all sure that I fitted the mould anymore. I'd been through too much.

Did I even relate to these people anymore? Could I really see myself plodding off to lectures every day, studying in the library and pulling pints in the pub? It seemed insane, but maybe I related more to Burke and George and Scouse. 'Snap out of it, Peter,' I said out loud, angry with myself for thinking such stupidities, and I got up and headed for the kitchen, where I grabbed two bottles of beer and then went out into the garden. A breath of fresh air would surely bring me to my senses.

Lying back on the old bench tucked away in the far corner of the garden, in the darkness I sipped my beer and calmly convinced myself that I'd just have to take things slowly and that eventually I'd get my old self and my old life back. I had to believe that in time everything would work out just fine.

Just as I was sitting up and about to go back to the house, I heard the back door open and watched the unmistakeable silhouette of Bob, with Bullet by his side, walk out into the garden. He was probably taking Bullet for a pee, but just as I was about to stand up to go and join them, the back door opened again and another figure quickly made his way out into the garden. Holy Christ, I knew that shoulders-back, purposeful walk—it could only be my captain, Declan. Instinctively I crouched low behind a bush.

Now old man McPherson was beckoning Declan over to his spot behind the big cherry blossom tree in the centre of the garden, and I watched as Declan briefly shook his hand. The two of them—not more than thirty feet from where I was—then started earnestly talking as if they'd known each other for ages. I wished I could have heard what they were saying.

But how on earth do they know one another? Had I not introduced the two of them just an hour or so ago? They'd acted as though they'd never met, with Declan politely asking the old boy a bunch of polite questions. *Have you retired to St Andrews, sir? What was your profession, sir? What was it about St Andrews that attracted you, sir?* What a lying toad.

Now it was all becoming clear. Declan must be in the Firm—not surprising considering his late father's position in the Ulster Constabulary. He'd organised the rugby team run along West Sands and must have told Bob about it. The wily old bastard had been lying there out on the tide line, probably to test how curious and observant I was, and, unbeknown to me at the time, I'd gone and ticked the boxes with flying colours. They *had* been trying to recruit me, and Dad had been spot on when he'd said that the Firm doesn't do coincidences.

I should have been angry, but I wasn't. I'd left all that, and my pain, behind in Snowdonia. In fact, I just smiled to myself. At least now I knew.

They finished talking, shook hands again and Declan headed back to the house while Bob waited, lit his pipe and took a few puffs before tapping it out on the tree. 'Come on, Bullet. Let's go back up to the house,' I heard him say loudly. But Bullet had his mind on other things. He was staring into the darkness in my direction and was beginning to strain at his lead, tail wagging. 'Enough,' bellowed Bob, giving him a yank, and to my relief, they went up the garden into the house.

I got back onto my bench and opened another beer. As I lay back, I felt the wind begin to pick up and trees begin to stir. *So there you go, Peter,* said my father. *Now you know once and for all.*

'Hi, Dad. Thought it might be you.' I laughed. 'I think I always knew. But what's more important is that now I know for sure that I don't want to be one of them. I want to work with our firm, not theirs, and I want to build on your legacy.'

Thank goodness. He sighed.

'Peter, is that you?' I jumped up. It was Ofelia's voice. 'Are you here?' She was making her way down the garden.

'Yes, over here.' A second later we were embracing.

'I've been looking everywhere for you,' she whispered. 'That kind old man in the kitchen with the dog said you were out here.'

Printed in Great Britain
by Amazon